Overload
The Human Element Trilogy
Book 2

Van Camp, Kevin

The Human Element Trilogy/ by Kevin Van Camp – 1st ed.

p. cm.

Summary: Zeke Laufor's story continues when he and his friends arrive in Colorado to help the second division of the Clade fight against the Agency. However, Zeke's greatest enemy may not be a part of the Agency but his leader instead.

ISBN-13: 978-0-615-72587-1

ISBN-10: 0615725872

Printed in U.S.A.

First edition, October 2012

The text was set in Garamond font

Book Cover design by Eddie Conlon and Sonja Thorgersen

"War, it's something that everybody gets hyped about. Kids play games in their homes and backyards pretending to kill each other, and we play video games about war, and the news shows broadcasts new information about Iraq and Afghanistan every night. It isn't until it's in your own backyard that you realize how terrible of a thing it really is."

-Zeke Laufor

Special Thanks to,

My Grandma, for telling me stories when I was a little boy, my seester (cousin) Kelly for all she has done, and to everyone else who enjoys stories as much as I do.

Chapter 1

The helicopter spiraled towards the ground at an increasing speed. Trish and Marcus couldn't have survived the long fall to the ground. My heart filled with agony and grief knowing that I was never going to see Trish again, and, for once, there was nothing I could do.

"Hold on!" Juliette yelled to Sarah and I as the ground finally reached the helicopter causing us to smash hard into the solid dirt. The force jutted the copter causing it to immediately smash into tiny pieces. The grinding sound was so loud I wanted to hold my ears because they stung so badly, but I couldn't. All I remember was the sound of crunching metal and blades scratching against the Earth. I blacked out almost instantly...

Water fell on top of my face. The cool drips were godsend after what had just happened. I opened my eyes to see the helicopter smashed to pieces on the other side of the clearing.

I tried to get up and find the others, but I was too sore and tired. My muscles ached with every movement. I wanted to just lie there for the rest of my life and forget all about the Clade, but that would never happen. I realize that now. They will always be after you to try to keep you safe, or at least, that's what they think they are doing. If they don't come, the Agents will, and they only know how to do one thing. To kill. Just like how the Agents killed Gabe. How long ago was that?

Thunder ripped across the gray and gloomy sky. When we were all in the helicopter, it was a bright, sunny day. We could have been lying here for hours or even days. I remember riding through the air in the chopper when the tail of it broke off and we spiraled towards our doom. I guess our dooms day was still a few days away.

How did we survive a fall like that? My hand resting its palm on the dirt made it feel as solid as any ground anywhere else in this world. There was no way that we could've have fallen and all survived. That thought gave me chest pains from the sadness. I wanted to cry at the thought of my friends being killed in a helicopter crash. One that was primarily my fault.

Suddenly, a rustle came from the bushes across the clearing. I had no idea who it was, or even where we were. Maybe this person owned the land, and they weren't so happy that a helicopter just crushed some of their trees. It could even be the Agency coming back for round two when everyone was either weak or dead.

I used all of my strength to lift up my palm and charge a bolt of electricity in my hand in case it was the Agency. The bolt would be weak, but it could give me just enough time to run. I was too tired to make this shock lethal. I feel like a nap may be in store for me if I survive this encounter.

The person cleared the bushes. He was an older man, maybe in his mid 50's with curly gray hair and a large round face. His whole self was round actually. He stumbled out of the woods, but caught himself before he fell to the ground.

He said to me through the pouring rain, "I am not as limber as I once was. I swear these trees are gonna be the death of me." He laughed.

I didn't know who he was, so I didn't let my lightning bolt diminish from my hand. This person was a stranger to me. He could be a good person, or an Agent for all I know.

I pushed out through aching lungs, "Who… are you?"

He smiled and said, "I am the person that saved you from becoming a red stain on the ground." He walked up to me. "Now, put down your hand and let me take you back to my house, so you can rest up and heal."

The person sounded genuine, and I couldn't stay out here in the rain. My body may be able to heal itself from cuts and other gouges, but it can't fight a cold for all I know.

Before I tried to stand, I asked, "Did you… find others?"

"Yeah, I got Marcus, Juliette, and the other two girls. Good thing you crashed in the right spot." He laughed. "I guess there really is a bright side to everything. Now, may I ask what your name is?" He tried to bend down to hear me better. Maybe because his ears can't pick up sound like they used to.

"My name is Zeke, Zeke Laufor," I pushed out.

His eyes opened wide and then he said, "So, you are Greg's kid, huh? Well, isn't that just wonderful." He didn't sound too happy about that. The bolt in my hand grew in strength.

He noticed and said, "Woah! Hey now, you don't have to fry me. Your father and I just never got along much when we broke away from the Agency."

"What?" This caught my attention almost instantly. Anything about my father I wanted to know about, but first things first, "Who are you?" I asked.

"My name is Liam Randalph. Would you please now come with me? Marcus told me all about what happened back in New York. The Agents may be on their way if they noticed the chopper go down, so if you would like to live, follow me!"

I didn't get to say another word. He grabbed my non-electrified hand and pulled me up on my feet. The pain in my side made me want to scream, but I held it in. My legs were wobbly underneath my weight, and I felt like I could have collapsed at any second.

Liam began to walk back the way he came when he said, "Are you gonna follow me? Your girlfriends are waiting for you back at my place."

Girlfriends? He was talking about Sarah and Trish. This grabbed my attention, and I immediately began to follow Liam. He must've noticed an eager expression on my face because he said, "Ah, teenagers. They only care about girls."

I made a face at him, but he didn't see it. He was already making his way through the thick of the woods. I trudged through the mud that was covering the ground due to the massive amount of rain that was coming down. The slop stuck to my shoes making it difficult to walk through the woods.

Who was this guy? He said his name was Liam Randalph. Do I know any Liam Randalphs? I don't believe so, but by the expression on his face earlier when he woke me up, he knew me.

He said I was Greg's kid. Who was Greg? It must've been my father. It is embarrassing to admit, but I never knew the real name of my father. My mom, or my fake mom, who deserted me just a few weeks ago and left me to the Recruits of the Clade, never told me my father's name. She was always quiet when I asked about him. I thought she was just too depressed to want to talk about it, but maybe she didn't know anything about him at all.

This got me thinking about the woman who was my mom for the past 16 years of my life before the Clade. The day the Recruits, as well as the Agents, came for me, my mom disappeared. The only thing that was left from her was a note that said "she was sorry." I wonder if she meant this. The thought of her gave me heartache even now almost a month later, but I want to know what happened to her. I'm going to find out because the same thing happened to Gabe…

Gabe…

I left him to die. How could I do that? He was my first and best friend in the Clade. We first met while we were locked up in a room the day we first arrived in the Clade. I remember everything so perfectly, and I will for a long time. The shot that blasted through the trees. Gabe screaming in agony. Sarah crying her eyes out. The torment was too much. I promised him I would find his parents someday, and I plan on doing that.

The woods were thick with brush and other plant life. I had to keep an eye out for Liam when he would push back a branch; otherwise, it would hit me square in the face. Liam said that his place was back in these woods somewhere. Why would anyone live out in the middle of nowhere?

Liam kept pushing forward, but he must've known I was thinking about things because he said, "You are awfully quiet back there ain't ya? Wanna talk about it?"

I responded, "Sorry, but I don't have any idea who you are, so no, not really."

"Alright, have it your way then, but I learned after years of being in the Clade that the only way to find any relief and comfort in a world of terror and nightmares is too open up about it."

I stopped as I heard that. Liam stopped and turned around at me and said, "What? Is something the matter with you?"

"You… you are in the Clade?" I asked surprised.

"No, not anymore, but yes, I was at one point in my youth. Psh, I was the toughest of all of them… uhh… what do they call them now? Recruits? Yeah, I was the toughest of them all," he replied putting his fist to his chest.

"What do you mean by 'not anymore'?" I asked. "Did you quit?"

"Haha," he laughed. "You can't just quit from the Clade, sonny-"

"Zeke," I interrupted him.

"Zeke? Yeah, what about you?"

"Nothing, it's just that you called me sonny, but my name is Zeke."

"Oh geez louise, sonny," he responded rubbing his face. "I just say that to all the kids unfortunate enough to wind up in the arms of the Clade."

"Anywho, as I was saying," Liam continued turning around and trudging through the forest. "You can't just quit from the Clade. No, they will hunt you down like the animals they all think we are."

"Who do you mean by they?" I asked interested.

"I'm assuming you had a run in with the Agency if you were trying to get away from the New York Clade division. Well, the Agency are the people who find you even if you are not part of the Clade anymore. All they want is to exterminate anyone with abilities, and if you're lucky enough to hide from them, then you have to hide from the Clade because they just don't let you quit. The main council of Head Instructors is like that. All they care about is their stupid little organization."

"Yeah," I replied. "I did have a run in with the Agency. They killed everyone except the five of us who crashed in the helicopter."

Liam said softly, "Wow… that's like 300 people killed in one attack. The Agency must be putting an end to this little game of theirs."

I got a lot of answers by talking to Liam as we walked through the rain back to his home, or cottage, or wherever he was taking me. He knew a lot about the Clade, and what we can do. I wasn't ready to talk to him about everything I had just learned. I didn't trust him yet.

We walked together in silence the rest of the way. The only sounds were coming from birds, tree branches, our feet slapping the muddy slop that covered the ground, and the rain falling down between the trees. The rain made me feel cool and damp. I felt like crawling under a blanket and falling asleep if I wasn't lost in the middle of who knows where.

Liam continued on through the brush for what seemed like fifteen minutes. Without a trail, it would be pretty difficult to know where you are going in a huge woods like this one. He must've been here a long time if he could navigate this well.

The silence stretched on until Liam asked, "Finally ran outta questions, huh sonny?"

I made a face at him, which he didn't see and said, "Nope, I have a lot more, but I'm going to wait until I'm with my friends, so they can here the answers too."

I just said that Marcus and Juliette were my friends. I laughed at the thought that a month ago they were my worst enemies, but now I know that they are all good people just trying to find safety and justice in the world.

"Well," Liam said. "You won't have to wait much longer then."

"Why?" I asked.

"Because," Liam said as he pushed one more large branch out of the way to reveal a small clearing with an old, two-story, white house in the middle. "We are here."

Chapter 2

Saying that the house was actually a "house" would be stretching the definition of what a house is. I guess a house is considered to have four sides with a roof and a door with a few windows thrown in.

This wasn't a house really at all. The building was leaning on its left side which caused part of the roof to slide off creating a small gap that let the rain through. The brown door was cracked and hung open and the white siding was falling off. It looked as though a tornado ripped through here many years ago.

Liam sure seemed to like it though. His smile was lingering almost by his ears it was so big.

"Aah," he said. "Home sweet home."

He began to walk into the clearing being careful not to step in a big puddle. I followed him trying to do the same thing. If I got wet, that house wasn't going to do a good job at keeping me dry.

"A house?" I said. "Is that what you call it?"

"Hey now, sonny. I have lived here for the past 25 years without it once ever falling down on me. It's reliable; otherwise, I wouldn't be living here."

The thought of Liam living miles from a town or store with no contact whatsoever having to live in a house that's barely standing was insane. I don't know how I would live without my T.V. or computer. He has lived without those things or technology in general for the past two and a half decades. This guy was way tougher than Nathaniel.

We reached the front door. There was a small, cracked step in front of the door. Liam entered first, and then I followed. As you would imagine, the inside of the house wasn't anything special either.

There was a wooden staircase to the left of the entrance that looked as though it was beginning to rot. The kitchen was in the back. It had cracked tiles and drops of water dripping down from the ceiling. That was the same for everything on the right side of the house. It was all very damp including the small living room, even though it didn't look like anyone could live in there. To the left, there was a larger dining room which surprisingly looked in pretty good shape. The table and the floor all looked nice. The only problem was that it was sloping downward with cracked walls.

Also, the dining room had my friends.

"Zeke!" yelled Sarah when she noticed me.

"Sarah!" I exclaimed back.

This caused Marcus, Juliette, and Trish who were all sitting around the dining room table to look up at me. They all said hi and were happy to see me, but I don't know if they were as happy as I was to see them.

We were all okay. The helicopter crashed hard into the ground leaving only shrapnel and pieces of broken helicopter, but we all survived without a scratch. How was that possible? I didn't care at all. I was just glad everyone was safe and sound.

"Yeah yeah, you are all real happy aren't ya?" Liam said sounding disgusted. "It's cute. Very cute don't get me wrong."

I didn't listen to Liam as I pushed past him to give my friends a big hug. We all were together. I felt much safer with them around, and I'm sure the feeling was mutual. However, Marcus didn't look as though he was happy. He kept his eyes on Liam with a hateful look to them. Maybe he was just worried about whether or not we could trust him.

Liam entered the dining room and said, "Break it up, break it up!" He flailed his arms around separating the group. He continued, "Take a seat somewhere and we can talk about why you all decided to disturb my peace out here with your little toy crashing in my forest."

We listened and took our seats around the table. I sat on the far end with Sarah and Trish on my left and right, and with Marcus and Juliette up near Liam at the head of the table.

It felt as though we were at the kids table and the adults had their own separate table in which they could talk about adult things. I always hated those. Of course, those kinds of parties were with my fake mom's friends and not with family. I had no family, aunts, uncles, cousins, or grandparents growing up. It was just my mom and me. The way it was supposed to be, but now she is gone, and I am alone. She wasn't even my mom to begin with. That was something else I needed to get to the bottom of.

The thoughts of my mom and my home made me think of school. In another few weeks, I would be starting my final exams followed by three months of sweet summer vacation. I'm guessing the Clade doesn't take summer vacations from getting shot at and doing missions.

School was always my number one nemesis. I would be the kid in the back of the class not paying attention to the teacher giving a lecture about atoms or presidents or something that didn't matter to me.

The only things that did matter to me were girls, particularly one. Trish Dawson. She was always the cutest girl in the class with enough brain power to light New York. Trish had it all. The day I first had a run in with the Clade and the Agency, I was going to ask Trish to the Spring Dance. Of course, with my superb communication skills with girls, that all backfired, and I was forgotten about in New Haven shortly after. Trish, it turns out, has an ability also, and found herself here after I recruited her. I still find her beautiful, but any hope of a relationship is over until the Clade or the Agency falls.

Liam, looking as annoyed as ever, kept a strong stare on our group. He knew we were a part of the Clade due to the black cloaks we were all wearing, and the fact that he knew about the Clade also would help quite a bit.

There was something about Marcus that gave me an off feeling. He was never aggressive unless he absolutely needed to be. He was the Head Instructor at the Clade in New York. I guess he still is, but that's not the point. Marcus never becomes angered easily. Sarah, Gabe, and I broke the rules about leaving the dorm rooms after hours many times, but he never cared one bit. What is making him become so angered now?

Liam steadied himself in his chair and complained, "Why the hell are you all in my forest? Can't a guy live in peace for 50 years? I'm only at half of that." Liam looked up to the tattered ceiling. "I better get this time reimbursed whoever is listening up there."

Suddenly, Marcus slammed both of his fists down hard onto the table. The shock rattled the table and almost broke the rickety, old, thing. Everyone jumped up in surprise.

"Marcus!" Juliette yelled. "What's wrong with you? Ever since we crashed here, you have been on edge. What is it?"

Marcus furrowed his eyebrows in anger. "You want to know why I am angry, Juliette?"

"Yes, I really do."

"This man," he pointed to Liam. "This man abandoned me when I was born. He left me to live with some random stranger for 13 years until the Clade finally caught me!"

"What are you talking about, Marcus?" Juliette responded.

Liam's lips slightly curled upward in an evil kind of smile and said, "I did what every person in the Clade must do when they have a child."

We all knew where Liam was going with this, but Sarah said it first. "Wait, you are Marcus' father!?"

"Yes, yes I am little missy."

The sound of Liam's voice saying that he is Marcus' father echoed inside my head. All along we wondered who this person was when Marcus knew the entire time. Marcus hated Liam for abandoning him like all kids are when their parents are a part of the Clade. Will I be that angry if I ever meet my father? I felt angry towards him ever since the Clade recruited me. The thought of him being alive and capable of visiting me and coming to my birthdays and taking pictures of me on the first day of school made my anger and frustration even more concentrated. I felt sorry for all kids in the Clade who had to find out about their parents. At least for Gabe, his were dead. He couldn't be pissed off at his parents. Well, he couldn't even if he wanted to anymore. Gabe is dead…

I regained focus back onto the conflict between Marcus and his father at hand. This fight could be a predecessor of all other Clade Recruits that meet their true parents for the first time.

Marcus continued, "You left me to live with a stranger. I thought you were dead my entire life."

Liam responded, "Yeah, such a shame to. Do you think I wanted to let you go live with someone who was only in it for money?"

"Money?" I asked curious. "Is that why our fake mom's and dad's stay with us until we are of age? You offer them a job babysitting until the Clade recruits us?"

"In a way, you are correct," Liam said. "There are people all across this effed up country we call America that are low life's. We find them, ask if they want a job, and then relocate them to wherever the safest spot would be for the baby."

"It's terrible! How can the original Head Instructors even think about considering such an idea!?" Marcus screamed.

"Marcus you need to relax. It's not his fault," Juliette pleaded.

"No no," Liam said. "I do take some of the blame. I was one of the original five who helped construct the organization of the Clade. I was a fool to accept the idea though."

This was all new information to me. I have heard earlier that there was an original group of five Head Instructors that created the entire Clade. Was my father one of them? They were like the founding fathers of America. These few people came up with the idea of the Clade and all of the rules along with it. It's hard to believe even for a Recruit.

If everything that was said was true, then that must mean that some of the original five that created the Clade must be dead as well. If that's the case, then who replaces them? There must be a backup system. A hierarchy of Recruits that show potential to take the places of those killed. How else would Marcus get the Head Instructor spot?

Marcus switched the subject, "Why did you leave the Clade? Are you a coward, father?"

Trish adjusted herself to feel a little more comfortable and whispered to Sarah and I, "This is awkward. Marcus has daddy issues."

Liam heard us and gave us a glare as if we had no idea on what was really going on between Marcus and himself.

Liam said, "I left because I knew the Clade was going to come crashing down at the hand of the Agency. It was only a matter of time, and if we don't do something quickly, the Agents will be knocking on my front door looking for you. For an added bonus, they will find me, and I will be killed. All my years in seclusion would be put to waste."

"Excuse me, Mr. Randalph," Juliette said. "Why did you run away, though. We understand that it would be much safer out here away from the Clade where you won't be targeted by Agents, but why run?"

Sarah whispered to Trish and I making sure Liam wasn't listening, "How did she know Liam's last name is Randalph?"

I shrugged and said, "It may be Marcus' last name. Did he ever tell us his last name?"

Trish shook her head and Sarah answered, "No, I have been here longer than both of you, and I have never known his last name. I always knew him as Marcus. Plus, Nathaniel was my Instructor, so I never really met Marcus too often."

That made me feel stupid because Marcus was my Instructor and I never knew his last name. For all I knew, his last name could've been Laufor, and we would be brothers. Wouldn't that be a plot twist?

"I left," Liam answered. "Because it was a smart thing to do. Granted, I was only thinking of myself, and I could've taken Marcus with me to grow up with his real father, but if this plan failed, and the Agents caught up to me right away, he would have been killed, so I left him with his hired mom like all of the other Recruits."

Liam refocused himself on the question at hand and continued, "The Clade was great in the beginning. It was a perfect place to go for all of us "Originals" that escaped from the Agency when our powers first manifested. All of the people who survived met up and five people were selected to be leaders of the group of fifty or so. I was one of them, same with sonny down there," He pointed to me.

I pointed to myself in surprise and said, "My father was one of the creators?"

Liam nodded and said, "Yes, your father was the one that everyone looked up to. Always full of confidence. That's why I knew he could be trusted, so when I left Marcus with his new mother, I requested that he personally Recruits him."

Wow, my father was one of the most important Recruits in the Clade. If it wasn't for him, the Clade wouldn't exist as it is today... I haven't decided yet though if he is an idiot or a genius. As of right now, he is an idiot. 300 Recruits died back in New York, and no one came to help. Shouldn't somebody have been aware of an attack? Nathaniel must've hid the information well.

"Anywho," Liam added. "As I said, the Clade was a great idea at first, but as time went on and the original fifty Recruits aged and had children with their lovers-"

I lost my train of thought when he mentioned lovers. Sarah and I both shuttered a little at the thought of our moms being with our parent. Trish kind of smiled a little probably thinking it was romantic. Gross.

I regained focus on Liam. "The Clade was becoming too large. We had to separate the Clade into three divisions across the country due to lack of space in the original Clade division that still stands today. I knew it was only a matter of time before the Agency would take advantage of our weakness and attack. As I figured, I was right. One Clade division has been eliminated except you five, and now you have one of the most important missions on your hands. You have to warn the other two divisions of the impending attacks, or they will fall, and we will cease to exist."

Liam pointed his finger out at us around the table. All of a sudden, I felt as though the weight of the world was on my shoulders. I'm sure everyone else felt it too. Even a Head Instructor like Marcus must have been feeling some strain. We were on a mission to save the Clade and all Recruits. If we fail, then the Clade dies along with all of the people with abilities in the world.

I remember lying on the couch when I was younger watching cartoons on Saturday morning. Jackie Chan Adventures was my favorite. I always wished I could be a superhero and make a difference in the world and save little kittens stuck in trees and defeat evil dragons like Shendu. It turns out that my future would be almost like a cartoon. However, now that I know that I have to save everyone from certain demise, I don't want it anymore.

Thunder rumbled gently shaking the house a little followed by the sound of pouring rain. I could see the living room off to the side across the entry way, and it was beginning to fill with water leaking through the ceiling. A storm must be rolling in. It will be tougher to move now in the mud around the house.

Juliette and Marcus remained focused on what Liam was saying trying to absorb every little detail on the impending mission that will determine that fate of everyone in the room. Sarah and Trish were as focused as the others. I felt out of the loop since I wasn't paying attention much and became lost in thought. Good thing I'm not the leader then.

Marcus said, "We should get going then. The next Clade division is in Colorado up in the mountains. What do you think is the fastest way to get there, Juliette?"

"I would say helicopter, but ours got smashed into pieces on the landing here. It wouldn't matter though anyways. We wouldn't have enough fuel for a one way trip to the Rocky's."

"Yeah," Liam said. "There is a town a few miles that way," Liam pointed behind him. "If you get there, you can ride a bus. It may sound silly, but it will be easy for the Agents to track you if you had to give any information to anyone. You can pay for a bus with paper money. No trail will be left behind when you leave here."

Liam made a good point. We were in a race now to beat the Agency to the Rocky Mountains. If they knew where we were, they could try and stop us. If taking a bus meant safer travel, I was all for it. Besides, I have never been out of the northeastern section of the country. This would be exciting if our lives weren't on the line.

Marcus said, "Sounds like a plan. Thank you, dad, for helping us out even though you did abandon me when I was young."

"Yes, no problem," Liam said. "I am sorry for ever leaving you. I hope you can forgive me someday. Maybe when all of this is over."

"Maybe."

"Now," Liam finished. "Go out the back door and keep heading west. You will find that town. Hurry before the Agents show up. They probably saw that helicopter crash if they were following it from New York."

Liam was right because right after he finished that sentence a grenade broke through the front window.

Chapter 3

All of us jumped back and moved away from the table. The grenade erupted in a cloud of smoke. Thankfully, it was a smoke grenade, but had to mean that the Agents were going to break in any second and kill us all.

I crawled on the ground looking for everyone through the thick fog. It was no use. The smoke was to thick to see anything, and I had to follow the sound of the others voices.

"Sonny!" Liam yelled from somewhere ahead of me in the smoke. "Get your ass back here, or you will be shot!"

He found me. I felt a strong grip on the collar of my shirt and got yanked forward out of the smoke and into the kitchen. Everyone was in there waiting for me. It makes sense because I was the closest to the window on the opposite side of the table.

Sarah and Trish were near the back door. It was a screen door, so we could see through it. It appeared as though an escape through the back would be a good idea. There was no one around in the back. I stood over by Sarah and Trish as Marcus, Juliette, and Liam discussed the situation.

"They are here. We need to get out now," Juliette said.

"You're right," Marcus said. "If we go now, we can probably make it safely away without them catching us if we move quickly. The longer we stay here, the more likely we are going to get killed.

That's when the bullets started ripping through the walls.

The machine guns the Agents were using were powerful because they broke through the front wall and through the kitchen wall. Sarah, Trish, and I threw down the kitchen table and hid behind it near the back door. Marcus and Trish moved over by Liam who was up against the far wall in the corner of the room.

Liam shouted through the sound of bullets, "Get those kids out of here! That Zeke boy is important! He can do things I have never seen before in all my years in the Clade!"

Sarah and Trish glanced at me. I just shrugged. I didn't feel like anyone special hiding behind this table for safety. If I was important, I would be able to stop all of the Agents from turning the walls into Swiss cheese, but I couldn't.

Our powers have a limit. The more practice you get with your ability, the longer you can use it. The toll it takes on your body is tremendous. I could see myself taking out all of the Agents in front of the house, but I got gassed fighting Nathaniel earlier, and he didn't even break a sweat. If I was going to be of any use to the Clade, I needed more time to train.

Time wasn't a luxury at the moment however. The Agents were on our doorstep and soon to be taking us out. We needed to make a move now before it was too late.

"Are we going to do something or just stand around and talk!?" I shouted over the sound of firing bullets.

"Yes!" Marcus replied. "Everyone head out the back and keep moving! Don't slow down for anything!"

For once, a plan was made. Trish bolted out of the screen door followed by Sarah and then myself. I took a quick look behind me to find Trish and then Marcus.

Trish didn't halter for one second through the even thicker goop. The stuff really stuck to our shoes which made it even tougher to move in than before. The rain didn't help either. It blurred our vision making us wipe our eyes repeatedly. The sound of thunder ripped through the air creating an ominous feeling only making us all push harder.

As Sarah, Trish, and I left the clearing and entered the forest line, we stopped and waited for the others. That's when we noticed that Marcus stopped Juliette and began to talk to her. There was a lot of yelling going on, but it was out of range for us to hear.

"What do you think is going on?" Trish said.

"No idea," Sarah replied. "But they shouldn't be talking at a time like this. The Agents could come around any second."

Sarah was right. I was shaking due to my nerves. The Agents could come around and get us any second and Marcus was talking to Juliette like we were back at the hospital in New York. This wasn't a good time. Couldn't he wait until later to talk to her? Unless, it was something that was so urgent that he had to tell her about it now. I had a worried feeling in my gut.

Marcus and Juliette just kept yelling at each other. Something I noticed was that Liam was nowhere in sight. He must've stayed inside to fight the Agents. He really loved this place. Even though it is a mud filled dump.

A scream broke through my thought. Everyone lost their train of thought, even Marcus and Juliette stopped yelling at each other for a little bit to hear the screams. It must've been Liam. It was a male voice and came from the house.

Marcus yelled a little more and took off running for the house! What was he thinking? He was going to get himself killed. There was no way he could take on all of those Agents. Actually, he did beat up a lot of them back at the Clade, but still. This is a whole different situation. Why would he risk his life? Unless, it was too help his father.

Trish didn't go back and help though. She turned towards us and began to run for the tree line. As she approached us, I could tell she had started to cry. Her eyes were bright red. Whatever went down between Marcus and Juliette must've been serious.

Juliette finally reached us. Her black hair stuck to her face hiding her red eyes from the others.

Sarah asked, "Juliette, what happened to Marcus?"

She wiped her hair out of her face and a few tears, I believe, out of her eyes. If I were to ask her if they were tears, she would say no. Juliette is a very independent woman and never likes to show weakness even to weaker Recruits like Trish, Sarah, and I.

More gunshots rang out from in front of the house. Marcus and Liam better get out soon, or they will be in serious trouble.

Juliette said through choked back sobs, "I will tell you what happened when we get a safe distance away."

She took off further into the forest. The rest of us followed, but not before taking one more look back at the house fearful for the lives of Liam and Marcus. I hoped they would catch up with us.

We moved through the forest carefully making sure we didn't get separated or lost. Due to that, we moved slowly making sure we were going in the direction that Liam pointed out for us.

There was a small trail cut through the trees that followed Liam's path. It definitely helped us make our way to the town at the edge of the forest. Liam could've created this path himself in case he needed an escape. Probably not though because he just stayed back there and fought the Agents.

Liam was the only person besides Nathaniel that I met so far that was one of the original members of the

Clade. I wonder if he knew Nathaniel back then. They would've been teenagers or at least in their mid-twenties back then. It's hard to believe that a group of 50 people elected 5 individuals to lead them. I'm 16, and I couldn't imagine doing anything like that.

Then again, I never imagined running through a forest in the middle of who knows where with a couple of people with supernatural abilities. I never imagined that my mother would be a phony and disappear from me never to be seen again, and I definitely never imagined my friend getting shot and killed by someone I trusted.

Nathaniel will pay for that.

We kept running and swerving between the trees and shrubs trying to be as quiet as possible. Thunder and lightning still shook and rattled the sky. The mud was not as tough to move through here thanks to the trees blocking a lot of the rain, but some drops still made it through. A few times one of us would stumble and push ourselves back up. We were soaked with water and dirt, but we kept moving.

The humidity was getting to me. I kept wiping the sweat from my forehead. One time, I wiped off my cheek and noticed that there was blood on my hand. I touched my cheek again and felt a cut.

I slowed Trish down and asked, "Trish, is there a cut on my face?"

"Hmm?" She said. "Yeah, you do. You could've been cut by a piece of glass when the grenade came in through the window...wow, I can't believe I just said that."

"Yeah, me either," I laughed. "If it helps, I'm sure there is more of that to come."

She put her hand on my right cheek and gently rubbed it wiping off the blood. I'm surprised it didn't gross her out. It only makes me like her more which is a feeling I didn't want, not now at least. With everything that is going on with the Agency, the Clade, and Marcus leaving us, it would be wrong for me to try to make any moves on Trish at a time like this. Also, I can't make any moves because I have no idea how to make a move.

Finally, after what seemed like forever walking and running through the thick foliage, we reached the end of the forest. What lay in front of us were a series of rolling hills that stretched far into the distance. The storm clouds approached us with increasing fury from over the hills on the horizon.

I noticed a few burrs on my cloak, so I reached down and picked most of them off. Everyone else noticed what I was doing and did the same. There was nothing we could do about the mud stained onto our cloaks though. The only thing that could help that was if the rain washed them away.

We looked around for the town that Liam talked about. There was no such town in front of us like he said there was. It was confusing all of us. Did we go the wrong way?

Juliette announced, "There is a highway around the bend of those trees." She pointed to our left where a small, rural, highway cut through the hills. "If there is a town anywhere around here, then it would definitely be near that highway. I say we follow it."

"Sounds good to me," I agreed and began walking for the highway.

Not everyone was in agreement with that decision.

Trish said, "Wait a minute. I'm not going anywhere until I find out what happened to Marcus. Doesn't he make all of the decisions because he outranks you?"

Lightning tore through the sky in front of us followed by a loud boom of thunder. The storm was becoming stronger and more fierce. It was beginning to be unsafe.

That was the opposite expression Juliette showed. Her eyes descended to the ground, and she gave a blank stare. It was as though her soul or being was completely removed leaving only a shell.

"What happened, Juliette?" Sarah continued. "Is everything okay?"

She shook her head and wiped her face. Juliette's lip began to quiver as she tried to straighten herself like she did before. Something serious had happened. She didn't have to say anything. I think Sarah, Trish, and I all had the same idea about what had happened with Marcus.

Juliette answered in a shaken, broken voice, "He stayed behind."

It wasn't much of an answer. I kept pushing her hoping that she would elaborate more on what happened. We could all tell that Marcus stayed behind.

Thankfully, I didn't have to ask. She continued on her own.

"Let me explain. On the way out of Liam's shack, Marcus pulled me to the side and said to me..."

She began to faulter. It must've been hard for her to leave Marcus behind. They have been Recruits in the Clade together since they were my age. They became Instructors together and best friends. Now he is gone, probably killed by the Agents. That even made me hurt a little bit.

"… he said he was going to stay behind and help Liam fight."

"Why?" Trish asked. "I thought he hated Liam for abandoning him?"

"He did, but as we discussed the Agents taking over the first division of the Clade, he thought about his life and what Liam did for him. Marcus realized sitting in his father's home that Liam only did what he thought was best for him, and he couldn't live with himself if Liam died. It would be his fault in some way because the Agency tracked our helicopter and found us when it crashed. We led the Agents right to Liam."

There was a long silence as we let the information of Marcus staying behind to help protect his father sink in. The only sounds were the thunder roaring overhead.

I wondered if we would ever see Marcus again. He was my Instructor back at the Clade. At first, I hated him and thought that he was working with the Agents. It turned out to be Nathaniel who was working with the Agents and Marcus did what he could to protect me. He almost gave his life.

The memories floated in my head and made me think we were at a funeral. I felt confident that Marcus would come back even if no one else believed it. He has a habit of coming back like the time when he recruited me. He wouldn't go away until I went with him. Well, he hit me in the head, but still.

Sarah broke the silence and asked, "He was our division's leader though. How can we go on without someone to represent and lead the New York Clade. No offense Juliette, but there were 5 Instructors including yourself who were all qualified to take up the reins as Head Instructor if Marcus was transferred or… killed, and you are the youngest."

There was another long silence as Juliette absorbed what Sarah had just said. It was true. Juliette and Marcus were the youngest Instructors in our Clade division, but if Marcus could become the Head Instructor being that young, then why couldn't Juliette? Also, who makes the decision of who becomes the Head Instructor?

I soon got my answer as Juliette said, "That was the last thing Marcus said to me. He told me that… that I was to become the Head Instructor from now on for the New York division, and to go on without him. If he was to survive, then he would be right behind us."

Trish said, "Does he have the right to hand over that kind of power?"

Juliette shook her head in response, "In times of war and turmoil, a Head Instructor can give the power over to another Instructor in the Clade, but the real decision comes down to what the Council thinks."

The Council? That was something I have never heard of before. What was it? It had to be a group of important people, but what do they do? I told myself to remember to ask that later.

I said, "Don't worry, Juliette. I'm sure Marcus will catch up with us, but until then, you are going to be our Head Instructor. I trust you."

Trish and Sarah responded by saying, "Me too."

Juliette finally began to cheer up. A smile stretched across her face, and her eyes began to become more pinkish instead of red. Her tears were drying up.

"Thank you," she responded in a shaken tone. "I'll do my best, but first things first. We need to find that town and switch out of our cloaks. It will be easier to hide from the Agents while we go to the Colorado division of the Clade."

"Sounds great to me," Sarah said. "Let's-"

She was broken off by a sound coming from the forest.

It was loud. Loud enough to be heard over the sound of the thunder and pounding rain that was really falling down hard now. You could hear a few branches being broken. It was as if the person or thing or whatever it is was stumbling through the forest disoriented. Maybe it was a deer or rabbit that got spooked by the storm, or maybe it was Marcus and Liam.

We all remained in battle mode ready for the worst. If there was an Agent or group of Agents about to attack we would be ready.

Good thing we were.

Out of the forest came an Agent in full black battle armor stumbling and spinning in circles disoriented and lost. He fell to the ground, but quickly got back up. He held his gun out in front of him ready to be used in case he found us. Well, he did.

"MOVE!" Juliette yelled.

Chapter 4

We all sprinted in the opposite direction towards the road getting as far away from the Agent as possible. It didn't take him long to figure out though that we were Recruits.

The Agent regained his focus on his targets, us, and pulled out his walkie talkie from his belt. "Captain! I found them! They are heading towards Highway 21 on the west side of the forest."

I couldn't hear the muffled reply from the Captain, but it couldn't have been good for us. I looked back behind us to see the Agent beginning to run for us.

"He's coming!" I told the others in between breaths.

"Get around the bend of trees and hide back there. We will take him out and make our way down the highway," Juliette responded.

We ran a little bit further and dove behind the bend in the tree line. We sat quietly in the brush while the Agent moved closer to us. He stopped and looked around wondering where we disappeared. The gun he held in his hands was now held up to his eye ready to blast anything that moves.

I looked over to Trish and Sarah on my right. What I saw surprised me. Sarah looked freaked out beyond imaginable. Her eyes were wide open and it looked as if she may pass out. Was she that afraid of conflict? She wasn't back at the Clade. What happened?

Trish, on the other hand, was watching Juliette. I looked over to Juliette on my left who began to swirl her hand in a circular motion. In front of me, the air began to shimmer and shake. What formed was a long band of air that held its shape in some magical way. It looked like a javelin.

Juliette waited for the Agent to move over a little so that she could have a clear shot. She didn't need one. Her air javelins were strong enough to break through ten trees and a soldier without slowing down or disappearing, but she still waited.

Finally, after what seemed like forever, the Agent moved into the spot that Juliette had hoped for. She pulled her hand back and threw her arm forward like a punch. A shimmer of air followed and launched itself at an incredible speed. The javelin connected with the Agent in the chest and before he even knew what hit him, his armor exploded sending him flying. One less Agent in the world to worry about.

Juliette quietly moved out of her hiding spot behind a tree and moved towards the highway. She held up her hand signaling for Trish, Sarah, and I to remain put. We listened and she continued on her own.

For being unsure of whether or not she was ready to be a Head Instructor and lead us, Juliette has done really well. Of course, it has only been 5 minutes, but still. We were confronted by an Agent, and she did what she thought was right, which saved our lives.

Juliette stopped and waved her hand signaling us to move out. I took the lead, and the girls followed behind me out of the brush and into the open.

"Everything appears to be clear. We should start moving towards the town before backups show up," Juliette ordered.

We made our way to the highway to our left. It was a paved, two-lane highway. There were a lot of cracks and bumps on its surfaces probably meaning that it was old and never redone. Not many people must travel this way around the forest. We should go relatively unnoticed as long as we stick to the highway.

The rain was still falling steadily making our cloaks drenched and heavy on our bodies. We all had to keep wiping the water dripping from faces. My mom always told me when I was young to stay out of the rain on a wet spring day; otherwise, I would catch a cold. I wished she was here now... I wished Gabe was here now.

Thoughts of Gabe never left my mind. Ever since his death, it felt like a hole had opened up inside me and most of my emotions got pulled down into it. I wasn't the only one who felt like that though. Juliette was a little sad just because she was Gabe's Instructor. Trish was only part of the Clade for a week or two, so she really never got to know Gabe like Sarah and I. Sarah, on the other hand, was a wreck. She hid it well, but you could tell by the way she acted that she was feeling distressed. She really liked Gabe, and Gabe was really starting to like her, but that will never be now because of the Agency and Nathaniel.

Suddenly, a group of thumping sounds rose out of nowhere from behind us followed by microphone sounds. That could only mean one thing…

The Agency's reinforcements have arrived.

The group turned around, and we saw at least a dozen fully equipped Agents ready for battle against us.

They were still moving down the highway. We had enough time to start running towards the town; although we had no idea how far it was, and if we didn't reach it in time, we were easy targets on the straightway road.

Juliette made the call, "We have to keep moving before they reach us. If we can get into town, we can hide out and wait for them to pass us by."

"But how far away is the town?" Trish asked.

Juliette looked down the highway that slopes downward on a hill into the town. It was at least another three miles away, which was too far to run.

"We will have to fight. The town is too far away to out run the Agents," Juliette said angered.

The marching grew louder as the Agents continued their sprint to us. It was going to be a fire fight now, and if we didn't win, then we could end up like Marcus and Liam. It was tough to think that Marcus could be dead, but how else could the Agents get here without running into Marcus and Liam? If that is the case, I will avenge them.

Anger filled inside me with hatred and rage for what could have happened to Marcus, Liam, and Gabe. I was going take them all out myself.

"Then we fight, and win," I said confidently.

"I don't know if my ability will be much help to you though, Juliette," Sarah said.

"Same here. My ability is only useful when I am in touching distance. If we stay back here, then I can't do much," Trish added.

"It's no problem," Juliette replied. "Zeke and I can blast these doofuses into next week."

"Yeah, I got enough rage to take them all out myself. You don't mind if I go first, right Juliette?" I asked.

"Not at all, Zeke," Juliette smiled.

Our confidence was building even though the Agents were almost on top of us. Soon they would be able to fire their guns without worry of missing. It was time to take action, but the new Head Instructor was all prepared for it.

"Sarah, Trish, stay behind us and keep moving down the highway towards town. We will catch up," Juliette said turning to face the Agent army.

I turned and stood next to her. She was a little bit taller than I was which gave her the powerful leadership qualities that leaders need.

Thunder rumbled one more time as Sarah and Trish began to run in the opposite direction. I was insane, but glad to be staying here with Juliette. I needed to unleash some rage upon the Agents for many reasons. Killing my friends would be the first and messing up my life would be the second. The only reason the Clade exists is because these guys tried to exterminate all of the people with abilities. If not for them, I would be home with my real mom and dad playing Wii with Thomas.

That is not the case though. In the here and now, the Agents were slowing down and coming to a stop. The leader of the group of Agents was in the back calling commands. The group began to get down on one knee and were about to fire.

We didn't let that happen.

"Go now, Zeke!" Juliette commanded.

I responded by charging up a bolt in the palm of my hand. The faint blue glow has become common to me even though I knew it was capable of killing people.

I unleashed my bolt of anger on the middle of the group. I blasted one Agent sending him flying back with a burnt uniform and scorched chest, but that's not all. The bolt arced and hit the man next to him who was down on his knee. It wasn't as severe as the first guy, but he did tense up and fall to the ground on his back.

Juliette was already prepared for her turn. She unleashed multiple air javelins at many of the Agents. She hit four of them without even breaking a sweat. The bolt I unleashed took some serious energy out of me making me feel a little tired. I guess that's why she was an Instructor, a lot of practice went into controlling her ability.

The remaining five or six Agents looked stunned as if they had never seen a power like ours before which was a plus for us. It didn't last long; however, they were already regrouping and prepared to fire a few shots at us.

The Agent on the far left unloaded his gun at us. Juliette and I noticed this and were ready for it. Juliette released a large amount of air javelins. These weren't like regular ones though. These were very small and not long at all. I guess Juliette can make many more air javelins if they are small.

The javelins, and you would not believe this, hit the bullets the Agent was firing at us. Small explosions creating tiny clouds of smoke and debris formed in the air in front of us. Juliette kept spinning her arms in circles releasing more and more tiny spears to block the oncoming enemy fire.

The other Agents were getting ready to fire. Juliette wouldn't be able to block those bullets. She was powerful, more powerful than I ever realized, but she wouldn't be able to block fire from another five Agents. I had to stop them.

"Zeke! The others!" She cried out.

"I know! I got it!" I replied.

I threw my arms up charging for a strong, lightning-like, blast. If it was strong enough, it would arc and take down most of the Agents again like it did last time, and then Juliette and I can finish them off.

I unleashed the bolt. It was strong. I could feel it. This bolt was a lot stronger than the last one. I was going to blast them all, and we would be safe.

All of a sudden, the bolt began to rise up towards the sky. It was no longer under my control. I tried to focus my energy and pull it down on the Agents, but it just wasn't working. Luckily, the Agents were distracted by it too. We all watched as the bolt arced towards the storm filled sky.

Uh-oh. A part of me thought I knew what was about to happen. It's like taking two wires and putting them by each other. If they are close enough, an arc of electricity would skip between the two of them. As I watched the bolt reach towards the sky, all I thought about was that.

"Juliette, you have to get away now," I said.

"What?" she said. "Why are you doing that?"

Thunder rumbled. This wasn't going to be good. Juliette needed to get away. I don't know what would happen to me, but I can handle electricity fairly well… as in I can take lethal amounts and only feel a small shock. Juliette would be fried. She needs to get away.

"I'm not controlling this. It's being pulled towards the sky," I answered.

"Why?" Juliette said looking confused.

Thunder rumbled again. She was running out of time.

"My lightning bolts strike whatever is closest to it usually. My bolt of electricity is an easy pathway for it to travel through to reach the ground."

"It's like a spark?"

"Sort of, but it doesn't really matter right now. The lightning will strike my bolt and use it as a pathway to the ground. I will be able to take most of it but still get a pretty big shock. You, on the other hand, will be a French fried Juliette if you stay."

Juliette thought it over quickly and realized that it would be smart if she got away. She turned and ran off the highway behind a small hill a few hundred feet away.

Just in time too. Lightning released from the dark clouds. It was surreal. Bright white light released from a black cloud and created a twilight setting for a few moments. The bolt bent and twisted through the air until it reached my bolt. It hit the end of the bolt. The energy in the cloud lightning was too great for my bolt to handle, for me to handle, and it surged down my bolt. I could feel it the entire time. It was overwhelming.

The lightning bolt continued downwards and landed on top of the remaining Agent soldiers. The power arced through their bodies leaving behind scorched, lifeless, bodies. If Juliette didn't leave, that might have been her.

The energy traveled down the bolt and finally connected into the palms of my hands. I only felt a shock and then, as if the sun burned out, everything became black.

Chapter 5

My body was too weak to move. The power of the lightning strike must have really knocked me down which is rare for me because usually electricity has no effect on me. Things like shocks, tasers, and sticking your finger in an electrical outlet brings no harm to me. I can absorb huge amounts of electricity.

Well, I guess lightning is the one exception. I never felt anything like it. I could feel the energy from the lightning travel down my bolt of energy like a wave until it finally hit me. At first, I felt warm and then everything turned dark. I must've passed out from the shock, or I may have died. I didn't feel dead. Can you feel if you are dead?

I couldn't be dead. I was aware of what was going on. Every once in a while, I would wake up from the dark prison I was in. The light hurt my eyes, and everything was blurry. I guess the shock had an effect on my brain. What I saw was Sarah, Trish, and Juliette carrying me. We were on the highway and getting to the outer edge of the town ahead of us. We passed a sign, but it was too blurry to read. The efforts of staying awake were too much, and I fell back asleep.

I awoke I don't know how much later on a bench. The sky was blue with only a few clouds passing by. I must've been out for a while if the storm had passed. That was one heck of a storm if it could take out myself and all of the Agents...

The Agents! What had happened to them? I quickly sat up causing me to become dizzy and disoriented. I fell back on the back of the bench keeping me upright. Also, where were Trish, Sarah, and Juliette? Would they just leave me here unconscious?

My memory started coming back to me. The Agents were blasted with the actual lightning bolt. They were all dead. I'm sure more will be here eventually. Wherever my group was, they have to know that we can't be here that long.

That's when I heard quickly moving footsteps off to my left. I looked over my shoulder to see a young boy, probably 8 years old, running for what seemed like his life. He sprinted past me leaving a trail of dust in his wake. Someone must be in a hurry. Then, two older guys, probably 18 years of age, ran by me from the same direction the little kid came from.

I overheard them talk as they ran by. The one with the letter jacket and short hair said, "When I find that kid, I am going to pound him into the dust."

The other, who was wearing a black jacket and had long, blond hair that hung in his face said, "Yeah, nobody steals from McMan!"

Confused and intrigued, I followed them. My legs were weak getting up but they quickly adjusted to my weight, and I was able to move as if nothing had happened to me. I hope the others wouldn't worry about where I went. I would be back in 5 minutes.

I followed the two older boys in a dead sprint across the park. Thanks to the Clade and all of its training, I was in the best shape of my life, which isn't really much because I'm only 16. Sports were never my forte in high school, so I felt that I never needed to work out.

The park contained a bunch of different playgrounds and swing sets with kids and parents on them. It was a pretty place. At one point, I followed the boys across a small, wooden bridge that crossed a creek. There were trees everywhere giving the park a forest vibe to it. If I had passed out in the forest by Liam's house, I would have no idea that I even left there.

The two older boys finally came to a stop just outside a brick building across the street from the park. It was a store called Goldman's Hardware. There was an alley right next to the old store that was a dead end.

The boy was cornered in the alley with nowhere to run. The two older boys moved closer and closer as if they were stalking their prey which was what the younger boy pretty much was. Whatever he did, he was about to pay for it in full.

I knew kids like that back in high school in New Haven. They were primarily jocks who were great at sports and good looking. In the hierarchy of high school, they were on top. Guys like me are somewhere near the middle which is just fine by me. Sure, I didn't get girls too often, or never, and I didn't have a lot of friends, but I was happy. At least I was going to have a future. Unlike them, or maybe not now that I think about it.

The bald-headed boy, McMan I believe, pointed at the boy and said, "You are in deep trouble kid. You're just lucky I feel a little kind enough to give you a few last words, so go on."

"I didn't do anything! I swear it!" The boy pleaded. This wasn't looking good for him.

The other blond-haired guy said, "Those are your last words? Ha, kinda lame even for a runt like yourself. We saw you touch McMan's jacket in the park. Nobody touches McMan's stuff and lives to tell about it. Sorry, those are the rules." He started to crack his knuckles.

The boy slid up against the back wall and fell into the fetal position waiting for the worst.

McMan said, "Look at what you're doing, Lars. You put him in the fetal position. How are we supposed to pound him good if he is all huddled up like that?"

"Sorry McMan, I wasn't thinking I guess."

"No, you weren't, but I'll think about forgiving you if you can beat this kid out of the fetal position."

Lars smiled from ear to ear and said, "Oh thank you, McMan, I will do it for you."

He flexed his arms and moved towards the cowering boy. He was a goner unless I stepped in and did something, so I did. I jumped in between McMan and Lars and stood in front of the boy with my arms out wide protecting him.

This took them by surprise. They didn't expect someone to step in and fight this kid's fight. Bullies were dumb like that. They played off of fear and hoped that no one would step in and help the kid they are picking on. They are strong and brave when it's one-on-one or two-on-one, anything in their favor, but once the tables are turned, they become fearful of the kids they are tormenting. I hope my theory is right. If I had to fight, I would win. I had more power than these guys knew about.

"Woah," Lars said surprised stumbling backwards. "Who is this freak in the ridiculously long, black, sweatshirt, McMan?"

"I have no idea, but he is asking for trouble by standing in front of that snot nosed kid. Unless you want to get pounded too, I suggest you make like a tree and get out of here freak."

What he said was so idiotic I couldn't help but laugh. I think the kid behind me even laughed a little, but then went immediately back into cowering. These guys were not bright… at all.

"Sorry," I said sounding tough. "I saw you two picking on this kid and had to step in. I hope you don't mind."

"Are you talking smart with us, freak!?" McMan screamed.

"Ya know, I think he is, McMan. I say we should teach him a lesson about messing with the two toughest guys in Wellsboro."

Wellsboro? Where was that? At least these guys weren't a total waste of space. Now I know where I am, but now all I have to figure out is which state. The helicopter couldn't have gotten far. We could still be in New York for all I knew.

"I will give you the chance to turn and walk away," I said casually. "Nobody needs to get hurt today. How about you put away your fists, and go home. Perhaps, you should study because by the sound of it, you two aren't going to graduate for a long time." The little boy laughed behind me out loud this time.

This really set them off. "Fine, have it your way," McMan said. "Lars, take them out."

"With pleasure," he replied grinning.

Lars stepped up with fists clenched tightly. He stopped just short of me and wound up for a shot. He swung at me, but I caught his fist and punched him right back in the gut. He flew backwards and landed on his butt besides McMan. I guess all of this Clade training was really paying off.

"What are you doing?" McMan asked Lars.

"I'm just toying with the punk. Don't worry, McMan, I can handle the freak."

He jumped back up and ran at me hoping to get his revenge for making him look like a fool in front of his idol, McMan. He dove at me and wrapped his arms around my chest. We fell backwards and hit the wall behind us.

That's when the weird thing happened, even for me. A small bolt of electricity shot out of my chest and hit Lars. He shuddered and rolled away from me back towards McMan. I rubbed my chest wondering how that happened because I didn't do it. My body just released electricity on its own.

"What the-" Lars said freaking out.

"Who the hell are you, and how did you do that?" McMan said.

"I…. have no idea," I answered truthfully.

I had no idea how I released electricity from my chest since I didn't will myself to do it. It did it all by itself. What did that lightning bolt do to my powers?

"I'll handle this," McMan said moving forward towards me now.

I tried to stand up, but my attempt failed when a fist flew in from my side view and hit me in the cheek. I spun around and hit the ground, but that's not all that had happened. Another bolt reached out from my cheek and up through the arm of McMan causing him to spin and contort through the air back to where he came from.

I felt my face and noticed that my cheek was bleeding just a bit. I couldn't feel the cut though. My powers must've healed it already. That is normal, yes, but it is also odd because my injury usually stays around a little bit before it is healed. Something bad was going on. I no longer had control over my abilities..

McMan and his puppy, Lars, had enough of what I had to offer. They screamed like babies and ran away from the alley down the street. They won't hurt this kid ever again. If they had any sense, they would stay away unless they wanted to go toe-to-toe with me again, or at least, that's what I hoped. I won't be in this town for long.

I gave the boy a helping hand getting up and brushing himself off. He reminded me of Gabe a lot now that I look at him. He was a little bit bigger built around the waist with a pudgy face to go with it. He had short hair and had the same knack of being afraid. It made me miss Gabe even more.

I said, "Sorry about those guys. What did you do to tick them off anyways?"

"Nothing," He said. "I was on my way home from my friend's house when I decided to take a short cut through the park. As I was walking through the park, there was a letter jacket resting on the park bench. I thought someone left it there by accident, and I was going to see if there was a name in the collar or something. When I touched it, those guys showed up and just started chasing me. Thanks for helping me."

I smiled, "It's no problem. My name is Zeke Laufor."

"Mine is Theodore Clemson, but everyone just calls me Teddy because I look like a teddy bear."

I laughed, "Yeah, you kind of do."

We started walking out of the alley when Teddy noticed the blood still on my face.

"You're bleeding," he said. He reached up and then jumped up and wiped it off with his hand. I forgot that the blood was still on my face even though the cut disappeared.

"It's fine really," I said. "Nothing to worry about. I can take punches."

He looked up at my face and asked, "I thought you got cut. What happened? Also, how did you shock those guys?"

I answered truthfully, "I have no idea, Teddy. I just have no clue about how anything has happened or might happen in the future."

He wiped the blood off on his pants creating a small, red, smear. This was a good kid and I was glad that I was around to protect him. What had me concerned was why I was left here? Where were my friends?

Teddy waved over to another kid across the park and said, "That's my friend. I am going to go with him now, but thanks a lot for helping me out before."

I smiled and said, "No problem, Teddy. It was nice to meet you."

He smiled back in reply, "It was nice to meet you to, Zeke. Hopefully, I'll get to see you around again sometime."

I didn't know how to respond to that. Teddy was a nice kid and I wanted to see him again, but that probably will never happen. As much as I yearned for a normal life and to be with my family and friends, it will never happen. I have a mission to complete, and if I didn't, the entire Clade and all of its members will be killed.

I choked up and said, "Yeah, hopefully." He ran away across the park to a boy that appeared to be his age.

I began to walk back to the bench in the park where I woke up when I noticed three girls running from that area. It was Trish, Sarah, and Juliette, but they looked different. Their outfits had changed and Sarah even dyed a purple stripe into a few strands of her hair.

I began to run towards them waving my hands in the air frantically. They noticed me and began to run towards me on the edge of the park, smiles on all of their faces.

"There you are!" Trish cried out. "We thought the Agency caught you."

"Psh," I panted putting my hands on my knees. "They couldn't catch a cold."

"Nice analogy, funny boy," Sarah laughed.

We all laughed, and then I said, "I like the new outfits."

Their entire wardrobe had changed since last time I saw them which was I don't know how long ago. Trish had a turquoise shirt on and jean shorts. Juliette had on a purple and blue fleece with the sleeves rolled up in the humid, spring day and also had jean shorts on. Sarah, on the other hand, wore blue basketball shorts and a white t-shirt with a few purple stripes on it which matched the stripe in her hair.

"I'm liking the outfits," I nodded at them. "Very stylish. Nice hair, Sarah."

She twirled the strand in between her fingers. "Yeah? Thanks. I feel more like myself now. This is what I used to look like before the Clade got to me two years ago and gave me that oversized sweatshirt. Ick."

The outfit definitely described Sarah's personality. Weird. She even called herself a little odd when Gabe and I first met her back in New York. She was the only person I really got to know besides the Instructors and Trevor. However, we never really got to see the weirder side of

Sarah due to the sneaking around, and the oncoming attack.

Juliette shoved a plastic bag with clothes in it into my chest. "Take these and change. We will explain more once you are done."

"You guys are like my mom," I said. "Buying me clothes and all."

"Yeah yeah," Trish said with a slight sneer. "Just get yourself changed before we miss the bus out of here."

I forgot about the plan to take the bus all the way to Colorado. We were going to have a long ride ahead of us if we were only in Pennsylvania. Perhaps, the clothes were just to make the ride more comfortable or to blend into the crowd, so the Agency couldn't pick us off on the way.

I stopped thinking and began to move across the street to a public bathroom where I went into a stall and changed. The girls had a taste for fashion, well, except Sarah. I had a bright blue t-shirt and a black, zip-up sweatshirt, which I wore but didn't zip at all. For my pants, they bought some regular jean shorts like Trish and Juliette's except that they were made for boys. I threw the cloak in the plastic bag and walked out of the bathroom.

"What should I do with the cloak?" I asked.

"Throw it in this bag," Juliette handed me a brown bag with other cloaks in it.

I rolled it up and dropped it down into the bag. The bag crumpled a little under the weight of all of the cloaks making me feel unsure whether or not I should hold it by the handles. I gave it back to Juliette just in case.

"Are we allowed to do this?" I said straightening my shirt.

"Do what?" Juliette asked.

"You know. Wear clothes other than the cloak we were given. It's kind of our uniform, and we had to wear it every day in the Clade."

"Well, we aren't in a Clade division. It will be safer for us all if we could just blend in with the crowd while we make our way to Colorado. The less we stop for fighting or any other annoyances, the sooner we will be able to warn the Clade."

"Okay, fine by me," I said.

Juliette began to walk down the street away from the park. The rest of us followed obediently like little ducklings following their mom.

Chapter 6

There were a few things that remained fuzzy in my mind. One thing is what happened after I shot my bolt of electricity at the Agents when they followed us down the highway. Another thing is why did I wake up on a park bench? You think Sarah, Trish, and Juliette would've stayed with me until I woke up. They were relieved to see me when I had disappeared from the bench. Trish thought the Agents caught me. Why did they leave me there then?

I decided to ask them since we had the time. "Hey Juliette, I got a few questions for you."

She raised an eyebrow. "Yeah? Like what?"

"My mind is a bit fried right now," I rubbed my forehead. "I was wondering what the heck happened to me back on the highway when we fought the Agents."

Juliette looked to the ground in thought and answered, "It was odd to say the least. What happened was that you released your electrified attack at the group of Agents, but the bolt didn't reach them. Instead, it rose into the air and connected with a bolt of lightning coming down from the clouds overhead."

"The lightning bolt itself continued straight into the ground that occupied the Agents electrocuting them all in a horrific way. Your bolt, on the other hand, was overpowered by the lightning and rebounded with more energy than it had before. You were fried and sent flying on your back."

The memories started to flow back into my mind. I remembered the lightning connecting with my stream of energy, but the part where I flew onto my back after it made contact with me was still unclear. It probably would always be.

"All of this happened and I didn't have a burn or anything? I can only handle so much electricity," I said.

"Right after you were hit, I ran up to you. You lied motionless on the pavement. I tried to pick you up when I noticed the many brutal burns on your skin where it actually seemed like the skin was gone."

"Ouch, that's gross," I stuck my tongue out at her.

"Sorry for being descriptive. Anyways, I noticed that little electrified strands of your skin began to stretch over the burn, and it healed itself almost instantly like it usually does."

I thought back to the time when Trish woke up from her shot after being captured and going psycho inferno on the place. I had a bunch of burns then, but they all healed but not instantly. They hurt for a few minutes and then healed. If Juliette was being accurate, then something had happened when the lightning struck me. My wounds healed instantly.

It was like my body had become overcharged. That would explain somewhat why those bullies received shocks after punching me. I didn't do that to them; although, I really wanted to. Was I losing control of my powers? I was scaring myself. I was sure that my body could fix it.

"I have one more question," I asked.

"Yeah?" Juliette replied. "And what is it?"

"I woke up on a park bench before, alone. Why was I there and how come no one else was there with me?"

"Trish and I," Sarah answered, "waited for you and Juliette to finish off the Agents and find us. We waited on that same park bench for both of you for longer than we expected it would take."

"Eventually," Trish continued. "We saw Juliette walk into the outskirts of the town carrying you on her back like she was giving you a piggy back ride, but you were unconscious. Sarah and I ran over and helped her."

"We brought you back to the bench and laid you down," Sarah said as we rounded a corner where a large blue and white bus loomed in the distance. "It was then we decided that we needed to blend into the crowd if we were going to make our way across the country, so we left you there because we couldn't bring an unconscious boy into stores."

"I guess," I rubbed my forehead again. "Wouldn't you be worried that the Agency would come and take me?"

"No, not really," Juliette said. "It would be a while before they could rally another strike against us. We defeated one of their squadrons, so it would be a while before another showed up. It has been a while, that is why we are rushing to the bus."

We kept pushing forward on the sidewalk towards the bus that was now beginning to load passengers. Juliette moved to a window with a small hole cut out of it to purchase our tickets for the bus. Sarah, Trish, and I stood in line to reserve our spots.

After waiting a few minutes and moving forward in the line, Juliette approached us and handed us our tickets.

"Here you guys go," she said.

Sarah flipped the ticket around. "This bus can't possibly take us all the way to Colorado. Are we stopping somewhere?"

"Yes," Juliette answered. "We have to make a stop in Missouri and wait for the bus the next day."

That's when I saw Sarah shudder slightly. I wonder what is wrong. Her face became pale and petrified. Something definitely has her afraid, but what was it? It must be something in Missouri. That is where Gabe was from, and anything that has to do with Gabe made her depressed and morbid.

I told myself that I would figure out what was bugging her on the ride there, but for now, I decided to change the subject quickly.

"How did you pay for these, Juliette? I'm sure the Agency probably has shut down your bank account."

"The Agency does close all accounts and take all possessions of the Recruits," Juliette said. "The money is from the Clade. During the assault while we were escaping out of the tunnel, I stopped in the storage closet where we hold all of the weapons. In there, there is a bin full of money that Recruits had on them when they were brought there."

"You robbed us?" Trish asked feeling her pockets.

"Sort of, I guess," Juliette answered. "Don't you remember waking up with nothing on you other than your clothes?"

The memory of myself first waking up on the cold, steel, table drifted into the center of my mind. What I had on me wasn't really an important issue to focus on at the time. I was more worried about where I was, and who wanted me. It was also the place that I first met Gabe…

We began to board the bus with Trish first and Juliette following behind. We shuffled our way through the rows of seats and other passengers until we found our seats. Trish and Juliette sat together, which kind of disappointed me because I wanted to be with Trish, but Sarah is one of my best friends, so it was okay.

The bus was a typical coach bus. Comfortable padded seats that are cozy at first, but by the time you reach your destination, no matter how far away it was, your butt got sore. Small air conditioning vents hung above our row which felt nice on a humid day like today.

I closed my eyes and let my head rest on the back of the multi-colored, fabric, seat. The only sounds to be heard on the crowded bus were the air conditioning, driver throwing bags on the bottom of the bus, and the radio playing "All Summer Long" by Kid Rock.

I felt Sarah reaching over my chest from her window seat and pushing a small button on the arm rest which caused my seat to fall back slightly making it more comfortable and creating an easier position to sleep.

"Try that," Sarah smiled.

I stretched. "Thanks, we haven't gotten much sleep over the last two days."

"Being passed out doesn't count I guess," Sarah said.

I giggled slightly then became embarrassed. I hope nobody heard me, but by the way Sarah was smiling at me made it seem like she had.

Now that I look at her, the purple strand in her hair, it really fits her personality. She was also kind of attractive, but I had my eye on someone already which would also have to wait until this mission is over with. She was also my best friend's girl. She was off-limits, even if Gabe wasn't here.

Pictures swarmed in my head about the assault on the Clade and the tragic death of Gabe. How we had to leave him alone in a burning forest. It caused me so much pain on the inside.

Sarah was feeling the worst of it. Everyone could tell by the way she acted around situations that involved fighting. It's how Gabe died. Fighting to save our lives. Maybe she thought that we would never die. A lot of teenagers have a belief of immortality and that nothing can ever hurt them. Unfortunately, that's not true.

Also, the reason why Sarah looked so hurt outside earlier when we heard the news about stopping in Missouri for one night might be because Gabe is from that state. Any little thing that reminds Sarah of Gabe tears her up. I wished I could help.

The bus shuddered and began to move down the street. After about five minutes, I opened my eyes just slightly allowing me to catch a glimpse of a sign that read "You are now leaving Wellsboro." It was going to be a long ride. I let sleep take me into its opened embrace.

My dream was a flashback of the war on the Clade back in New York. I remember the gunshots ringing in my head as if they were just now occurring. The girl collapsing next to my side as a bullet impaled her. The dark cave that seemed to stretch on for miles only to lead to our own demise and the possible execution of all of the other Recruits, and Gabe…

I felt a small shock run through my body causing me to jolt forward in my seat waking me up. The pain lasted for a brief moment before subsiding. What was that? Was that the electricity again?

Ignoring it, I glanced out the window. The moon was in the center of the sky creating twilight across the interstate and the cars on it. It was so bright that the driver wouldn't even need his headlights on.

A sound cut through the silence of the sleeping bus. It was Sarah sleeping next to me. She was sleeping with her head against the window with a little bit of drool beginning to run down her cheek. Sarah was whimpering very quietly in her sleep. She must be having a bad dream about something. It could even be the Clade, like me.

I glanced around the bus to find everyone else asleep as well. Alone, I tried to rest my head on the backrest and fall asleep. After trying for about twenty minutes, I gave up and accepted the fact that it was going to be a long night.

My stomach grumbled. I just realized that I hadn't eaten a single thing since we left the Clade last night. I wished I had a cheeseburger to munch on all night. Perhaps, a Big Mac from McDonald's. That would be delicious.

My mom never really liked it when I went out to eat at fast food restaurants. Being a nurse, she always complained that I would get sick and end up in the hospital with a hose in my stomach. I told her she was a worry wart and went with Thomas whenever I got the chance to.

A few hours passed. I sat in silence on the sleepy bus as the sun began to rise behind us. It must have been around six in the morning if the sun was rising. We have been on the bus for more than twelve hours which probably meant that we were approaching Missouri.

I have never been out of Connecticut when I was a kid. The only time I had ever left the state was when Marcus kidnapped me and brought me to New York to recruit me. Even then, though, I never got to leave the Clade except to go back to my high school to get Trish.

The bus ride was a perfect way to get some sightseeing in before I was put on lock down in the Colorado Clade. I ooed and ahhed at every little thing I saw even if it was a field. I'm glad everyone was asleep for that part.

Another hour passed. That is when people began to stir on the bus. A few people in the back of the bus woke up first because of the sun shining down on their resting heads. The rest of the bus followed from back-to-front. It wasn't too long before Sarah woke up next to me.

She stretched out and gave a big yawn. "Good morning, Zeke," she rubbed her eyes. "Did you sleep well?"

"Not really. I woke up in the middle of the night. I kept having nightmares."

"Same here. A lot of them were about the Clade falling and other things."

Sarah didn't elaborate on what 'other things' meant, but I had a strong suspicion that they had to do with Gabe. I didn't want to push her, so I just let it be.

The bus continued down the interstate for many more miles, more than I can count. It was just a few hours later when a sign passed that read: "Welcome to Missouri." We had reached our destination safely, but this was only the first half of the trip, and we had already lost Marcus and Liam. What fate should befall us if we are surrounded by Agents? I sure can't pull a lightning bolt out of the sky again. The odds of that happening again are probably... well, the odds of getting struck by lightning.

We turned off the interstate at the very next exit and began a slow and curvy descent to a rural highway only populated by a local McDonald's and green, grassy, fields. It would be at least a half an hour before we reached our stop.

I nudged Sarah and whispered, "Have you ever been out here before?"

Sarah's eyes began to fill with tears as she said, "I really don't want to talk about it. I'm sorry Zeke."

Something was really bothering Sarah, and it had to do with wherever we were. Was it because Gabe was from this part of Missouri originally, or is it something else? I never really got to know Sarah all that well. It was usually Gabe and I then she tagged along and ended up getting us in some deep trouble with sneaking onto the second floor in the middle of the night. However, if it wasn't for her and her mischievousness, we probably would've died when we were attacked.

Sarah rested her head back on the window and shut her eyes most likely wanting sleep. Whenever I feel terribly or possibly on the verge of tears, I sleep. Sleep can take away almost any kind of pain. I shared her idea and slept for the rest of the bus ride to ease my mind of my thoughts.

Chapter 7

Hands shook me awake. Groggy, I slowly peered around the bus to find that most of the seats were empty and the rest of the seats were being abandoned by their passengers. Outside, it was sunny. Summer was on its way. The sun cast a large shadow behind a gas station that almost reached the bus.

Juliette said, "We reached the halfway mark. It's time to get off the bus and find somewhere to go for the night. The next bus won't leave until tomorrow morning."

I sat up and stretched my arms almost hitting Sarah and some random stranger in the head. I stood up and fixed my jeans then strode down the aisle and out of the bus rubbing my eyes in the process as they adjusted to the blinding light.

The surroundings consisted of a large parking lot that we were dropped off in that hosted a white gas station in the middle of the lot. On the other side of the road, a corn field stretched out into the horizon over a hill. Down the road to the West, more buildings emerged as if a city was approaching.

I asked, "So, where are we?"

"We are just outside of St. Louis. The city may provide a great area for concealing ourselves until tomorrow morning comes. The only problem is that we need to figure out a place to stay," Juliette answered.

"I'm guessing that a hotel is out of the question?" Trish asked.

"Afraid so. Unfortunately for us," Juliette began. "We will have to most likely rough it in the cornfield or in the sewers. Something disgusting for sure to keep the Agency off our trails."

"Dang, I really could've used a shower." Trish snickered.

Juliette laughed quietly to herself and added, "I agree. I could've used one too. The showers back at the New York Clade were decent, but since water was cut off there, a few individuals with water abilities had to create the pressure in the pipes from an underground lake about a half mile away."

"There were people creating that?" I asked surprised.

"Yes, after your initial month of training is complete, we get you to work in a way that will benefit the Clade and all of the Recruits in it," Juliette said. She waved her hand over in Sarah's direction. "Just ask Sarah."

"Sarah?" I asked. "What did you do?"

She shook her head. "I had the fun job of washing the dishes in the kitchen of the cafeteria. Since we had a limited amount of dishes, I had to clean them quickly. That's where I went when you and..." She went quiet.

An awkward silence spread out over the group. I even think that some of the tourists or travelers from the bus leaving the gas station became quiet. We all knew whom she was referring to. It was Gabe. Again, his name made Sarah feel terrible.

The silence ended when Juliette said, "Yes, so we need a place to go. Any ideas?"

I said, "Anywhere but the sewers. That doesn't sound to inviting."

"Agreed," Trish said.

Juliette began, "Well, we-" She was cut off.

Sarah interjected softly, "I know a place where we can go to."

Juliette perked up, "Really, where?"

"I lived in the suburbs of St. Louis before Nathaniel recruited me two years ago. It's my old house. It was partially destroyed a while ago so there is no power or water, but it could be a good location for us to hide out until tomorrow morning."

Juliette said, "Then we'll go to Sarah's house. First, we need a means of transportation, then Sarah, you can lead the way." Sarah nodded without breaking eye contact with the ground.

Sarah pointed over to the back corner of the gas station. "There is an employee's car behind the gas station. The only way they would catch us stealing it is that security camera," she pointed slightly above the car to show us a camera mounted on the corner of the building. For staring at the ground, Sarah really took in her surroundings.

Juliette said, "Good plan. Zeke, when I say, blast the camera with your electricity. That should either destroy it or at least make it non-functional. Then, I'll break into the car, and Zeke can start it."

"I can start it?" I whispered. "I don't know how to hotwire a car."

"You have electrical abilities," Juliette began. "Just give the vehicle a small but steady stream of electricity until the car starts. Hopefully, that should be enough to start it up."

"Umm… alright. As long as you know that I am not a felon when I do it," I replied.

"Zeke," Juliette explained. "In the eyes of the American people and the Agency, you are a felon for having abilities to begin with."

There was a silence then I said, "Good point."

We cautiously made our way to the back of the gas station without being noticed by any unwanted visitors. Thankfully, there were only a few people outside the gas station, and they just kept to themselves and chatted while we rounded the back corner of the building.

A few dumpsters that were pushed up against the building separated us from the car and the camera. I was close enough that I could fire a shot at the camera. I slowly raised my hand when Juliette grabbed it.

"Wait for us to move closer. If you miss, it may appear on camera and then the worker inside has us," she said.

"I can totally make the shot from here," I argued, but it was no use. She began to move forward along with Sarah and Trish.

We approached closer and closer until we were practically underneath it. Juliette then looked over to me and nodded. I slowly raised my hand towards the camera and let a charge build in my hand. The blue light began to emit from my palm and around the edges of my fingers. I could feel the power I was containing in this single shot.

That's when all hell broke loose. The energy ran back up into my arm out of my control and blasted out of my eyes. I shut them quickly and fell backwards. The electricity from my right eye sailed right in front of the lens of the camera, and then shortly after, the electricity from my left blasted it to pieces. Plastic and metal chunks of camera littered the floor.

"What was that!?" Trish shouted.

Juliette made a 'shushing' sound then whispered, "We will worry about what happened later. We need to get that car going and get out of here."

She quickly walked up to the red Buick and held her hand against the door. Juliette peered into the car and looked down at the lock. It was an old car and had the old push-up locks. She waited patiently as a small shimmer of air swirled. She clenched her hand into a fist and thrusted upward pushing the small dart of air into the lock and pushing it up unlocking the door.

Juliette quickly opened the door and unlocked all of the car doors. "Get in, quickly."

We all jumped into the back seat of the car. I was squished in the middle, which wasn't that bad because I had a girl on either side of me. I leaned forward to the front of the car, and put my hand on the empty ignition slot when a man wearing a bright yellow t-shirt walked around the corner in front of us.

"Hey! My car!" He screamed and began to charge us.

"Zeke, go now!" Juliette cried out.

I unleashed a charge in my hand and out my fingertips. This time there was no problem with how the energy flowed out. The electricity sailed through the metal and down the wires. A few seconds passed as the man sprinted closer.

"Hurry, Zeke!" Trish yelled from the back.

I kept the charge going when the man began to pound on the window and pulled on the door trying to get in. It was no use. That is until he bent over and picked up the metal mount used to hold the camera up on the building.

He smashed the glass in front of Juliette. She covered her face as the glass littered the car. I closed my eyes and prayed to some unknown car god to make the engine start when, suddenly, it did.

The engine roared to life as the man grabbed Juliette by the collar and reached for the lock on the door. Juliette shifted the gears and punched the gas. The man flew from Juliette's grasp and hit the side of the gas station wall. We turned on the street and headed west towards the city.

"That was climactic enough," Trish said leaning against the front passenger seat.

"Hey," I said. "I tried to get it to start."

"It's no matter," Juliette said. "We got out of there. The only thing we have to worry about now is the Police. The man saw our faces. He probably knew we were back there from the bolt of electricity that sailed in front of the camera."

"Yeah, Zeke," Trish said. "What happened there. It looked as if you had control of it, but then it came out of your eyes!"

"You tell me," I answered honestly. "I tried to control it and send it out of my hand, but ever since that lightning bolt struck me, my powers have been acting funny."

"Uh-oh," Juliette whispered to herself.

"What?" I asked.

"Nothing. I'm sure it is nothing."

All of us in the backseat knew she was lying. She was acting like our parent, keeping important information from us. What made that analogy even worse was that we were all in the backseat with no one in the front.

"Sarah," Juliette switched topics. "Come to the front and direct me to your house."

Sarah crawled over me and Trish and sat in the front seat. She sat quietly just pointing where to go. Sarah was still depressed. This has to be bigger than Gabe. What was the problem then? I really wanted to help her, but not with Trish and Juliette here. I would wait until we were alone.

The old Buick maneuvered the busy city streets like an old, rusted, dream. We barely hit any red lights and there were not very many pedestrians since it was ten in the morning. Everyone was at work or at school.

Juliette followed Sarah's instruction throughout the city. Her old house must've been on the far side of the city because I got to see a lot of the sights like the Arch. The city was awesome, and I wish it had lasted, but ten minutes later, the skyscrapers all vanished, and we were back on country highways.

We followed the highway and many others around fields and forests until we came across a small but long driveway that stretched into a large patch of woods.

"Go down here," Sarah said.

Juliette listened and turned down the driveway and slowly swerved through the trees and other plant life. I got a glimpse of the wooden mailbox at the end of the driveway. It was beginning to rot away, and moss was beginning to make it their home. It was true I guess that this house hasn't had a lot of living in for a while. What happened that made Sarah's "family" leave here?

The driveway continued on for what seemed like forever. I checked the clock on the dashboard. It showed that five minutes had past while we were on the driveway.

"How long is this driveway, Sarah?" I asked.

"We are almost there. It's just passed this line of trees."

Just after Sarah finished her sentence, like magic, the woods cleared into an open space of dying grass on a large hill. What lay on top of the hill was amazing. It was the biggest mansion I have ever seen! It had to be at least ten thousand square feet if I could accurately predict the dimensions of a house. The walls were made out of stone and white marble that made the house look like the White House. It gave me the impression that somebody powerful or famous lived here.

Juliette maneuvered the car to the top of the hill. The driveway separated into two paths that connected again in a circle at the front door. The driveway surrounded a large fountain that had a replica of the Statue of David with small water jets pulsating on it. Spotlights were placed around the rim of the small pool to illuminate the figure in the dark of night.

The car slowed to a stop in front of the steps leading up to the large door. Sarah opened the door and stepped out her side. Trish, Juliette, and I were dumbfounded at the sight of the monstrosity. How could Sarah have come from a place like this?

"Sarah... this is your house!?" Trish shouted. I thought the same thing.

"Yeah, well, it used to be," she replied as she climbed the stone steps to the wooden doors.

"How could your foster family afford this?" Juliette asked.

Sarah remained quiet as she threw her shoulder into the door breaking it open. The rest of us followed her up the steps and entered into the foyer. As I passed the front doors now standing open, I noticed two large, bronze knockers that had the shape of a lion's head with the ring hanging out of its mouth. On the ring, it read, "Irving."

The foyer was immaculate. The floor was pristine marble that spread out all around to the multiple rooms that were connected to the foyer. I could tell that there was a dining room, a kitchen in the back underneath the large staircase, a hallway on the other side of the staircase that probably led to the pantry and basement, and a living room that contained an old piano.

"It's almost exactly as I remembered it," Sarah sighed.

I walked around the house and noticed that there was something funny about it. On all of the expensive floors, walls, and decorations, like the large, golden chandelier that swung overhead, a small amount of mold was beginning to grow. It was disgusting to say the least, but I didn't say anything; although, I'm sure the others noticed.

"Sarah, I have a question," Juliette said. "What happened to your foster family who lived here with you? I noticed that the windows in the living room were boarded up."

Sarah answered, "They are long gone from here. There was an accident, you see, during a huge party in my family's honor. During the party, the house had to be abandoned when there was a bad flood after a storm that lasted two days. We weren't prepared for it, and it destroyed a lot of the stuff in here, including the grand piano. It wasn't hospitable for a few years. It should be fine now. The storm passed over two years ago. Right after that, Nathaniel recruited me."

We all listened to Sarah's story intently, even Juliette who kept examining the house. I followed Sarah around and saw that she was extremely depressed. How could you not be happy in your old home? It confused me even more and made my head ache. I just wanted to help, but Sarah was stubborn; I would find out eventually.

Sarah began to ascend the staircase waving for us to follow. She made a right turn and headed down a long corridor with more wooden doors on the left and right. We passed a boarded up window, like Juliette said, and turned left down another long hallway. A person could get lost roaming through here.

The mold began to disappear as we made our way further down the corridor and away from the foyer. Did the flood only wreck that part of the house? Perhaps, it entered the vents and it made the house impossible to live in. That would be a health concern especially for anyone who had power like Sarah's family.

She stopped in front of two shut doors standing side by side. Slowly, she opened them and poked in her nose in and sighed.

"Here is my room," Sarah said stepping away from the now open doors. "We can stay here until tomorrow morning. Nobody should suspect us being here."

Chapter 8

Sarah's room provided us the perfect spot to make camp for the night. Unfortunately, none of the showers or toilets worked, but at least we had a roof over our heads.

The room was huge. It was about the size of my apartment back in New Haven. The walls were decorated in bright pink with a white trim around the floor and ceiling. There were old stuffed animals piled up in a corner of the room next to the large wardrobe that was empty except for a few bugs. The bed was circular and on the opposite side of the wall. Two windows were by the bed that gave us a spectacular view of the now green, algae infested, pond in the back yard. If you called it a yard, it was the size of a field.

I found a spot on the teddy bear pile and threw myself onto it. Sarah said that she would sleep on the floor with a pile of blankets she brought up from the basement, and Trish and Juliette shared Sarah's big bed.

Night arrived later like it has for the last month. The moon shone through the atmosphere on the cloudless night. It blocked out most of the stars around its glowing aura. I slept away from the boarded up windows, so the moonlight didn't bother me.

How could Sarah grow up in a place like this and not talk about it? In fact, she never really talked to Gabe and I about her past. We got to know her personality and what she enjoys, which is doing anything mischievous. If I lived here, I would brag about it all the time, but that is just me.

The pile of teddy bears that I slept on was comfortable, but as the night stretched on, my back began to ache. I slowly awoke to find myself sunken into the pile bent in a way that would make my back ache terribly. I tried to move myself out quietly, but it was difficult because the stuffed animals kept tipping over. I had nothing to grab onto.

Eventually, I pulled myself out and fixed my sleeping spot and my posture. I rested my head back down next to the stuffed giraffe and began to shut my eyes when I noticed Sarah was lifting her head up from her pile of blankets.

I squinted my eyes making it seem as though I was sleeping; although, I kept my eyes on Sarah the entire time. She looked cautiously around the room probably wondering if anyone was awake. She scanned over me, but I just lay still. Quietly, she rose from her bed and began to silently shuffle her feet towards the door and down the hall.

Where was she going? A part of me was exhausted and just wanted to sleep, but a larger part wanted me to follow her and see where she was going. Maybe this was my only chance to get to talk to her in private.

I did the same as Sarah, examining the room to make sure nobody was watching me. I pulled myself up out of the teddy bear pile, which began to reek of sweat and mold, and silently headed down the hallway.

The hallway was dimly lit. The only light source was the pale glow of the moon shining in through the cracks of the boarded up windows. A few portraits were dimly illuminated by the light of the moon. I slowed to examine one. It was a painting of a man and a woman. The man had black hair and a thick beard which looked odd on him because he was fairly thin. The woman who was sitting on a chair next to the man had red curly hair and a thin face. Her blue dress really made her stand out in the dark picture.

I noticed another element in the piece. There was a small girl sitting on the woman's lap. She had blond hair, still growing, and didn't focus on the camera at all. She held a little rattle in her hand which gave her a big smile. It made me smile.

"What are you doing up?" Someone whispered next to me.

I jumped sideways and almost screamed. Sarah stood next to me with her index finger over her lips signaling me to be silent.

I said, "I woke up and noticed you were gone. I decided to find you and see if you were okay. That is, until I saw this painting."

Sarah examined the painting with me. She stood next to me in the faint, blue light from the moon which helped illuminate the portrait. I watched Sarah's eyes look over the painting. I noticed that they froze on the small girl sitting on the woman's lap.

"Do you know these people?" I asked quietly.

Sarah whispered, "Yeah, the man and woman were my mom and dad. That is, until I found out who I really was, and who they really were."

I listened to Sarah. I heard a hint of pain in her voice. Perhaps, she never wanted to have her childhood end? It sounded as though she really liked her fake parents.

I know how she felt. I still missed my mom and apartment and my life back in Connecticut. It has only been a month after all. Do I have this to look forward to? Will I always be in pain from being torn away from my "family?" Sarah still looked as if this place brought up memories that she wanted to forget. Are they sweet? Or are they one's of pain? I was determined to figure these answers out.

"Who were your parents? They seemed to have quite the life," I asked.

"My dad was a CEO of the popular computer software company Delfire. My mom, on the other hand, was raised by a wealthy family. She attended very prestigious schools and lived the life of a queen. When her parents, my grandparents, unexpectedly died in a terrible accident, she inherited everything from them. Together, those two were able to afford the life everyone wished they could have. A mansion, ten cars, and butlers and servants."

Sarah paused for a little bit as if she was debating whether or not she should tell me. I didn't push her. I listened and kept quiet. I wasn't going to ruin the only chance I may have at listening to her open up about her family and her life prior to being recruited two years ago.

Sarah continued, "The only thing my parents didn't have was a baby to pass on their legacy. They tried to have kids, but unfortunately, they were not able to have kids of their own, so, sixteen years ago, they applied to be parents of an orphan child, a child that her real parents didn't want."

"And this child was you," I broke in.

"Yes, that child was me. They met a man named Leonardo Irving when they went to a conference in North Carolina. He said that he and his wife, Barbara, were having a baby girl, and they wanted a great life for the baby. He said that adoption agencies would be too risky. There was always a chance that the baby could end up in a terrible home, so they are looking for potential parents."

I nodded at Sarah's story. That man, Leonardo, must've been in the Clade as well, and one of the Originals. Sarah paused and let me absorb all of the information I had been presented with.

After a few moments, I said, "So, Leonardo was your real father? The one from the Clade?"

"Yes," Sarah said. "I was told when I first was recruited by Nathaniel that he died right after I was born. He was killed on a reconnaissance mission like most Originals are. However, my mom, Barbara Irving, is a Head Instructor in Colorado."

"She is in Colorado?" I responded. That was where we were headed now. Is there a chance we would meet Barbara Irving?

"Yeah… a part of me feels like I'm not ready to meet my mother. I mean, you saw how Marcus reacted when he met Liam. He was incredibly angry with him. I don't know if I want to meet my mother if that is how I will act," Sarah thought to herself. "I just want to live in my own little world where all I have are the memories of my family growing up," She pointed to the picture. "These people are my family, but I guess I'll never be able to be with them again…"

I broke in, "Nonsense, you can be with them when this is all over."

"When what is all over?" She asked looking at me now.

I didn't know what I meant. I knew there was a war brewing between the Clade and whoever the Agency was, but could that really end soon? It has been going on for almost fifty years, and we have no idea just how powerful the Agency is. We don't even know who they are. My thoughts made this dark hallway feel even darker.

I had my own issues with my dad. Marcus already told me that my real mother was killed by the Agency after I was born. Thankfully, I was given away to my foster mother by then if you want to use the word thankfully to describe it.

My answer slipped out quietly, "When either the Agency is finished, or we are."

Sarah just smiled a little bit and said, now looking at the floor, "If only it was that simple. We can barely fight the Agency mainly because we have no idea who they are. At least our generation has no idea, and I think there are only a handful of Originals left. If this enemy is part of the United States government, then how can we fight against that?"

Sarah had a strong argument. We have no intelligence at all about the Agency other than they wanted us captured or dead.

She began to walk down the hallway and around the corner. I silently shuffled my feet after her keeping an eye on the other portraits, and the walls to make sure I woudln't run blindly into one.

The large foyer was dimly lit with a ghostly blue color that seemed to come straight out of a horror movie. The only thing missing was a damsel in distress, a large monster, and spider webs hanging on the chandelier and walls. Sarah descended the marble staircase and entered the living room on the left.

The walls were chipped from the mold and water damage. It must have been quite a flood. By looking at the walls, the chipped paint and mold rose all the way to the very top of almost every wall. Could a flood really fill this house with water up to the ceiling especially with it being built on a hill? Something wasn't making sense. Perhaps, Sarah would reveal more to me now that she had opened up about her past life.

I sat next to her on the piano bench which was moved in front of the large, partially boarded, window facing the driveway.

I said, "I saw there was a lot of mold and water damage on the walls and furniture. That must've been quite a flood."

Sarah didn't respond with words. She just nodded and stared out of the window through the gaps between the boards.

"You know," I whispered. "If you need to let anything off of your chest, you can tell me. I'm your friend. You can tell me anything."

Sarah nodded again. We sat in the room in silence for a few moments. I looked around awkwardly at the grand piano that would never play again due to water damage, the fire place that had a few bricks missing from the frame of it, and the furniture pushed into the corners and stacked on top of each other. Nothing in this room survived the flood.

I thought back to when Sarah said that she was recruited shortly after the flood. Almost the next day she said. I began to piece things together in my head as I sat next to Sarah. Gabe said back in the Clade he burned his house down and then he was recruited. I created a power surge through my school and probably most of New Haven without even realizing it. Was this flood hers?

Sarah broke the silence with tears dripping out of her eyes softly to the ground. "I caused the flood, Zeke."

I had a feeling, but I didn't accuse her of being a bad person. It happened to me, Gabe, and everyone else who was recruited by the Clade.

"I had a feeling," I said putting an arm around her and pulling her close to me, trying to comfort her.

"It happened two years ago," Sarah began. "My family at the time was having a huge, expensive, party. Only the richest and most powerful people in corporate America were allowed to come. I remember the night so well. Women wore long, elaborate, dresses that sparkled and shined in the foyer's light. The men wore black tuxedos with a tie or bow tie."

"I was up in my room dreading attending the party. My parents wanted to show me off at the gala. When they adopted me, I was a new born, and since then I was kept sort of like a secret. Of course, there were pictures of me in the newspapers and tabloids and rumors of me attending prestigious elementary level schools, but I was kept away from all of the glory. When I was growing up, my rules were simple: Go to school, and then come right back home. I don't know why. My only suspicion is that my parents were afraid of me getting kidnapped or something."

Sarah laughed a little and then I added, "Yeah, like who could kidnap you?"

She laughed a little louder finally coming out of her shell, "Exactly!"

The laughing died down then Sarah continued with her tale, "I put on my pink, sparkling dress and descended the staircase with everyone's eyes locked on mine. I felt like a princess, but to this day, I still hate the color pink. Anyways, the night stretched. Important figures introduced themselves to me, and I greeted them warmly with a fake smile painted on my face. At one point, I got tired of the party and hid back in this room. I sat on this very bench and looked out of this very window..."

Sarah grew quiet. Tears began to swell in her eyes. She had always seemed happy and energetic, even a little eccentric, around Gabe and me. Is this her true self? There was a lot of pain built up in her that was just waiting for a moment to explode. Gabe's death must've done that to her. That would explain why she felt so awful since we escaped the Clade.

Sarah choked on her words as she finished her dreadful story, "A man then walked in on my break from the party. He was a younger man, probably around twenty. He said I was beautiful. He was handsome himself, but I didn't tell him that. I was too infatuated with the moon glowing in the nighttime sky. He sat down next to me, like you are now, and slid closer and closer until eventually he was holding me at his side. I pushed away, but he didn't back down. I yelled and screamed for him to leave, but he resisted."

"He said, 'C'mon Sarah. I know you have been eyeing me up from across the hall. Why don't you want to be with me?'"

"He acted as if I actually liked him. I said, 'Listen perv. How about you go back into that party before I get pissed off!?'"

"He laughed at me as if we were playing. 'Please Sarah. Let's stop resisting.'"

"He jumped at me and pinned me against the wall. The boy was big, too big for me to push him off. I just kept screaming and then I felt something strange tingle inside myself. It was as though a huge weight was lifted off of my shoulders."

I clenched my fists listening to Sarah speak. Whoever that guy was, I wanted to clobber him myself. How can some guys be so cruel? I had my own run in with a guy like that, but all he wanted to do was hurt me. What he was doing to Sarah was way worse. I felt so bad for her. My heart ached in pain for her.

"Suddenly," Sarah said tears freely flowing from her eyes. "The walls began to creak and break open. Large cracks appeared followed by a large wave of water knocking the boy off of his feet. I took this strange occurance as my chance to escape. I ran past him, but he grabbed my ankle. I looked down to see the water rise just over his eyes. I pulled hard and screamed. I heard more walls crumble from the water being released from the pipes in the walls. Another wave came and knocked both of us off of our feet. It was now up to our waists. I swam out of the room and into the foyer to see that water was pouring from all of the walls."

Sarah waited a little bit as she wiped tears out of her eyes. I put my hand on her back and gently rubbed it trying to help ease the pain. It wasn't much, but I didn't know what else to do.

"What happened then?" I whispered to her softly.

"I reached the staircase and climbed. I looked back down to see..." Sarah began to cry fiercely. I held her close to me. She wiped her eyes on my shirt and then finished, "A lot of the guests were dead. They drowned. Most of them crushed by the collapsing walls. If they survived that, then they drowned due to the rushing water. I hid in my room until the water finally stopped. I cried all night, and by the next day, Nathaniel arrived telling me about what I had done."

My eyes were wide open. I couldn't believe what I had just heard. Sarah, one of my best friends and the sweetest person, killed almost an entire party. It wasn't her fault though, but she still blames herself.

"I..." I stuttered. "I don't know what to say."

She just wiped her eyes with her sleeve and slid away from me staring out the window through her red, swollen, eyes.

"I'm sorry, Sarah," I said.

90

"Yeah… thanks," she said not looking at me. "I know it wasn't my fault, but the pain is still there. This place reminds me of that night. The mold is growing there because of all of the water damage I brought to this place. The only optimistic thing I could say was that my parents survived, but when Nathaniel showed up, they would've done anything to get rid of me. They told me on the way out that they were even going to pretend like I never existed. That hurt the most…"

Again, my mind kept racing but I couldn't find anything to say to comfort her.

She continued without me saying anything, "I was fine at my new home. I repressed all of those memories and became the fun, perky, Sarah Irving. Then, I met you and Gabe and that made everything a lot better. I felt as though I had a family again. In fact, I thought Gabe was… pretty cute."

She smirked a little and I did the same. "I had a feeling you had a crush on him."

She giggled, "Yeah, I did. Everything was perfect again, and then we found that room on the second floor. The one Marcus kept hidden from us. The one that can only be accessed by muttering '*Zeke Laufor is our key to freedom.*' We also found the file with your picture in there, remember?"

I shrugged and said, "I'll be honest, Sarah. Ever since we barely escaped there with our lives, I can barely remember anything about the Clade other than the people we met."

"Oh…" Sarah said. "Well, just know that I was having the time of my life. Sure, it was in hell, but it was still great. Then, we came up with the idea of escaping. It was risky, but I wanted it so badly I would've done anything for it, but we all didn't make it out…"

"No, you're right," I said somberly.

"Gabe was killed. I couldn't believe it. It made everything in life seem so… I don't know. It made me get off cloud nine and get back to Earth. I still have images of him dying in my head all the time. I'm sorry if I have been a jerk to you today and yesterday. I just had all of this on my mind."

"Sarah, I completely understand," I said trying to sound comforting still. "I don't blame you at all. That's a lot to take in."

We sat together in silence for a little while longer. I finally got what I have been waiting for for a long time. I knew why Sarah had been acting so depressed and strange. A part of me wished I didn't know now. It was horrifying, but it would help me be able to connect more to her now.

"Ready to go back to bed?" I broke the silence.

"Yeah, I guess so." Sarah laughed a little to herself, "I don't even know what time it is."

I laughed a little also, "Yeah me either."

We rose up off of the bench and began to turn towards the door when something strange happened. The walls began to glow with flashing red and blue lights followed by a loud whirring sound. We looked at each other knowing that the other knew what it was.

We slowly turned around and peered out between the boards of the windows to see a squad of police cars waiting in the driveway.

They found us.

Chapter 9

It seems as though when we feel like we have a break, all hell breaks loose again. If it isn't the Agency, it's the police, and if it isn't the police, it's the Clade itself trying to stop us from reaching Colorado. At the rate we were moving, the chances are the Agency will have the Clade crushed and moved on to whatever district of the Clade comes after Colorado.

Sarah and I found ourselves rushing up the staircase and shaking awake Trish and Juliette before the cops were able to break in. They were slow to stir mainly because it was still the middle of the night. The clock flashed 2:00 A.M.

"What is happening?" Juliette said groggily.

We told them about the police waiting for us outside, and the possibility of them breaking in any second. Juliette threw off the covers of the bed and jumped to her feet. Trish was right behind.

"Alright," Juliette said rubbing her eyes awake. "We don't have a lot of time then." She turned to Sarah, "Is there any way out besides the front door?"

Sarah nodded, "Yeah, we have a patio deck. We can access it from the basement."

"The basement?" I asked.

"Yeah, it is one of the problems of living on a hill. You have to build a patio almost below the house because of the steep slope."

"How many were out there?" Trish asked.

I said, "There were for sure three cars, but the driveway is endless. Who knows how many are really waiting back down the driveway."

Juliette commanded, "Alright, then let's move. Be silent but swift. The police will be in any second and we can't be caught. Once we are outside, we will make our way for the forest on the North side of the yard."

I asked, "Which way is North?"

Juliette pointed out the window behind her. "If you don't remember, just follow the rest of us. I don't plan on any of us getting separated from the group unless something drastic happens."

We all agreed on the plan and began to make our way downstairs. The hallways stretched endlessly into the darkness. It was almost disorienting. The fear of being stalked by police officers in a maze of a house like this stuck in my mind. It gave me the chills, and I wanted to get out of there as quickly as possible.

The group turned the corner almost in unison. Together, we moved a few more feet and began to descend the flight of stairs. The lights stopped flashing outside. I guess they wanted to be hidden in case we were stirred by the lights, or maybe, perhaps they saw Sarah and I through the cracks in the boards on the windows? All of these questions rattled in my mind as we turned around and headed towards a hallway in the back.

There were more pictures and paintings hanging in this hallway which also seemed to stretch on forever. There were a multitude of doors with brass knobs. Some with intricate designs like lions or griffins.

We turned another corner where almost an entire wall was made of glass. Beyond that glass was a small courtyard that lay in the middle of the house. A small, square, section of the building was left open. No roof, no floor, nothing. It was a small patch of grass with a small garden and a few benches. A basketball hoop and a soccer net rested in the corner with long, unkempt grass crawling up its edges.

Throughout our entire journey through the depths of Sarah's home, I kept getting the unnerving feeling that the police were stalking us, waiting for us in the shadows until they have a chance to strike. It reminded me of the cave in New York.

As we turned a few more corners, a window allowed me to see the backyard. It stretched for what seemed like a mile to a pond almost touching the wooded barrier. Before the pond was a small hill. Just beneath that hill, I noticed a wooden platform. That must've been the deck. If so, the basement was huge, way bigger than the main levels of the house, and that part was huge to begin with.

"Sarah," I panted. "Is your patio deck all the way down there?"

"Unfortunately, yeah it is," She replied.

Juliette commented, "That is probably more beneficial for us. The further away and more concealed the entrance to the house is, the better chance we have of escaping with no confrontation. It concerns me that we haven't had any disturbances yet from the police force. Are you and Zeke sure there were police officers out front?"

"Yes," Sarah and I said in unison. Sarah continued, "They were at least three, like Zeke said earlier. I don't know where they went."

"Well, let's keep moving then and be quiet," Juliette finished.

We turned another corner and began our sprint down another hallway. Most of these didn't have windows which made them almost completely pitch black. I was surprised that Sarah knew her way around here so well after being gone for two years, but I guess when you couldn't go anywhere as a child, all you could do was explore and make your own games.

Eventually, we reached a double door with two brass handles, one on each side. Sarah carefully pulled open the right one and stared into the darkness below her.

"We won't have any light," Sarah whispered. "There is no power here."

Trish looked over to me in the back of the pack. "Zeke, you go up in front by Sarah. You can provide us with a light."

"Are you sure?" I asked quietly. "I don't want to fry everyone. How will I know that my electricity will work for me?"

"It will just have to," Juliette said firmly. "Go on up with Sarah."

I shuffled to the front with Sarah and focused my power to collect in my hand and fingertips. I clenched my hand into a fist and closed my eyes. A few moments passed when I noticed a small glow radiate through my eyelids. I opened to see my right hand glowing, cutting through the darkness below providing us with a path.

We moved a lot more slowly this time. The basement was like a labyrinth. There were no windows. If you were caught down here without a light, you would be in for a long night of being lost.

I stood right next to Sarah with my hand slightly gripping her t-shirt, so that we wouldn't get separated. The difference between down here and upstairs, besides the lack of windows, was that the hallways were much shorter and narrower. One wrong turn meant losing the group. I hope Trish and Juliette kept following my light from behind me.

The hallway branched off to the right. This hallway was much wider as if it was the highway among hallways in the basement. The one most traveled.

Sarah whispered, "We just need to follow this one all the way to the door. It should only be a short walk."

We all nodded and began to stroll through the dark; my hand illuminating the hallway just around our group. More doors of all shapes and sizes passed us by. How many rooms does one house need?

Another hallway branched off up ahead. I turned slightly to peer down it when a bright, white, light cut through the darkness towards us. We were spotted by a flashlight followed by a loud voice, "Freeze! Police!"

We were found. "Run!" Juliette yelled.

Sarah took off first, and I tried to stay right behind her to keep the hallway lit up ahead. I looked back to see the flashlight shrink and turn towards us as the officer turned the corner. He was closing in.

The hallway was too long. He would for sure catch us if we kept running. We had to do something, but what? I came up with an idea almost instantly.

"Juliette," I asked. "Can we use our powers to slow down the officer?"

"Are you crazy?" Juliette answered sprinting as fast as she could. "If we harm the officer, the world will know about our secret unless we kill him, and I am not doing that. He is innocent."

"I know. Trust me. Can we use our abilities to turn off his light?"

Juliette looked back. The officer was almost in complete view for us. The light of his flashlight hiding him in the shadows beyond.

"Perhaps, if we can hit the flashlight," she answered.

I looked up ahead as far as I could. I noticed a very dim light shining through a glass door. It was the exit. The end of the maze, but would we make it? I noticed there was a hallway crossing the one we were running down now. It would be perfect for my plan.

While it was still too dark to use the moonlight from the glass door, I said quietly, "I have an idea. I'm going to turn off my light. You guys keep running forward. The door is just up ahead."

"Are you sure?" Juliette asked. I noticed Trish furrow her brow. She was worried. It made me smile on the inside.

"Yes, trust me," I said confidently. "I know what I am doing."

Juliette didn't respond. I took it as a "do what you want as long as you don't kill us all." I squeezed my hand, and the light vanished almost instantly. The warm feeling quickly replaced by a cool breeze.

I rushed down to the hallway and crouched around the corner. I watched as Juliette, Trish, and Sarah made their way to the door. They were clearly visible by the intensity of the light from the flashlight the officer was wielding. I hope he didn't see me.

I waited silently, listening to the approaching steps of the oncoming officer. I slowly poked my head out from the corner to find the officer almost right in front of me. I concentrated some electricity into my fingertips. I didn't want a big blast. Just enough to be able to break the flashlight. It would be easier for us to escape without being noticed.

I held my hand up like a gun and watched as the officer ran directly in front of me. I took aim and unleashed the small bolt of energy from my fingers. It successfully connected with the light. The lightbulb shattered littering the floor with glass. The officer stopped in his tracks looking around for what had caused his light to break. I silently slipped back behind the corner and tried to breathe softly. Any noises could give me away now. He was almost on top of me.

I slipped further down the hallway and found a door. I opened it and quickly shut it behind me hoping I didn't make too much of a sound. I felt it was safe to light up the room, so I built up a charge in my hand. The warm sensation spread throughout my palm once again as the room lit up.

A bed was situated in the middle of the room. A dresser rested next to it. There was a small bathroom in the far corner with a door to another hallway. That would be my way out.

I paced through the bathroom and slowly opened the door causing an eerie creak throughout the basement level. I waited in the darkness for a few moments and then decided that it was safe to move. I edged outwards into the hall and turned left away from the connecting hallway I ran down.

The darkness was beginning to lighten as I moved further down this hallway. I knew I was moving closer to the exit, but I didn't know how close I was.

The air was thick. Either that or I was so nervous I could barely breathe. The thought of a man waiting for me, wanting to catch me and possibly lock me up and throw away the key will do that to you. I just continued to stay low and move silently.

At the end of the hallway, there was another hallway stretched out to the left where the door waited for me like it was the end of the yellow brick road. Its radiance called out to me.

I decided that being stealthy wasn't as important anymore, not with the exit staring me in the face. I rose and began to sprint. I didn't know where all of this extra energy came from. Just before, I was exhausted. I was surprised I still had enough strength to push out more electricity, but it worked. I guess that is what adrenaline will do to you.

The door was calling out to me. I was so close I outstretched my arm opening my hand ready to grab the handle. Suddenly, the officer stepped in front of me. I yelled and tried to slow down, but I couldn't. I flew head first into the officer throwing him off his feet.

I glanced down at him as I grabbed the handle. He looked up at me and screamed, "Hey! Stop right there!"

That's when he started to pull out his pistol.

I didn't think. I just acted. My hand grabbed the handle and I pulled open the door. My legs moved as quickly as possible. I ran through the door and out into the open air.

The deck was massive. It stretched all the way down to the banks of the pond which had to be almost fifty yards away. At the end of the deck, two fishing pole holders were screwed down onto the handrails.

I stopped admiring the sights and ran down the first flight of steps and then the next. A part of me willed to keep moving, but a stronger part wanted to look back. When I looked back, I saw the officer sprinting through the doorway after me.

Another flight of steps stood between me and the solid ground. The officer was gaining though, his training definitely paying off. I looked over to the railing and saw there was about a ten foot drop to the ground.

I decided to take the risk. I moved for the edge of the patio deck and gripped the railing. In one quick move, like a gymnast, I rolled over the railing and tumbled through the air and onto the ground. It was cold and wet from the dew.

I stood up and quickly began to run for the forest edge where Juliette told us to meet. Soon into my sprint, I realized I forgot which edge of the forest I was supposed to run into. Was it the one to the right, or straight ahead? I couldn't remember. All I remember was that there were two windows next to each other. One pointed out straight ahead beyond the pond, and the other went to the right of it.

Acting quickly, I chose to go behind the pond. Even if that wasn't right, I would at least be as far away as possible from the police cars parked out front, and the officer would have a hard time shooting me from across a pond. Pistols don't have great accuracy from long range.

However, that didn't stop him from firing a shot from the deck. I heard the bullet sail behind me, and I witnessed a little patch of dirt hop out of the ground. This only made me run faster.

I rounded the far edge of the pond next to the stone edge and a tall, grassy, patch. I leaned forward to help conceal me behind some of the tall grass blades.

The forest approached, and I dove into it. I looked back from behind a tree to see the officer running back towards the driveway talking into his microphone on his shoulder. He was probably calling for reinforcements to come find me. I needed to move quickly.

With sweat dripping from my face, I kept moving through the woods. I jumped over fallen logs and rounded large trees. I ran for who knows how long. I felt like I ran a mile into nothing. The darkness made it difficult to see anything in front of me. I slowed my pace when the house was completely out of sight out of fear that I might run face first into a tree.

I gripped my sides and walked slowly trying to catch my breath in case I needed to run for my life again. That bullet was close enough to me that I could hear it whiz by. If I was a little bit slower, I could have been dead.

Did the officer have the right to shoot me? For trespassing, I don't think you can shoot the perpetrator. What about stealing a car? Could they even prove that Juliette, Trish, Sarah, and I stole it? Even if they did, I don't think they can kill. Maybe, but I'm not a cop. Perhaps, it was when I ran into him. That would be assaulting an officer, and he does have the right to protect himself.

I stopped thinking because it was giving me too much of a headache. I found a log a few yards ahead almost near the far end of the property. That's where the road cut through, and I decided to rest. I wiped off my forehead with my arms. Since it was a spring night, the air was cool at this time of night. It wouldn't last for long though. Soon, summer would come around, and then everything will be warm 24/7.

I shut my eyes and listened to the silence. It's hard to imagine that you can actually listen to nothing, but you can. It was peaceful. I didn't want to leave this spot unless I had to. I just hoped that the girls were okay. I'm sure they were. They could each take me in a fight single-handedly. I laughed at myself for thinking that.

All of a sudden a loud, squealing sound penetrated my silence. I looked down the country road to see a police car heading right for where I was standing. Could they see me? I moved slightly into the woods just in case.

The lights then began to flash almost blinding me. Yup, they saw me for sure. I started to run in the opposite direction, back into the thick of the woods, when a voice came over the loudspeaker.

"Zeke!" The feminine voice cried out. "We saw you. Get your butt over here and jump in before we are found!"

It was Trish. I couldn't believe it. I ran back over to the road cautiously. A part of me wondered if the officers were using Trish as bait to get me to come out, but if she was being used as bait, I would still have to come out and help her escape.

I stopped on the gravel on the side of the road as the car came to a stop. The back door popped open and Sarah looked out at me.

"Hurry up and get in!" She yelled to me.

I listened and jumped into the car relieved that it was them and that they were safe. Juliette slammed on the gas causing the car to perform a burnout and accelerate forward at great speeds leaving that insane mansion of terror behind us.

Chapter 10

I fell asleep about an hour after we escaped from Sarah's mansion. The adrenaline still pumping through my veins kept me awake for much too long, but I couldn't help it. My wired body trembled and shook as the car sped out of the country and headed westward. We avoided most interstates trying to conceal where we were heading. The cops didn't figure out where we went, which is good because Juliette stole the police car we were driving in.

A few more hours passed after the city faded from view in the rearview mirror, and the sun was beginning to rise. We were close to being out of Missouri and another state closer to Colorado.

Trish's unconscious body gently bounced onto my lap. I gently picked her head and shoulders up and moved her back to her side of the car; although, I really liked her head on my lap.

Juliette was in the driver's seat on the other side of the bullet proof glass. She had been driving since she picked me up. I never got the chance to ask her how Sarah, Trish, and she stole the police car with all the cops out front. It had to be difficult not using their abilities. I would ask, but it would be difficult to talk through the glass, so it would be just Trish and I.

And I really liked that plan.

I rested my head back down onto the cushioned part beneath the window and stared out the window across from me. I have come a long way in just over a month. I had no idea that my life would turn this way. Of course, I didn't plan on Marcus kidnapping me only to drop me off as a Recruit at the Clade, but this kind of reminiscing is only going back to two weeks ago.

My powers have increased in strength by far, and it is easier for me to control without exerting much force to do so. I remember when Trish began to torch the basement level, and Sarah and I stopped her. Sarah's nose bled, and she passed out after we got to Trish. I haven't felt that kind of pain in a while. I must be either gaining control over my ability more, or I just haven't been using it enough. It could really be either.

The clouds floated overhead like large hot air balloons moving wherever the wind takes them. They were kind of like us. Moving from one place to the next just trying not to get caught. What do clouds run from though, and are they even in a rush to get anywhere? I don't know why I began to think these things, but it felt good.

It was nice to get my mind off of the chaos my friends and I were in. I guessed that as long as I stared out at the window, life wouldn't catch up to me. No lives were in danger and everything was okay and at peace.

But that wasn't the case. If we didn't reach the Colorado Clade soon, then we would have a massacre to clean up, and I don't know if I can watch more people die. I know I couldn't kill.

The images of the battle raced through my mind like an out of control train. It shook and rattled my brain giving me a headache. I hated the images, but they stuck in there so tight that I couldn't help but think of them. Did I really kill those Agents that shot at us? I know I blasted them, but did I kill them? I remember myself shaking after I attacked them. A part of me hoped that they survived, but a darker side of me wanted to know they were gone and couldn't hurt anyone anymore. Is that wrong of me?

And of course, there is Gabe…

I rubbed the corners of my eyes as I slowly lifted my head. I must've fallen asleep while I day dreamed. The exhaustion was finally catching up to me. It felt as though it drained my entire being. If I never had to get up, it would still be too soon.

Trish was sitting up in her seat on the far side of the car. My legs were perched up on her lap. I slowly tilted my head to see Sarah looking forward and Juliette still driving. I swear Juliette must be on caffeine pills or something. How can she just keep going? She had less sleep than all of us.

I flung my legs off of Trish's lap causing her to look at me. We both smiled at each other as I wiped some of the crud out of my eyes.

She said, "Good morning. Sleep well?"

I stretched my arms into the open spaces and said, "Yeah, I guess." I yawned. "As well as I could sleep in the back of a police car I guess."

We laughed.

"I guess that is pretty good then," she said.

"Yup, I guess so," I finished.

I couldn't let the conversation die on me now. This is a really good opportunity to get to know Trish more. Better yet, nobody could interrupt.

I decided to ask her about the police car. "So, what happened back at the mansion when I was separated from you?"

Trish answered, "Well, we ran to where we said we were going to meet. You gave us a great head start. As we waited in the woods for you to come out, Sarah snuck further into the woods and ran to the front of the house at the top of the hill. That is when Juliette and I saw you run out of the door. The cop was right behind you, so Juliette and I ran deeper into the woods just in case he saw us."

I said, "You saw me and didn't bother to help?"

"What were we going to do?" Trish shrugged. "We couldn't use our abilities, and he had a gun. Thankfully, you managed to pull yourself away from the cop and dove into the woods after the bullet fired just barely missed you. That is when Sarah came back glistening with sweat.

She told us that there were cop cars lined down her driveway all the way to the road."

"And you stole one?" I cut in.

"Yup," she said. "We ran out of the woods and down the road to where a cop car sat in a row of cars. We lied low as we approached the rear of the vehicle. An officer was sitting in the car waiting for a call probably. Just as we were about to jump him, he got a call from an officer near the house and he sprinted up the driveway. He didn't see us; otherwise, we probably wouldn't have been able to take it. Before we stole it, Juliette blasted off the plates, so we couldn't be tracked. After that, she just started the car and we drove to where you entered the woods. Easy as pie and no one got hurt."

"I guess, but I almost got shot!" I began to yell.

I felt as though anger had begun to boil inside me. I didn't want to be angry, but they saw me get chased and shot at, but they did nothing to help, other than run in the opposite direction. I know their intentions were good, but I couldn't see that right now. I was too angry.

"Easy," Trish put up her hands in front of her. "We did what we could. We found a way out of there with all of our lives in one piece, and we have a good mode of transportation to Colorado. No more having to ride busses or hitchhike or whatever we would have had to do."

"Yeah, I guess," I responded somberly. I rolled back over to my side of the car and crossed my arms.

Trish looked at me and then stared ahead at the back of Sarah's head. She bit the bottom of her lip as if she was becoming slightly angered as well. Could this be our first fight? That thought made me chuckle silently a little bit.

I guess I should apologize then. "I'm sorry. I know you did what you thought was right, and it was."

Trish smiled, "Yeah, I know." She stretched her arms and relaxed them behind her head. "I'm pretty good at faking emotions."

I let that sink in which made me a little ticked off again. She glanced over at me and laughed. I joined in. Phew, a fight was the one thing I didn't want to have. That would ruin my chances with her for sure.

I looked back out my window and noticed a mountain range in front of me. It stretched all the way out into the distance. We were getting closer. How long was I out? We must almost be in Colorado.

That's when a loud crash broke through my thoughts. Little bits of glass rained down from above. I instinctively covered my head and slid to the floor. I looked up and saw where the glass came from.

The barrier between the front and back seats was shattered. Juliette or Sarah could've given us some warning before they decided to blast it. Geez.

I sat back up in my seat shakily. "What the heck was that!?" I yelled.

"Sorry, Zeke and Trish," Sarah said. "We couldn't get your attention. You just kept staring out the windows day dreaming about who knows what." Sarah scanned from Trish to me and then gave a slight wink and nod towards Trish. I just stuck my tongue out at her.

Juliette looked in the rear view mirror and said, "Yeah, sorry about that you too. I just blasted it with my ability. I hope nobody is hurt. I didn't use a very big blast."

I rubbed my face and checked myself over for bumps and bruises. I was fine, but Trish had a small cut on the side of her forehead. There was no stream of blood or anything, just a little scratch.

We both said we were fine, and Juliette nodded in agreement.

Juliette began, "We are about two hours from the Clade. Before we get there though, there are some things you should know. First, the Colorado Clade has two Head Instructors, Barbara Irving, an Original from Liam's generation, and Callon Alton, another Head Instructor from our generation."

Barbara Irving. She is Sarah's actual mom. I wonder how she would handle seeing her for the first time in her life.

I looked up at her to see her expression blank. She appeared to be cool, calm, and collected, or she was completely faking it. Nobody else, except maybe Juliette, knows that Barbara is Sarah's mother.

"So, what's so special about us knowing that? Are they like slave drivers or something?" Trish asked.

Juliette shrugged and said, "I have never really been there. I just heard stories from Marcus. You see, Head Instructors are the ones that travel from district to district. Usually they are accompanied by one other Instructor, and Marcus always took Nathaniel, since he was there before I was."

Nathaniel knew all about the other Clade districts. That was an advantage for him. He knew the weak spots and unguarded areas of the Clade.

The Clade, at least the New York district, didn't have guards, at least I didn't think so. We relied on the natural surroundings to keep cover for us. Nathaniel knew where we were hidden, that's how the Agency were able to attack, and we weren't prepared for that fight.

"That doesn't really answer my question," Trish continued. "What kind of stories did you hear?"

"Let's just say Callon runs a very tight ship up in the mountains. It's pretty much boot camp for the fifty unlucky Recruits that had the misfortune of living near there," Juliette said.

"Only fifty Recruits!?" I asked shocked.

The Clade in New York had just over two hundred. How could the Colorado Clade have only fifty?

Juliette answered, "The Clade districts were formed in a triangle. One in the Northeast, one in the Mid-Western region, and one down South. The Recruits were naturally born in the middle of these districts and are placed in the Clade that is closest to them. Where do most of the people in America live? They live on the East coast, so our district of the Clade actually had the most Recruits."

We all let that sink in for a bit. I think we all thought the same thing, but nobody decided to say it. If our Clade division had the greatest number of Recruits and we lost to the Agency, how can we possibly be able to fight them? Also, we now had less Recruits. Who knows how many troops the Agency has? That just made the fight a whole lot tougher.

"Alright…" I said trying to break the ominous silence surrounding us. "Anything else we need to know?"

Juliette remained silent as she pondered on how she would answer my question. It seemed as though she was waiting to reveal information to us. If so, there was a lot to choose from. Most of the Recruits, including myself, had no idea about our parents' history like why we have the powers and what the Agency has to do with it all.

Juliette answered, "Nothing at all. However, if the Clade is still standing, then I suggest to sleep now because when we get there we will be working non-stop."

"Non-stop like how?" Sarah asked from the front seat.

"You'll see. Like I said, Callon runs the place like an army general."

The thought of going to a boot camp for special individuals didn't seem all that appealing to me. I couldn't imagine myself doing twenty push-ups. I could barely do five. I shivered and prayed that I will never have to embarrass myself by my lack of strength.

We rode silently for a good hour and a half or so. The mountains rose up in front of us like earthly spears reaching towards the sky trying to stab a cloud floating by.

The ascent up the great rocky structure began with a small slope and continued to climb as we swerved around hairpin turns with a near endless drop. Snow began to become clearly visible the higher we climbed. I hoped the Clade wasn't that high up in the mountains, I forgot my coat.

Another few minutes passed as we climbed the steep mountain highway. The drive was beginning to make me car sick. All of the twists and turns and the slowing and speeding up were really taking their affect on my body.

Before I blew chunks all over the back seat, we slowed to a stop in front of a small, chalet style diner. The sign read, "**Wintry Slope Diner**." It was a quaint place with a few parking stalls and only enough room to seat fifty people at most.

We jumped out making sure no cars on the highway slid off the road and rammed into us. I rubbed my arms to try to stay warm. It may have been summer soon, but I could see snow in the distance on top of the nearby mountains. I shivered.

We stepped up the wooden steps to the small patio deck around the diner and stepped inside. There was a small bar area with stools all around it in the main room. To the right, there was a small dining area with a few booths and a few more tables. It was very tiny.

Juliette went to the counter and rang the bell and waited patiently for someone to come.

Trish walked up to Juliette and asked, "Why are we here? Are you hungry?"

I hoped she was because I was starving. The last time we all ate was the night before at Sarah's home before we went to bed. There were a few cans of soup in the kitchen that Sarah stumbled upon. Then, Trish used her ability to cook it.

"No," Juliette said staring at the kitchen door. "We are going to buy some sweatshirts." She pointed to the rack near the entrance where a few blue and white sweatshirts hung on racks. They were very tacky.

Juliette continued, "The final part of our ascent requires us to travel on foot. We will hide the car, and then begin our climb."

Trish stepped away as an older man stepped out from the kitchen. He wore an apron with a few grease stains on it, and his long, gray beard shed slightly on it also. It grossed me out and suddenly, I didn't feel very hungry anymore.

He rubbed his round stomach and grumbled, "Yeah? Anything you want?"

His physique and manners made me sick. I think it made Sarah sick too because she looked in the opposite direction.

Juliette casually replied, "Yes, we would like to purchase four of your sweatshirts over there." She pointed.

"Oh yeah, that's eighty bucks," He replied being extremely rude to us.

Juliette reached into her jean pocket and pulled out a roll of cash. She counted out the bills until she had four twenties in her hand. The man snatched that up quickly and then went into the kitchen again leaving us to ourselves.

"Well, isn't he friendly," Sarah said sarcastically.

"Doesn't matter," Juliette said. "We got what we wanted."

She pulled off a few sweatshirts. They were all roughly the same size, and they were all the same blue color. We all slid them over our short-sleeved shirts.

Juliette said heading for the door, "It's good that that man is cranky and unhappy to his customers. It keeps tourists and other people away from here."

"Um, why is that?" I asked.

We crossed the parking lot and headed for the car. Juliette entered the driver's seat. When Sarah, Trish, and I were going to get in, she held up her hand and told us to wait there.

She started the car and drove around the back of the restaurant and began to drive up the wooded slope. She maneuvered the car behind a circle of trees until we could no longer see it from the parking lot. It was completely hidden from sight.

Juliette got out and walked over to us. "Alright, follow me, and you'll see why."

We listened and followed her to the back of the restaurant. She led us to a small path cut out in the shrubs next to where the car was parked. Juliette began to climb the slope hidden in the foliage. As we passed by the cop car, I noticed that there was another car sitting next to it. Why was that there?

The path continued for a few yards and then cut to the right when the bushes ended and the thick forest began. We followed that path for about twenty minutes twisting through trees and mountain sides. At one point, we had to push our bodies up against the sheer face of the mountain in case we fell off the trail and broke our legs. We wouldn't have been killed, but it was a huge drop.

We kept climbing up the mountain path hidden in the forest. It looked as if not too many people walked this. How did Juliette know about this?

The weather began to take a turn for the worse. The temperature dropped to right around freezing, and it began to snow lightly. I was glad we got the sweatshirts, but I was still cold.

We had reached an opening in the forest near the edge of a cliff. I looked down to see jagged rocks. I got a sense of vertigo and stumbled backwards towards safety. I couldn't even see the highway anymore. We were really high up. I looked up to the mountain and saw that we were about halfway to the summit. Where were we going?

Sarah asked as we kept moving forward, "Where are we going, Juliette? I'm freezing and extremely tired."

Juliette just laughed to herself and said, "That's not good. Callon will have you running this path five times a day."

"Wait," I responded. "Are you telling me that the Colorado Clade is-"

Juliette broke in, "Yes, The Colorado district of the Clade is up this mountain." She pushed some brush out of the way to see a cave dug into the side of the mountain, away from all cliff sides and edges. "In fact," she finished, "we are here."

Chapter 11

The cave rested on a ridge on the mountainside. It resembled a sanctuary to me. It was such a long trip filled with danger around every corner. It may not be much, but it was finally a place where we can all just relax for a little bit and wrap our minds around everything that had happened the last two days.

How would we tell Callon and Barbara about the fall of the New York Clade? How would we tell them that Marcus stayed back to fight with Liam?

These questions buzzed in my head as we climbed up the trail that cut through the trees towards the cave. I had to squint looking up at it due to the intensity of the sunlight at this altitude.

As we got closer, I saw two hooded figures standing outside the cave entrance. It reminded me of when Marcus recruited me. They must be Recruits.

They noticed us arrive from the ridge that they stood up on. They were about fifteen feet above our heads. They were much too high for us to jump up to and climb up.

We stood in front of the ridge. They looked at each other, and then suddenly, they each pulled out a small pistol from underneath their cloaks. They jumped off the ridge and stood on either side of our group with the pistol held up to Juliette's and my head. We held up our hands.

"Woah!" I yelled. "What are you two doing? We are on your side!"

I couldn't see their faces, but they glanced at each other and nodded.

Juliette took over. "My name is Juliette Stratton. I am an Instructor from the New York Clade Division. We come together as a group because we bring important news."

The two hooded figures looked at each other for a while. They stared into the blackness of their hooded faces.

The figure by my side said, "You aren't dressed in the attire of a Clade Recruit. Why is that?"

Juliette told them about how we needed to change clothes to blend in. Their lives were in serious danger, but that is for Callon and Barbara to hear about.

Then the one near Juliette lowered his pistol and said, "Follow us, then. Do not stray from our path. We know how to use these." He shook the pistol in his hand.

"You have nothing to worry about," Juliette replied.

The Recruits stayed separated. One in front of the group leading us, and one behind the group, more specifically me, making sure we didn't try anything funny.

The lead Recruit took us around the ridge where it began to slope up. We jumped on that trail and continued around the bend, up the slope to the entrance of the cave.

We entered the dimly lit, hollowed out space in the mountain. There were metal tubes that were nailed to the cave's ceiling that connected to a few, small lights. My eyes still had to adjust to the intense darkness. It was as if you were in a pitch black room with only a lamp for light, but the lamp was covered by a blanket.

The cave was deep. There were a few branches that stretched off to the sides of the cave until it became impossible to see how far they went. We continued down the main shaft of the cave until daylight from the cave entrance was completely gone.

As we followed the Recruit down into darkness, I noticed many other Recruits, boys and girls, teens and adults, stand to the side as we passed by. I saw them whisper to each other and gossip as if this was high school. They probably didn't see too many visitors around here, being on top of a mountain and all. This could be the most exciting thing they have seen in a while.

I looked off to my left and noticed a walkway that sloped downward and wrapped around the main cave like a spiral staircase. I wondered where that went. How come none of the other branches of the cave sloped down like that?

The cave came to an abrupt end. A solid wall appeared before us that had a small opening with a dim light shining through.

The front Recruit stopped and turned around. "I shall enter and then come back. If Callon allows you to enter, then you may, but if he does not, then you will have to leave no matter who you say you are."

Juliette nodded and then said, "Tell him 'Juliette Stratton is here.'"

He nodded under his shadowy hood and entered into the room and disappeared.

We waited outside in the darkness with the other Recruit who stood stiff and still in the shadows of the cave, watching us as if he expected us to run.

I looked over to Trish and Sarah and whispered, "This place gives me the creeps. How could people live in here? Couldn't they find a more humane place to hide from the Agency?"

Trish just shrugged, and Sarah said, "Perhaps, but the Agency would never look in a cave on top of a mountain. The Clade could be hidden anywhere over the entire country. The odds of them thinking that Recruits were hiding in a man-made cave on top of a mountain in Colorado would be extremely low."

Trish asked, "How did you know it was man-made?"

"I can tell by the wiring." Sarah looked up at the bulb that barely let out a spark of light. It whimpered and flickered creating a kind of candlelight feeling. "The cave was built to support this kind of system. We passed bathrooms and a generator for the electricity."

"Where did you see that?" I whispered. The Recruit stepped out of the shadows and began to approach us.

Sarah rushed, "I heard a whining noise coming from the only sloping tunnel. It must be a generator creating this power."

I didn't even hear the generator. I guess Sarah was much more observant with all of her senses than Trish and I were. She seemed as surprised as I was that she noticed it.

Just then, the Recruit stepped out of the passageway and said, "Callon will speak to you. Go in and only speak when spoken to." He pointed at the archway.

Juliette nodded at him and walked in followed by the rest of us. There was a small, dark and dank, alleyway that led to an opening cut out of the cavern wall where light shone through creating a twilight effect.

We all entered in a single file line with Juliette first. The room was small. A wooden desk sat pushed up against the far wall with just enough room for a person to squeeze in and sit down. Juliette stood off to the side to fit the rest of us in. Unfortunately, however, I got stuck looking over the girls.

There was a man sitting behind the desk. He stared at some papers intent on not moving until he finished the work he had begun. A lamp was the only source of light in the room. It created twisting shadows on the narrow walls giving me the creeps. How could he work in here?

I examined him closely as he stared downwards at his desk. He had hard, dark eyes, almost black. His hair was light brown and trimmed to be short like an army soldier's hair would be cut. As he flipped a page in his stack of papers, I saw a scar come down from his right eye to about his nose level. How did he get that?

Overall, the guy seemed as though he shouldn't be messed with. He appeared as though he worked out often. His arms bulged and rippled against his Clade cloak. It looked as if it was just a few sizes too small, but nope, he was just that in shape.

Callon looked up from the stack finally to acknowledge our existence. "Juliette," he said slowly turning towards her. "This is unexpected. What do I owe the honor of your and these kids presence here?" He glared at us scanning our faces for signs of fear.

Because they can smell that sort of thing.

Juliette answered, "We are here to discuss some important matters. I'm afraid the worst has happened back in New York."

Callon turned his attention back over to her with his eyes slowly widening. "Go on, and how come Marcus isn't with you? Did he send you?"

"N-No," Juliette began to shake and falter under the weight of her words. "He was with us, but the Agents showed up... and he stayed behind to fight them off, so we could escape."

Callon's eyes grew wide. He looked down at his desk and shut them slowly and exhaled deeply, obviously in pain. He and Marcus must have been close in some way. His absence has really hurt him.

Suddenly, his eyelids shot back up over his eyes and he said with force, "You will tell me everything that has happened, and I mean everything!"

I swear the walls shook, possibly the entire cave when he finished his sentence. I hadn't realized this, but I had slowly moved towards the exit. Callon was definitely intimidating.

Juliette began the story of all of us back at the Clade. The same story I keep having nightmares of. The Agents approaching the hospital, the shooting, the killing, and the death of Gabe… She repeated everything up until where we are now. Callon just listened and absorbed the information.

"I don't believe this…" Callon leaned backwards on his chair legs. He rubbed his face and yelled at no one, but I still stumbled backwards. All of us did.

There was a silence while Callon sat back in his chair. Nobody wanted to say anything in case he needed an excuse to take his rage out on somebody. I would much rather face Nathaniel any day than him, and I don't even know what Callon can do.

Callon shifted his chair back on solid ground and said, "That explains a lot then."

Juliette answered as confused as the rest of us, "What do you mean?"

Callon bent down under his desk and heaved onto the surface a large, black radio. It had some of the biggest antennaes I had ever seen. I guess you need them to get a signal in a cave.

"There have been special broadcasts and news reports over the radio waves about a wild fire in northern New York. I worried if the Clade had something to do with it, and it turned out I was half right."

Callon flipped a red switch on the machine and twisted the black knob through static until a voice broke through the air waves.

The voice was female, and it sounded as though she was in panic. *"The fire has been spreading for the past three days now. Local fire departments have been trying their best to stop the wildfire; however, due to lack of precipitation and the sheer strength of this inferno, there appears to be no real hope to stop this catastrophe. The Governor of New York has declared an evacuation for most of the northern counties in the state and has asked for the National Guard for possible assistance."*

"In regards to what actually started the fire, a few citizens report hearing what sounded like thunder and gunshots in the background followed by strange seismic events. Some townsfolk say that there was an old hospital built in the mid-1940's that was abandoned about thirty years later because it was not up to proper code. Local officials checked on the building, and it appeared to have collapsed, and the officials say, from what was left of the smoldering heap of charred rubble, that the building may have collapsed due to natural causes which could have sparked a fire due to faulty wiring.

"The important thing however to take from this is that no bodies have been found and the local officials expect to find none due to-"

Callon clicked the radio off. We all stood in silence, like little children waiting to be punished, as we waited to hear how Callon would probably kill us.

He pushed the chair back a fraction of an inch until the chair hit the wall. I swear I saw the metal frame bend underneath the force of the push.

Callon screamed, "Did you hear that! No bodies found, but you almost gave away the Clade! If society would've found out about us, the Agency would find us and kill us!" Silence rang overhead again.

Callon stepped out from his desk and pushed us all out of the way as he made his way for Juliette, still standing as straight and stiff as a board.

He got close to her face, "How many died back there?"

I've never seen Juliette so afraid before. She whispered trying to control her shaking, "About two hundred. We were the largest division of the Clade."

Callon quickly turned and slammed his fist into the desk creating a crack in the wood. Juliette shuttered and stumbled slightly backwards into the corner of the room.

"You should have known that the Agency was coming," Callon said trying to calm himself down. "You should've had guards on night watch. You should've been ready for such a fight and maybe they all would be alive here still!" Callon stood in silence a moment then said to her in a whisper, "Maybe Marcus would still be alive if you all weren't so careless."

Suddenly, I don't know what happened, I knew I had to speak up for Juliette.

"Hey, it's not her fault!"

The room got quiet again. Sarah and Trish slowly turned their heads back towards me with wide eyed expressions on their faces and their mouths open. I probably looked the same.

Callon pushed Sarah and Trish out of the way and stepped right into my face. I could feel his breath and spit as he spoke.

"And who might you be, boy? Don't you think you are in a little over your head here? I think that if you weren't all so careless back in New York, your friends and my best friend, would still be alive today," He said.

"Marcus is alive," I replied trying not to make eye contact.

Callon just whispered, "I wish… but the Agency doesn't leave Recruits alive. They just kill them because to them we are nothing but animals. For Liam though," Callon stepped back to the middle of the room. "I don't care at all about whether or not he lives or dies. For all I know, that man left us as a traitor. You don't abandon your allies in the middle of a war!"

Juliette said, "The Clade was built to reflect America. Three districts with three separate ways to govern depending on how the Head Instructors wanted it to be run. He had the freedom to leave whenever he wanted to."

"He was a Head Instructor though!" Callon spat at Juliette. "The president doesn't decide to resign and flee the country if a war isn't going the way he hoped! He stays and fights for his country or dies trying!"

Juliette replied trying to settle Callon down. "We had no idea that the Agency was planning this. They initiated a whole new war. This isn't just a race to get Recruits anymore. This has now come down to battles until one stands and the other falls."

Callon walked back over to me. He liked to be in control and always moving. I didn't want to get in his way, so I just stood still and hoped he wouldn't yell at me too much.

"What do you think, boy?" Callon asked me. "Do you think it is right for a leader to abandon his troops?"

"I... I," I could barely speak. I put all my effort in the last few words. "I think that a leader shouldn't, but he wasn't the only leader. He could back out whenever he wanted to."

Callon gave me a funny look. "Really? So, do you think it was okay for Marcus to die because we had backups? I mean it's no big deal because we can replace Marcus with another Instructor. Promote them to Head Instructor. Do you know what that entails? You are the head of your division of the Clade, and, along with four other Recruits, you decide every action the Clade makes."

"This is true..." I said trying to gulp down my choked throat. "...But I think Juliette will fill the required spot well until Marcus returns."

That is when Callon lost all control. His eyes grew wider than ever since we met him. He turned and literally ran to Juliette. She fell backwards and hit her head on the wall with a loud thump.

Callon yelled, "You are the Head Instructor! Who decided that!?"

Juliette said, "M-M-Marcus told me to be the Head Instructor before he left to go fight the Agents with Liam."

Callon stepped back and threw his fist down on the desk again causing a leg to literally snap under the sheer power. I wanted nothing more than to run down the hallway and out of this cave.

Callon said, a little more in control, "Marcus doesn't have full right to bestow upon yourself that kind of power. You must go to Council, which I can promise we will have especially with everything going on."

Callon spun and glared at all of us again. It was as if I could feel the searing heat radiating from his gaze. When his eyes landed on mine, I felt as though my body would turn to stone or combust. Maybe that was his ability?

Callon said, "I will have a word with Barbara about this. Until then, you are welcome to stay with us as fellow Recruits, but know that as long as you are a part of my division, you will abide my rules and regulations!"

We all nodded to make Callon feel as if he had the power. I didn't want to stay here at all, but we had to. There was no place else out there that would take us in. Nobody would accept and protect people with extraordinary abilities.

Callon asked for all of our names. Trish gave Callon her name, and then Sarah followed. Sarah also confirmed that her mother was Barbara Irving, the Head Instructor. Then, he approached me.

"And you, boy?" Callon said.

"My name is Ezekiel Laufor," I pushed out.

His expression changed from hate to an expression of curiosity. Suddenly, I appeared to be something of a treasure to him. What did he find so interesting about me?

"So, you are Greg's child," Callon said slightly smiling as he stepped past me. "I would say it is an honor, but I have never seen you fight. But, I'm sure we will soon enough. Let's find out if you are as great as your old man." Callon laughed to himself and said, "More importantly, I want to see if your ability was all that Marcus bragged it up to be."

Those words scared me, but as long as I didn't have to fight him I think I would be okay. However, I noticed that almost everyone here is ripped beyond all belief. Does he expect everyone to take steroids while they are here? I'm against that, but I wouldn't mind adding a few pounds of muscle.

Juliette stepped in front of us and began to follow Callon down the main shaft of the cave. Sarah, Trish, and I were right behind. We all gave each other a fearful glance as we walked down the main tunnel of our new home.

Chapter 12

Callon led us down the dank tunnel. The more we walked, the more the other Recruits stopped and stared at us. Their pale skin all gawking at the fresh faces. I also heard a few of them whisper things about Callon. Do they not see him very often, or was it an honor, or dishonor, to be escorted through the cave by their dominant leader?

"What do you think?" Sarah asked Trish and I barely under her breath.

"About what?" Trish answered. "Do I think that this Callon guy is insane? Then, yes. I think that he is insane and the sooner we get out of here the better."

The thought of trying to break away from Callon's controlling grasp was appealing, but the more and more I continued to contemplate how we would do this, the more that it seemed improbable to try and escape.

Callon had guards posted at all positions of the mountain. He had guards at the entrance, at his office, and most likely random locations throughout the entire cave. Also, if we were to actually make a break for it, where would we go? This wasn't New York.

I said, "I think we are going to have to stay and tough it out. Callon is very controlling, kind of like an army general, but we have to just act like his troops and stay on his good side, and I think we will be alright."

"I don't think I could be cooperative with a leader like Callon," Trish shook her head.

Sarah said, "I think we can manage. Just do what Zeke suggested, stay on his good side, and we should be able to blend right in with the other Recruits."

Trish, still uncertain of our plan, said, "I guess I will try that also, but what happens if we find out that this guy keeps prisoners? Let's agree that no matter what we do, we do together."

Sarah and I nodded at Trish and each other and said, "Agreed."

We were about halfway back to where the guards escorted us into the mountain when Callon took a left down an adjacent connecting tunnel. However, this shaft of the cave did not stretch on for long. In fact, it was so short and abrupt that it was illuminated completely by only two flickering blue lights.

Callon halted at a small opening with a curtain shade hanging down in front of it, kind of like a makeshift door.

"This is the boy's dormitory," Callon pointed at the curtain. "Zeke, you will be sleeping in here along with the other twenty-five or so boys that inhabit this division of the Clade."

The group followed Callon down the short remainder of the tunnel while I stayed behind and took a quick peek beyond the curtain drapes.

There were three rows of bunk beds like an army camp. However, only about half of them were taken by other boys. I could tell because their beds were not made nor were there clothes picked up off the frames of the beds. I looked up at the ceiling to see one large, plastic covered light bulb give light to this portion of the cave.

There were no closets or places to keep your clothes the more I looked. By each bed, however, I noticed a small bag. It looked almost like a garbage bag and clothes were piled up inside of them. I guess those were the makeshift closet space that the Recruits came up with. Suddenly, I missed my tiny dormitory back in New York.

I noticed that the group was already down at the very end of the cavern, and I raced to join up with them.

I popped in just in time to hear Callon say, "This is the girl's dormitory. Sarah and Trish, you will share this sleeping space with the other twenty-five or so girls that are Recruits here as well."

Sarah and Trish peeked in through the gray curtain. They made scrunched faces at each other, apparently not liking their new living space, and backed out.

Juliette asked, "Where will I be staying then if only Sarah and Trish are staying here?"

"You will be sleeping in the dormitory directly across the main shaft from this one. That is where all Instructors and Head Instructors reside while here."

Callon then glared at Juliette ever so slightly that I think only I noticed. "So, to me it sounds like you are perfect for staying in there with us. Isn't that right, Juliette? You are an Instructor and maybe even a Head Instructor. We will find out what you really are soon enough."

It sounded like Callon just threatened Juliette. Juliette just turned her shoulder the other way and began to make her way towards her new dormitory. I felt really bad for her. She would have to sleep in the same room with Callon. If I was her, I wouldn't sleep an hour. The thought of Callon sleeping next to me gives me chills.

Callon watched her walk away from us and cross into the opposite shaft. He then walked across the shaft and back in between the two dormitories where another curtain hung down covering a hole in the wall.

"This," Callon began, "is the bathroom. It's divided with boys on the left and girls on the right. If I catch any one of you in the opposite bathroom, I will just have to think of a punishment severe enough to make sure you follow the rules next time."

Sarah spoke up, "But, what if it was just a mistake like we were sleepwalking or something."

Callon just laughed lightly to himself and said, "Trust me, Sarah Irving. If for any reason I find you, or anyone else in the Clade, break a rule that either I or Barbara have established, then you will be punished to the point that you will make sure not to 'sleepwalk' into anything prohibited again. Is that understood, Ms. Irving?"

We all remained silent. Even Sarah, the person who had a smart answer to anything thrown her way, was too intimidated to answer. This guy wasn't a ruler, he was a dictator.

Callon, in a more uplifting tone said, "I will allow you to get accustomed to our rules and daily routines here, so go to your rooms and pick a bed. There should be a bed that has a garbage bag containing a cloak on it. Switch into that so my Recruits will stop staring at you and possibly get back to their jobs. Tomorrow, we will decide what to do with you, and trust me, it will be fun."

Callon just smiled an eerie smile as he walked through Trish and I and back towards his office.

Trish, Sarah, and I all stood in a circle waiting for one of us to make a move or decision. None of us wanted to do anything. I sure didn't. As long as I was near them, I would be safe and okay. I kept thinking about Callon sneaking up on me while I slept. The chills wouldn't go away. It looked as if that applied to both Sarah and Trish.

Trish said, "I guess I'll go pick out a bed then. I'll see you soon, Zeke. Hopefully." She turned around headed back to her dorm.

Sarah flashed me a fake smile. It was more of a "I hope you don't get killed by the brutality of this place" kind of smile. I did the same and headed back to my dorm to pick out my bed.

I hoped I would see them soon. It felt like I was the new kid in town, if this was high school. Everyone watched as I moved into the dormitory and shut the curtain behind me.

I walked down the rows of beds looking at each of the garbage bags next to them. Some of them were open with identical looking cloaks piled up outside of the bag. I guessed that those beds were taken.

Something I noticed was that the beds alternated every other. There was one person to an entire bunk and every time I saw a bag opened on the top bed, the next bunk would have the bottom bag opened. I wonder why that was?

I kept moving down the aisles of the wooden bunk beds. There were three rows of about twenty each. Not even close to all of the bunks were used. At times, I would hit a stretch of bunks that weren't even occupied by a single person, and then I would find one where someone had taken a bed, and then there would be another long stretch where no bed was taken. I guess that the boys were trying to spread out and not be too close to each other while they slept.

All of a sudden, as I approached the end of one row of bunks, I heard a rustling sound coming from the very far corner of the dorm. I silently maneuvered my way to the end of the bunks, trying not to be heard to find out what that was. Could it be a person?

As I closed in on the end of the aisle, the rustling stopped. I froze in my place and waited for the sound to come back, but it never did. I stood up tall and straight and figured it was a mouse or a bat or something, if they had bats here.

Suddenly, a voice came from behind me, "Hey."

I jumped and spun around too quickly, causing myself to fall down right on my butt. I looked up to see a guy lying on the top bunk in the middle row. He had long blonde hair that fell over his eyes. Height wise, he wasn't much taller than I was, but I could tell that he was full of charisma and energy.

He hung upside down looking down at me and said, "Oh man, sorry for scaring you like that." He paused and then gave a confused expression. "Are you a new Recruit? Did Brody get you?"

My heart felt like it was going to pound right out of my chest. I stood up, still shaken, and said, "My name is Ezekiel Laufor, but everyone just calls me Zeke, and I'm not a new Recruit. I'm from the New York division, and I came with three others. Who are you?"

The boy gripped the edge of the bed frame and did a really cool flip down and stuck the landing perfectly. He brushed the hair out of his face and moved towards me with his hand outstretched towards mine.

He said, "My name is Riley Patterson. I am a Recruit in this lovely place we call hel- I mean the Colorado division of the Clade." I took his hand and shook it. "I have been here for almost a year now and I still haven't been able to go on a mission. In fact, I only see daylight about once a month when I have to take the Course."

I looked at him more closely and noticed that he was just as pale as everyone else. Do they really only get to see the sun once a month, or did that rule only apply to his position here?

"I guess I have a lot of adjusting to do," I said.

He laughed. So far, he has never wiped off the smile from his face. He must be that happy of a person.

"You have A LOT of adjusting, my friend," Riley replied. "Thankfully, for you though, you don't have to stay that long. Soon, you will be back to your division of the Clade."

I felt a little uneasy talking about the New York division of the Clade. However, I did open up to him and told him everything that happened. I told him about my being Recruited up to my meeting with Callon. His smile vanished when I reached the part about everyone else in the Clade getting killed by the Agents.

When the story was over, Riley just stared at the floor with his mouth still wide open. The silence continued for a few moments longer as he thought about the horrifying deaths, and the sudden betrayal of a trusted ally.

He said somberly, "I'm really sorry, man. I don't want to say I know what it's like to lose a friend because I truly don't."

I just shrugged and said, "I didn't lose one friend. I lost possibly hundreds of friends. War took me from my home and brought me to this place only to take me away from my new home again."

Then, for no apparent reason, I spoke softly, "War, it's something that everybody gets hyped about. Kids play games in their homes and backyards pretending to kill each other, and we play video games about war, and the news broadcasts new information about Iraq and Afghanistan every night. It isn't until it's in your own backyard that you realize how terrible of a thing it really is."

Riley, removing his hand from my shoulder, said, "That is very true, my friend. War is terrible, and hopefully, we can put an end to it before it's too late."

Riley gave a huge grin. It forced me to smile back at him. He was such a hopeful person. It would be nice if everyone else in the Clade would have such high hopes as he did. I only knew one other that believed that this war could end...

And that was Marcus.

The air was thick with sadness and depressing emotions. I decided to change the subject, "What are you doing in here? There are roughly fifty Recruits here, right? How come I have only seen a few in the cave?"

Riley answered, "This is my job. You see, we have this sort of *test* once every three months. Those who do well get the nice jobs like going on recruitment missions with Instructors while the ones that don't do so well end up with the terrible jobs like cleaning the bathrooms or melting snow on top of the mountain for water."

I imagined a person shivering on the peak of the mountain as they tried to melt the snow and collect the water. That was like worker cruelty.

"Can Callon do that?" I asked. "You know, make someone go up to the top of the mountain and melt snow?"

"I guess so," Riley said. "I know because my best friend here, Cooper, has that job. Every morning he wakes up and climbs this barely visible path to the summit and melts snow with his ability. He can have snow become a liquid, gas, or solid just by clenching his fist. It's quite amazing really." That smile came back on Riley's face.

"Okay, what do you do then?"

Riley pointed to the far corner of the room where there was a little outcropping in the wall. Inside of the small compartment was a fire burning in a steel bin. The closer I got to it, the warmer I got. Soon, I felt like I was going to sweat right out of my clothes.

He said, "I have to make sure this fire stays lit by using either my ability or throwing in some branches and leaves from the trees on the mountainside. Some people also have the fun job of carrying sticks in, so in comparison I really don't have it too bad."

Riley really didn't have it that bad. Compared to some of the possible jobs someone could have, he gets to sit in a warm room on top of a freezing cold mountain and do really nothing all day other than make sure the room stays warm.

This got me thinking about what Riley could do. If his job revolved around him keeping a fire lit, then I guess he has to have an ability to somehow manipulate fire, but how? I thought of some of the cool ways a person could control fire, like Trish and how she can literally set her appendages aflame, and Gabe... how he could make things explode into flames.

"What can you do?" I asked curious.

Riley laughed a little and walked over to a bag of leaves sitting in the corner of the room opposite of the fire. I suppose those were over there so they wouldn't start burning randomly from the intense heat of the fire.

He brought back a handful of small twigs and brush and held them in his hand. He then began to break the sticks in half repeatedly until the pieces were small enough to fit in both of his hands. He filled his right hand with brush and placed it on his left and filled with brush.

He said, "I would stand back. Just in case, you know?"

I took his advice and stepped back not knowing what to expect. I watched closely as he formed a cocoon with his hands around the brush. He looked up at me and smiled yet again.

Just then, flashes of light escaped between his barely parted fingers. I felt even more heat coming from his hands than from the fire behind me. It was incredible. He was an incinerator.

He opened his hands to show that nothing but a little bit of dust and blackened ash remained. He tilted his hand and the powder gently glided to the ground with some of it vaporizing into the air, exiting existence.

"That's awesome," I said. "You are like a human incinerator!"

He wiped his hands on his cloak and said, "You think? 'Cause, I was coming up with this idea of being a superhero, and Heroic Hot Hands kept coming to mind. Maybe Captain Incinerator is better?"

The question caught me off guard, but I just shrugged and said, "Uh… yeah, that sounds perfect."

Riley walked over to the opposite row of bunks up against the far wall and pointed at the fourth one from the fire.

"This will be your bunk," He said. "You can choose top or bottom, but, if you asked me, I would take bottom because more people sleep on top in this row."

I walked over and flopped down on the bed deciding on whether or not I liked it, even though it wouldn't make a difference. I rolled over a little bit and noticed the black, unopened bag resting next to the head of the bed. I opened it and pulled out my black cloak.

"You can change," Riley said. "I can turn around."

I looked back down at the cloak. A strange feeling swept over me. It was a feeling of acceptance and belonging. It was like holding this familiar cloak in my hands makes me feel like I'm right where I belong. I'm with my own kind in the end, but just because I'm in a new place with all new faces and leaders, that doesn't mean I will forget everyone back in New York. They still live on inside my head and heart and especially in my nightmares.

I quickly undressed and threw on the cloak. It dropped below my knees and hit the tops of my shoes. I wiggled and moved around a little trying to get that familiar feeling back. It was just like I was back in New York.

Riley spun around and said, "Nice. Looking good for a kid from New York."

We both laughed, and he went back to take care of his fire.

I didn't know how long I would be here in Colorado. I didn't even know how long I would have to deal with Callon which unfortunately, I had a bad feeling would be a long time. No matter how long I had to stay here, one thing was for sure, it was going to be weird, fun, hard, and exhausting with Callon and Riley here.

Chapter 13

This night, as well as every other night since we narrowly escaped from the clutches of Nathaniel and his army of Agents, has been filled with thoughts and nightmares about the Clade in New York. They aren't all depressing though. Sometimes, I think back to when Gabe, Sarah, and I first met, or it could even be the nights we snuck around on the second floor only to find that hidden computer room. But most of the time, my thoughts were filled with the gruesome deaths of my friends.

Especially Gabe...

It's odd that thoughts of depression occur at night, at least for me. Even back when I lived with my "mom" in New Haven, I would have great days, but if something was truly bothering me, it would arise every night in my thoughts and nightmares. I hated it, and soon, you begin to fear sleep because you know that you will soon see the thing you have been fearing and dreading for the last few days or weeks.

I started getting used to that feeling. Thankfully I've come to accept it almost like a friend. Every morning I wake up and have a pretty good day, but I know that my special friend of pain will show up again to remind me of what I am missing out on, whether it be a missed chance at a girl, death of a friend, or betrayal from someone you trusted.

The lights in the cave are on timers. Every night, all the lights in the caves click off. Along with that, the generator can be heard dying down for the night. At least, that is what Riley told me.

Riley has been a big help in adjusting to the differences of this division of the Clade and the New York one. While everyone was on duty, he gave me the "rundown" on how things operate around here. First of all, each Recruit follows the same schedule every day in order to keep the Clade running. Riley wrote down a schedule and handed it to me. It read:

1. **Lights turn on followed by fifteen minutes of showering and dressing**

2. **Ten minute breakfast in commons**

3. **Attend job until ten minute lunch bell rings**

4. **Attend job until ten minute dinner bell rings**

5. Remain in barracks until lights turn off or Callon or Barbara request your attendance.

It was a fairly straightforward schedule for its length. It shouldn't take me more than a day to figure out what my role is here and how to blend in. The only thing that was still on my mind was what my job was going to be.

Riley told me, "You will find out soon enough unfortunately, and for your sake, I hope you do well on the test Callon puts you through."

I asked, "I have to take a test?"

Riley nodded. "Usually, all new Recruits must go through a physical test to find out where they are strong and where they are weak. Then, Callon analyzes the results, and determines what is the best job for you. You see, I can keep fire going, but I am not the strongest or fastest Recruit here, so I get stuck with the boring job of sitting around watching sticks burn."

I watched Riley perform his job in the Clade for a few more hours until a loud chime jingled through what sounded like metallic ventilation shafts. Riley hopped off the top bunk of his bed and headed through the curtain. I followed close behind.

Riley turned right and headed down the main shaft of the cave. At the same time, a lot of other Recruits began to shuffle out of different rooms and follow in the same direction. They acted as if they were a herd of cattle following one another in procession.

It was kind of like high school.

Teenagers of all different ages and sizes gawked at the new kid in the crowd. As you could guess, that was me. I constantly had eyes pointed in my direction making me feel very uncomfortable. I felt as that any wrong move I made would be brought back to haunt me in the future. Making a good first impression was vital.

Riley followed the crowd down a wide adjacent tunnel that led to a hole in the rock wall larger than any other doorway. We walked through it holding the curtain for the others behind us.

The room was larger than any of the other areas that I have been in so far in the Clade. It was an open area with two rows of wooden picnic tables that ran parallel to each other. A few kids were already sitting at a table chatting with full mouths.

We continued to follow the group around the tables to a line that formed against the far wall. Recruits stood in lines grabbing their trays and continuing to shuffle down the line grabbing whatever food was sitting outside of the opening in the wall.

I was surprised by how fast these kids were moving. My legs began to ache from the constant rushing of the line and the atmosphere. I grabbed my food as quickly as possible, something that resembled meat loaf with bits of green vegetables in it, and followed Riley to a table.

Just like the others, Riley began shoveling food into his mouth faster than he could chew. I took my time just trying to make sure I didn't choke on my food, and so I wouldn't get a gut ache later tonight.

Riley shook his head at me after swallowing a huge helping. "You are going to starve if you eat at that rate."

I said, "I think I will be fine. I can usually last a while without that much food in me before I get light headed and weak."

Riley laughed, bits of green pieces stuck in between his teeth. "Really? I thought that too, but then I started my first day on the job and, wouldn't you know it, I got sicker than a dog."

I kept eating at my pace while I continued to watch the others eat as quickly as possible before the bell rang for the end of the day. As usual, all of the other kids were staring at me between bites and whispering to each other.

However, two girls in line were not. It was Trish and Sarah. I watched them approach the window and grab their food quickly before the kids behind them began to start hurling things at their heads in anxious anticipation. I waved, trying not to make that big of a scene, for them to sit by Riley and me. They plopped down their trays on the table and sat next to me with a girl on either side.

Riley said, "Hey, are these your friends, Zeke? Are they from New York as well?"

I nodded. "Yup, these are my best friends. This is Sarah Irving," I looked to Sarah on my left who waved gently. "And, this is Trish Dawson," I looked to my right. Trish nodded and said "hi" back to Riley.

An awkward feeling swept over the group. It must've been even more awkward for Riley who was just introduced to my friends with none of his present. The question then arose through the silence in my thoughts, did he have friends?

Almost on cue, Riley smiled with a full mouth and waved to the line behind us. It was almost disgusting the way he smiled with a full mouth.

I turned around to see nobody in general. I had no way to pick out who Riley had been waving to. Sarah and Trish did the same. They looked as confused as I was. They looked at me as if I knew who he was trying to contact, but I didn't have the slightest clue.

Then, two figures, a boy and a girl both a little older than I was, strode to the table. The boy plopped his tray down causing the table to gently shake underneath my tray. The girl casually sat down next to Riley on the opposite side of the boy.

Riley said, "Guys, these are my friends. This is Conner Mitchells, and this is McKayla Forwing. We were all recruited at roughly the same time, which is how we met."

Conner waved to us but kept focusing on his food. McKayla, on the other hand, just rolled her eyes and stared vacantly into space as if she was annoyed by our presence. Riley noticed but didn't wipe the smile off of his face.

The awkwardness didn't go away with that introduction. The three of them seemed as though they had nothing in common. How could they have ever become friends?

Conner was a little bit taller than I was and very lean. His eyes were dark and shady which gave him the persona of someone who liked to cause trouble. I knew a few boys like him back in high school that were strong for their meek appearance and quiet and were on top of the principal's "Most Wanted" list.

McKayla had long, blonde hair that fell to the middle of her back. A hole stood out above her lip where a piece of jewelry would slip through. She pushed her hair back over her ear revealing many small holes that would be for her jewelry. I counted four or five empty sockets.

To me, she resembled a rebel. A girl who wanted to rebel against her parent's wishes and create a life for her own somewhere else as long as it wasn't there. That could be my own personal thought, or the hours of television I watched after school.

A part of me felt kind of bad for judging them. I know that they would have no knowledge of me doing this, but I didn't even know them that well. It was as though my high school, immature, judging self was released. I liked that I could be a kid again, but my more mature self knew to stop.

I broke the awkward silence that hung around our group like a thick haze. "So, where are you all from?"

Riley immediately answered lifting his head from his tray, "I'm from Chicago. It was a nice place, but awfully busy. The Clade was a big change for me."

He then turned to Conner who said sternly, "I'm also from Chicago." He went back to his tray and kept eating.

McKayla then spoke seeming distant, "I'm from here. I lived in Colorado all of my life unfortunately. Not much to do other than ski or snowboard, and lucky me, I don't do either." She made it sound like it was an insult to ask her.

I remained silent after that and tried to eat my food. I barely touched it, and Sarah and Trish were about halfway done. Almost all of the other Recruits were finishing the last few morsels of mystery meat on the tray or even giving the tray back to the window where a hand reached through and pulled them back.

I chewed quickly to try to catch up to the rest of the Recruits, but once again, I got distracted by someone calling my name. I looked over to the curtain to see Callon standing under the rock arch.

Just then, the entire room became dead silent as if I was called out to a duel in the Wild West. Not a single Recruit dared to eat or even make a move towards their food. I felt as though I was in deep trouble.

Callon said, "As you were, Recruits."

The room then resumed back to the way it was just a few moments ago before Callon showed up. He has the authority of an army general around here. Juliette was right.

He walked over to me taking long, powerful, steps that felt as though the earth should've shook beneath his laced boots.

"Zeke Laufor," he said to me not breaking eye contact. "I have news for you as well as you, Sarah, and you, Patricia."

I asked him trying to sound polite, "Yes? What do you need?"

He gave me a dark look and said, "You will stand at attention when I demand your presence."

I quickly pushed my tray back and stood up on my feet. My knees bumped against the edge of the table giving me a nice bruise.

"You should learn your place here, Laufor. You are a soldier now. I don't know what you did back in New York when Marcus addressed you, but here, you will treat me as your commander. Is that understood?" Callon commanded.

Riley and the others were all looking up to me as I said, "Yes, sir."

I shook in his presence praying that he would hopefully leave and find someone else to pick on but that never happened.

Callon said, "Good. Now, since you are a new Recruit under my command, I need to know what you are capable of. So, tomorrow, you, as well as Ms. Irving and Ms. Dawson, will go through the Test."

I said, "Yes, sir." Although, I had no idea what a "Test" was. I think Riley was talking to me about it earlier today.

Callon continued, "The Test will be held right after breakfast tomorrow morning. You and the others will meet me at the entrance to the cave no later than one minute after."

"Yes, sir," I kept responding.

"The Test," Callon explained, "is a procedure used to measure what a Recruit is capable of. Usually, this is only given to brand new Recruits, so I expect you all to do quite well."

"Yes, sir."

"Good, now go back to eating. You have about..." Callon pulled up his sleeve to reveal a silver wrist watch.

He laughed to himself and said, "You have about three seconds." He began to walk out of the room when a ringing sound echoed through the vents again.

All of the Recruits followed the implicit orders given by the bell and rose to their feet. Those who were not finished dropped their trays off at the window with food still left on it. All of the others followed one after the other out of the room passing Callon on the way out.

Callon was giving orders to the Recruits like, "Let's move!" and "Faster!" and "No wonder why you are so large." It was pretty cruel, but he believed it's what every leader should be.

I quickly dumped my tray off at the window letting the hand pull it back. My stomach growled as I watched the food get pulled out of sight with barely a bite out of it.

We quickly rejoined Riley, Conner, and McKayla who were now in the line marching out of the room. We passed by Callon who flashed us a death glare followed by a small laugh. He knew how much food I had left and it made him happy knowing that I was going to be starving tonight.

I guess I better learn his game before the Test comes or else I will be starving and weak. If what Riley said was true, then we all better get enough sleep and warm up before the Test. This decides whether or not I will get a job that is easy and fun or boring and tough.

Sarah and Trish split off from the line with the rest of the girls as we headed towards our dorms or "barracks" as Riley calls them. I waved to them with sorrow-filled eyes as they passed through the curtain out of sight.

I entered the now partially filled boys barracks. Teenagers of all ages crowded around the blazing fire in the corner while others dangled from their bunks laughing at jokes others were telling. A few of them were even asleep.

Almost immediately, all eyes were directed towards me. All chatter that had been occurring between Recruits had been silenced by the odd figure in the bunch. This place was small enough that everyone knew everyone, so one new person really stands out amongst the crowd.

I slowly made my way to my bed across the room, but I was cut off by a large man with muscles almost as large as Callon's. My neck hurt as I looked up into his bearded face.

"So, you are the new kid that Callon has made a big deal about?" The man said.

I stepped backwards a little and said, "No, he isn't interested in me. I'm just from the New York Clade, and I need to take my Test."

He pushed me a little causing me to stumble. The wall caught me, but now I was stuck between a rock wall and a hard place.

"Do you think I'm some sort of stupid?" The man asked menacingly. "Callon doesn't just announce when someone is going through a Test. Oh no, he made it loud and clear to everyone in the cafeteria that he has some interest in you. The only thing I can't figure out is why that would be?"

"I have no idea what you are talking about, and why would Callon have any interest in me? Look at me?" I pleaded.

The man laughed. "I know. You are a little pipsqueak compared to us here." He spread his thick arms out over the crowd. I looked and noticed that everyone in the room had pretty large muscles even Riley, but this guy still had the biggest.

He continued, "I have been here longer than any of these little Recruits. I have been on a dozen recruitment missions to get them, and I will be damned if anyone thinks they can take that away from me!"

He closed in on me to the point where I could smell his breath. It made me gag.

I said, "I won't take your job, I swear! I have only been a Recruit for a month!"

The man backed off and bellowed a deep laugh. "Only a month!? Wow, you are a pipsqueak. Then, I really don't have anything to worry about." He then gave me a death stare that seemed to penetrate right through me. "You just watch your step, Zeke. Figure out how things work around here soon because otherwise you will have to deal with me."

I just nodded, and he went back over to his bunk at the opposite end of the room next to the fire.

I slid down the wall breathing deeply. My life flashed before my eyes, I swear. Riley ran up next to me and sat down patting me on the back.

"Who was that guy?" I asked.

Riley shook his head. "That is Bruno Jagger. He has been around here just as long as Callon. You don't want to mess with him dude."

He helped me up on my feet. "I noticed that, but thanks for telling me."

The rest of the night was pretty boring. I stayed near my bed hoping that nobody would come up to me and challenge me to a fight or something stupid like that. This place was scary enough, and my bed was my only safe haven.

Unfortunately, it was right where everyone else was.

After a few more moments, a loud whirring noise hiding in the background of everywhere I have been today began to slow and come to a stop. With it, all of the lights in the cave shut down. The sheer blackness brought back with it the pain of losing my friends and being thrown into a new environment where it seems like it's every man for himself.

I'm glad I at least have one friend around here.

I fell asleep listening to the sound of my grumbling stomach craving the sweet nourishment of food.

Chapter 14

The following day rolled around faster than I hoped it would. My body still ached from all of the climbing and running I went through the day before. At least, I got to sleep on a regular bed for once.

All of the Recruits in the barracks raced to the showers. There was barely enough room for all of us, and then we rushed to get dressed and get to breakfast before the bell rang. If we did, then we had more time to eat, at least that is how Riley described it to me.

Breakfast was just as rushed. I grabbed my food and sat down at the same table I did yesterday. Shortly after, Sarah and Trish joined in with Riley and me. Conner and McKayla sat down afterwards.

This go around, I didn't spend time talking. I shoveled down my runny eggs and hash browns (I think they were hash browns) and threw my tray on the window sill waiting for the hand to grab it and pull it in.

After I sat back down, Riley asked, "Are you all ready for the Test today?"

Trish answered, "I don't think it should be a problem. If it is a test about how we control our abilities, then Sarah and Zeke should do great. They both completed their month of training. Well, Zeke almost did."

"I think you will do great too," Sarah said. "We are a team, remember. We need to have confidence for everyone, but no matter what, pass or fail, we are sticking together."

I nodded, "You got that right. No matter what they throw at us, we will be ready for it."

Riley smiled, as usual, and said, "Your teamwork cheers me up, but you should know that the Test is only partly about how much mastery you have over your ability. A bigger part of it is just about how physically fit you are. It is just an extreme obstacle course after all. Sure, there are a few spots where an ability may come in handy, but none really help when you have to climb over a ten foot wall."

The ten foot wall made me gulp loudly. I began to sweat at the thought of a rigorous, army like, obstacle course. I could run, but I wasn't the most physically active kid. I do my "hour a day of play" and then would crash on the nearest couch.

"I think we will do fine," Sarah said noticing my horrified expression.

"Okay," Riley said. "Way to stay positive."

That's when the bell rang out. Conner and McKayla silently shuffled out of the room with the rest of the group.

Riley waited behind for Sarah, Trish, and I to gather. "Good luck. I hope you all do well," he said joyously.

"Thanks," Sarah smiled back. "We will do our best."

While Riley headed to the barracks to maintain the fire, Sarah, Trish and I headed to the entrance to the cave to begin our Test.

The walk was longer than expected. On our way there, I thought about what we may come up against. Riley told us about a large wall that we will have to handle by ourselves, and he said there are a few obstacles that challenge our specific abilities; however, all of them can be cleared with the help of an ability.

This course sounded to be biased. People with abilities that allow them to leap higher, move faster, and pull harder would be better suited for such a test. Whereas Sarah, who can only move water, may struggle because she won't be able to use her ability to allow her to maneuver obstacles faster than others. That is really what this Test is about- to see how we stack up against Callon's Recruits.

We arrived at the entrance just as the bell rang for the first shift of jobs in the morning. The air was warm even at this high of an altitude, but the wind gave it some bite that sent chills along my exposed face. I squinted at the bright sun hanging barely overhead due to the height of the mountains.

Callon appeared shortly after eight, apparently not following his own rules about being on time. "Recruits," he said in a commanding voice. "Today, you will be running the Test. Something all Recruits must go through before they are full Recruits in the Clade."

We listened to Callon as he gave us our "orders." To be honest, I felt like dozing off listening to him preach about how we are not really going to be respected until we run this dumb little obstacle course, but I just nodded and followed the motions of Trish and Sarah.

Callon folded his arms behind his back and stepped through us nearing the edge of the rocky path. "First to attempt the course will be Sarah followed by Patricia and then last, and of course," Callon narrowed his vision and slowed his speech as he focused on me, "not least, Ezekiel."

Sarah inhaled deeply and moved towards Callon. Callon pointed to the ground and said, "Ezekiel and Patricia, you shall remain here until Sarah has finished her Test. When I direct you too, Patricia, you will move down here and follow me to the testing grounds."

We all nodded. Callon led Sarah down the rocky slope and into the forest ahead of us, out of sight. I leaned up against the cavern wall next to one of the two guards protecting the entrance. I wondered if Callon was secretly trying to separate us so that Trish and I would have to fight Callon's guards. It wouldn't surprise me even a little bit. He seemed like the egotistical leader who would want to show off how strong his Recruits are.

Trish sat down and let her legs dangle over the edge of the path. She turned and said, "How long do you think this will take?"

I left my spot against the wall and sat down next to Trish a little paranoid that a guard may sneak up behind us, but they didn't evil wiggle.

"I have no idea," I said. "I guess it will take as long as Callon needs to make Sarah pass out from exhaustion."

"Then, we could be here for a while. Sarah is tough. I think Callon may be in over his head with her," she said. We both laughed together.

Trish leaned back on her elbows and basked in the radiance of the sun. Carefully, she raised her arm and moved a few strands of hair covering her eyes. I couldn't help but watch in amazement. How could someone be so beautiful?

She looked over at me, and I suddenly realized that I was staring at her… with my mouth wide open. I quickly fixed myself and stared down into the woods without a word as if that was my plan all along. I don't know how she reacted, but I think I heard a small giggle come from her. Great, now she probably thinks I'm a creep.

The rest of the time we sat and waited I kept checking myself to make sure I wasn't doing anything embarrassing or wrong that could ruin my chances with her. Although, my chances are probably slim to none. All the more reason not to mess up anymore than what I had already done in my thirteen years of us knowing each other.

About fifteen minutes had passed as we waited perched up on the slope. Dark clouds had begun to move in over some of the mountains in the horizon. It appeared as if rain was in the forecast for today. Hopefully, they go away or hold off until I am done with my Test.

As I stared at the gray clouds, a guard said, "Don't worry about those clouds. The mountains usually stop the rain from reaching us this time of year."

I guess he had been watching us. I stared at the gray clouds some more, and it turned out that he was right. The clouds advanced, but they were stopped by an even taller mountain than the one we were stationed on. They lowered and dissipated into the air like magic.

About fifteen minutes later, a rustling sound caught our attention. Trish grabbed my shoulder and launched herself upwards to watch as Callon stepped out from the tree line. Sarah was right behind with a bunch of scratches and cuts on her face, legs, and arms. Mud covered her cloak from head to toe. What did she have to go through?

Callon said, "Patricia, you are next," as if he was sentencing her to death. Trish stood up and began to follow the path down as Sarah walked up next to me.

"How was it?" I asked.

Sarah didn't respond. Instead, Callon said, "No questions about the Test, Laufor. Sarah, go inside and wash up and then begin your new job until the bell rings for lunch."

Sarah just nodded and began to walk inside. I looked down at Callon and Trish to find them gone. I was left alone with the two guards. This was going to be the longest wait of my life.

The time passed until finally Trish emerged looking shaken and broken just like Sarah. Callon stepped out just from behind her and said, "Ezekiel, you are last."

I walked down the slope watching as Trish slowly passed me looking tired, sore, and completely lost. How bad is that Test?

I began to fill with worry thinking that this was like going into the doctor's office when you were a kid. You don't know what they are going to do or find, and you don't know if you have to get shots. My anxiety relieved itself slightly as I thought about getting a shot deep in the forest. That was just ridiculous.

Callon noticed my slight smile as I walked towards him. As if Callon was allergic to smiles and his goal in life was to erase all happiness in the world, he said, "What's so funny? I promise that when the Test is over, you will be as broken as Sarah and Patricia." He smiled as mine faded.

Callon led us through the forest on the same path Juliette led us in on. The path diverged off through a few bushes, barely noticeable if you were to come from the other direction. We jumped onto that path and continued.

After a few minutes, I thought we were going to walk off the edge of the cliff, but instead of falling to our doom, we stopped at a podium with a red horn on the shelf.

Callon stepped up onto the brown platform the podium rested on and said, "You're Test should be set up by now. All of the obstacles are the same as your friends, but they are slightly modified so that you must use your ability in some way to allow yourself passage."

I just nodded as Callon focused on me with a creepy smile.

"If everything I have gathered from the other Instructors are true, then you should be a unique specimen to watch," he said as if I was some sort of science experiment. "Electric abilities are unheard of in the Clade, so we had to make special obstacles just for you. You should feel honored."

Sarcastically, I said, "Yeah, I feel so great about being the freak among freaks."

Wrong thing to say. Callon stepped off of the platform and grabbed me by the collar of my cloak. "How dare you say that about your own kind!" He spit a little on my face as he threw me onto the platform.

I slowly stirred and got back onto my feet. "I didn't mean what I said. I'm just sick of people making a big deal of an ability that I have. I don't know why I'm so different from everyone else."

Explaining things calmly to Callon wasn't helping much. He kept his anger built up inside of him and unleashed it whenever he needed to scare his Recruits.

"I am only yelling at you now," Callon exclaimed, "because you are the son of one of the original five Head Instructors, Greg Laufor! We all have high expectations for you!" Then, Callon slowed and looked at the ground. A small smile broke across his face when he said, "Maybe, you are weak. Perhaps, we made a mistake and you aren't Greg Laufor's son. Wouldn't that just be funny?"

I didn't know what game Callon was trying to play, but what he was saying somehow made me clench my fists and grind my teeth. Rage began to consume me whole.

I may not like my father that much, but being told that you are nothing like the father you never grew up with, who never took you to baseball games, who never talked to you about girls, who never taught you how to

163

drive a car, can make you really angry. It was as if Callon was saying that I don't have a father. This person, Greg, may not even be my father, but for once in my life, I have a name to put with the imaginary face in my head. For once, I felt like there was a person out there who somewhat cared for me a little even if it was just to become a soldier in this war.

And now, Callon was trying to take that away.

"Don't say that!" I yelled. "I am more than my father ever was or will be!"

Callon just laughed more and said, "Wow, someone has a little bit of anger kept up inside of him. What's wrong?" Callon spoke in a tone that parents would speak to babies, "Did your daddy not care about you?"

That's it. I forced all of my energy into my palm creating the warm, fluorescent glow that shone on the dim forest surroundings.

I lunged from the platform toward Callon standing still with his hands hanging at his sides. I threw an electrified fist at his face. Quickly, before I could even react, Callon ducked under the punch and threw his knee into my gut.

The power surging through my body and into my hand vanished as I collapsed onto the dirt. I held my chest as I vomited once before rolling onto my side coughing. That was stupid of me. I couldn't help it though. Callon really irritated me to the core.

Callon stepped over to me and picked me up by my collar again. "So, you do have some fight in you. Well, this is interesting." He threw me again onto the platform. I didn't get up as quickly this time as I tried to regain the wind that was knocked out of me.

Callon continued, "First of all, you don't attack me unless you want to die. Secondly, no matter how mad I make you, no matter how much you want to kill me, you will address me as 'sir.' Finally, are you going to shut up and let me explain the rules of this obstacle course?"

I just nodded, rage evaporating from my body and said, "Yes, sir."

"Good," Callon said. "As I was saying, I am interested in what you can do. Marcus informed me before his untimely passing that you have an ability to control electricity within your body." Callon became quiet after saying Marcus' name as if we were having a moment of silence in his memory.

After the silence, Callon continued, "This appears to be true. I would expect nothing less than the son of Greg Laufor to have an incredible ability. Now, let's see what you can do with it."

Chapter 15

Callon approached me slowly. I stepped out of the way while he pulled out the red horn from the podium shelf.

He said, "There is a dirt path in the forest that creates a large loop." He pointed to our left at the clearly visible dirt path. It looked as if the entire path was paved by the feet of other Recruits who had done this before. "There are five obstacles that you will need to overcome. At the end of each obstacle, a white flag will be hanging on a wooden post. You will grab all five flags and return back to the podium. That is when the time will stop, and I will rate your performance along with the other Instructors."

I nodded and prepared myself for the horn to sound. Adrenaline surged through my body giving me the jitters. When would he push the trigger? When will this start?

I could barely focus on the task at hand. My mind kept drifting from this moment to the Clade in New York. In some way, this was testing more than my physical strength and my skills with my ability. This was to see if Marcus and Juliette trained me well enough to stand up against my enemies no matter what the challenge. Granted, I did fall a week short of completing my training, but if Trish could do it with hardly a week's worth of training, then I can do it.

I kept thinking of Marcus and everyone who helped me to get to where I am now.

Especially Gabe...

The horn pierced my peaceful thoughts. It caught me by surprise causing me to stumble at the start, but I regained my composure and hopped off the platform heading for the first obstacle.

I think I could hear Callon laughing behind me as I headed into the woods out of hearing distance.

The ground sank beneath my feet creating a small puddle with every stomp I took. It was drenched with melted snow from the mountain peak. I looked down and saw the water-filled tracks of Sarah and Trish. I focused on that as I made my way around the track.

The circle was huge. I felt like I hadn't turned at all yet and it had been a full minute. My lungs began to ache and burn as I inhaled through my mouth slower than I exhaled. It was going to be a long Test, but I couldn't slow down. I couldn't give Callon that satisfaction.

Suddenly, appearing through the brush, a large wooden wall loomed. This must've been the wall that Riley was talking about. It didn't look so menacing...

...that is until I reached it. It was a monster. I stopped short of it just before colliding face first into its heavy stature.

I looked up at the imposing menace and wondered how I would climb something so tall. It was approximately ten feet high. It was tall enough to reach some of the bottom branches of the lower trees.

I poked my head around the wall and saw the flag about twenty feet from it. My mind raced as I saw that flag. Perhaps, I could just run around the wall and grab the flag. Callon wouldn't know that.

The temptation to just skip the obstacle and grab the flag was just too much. I couldn't resist. Cautiously, I glanced around the forest to make sure nobody was watching. Callon said that the Instructors were watching, but I didn't see any.

Time was wasting away, and I decided to try it. I stuck close to the wall for added protection from... nothing really. I was paranoid that Callon would have some defense set up. I stepped out slowly onto the yellow grass covered ground on the side of the wall.

Wait! The entire ground was dirt and mud. Why was there a random patch of grass on the sides of the wall? But, it was too late. My foot landed on the soft patch of dead grass causing it to collapse into a large pit it was covering.

What was that!? I quickly jumped backwards causing me to land on my butt. I carefully stood with my legs still shaking from the almost impending doom. I crept back towards the edge to see what was down there. There was nothing. It seriously looked like a bottomless pit.

What kind of sick Test is Callon trying to run me through? Maybe this is why Sarah and Trish looked so shocked and disoriented when they finished. Their lives were on the line, and now so is mine.

I guess I will have to play by Callon's rules. The pit was far too wide to even try and jump over, so I would have to go over the wall.

I took a few steps back to give myself a running start. Hopefully, I wouldn't slam into the wall and break something. I'm not the most coordinated person. After taking a deep breath, I started my dead sprint at the wall and leaped.

My fingernails scratched at the boards. A few splinters stuck themselves underneath my nails sending a few jolts of pain through my hands, but I couldn't let go. I got my fingers wedged between two boards and dangled in the air. I used my feet to pull myself up and reach the next board. A few speckles of blood smeared on the light colored wood as I progressed up the wall.

My strength was wearing out, but I managed to reach the top of the uppermost board and pull myself up. Before dropping down, I took a quick look to make sure there wasn't a pile of dead grass below me. There wasn't so I jumped. I hit the ground and rolled like the professional stuntmen do in movies and ran for the flag. With one smooth move, I swung my arm around and grabbed the flag and kept moving through the forest to the next obstacle.

I kept my eye out for the rest of the Test for other piles of dead grass. I know Callon is tough and strict, but he would go to such extremes that he would risk hurting and possibly killing new Recruits to see where they stand? It's absolutely insane!

Before I knew it, I approached the next obstacle. Just like the wall, there were piles of dead grass surrounding the barrier making sure you couldn't run around it.

This obstacle consisted of a bunch of small posts in uniform rows and columns with thick, silver wire running from each one interconnecting them. I was confused. I didn't know if I had to just run through or if there was something special I had to do. To answer my question, I saw a large note pinned to a tree. I grabbed it and read it: **Dig for the flag, but watch the wires**.

I took the warning whole heartedly as I carefully stepped into the first square. The square could fit barely three people, and I had to crouch and dig for a flag? How was I supposed to do that without hitting the wires?

The area was huge. It took me a while to carefully dig for a flag without hitting one of the ominous silver wires. I knelt down onto the soft mud and began to dig for the white flag while checking to make sure my legs weren't getting close to the wires.

After digging for a few minutes, I stopped. Callon wouldn't have buried it deep enough that it would take more than ten minutes per square to find it. I moved to the next adjacent square and began to dig there. Again, another few minutes passed of getting my hands dirty for nothing.

I stood, preparing to move to the next square along the row, stepping over the wire when I lost my balance on one leg and began to fall backwards. I screamed twirling my arms in the opposite direction to keep myself up but it was no use. I was going to fall and hit the wire. Time seemed to slow itself that last second when my back crashed into the ground with the wire underneath it.

My body tensed preparing for some sort of deadly trap to spring on me, but nothing happened. I slowly opened my eyes and saw that nothing happened other than the post that the wire was on snapped causing the wire to rest in the muddy concoction beneath it.

Forcing myself up, I brushed some of the mud off myself. I stared down at the wire, and anxiously, I touched it and then grabbed it and nothing happened. What was so scary about this? I pulled on it a little bit and nothing happened still. I probably shouldn't have been doing this, but my curiosity was winning the fight with logic.

Suddenly, I felt a small vibration within the wire that made my skin crawl. It shook in my mind very slightly, barely noticeable. I wondered what that was.

Well, since I had nothing to worry about, I ran through all of the other squares without care and dug for the flag. This could be my chance to make up some of the time I lost. It wouldn't be much, but every little bit helped.

Four squares of digging later, I found the flag. I stuffed the two flags inside my shoe, so I wouldn't lose them. It was uncomfortable running, but at least they were safe.

It was another five minute run on the beaten trail until I reached the third obstacle. It was a fairly simple one too. A long, black cord hung from the highest tree around. At the very top of the cord, a small key hung on a twig that the cord was tied to. I looked further down the trail to see a metal box resting on top of a post with a small keyhole. The flag must be inside the box.

I didn't waste any time. I ran to the rope as quickly as I could and jumped. I wrapped my hands around the highest point I could reach and began to climb.

The rope climb was my all-time favorite activity in my P.E. class back at school. It sounds odd because most kids hate it, but to me, it was easy. I had no upper body strength, but I could still move faster than any of the football players who were ripped to the core. How did I do it, you ask?

Well, I kinda cheated. I wrapped the cord around my leg and shimmied up the rope instead of actually using arm strength which is what our teacher wanted. I could go as quickly as I wanted, and if I got tired, the cord wrapped around my leg supported my weight. I learned that on Man vs. Wild. Maybe that's why I lack big muscles.

And parents say watching T.V. is bad for you.

That is exactly what I did here. I hung on the cord and tried to twist the cord around my leg. To my surprise, I couldn't get it. I kept swinging my leg around it trying to kick it up off of the ground, so it would slacken and my leg could slip through. That never happened though.

I slid down the rope and looked at the end of it. I found it cemented to the ground! The cord was stiff all the way up to the top of the tree. How did Callon know I was going to, in my way, cheat? Unless, it's like this for all Recruits.

With my muscles burning, head spinning, and lungs aching, I fell backwards and stared up and the giant that would be my downfall. There was no way I could climb that in the state I was in. The key twinkled from the sunlight shining down on it as if it were taunting me.

I closed my eyes and got lost in thought. There must be some way to get that key down without climbing that cord. I just need to think.

The key was far too high for me to throw something at it and knock it off the twig. The twig was fairly long, and the key would need a firm push to get it off.

My head was aching to the point that my eyes were going to shoot out of my skull. I thought of all the things that came before this moment like I usually do now to relieve stress. Gabe, Liam, the lightning striking me…

That's it! Maybe I could shoot it off with my powers. It was worth a shot. I jumped onto my feet and began to charge a shot in my hand. The warmness surged through my entire body relaxing me. I pointed one finger up at the twig and aimed carefully.

After a few seconds of aiming, I released the charge sending the warmness away and into the sky. The bolt missed the twig and the key, but barely. I began to charge another blast when the lightning arced from my hand randomly and hit me in the arm. It sent a wave of electricity flowing through me causing my muscles to tighten. I collapsed on the ground in pain.

Why does this keep happening? Is there something seriously wrong with my ability? I thought for sure that the first time that it had happened that it would just go away and there would be nothing to worry about, but it hasn't. In fact, I think it is getting worse. It never hurt that badly before.

Like I had been doing, I forgot about it and tried again. I pushed myself up from the ground and just fired a weak bolt at the key. It was a long stretch of electricity that never stopped being emitted from my palm. Thankfully, it hit the key, but it didn't get blasted off like I thought it would. Instead, the electricity just surrounded the key and hung there creating a sort of electromagnetic field. I also learned that on the Discovery Channel.

Whatever was going on, it was useless. It wasn't helping with getting the key off the twig, and time was ticking away. The electricity hung around the key giving it a slightly blue aura. The electricity created almost a perfect line that jumped and moved around itself sporadically all the way back to my hand as if they were connected by a string.

Thinking, I closed my hand around the string of electricity and pulled backwards. The key slid slightly towards the end of the twig! I couldn't believe it. Is this something else my ability is capable of? I never did fully complete my training sessions back in New York. Maybe this was what Marcus was going to teach me next.

I stepped backwards trying to tighten the electric string and pulled back hard. The key slid forward and fell off the twig! I ran up and caught the key in mid-air just as the electricity faded away.

Reminder to myself: Don't forget how to do that electrified string thing.

I ran to the box and jammed the key inside and turned it hard to the right. A clicking sound echoed through the silent forest and the door opened revealing the white flag. I grabbed it and took off down the trail for the next obstacle. Three down, two to go.

The trail was beginning to circle around now back towards the starting podium. I can just see Callon now as I step onto the podium with all the flags being pulled from the sole of my shoe after about a half an hour has passed. He probably won't be the happiest, but these obstacles are ridiculous. It was like taking a final exam that you didn't even have a class for.

The sun was peaking in the middle of the sky. Lunch would be soon, and if I wanted any, I needed to finish soon. Callon wouldn't be reasonable and give me food if I took too long on the Test. It's as the old saying goes: "If you give special treatment to one person, then everybody expects it."

The next obstacle loomed in the distance between a line of trees. I passed through them and found myself staring down a wooden post in the middle of a clearing. On the post rested a dummy, like the one I trained on back in New York with Marcus.

I looked to my right and saw a wooden sign with the message: **Destroy the Dummy, Find the Flag.**

The flag must've been hidden inside the dummy, and I had to destroy it to find it. This should be the easiest challenge. I stood a relatively fair distance away from the dummy, charged a blast and released it. The bolt arced and coursed through the dummy. I thought for sure that would fry it and destroy the dummy, but it did nothing. Instead, the bolts arced all around the dummy making contact with it at multiple points, but it didn't even make a mark on the thing.

I ran up to it and rubbed the dummy feeling the material it was made out of. Of course, it was made out of rubber, and rubber doesn't conduct electricity. I probably gave it a decent shock, but nothing powerful enough to destroy it. Callon did say that he would test my strength and my use of my ability. I guess I can't use my ability on this one.

I started pulling and tearing at the dummy hoping that it would fall apart nicely for me, but that wasn't the case. It was put together really well, and no matter how hard I pulled and tore at it, it wouldn't rip.

I put my hands down on my knees and rested in front of the dummy. It stared up at me like it was mocking me. My head began to drip from the sweat even though I was a mile above sea level.

The dummy and I had a stare down as I tried to think about how I could destroy it, when I noticed a bright light from behind the dummy. I looked and saw an axe stuck into a stump. The light was being reflected from the bright sun.

I ran to it and grabbed it. It was heavy in my hands. With it I felt unstoppable, like I could take on any opponent, even Nathaniel again. However, I never used an axe before in my life, so I had no idea how good I would be with it.

I slid my hands down the shaft of the axe and kept them a good distance apart for leverage and speed purposes. I eyed up the dummy and focused. I raised it over my head and gave a grunt as I threw it down at the dummy... but I missed just to the left of it.

How could I miss? The axe was big and the dummy was even bigger? Oh well, at least I have all my fingers and toes, and I can retry.

I pulled the axe from the ground and took a deep breath. I heaved it over my head, grunted again, and threw it down right onto the dummy slicing halfway into its arm. I removed the axe to find a large gash in the dummy.

Pulling the arm down to increase the size of the hole, I dug my hand and arm into the dummy to try and find the flag. I dug deep within its chest area until I felt a piece of plastic that felt like a flag, but I just couldn't reach it.

I picked up the axe and took two more accurate swings at the dummy completely severing the arm. I threw the axe down and pulled the flag from inside of it. I took off my other shoe this time and threw it in its sole. Only one obstacle remained, and I would be done with this.

The path now was almost all the way back to where I began. I never thought I would make it this far. I was probably doing terrible with time, and I wouldn't be able to go on Recruitment missions, but I didn't care. The only thing on my mind at the time was finishing and then taking a well needed nap; although, I knew I wasn't going to get that nap.

With the forest beginning to thin, I knew the final obstacle was up ahead. What would be waiting for me this time? Saws I have to run through? A tank full of sharks? Callon was making the obstacles tougher the further I went. When I climbed the wall, my arms were aching, and then I had to dig. After that, I had to climb a rope. My arms were already on fire along with the rest of my body, and the dummy slaughter should be fairly self-explanatory.

Whatever was coming up next would push me to my limits and play off of whatever was my weak point that arose through the other obstacles. I thought about the other obstacles and decided that the next obstacle must work off of upper body strength. Most of the other obstacles already worked me to the core in that area, why not have one more just to make it burn? Is Callon really that sadistic, or is there a purpose for all of this?

I crossed the threshold of foliage and approached the final obstacle. Before me, rested three tree trunks with all of the bark removed connecting in a zigzag fashion on top of wooden posts. That didn't seem to bother me; at least, not as much as the layer of dead grass that stretched around the trunks.

I inched towards the grass carefully. I had to make sure it wasn't what I hoped it would be. The tip of my shoe touched the nearest blade causing a large stir. The grass shifted and shuffled until, like an avalanche, the grass fell down the deep pit it was covering. The grass dropped into darkness, out of sight.

I leapt backwards stopping myself before getting vertigo and tipping over the edge. The pit was immense. It covered the entire clearing and stretched into the forest around trees; their roots sticking out from loss of dirt.

The trunks of the trees remained suspended over the pit. The flag stood on the post just on the other side. I would have to cross the three logs without falling into the unknown and grab the flag.

This obstacle played on my weakness just like all of the other obstacles: Exhaustion. I would have to keep my balance across three logs without succumbing to my uneasiness. I could barely stand as it was. My legs shook underneath my weight.

I took deep breaths and relaxed myself. Then, I put my right foot on the log and began my walk or fall.

Chapter 16

Time became less of an issue as I began to move slowly across the trunk step-by-step. With every little movement I made, dead bark scraped and fell into the pit below. The tree has been long dead creating a slightly squishy and slippery surface.

I almost reached the end of the first trunk when a strong gust blew through the trees. My foot slipped off an edge of the trunk and I fell to my side. I quickly grabbed the edge of the trunk with both of my hands catching myself before I plummeted.

My hands began to slip quickly due to the slippery surface. I pushed down hard and forced myself back onto the log holding it closely to my chest and wrapping my arms around it.

I shimmied until I reached the intersection between the log I was on and the adjoining one. It wasn't a straight connection either. Instead, there was a slight turn which would be difficult to maneuver on foot. However, the wooden beam that rose from the darkness and suspended the two in the air was too thick to get my legs around, so I had to stand.

My legs wobbled uneasily as I stood putting my entire self on top of them. With one little slip, I could be off tumbling into the darkness below. I inhaled deeply and tried to concentrate. I moved my left leg first. Since the log bent at an angle to the right, I figured moving the left first would make it easier for the right to get on and provide stability for myself. My foot planted firmly on the next log. After another deep inhalation, I lifted my right foot and swung it over to my side. I stood confidently having moved on to the next trunk.

I walked the rest of the second log sideways keeping my arms spread out wide to give myself better balance. I didn't know if it actually worked or not, but I see people do it all the time in the Olympics on the balance beam and the tightrope walkers at the circus, so at the very least, there must be some voodoo magic involved in doing it.

The next log approached quicker than the last one. This one moved off to the left where it ended on solid ground by the white flag.

My palms were beginning to sweat in the cool, Colorado, air. This wasn't exhaustion. It was nerves. I felt like throwing up from this obstacle. One wrong move and I don't know what would happen to me. Would I die? Get injured? Get teleported to a parallel universe?

…Alright, the last one probably wouldn't happen, but I was afraid of what would happen to me if I did fall. Callon was far more sadistic than I could have ever imagined. Who would promote him to Head Instructor? I would like five minutes alone with them.

The next intersection approached. I stepped carefully watching my foot swing over onto the next log and land safely. Putting slight pressure on my foot on the other log to keep my balance but not slip, I swung my other leg over. I lost balance for a second, but I twirled my arms in a circular motion and that kept me stable.

The last log was a little longer than the middle and the first log. I side-stepped my way over the deep chasm while trying to keep my focus on the flag hanging on the post. If I kept my field of vision above the chasm, then I wouldn't think about it and miss a step.

A few more steps later, I reached solid ground. I wanted to bend over and kiss it like you see in the movies, but I was already running out of precious time. I grabbed the flag and sprinted through the trees to the podium that began to become visible through the brush.

The flag flapped in my sweating hand, tickling my palm gently. I didn't bother putting it in my shoe like the others because I was so close to the end already.

I circled the pedestal that the podium stood on and broke through the tree lining into the clearing. Callon stood with his arms folded watching as I ran past him and onto the podium, stopping the ticking clock once and for all.

Callon unfolded his arms to reveal a black stopwatch in his hand. He gazed at the number and said, "Hmm, not terrible, I guess, but it could've been much better."

He looked at me and spoke like I was being punished for not living up to his expectations. He barely knew me. Did he really think I would be as great of a Recruit as my father? I don't even know who my father is! How can he compare?

I stepped off of the pedestal, my legs shaking from exhaustion, and said, "Sorry, I'm not my father. I don't even know who he is, so how am I supposed to know anything about him?"

"Your father is the reason why the entire Clade exists. Yes, he was one of the five Original Head Instructors who helped organize and lead, but he was the one who originated the idea for the Clade," Callon said as if my dad was some omnipotent being. "Without your father, none of us would probably exist, and that especially includes you because you are his child. The Head Instructors now expect great things from you, Ezekiel and, after looking at your time on the Test, I have a lot of work to do with you."

I did not like the sound of that. Riley said that your job depended on how well you did on the Test. If Callon believes I did poorly, then what will my job be? He doesn't like me, that's for sure, so I won't get a Recruitment job with an Instructor. That's fine. I want to stay close to Sarah, Trish, and Juliette. We are stronger in numbers.

Where was Juliette anyway?

Callon began heading back to the cave. "Are you coming?"

I didn't answer him. I figured if I answered he would only have more ammunition to ridicule me with. Instead, I walked silently behind him keeping the same pace as him while I watched the clouds roll by through the trees overhead. I wanted to fall back and watch the clouds roll by until I passed out, but that wasn't going to happen.

The cave appeared before us. The two guards stood attentively as Callon passed by and climbed the slope. As we entered, they clicked the heels of their black boots together and held their pistols against their chests. It was a salute of respect to Callon, as if he was an army general.

I've noticed that about Callon as we walked down the dark tunnel barely lit by the overhead lights. Recruits that passed by would stop and salute him just as the two guards did guarding the entrance.

He runs this division of the Clade as if it were an army. Each person has a specific role to play in creating a perfect, organized unit. We go through a sort of "boot camp" on our first arrival here. I just took a Test that decided our rank. Callon has guns available to all of his Recruits. Marcus, on the other hand, kept all firearms locked away until they were absolutely needed.

Callon moved to the cafeteria curtain and said, "Lunch will begin soon. I have already given Sarah Irving and Patricia Dawson their jobs. Don't expect them to show right away when the bell rings. You, however, will be able to eat right on time; something that most Recruits never have the chance to do. Don't take this gift of time for granted because it's the only one you are going to get. You will report to me in my office after you are done with lunch, so I can give you your job."

I just nodded and said, "Yes, sir."

Callon gave a stern nod to me as if I was earning his acceptance through all of the subordinate acts. He strode briskly down the tunnel and turned around the corner just as the bell rang.

I entered and walked towards the lunch trays where the line began. It was a weird feeling. I was only here for one day, but I already got used to the normality of always having the cafeteria completely packed after a bell rings.

It didn't take long though. Right after I grabbed my tray and my fresh grool from the hole in the wall, Recruits began to fill in behind me. There were only fifty Recruits in this division of the Clade, and I didn't recognize a single guy from my barracks.

No matter what Callon decided my job would be, my real job would be to know as many people here as possible and make friends. Back in New York, there were roughly two hundred Recruits, the largest division of the Clade, and I only knew about six of them. It eats me up thinking that almost everyone was killed and I only feel sorry for Gabe.

Poor Gabe... I need to stop feeling like this. He is gone, and I needed to get over that. He was gone, and there was nothing I could do about it.

As I sat down, forcing myself to finish thinking about Gabe, Trish walked in. I waved for her to sit by me. She smiled and went back to waiting in line. I saw no sign of Sarah though. I thought those two would be together.

Shortly after Trish entered, Riley, Conner, and McKayla walked through the curtain and stood in the already long line. They waved to me, or at least Riley did. The other two didn't seem to care at all. What was their problem? They always seem so gloomy, angry, upset or all of the above.

Trish sat down next to me dropping her tray on the table hard enough for the grool to jump on the tray. The grayish-red substance moved to a different section on the tray and slightly jiggled. It was disgusting to say the least. I felt like a prisoner in a jail cell.

Trish picked up a spoonful of grool, made a disgusting face, and let it drop back down onto the tray. "Do you believe Callon makes us eat this stuff?"

I smelled mine and made the same face. "No, I don't even think a dog would eat this."

I kept a lookout for Sarah but she never showed up as the flow of people from the tunnel stopped. Either everyone was in line already, or they were eating. Is she okay? She looked pretty beat after her Test, but then again so did Trish and I don't want to sound rude, but Sarah is tougher than Trish. I mean, she was in the Clade for two years before I even showed up.

Granted, Marcus was the Head Instructor, and he didn't have harsh rules or make us take any tests. Also, he gave us better food.

"How was your Test?" I asked Trish. "You seemed to move fairly quickly. What did Callon think?"

"It was easily the toughest and quite possibly, the scariest thing I have ever done. There were pitfalls and electrical wiring and who knows what. Thankfully, I didn't fall down any of the pitfalls; otherwise, you may not be enjoying this lovely lunch with me," Trish said sarcastically.

"Yeah, the same for me," I added.

Trish continued, "What's worse is that Callon didn't even say a word to me out there. He gave me the instructions and said 'Go' without even a 'Ready, Set.' I finished it probably around a half hour."

"Probably a half hour? Didn't Callon tell you your time?" I asked.

"Nope, he was quiet the entire time. I made it back to that wooden podium in the middle of the woods and collapsed trying to catch my breath. I was so exhausted. He just looked at his watch and began to walk back. I forced myself to follow him in case I would get lost or punished or something."

"That's weird," I said thinking. "He didn't give me my time either, but he just went on and on about my father and how I am supposed to be as strong if not stronger than him. Callon kept talking like someday I'm going to have to be a Head Instructor and lead the Clade. Is he serious? I can't lead anything. I'm only sixteen."

Trish stared down at her food. She was deep in thought.

I said, "I think he has something out for us. I don't know why, but he doesn't seem to like us at all."

"I don't really blame him though. He thinks we killed Marcus," Trish said.

"But we didn't!" I said a little louder than needed to be.

The other Recruits began to stare at us. They were giving us looks like, "Those are the new Recruits from New York? Freaks." I felt bad for Trish. I didn't want to embarrass her.

I looked back over to the line to see it almost completely reduced to nothing. Riley, Conner, and

McKayla stood next to the trays anxiously waiting to get their food.

I whispered to Trish quickly before Riley and his friends sat down, "What happened to Sarah? Did you see her after your Test?"

Trish shook her head. "I have no idea where she went. I didn't see her since she left for her Test and came back looking like a zombie."

"I did too though, I don't blame her," I said.

"Same here. When I came back in, an Instructor named Stewart allowed me to catch up on some sleep and rest. I woke up when the bell rung. He caught me on the way out and told me that I would have a job after this and that I would have to report to him."

"At least you got some sleep," I said. "I was sent straight from my Test to here. But that still doesn't answer the question of where Sarah is?"

Trish was about to answer when Riley and his group sat down across from us. I guessed that they had about six more minutes to eat before the bell would ring, and we would be off to our new jobs.

Riley said "hi" cheerfully, and Conner and McKayla remained silent stirring their forks in the sludge and then taking a bite.

Riley asked Trish and I how the Test went. We told him about all the things we had to go through and how long it took us to go through all the obstacles. He shook his head as he listened and spoke up when we mentioned how we thought we did. Riley thought we did well compared to him for even making it to lunch. That must mean that Trish and I are going to have good jobs. Sarah, wherever she is, must have done just as well also because she finished just around the same time.

We asked Riley if he had seen Sarah between bites of our grool. It tasted horrible. It got stuck halfway down your throat and then it slowly slid down. On top of that, Riley said he didn't see her. Then again, he works in the boys barracks. Conner, he works on the summit of the mountain, so he wouldn't see her at all, and McKayla… well, she isn't very sociable and never told us what she does for a job. In fact, I don't even know her ability.

Suddenly, Sarah erupted through the curtain in a frantic rush. She grabbed her tray; the only meal left in the window, and sat down next to us. Immediately, she started to mow down the food on her tray no matter how gross.

"Sarah!" Trish and I yelled at the same time ecstatically. "Where were you?" Trish continued.

Sarah swallowed her food as said, "I finished that crazy Test and was told by Instructor Stewart to rest for a little while, so I did. I was so exhausted I could barely see straight. I slept for an hour when I was woken up by a girl and told to go out into the tunnel. I jumped off my bunk and went into the tunnel to find Stewart standing there."

Riley and the others listened closely and ate their grool as Sarah explained what had happened to her. They were as interested as we were.

Sarah continued, "Stewart told me to follow him to my new position here. He said, 'Callon gave me your new job. I will take you to it.' So, I followed him. He took me down past this shaft of the cave and into the next one. Instead of a tunnel though, all there was was a curtain covering a hole in the main shaft. He showed me around and inside was the kitchen behind this wall where the food comes from."

We all looked at the wall where Sarah pointed. She works on the other side of it in the kitchen. I wonder if she had to make the grool or if this stuff just came from the ground. I felt bad for her if she had to make our food. The stuff was making me sick.

"What is your job?" Trish asked.

Sarah groaned and said, "I have to do dishes before every meal. And when that is done, I have to make grool for the next meal. It's basically water, hence, why Callon wants me to do it. It's pretty much identical to the job I did back in New York, but it was much less stressful."

Silence overtook our table. "I'm sorry, Sarah," I said somberly.

Sarah just nodded and said, "Don't worry about it. It's not a big deal. I have done it before, and I can do it again. What about you two?"

We told Sarah between bites that we have no idea of what our jobs are other than we will find out after lunch. However, the more I thought about how Sarah got her job, the more I questioned whether the Test that Callon puts all Recruits through really mattered. He never spoke to the Instructor Stewart once the Tests began. That must mean that he had our jobs planned out from the beginning. Then, why have us go through them? Also, why only speak to me and not Trish or Sarah? Things weren't adding up and I planned on figuring them out.

I quickly finished eating my food while speaking a little to Riley. Conner and McKayla remained quiet as usual. Not so long after the bell rang and we separated.

Sarah walked back down to the curtained passageway, Trish stood outside of the entrance of the cafeteria, and I began to walk down to Callon's office to find out what he wanted to me to do for as long as I was here.

If Callon doesn't do something soon though, there won't be much of a Clade left for me to help support. The Agency can't be far behind. Nathaniel knows the location of this division for sure. He was an Original and an Instructor after all, but then what was taking them so long to get here? I'm glad they aren't, but still.

I thought about Nathaniel and the mysterious Agency as I walked into Callon's office.

Chapter 17

Callon was sitting behind his desk looking at papers in a manila folder when I stepped in. He quickly folded the papers and slid them in a drawer in the side of the desk. How he can open them is beyond me. He has such little space behind him.

As he folded the files, I thought I noticed a photo on the top of the papers. Perhaps it was my imagination, but I swear I saw a picture of someone, and the way Callon hurried to hide the files from me...it was very suspicious.

Callon became fierce quickly, "How dare you not knock before entering my office! All of my Recruits treat me with respect! You are finally understanding how to call me sir because I am your superior, but yet you still don't know manners. Well Ezekiel Laufor, I know that your father isn't here, but I plan on becoming a father figure to you in that I will show you how to treat your superiors."

I gulped deeply and maybe a little too loudly and said, "I apologize, sir."

Callon relaxed his shoulders but only slightly. "Alright then. As your punishment, give me twenty push-ups right now."

"What?" I asked being caught off guard.

"I said twenty push-ups, and if you disrespect me or any of the other Instructors or Recruits here, then you will do more until you figure it out," Callon paused to take in a deep breath and exhale. "You are the bottom of the bottom here. A new Recruit. Yes, perhaps you have been in the Clade as a Recruit in another district, but here in the eyes of my Recruits, you are fresh meat. They are tough and ruthless. If a fight ensued, they would be the victors, and I am going to make you into one of them."

I gulped again. Callon pointed his finger out into the hall where there was more space and I began to do my push-ups. I was still tired from the Test and unlike Sarah and Trish, I didn't get any time to nap. My muscles burned when I was on number seven. These were the longest push-ups of my life, but I finished them with sweat beginning to form on my face.

I knelt on the ground and began to cough uncontrollably. I felt as though I may puke again like I did in the woods, only this time I may be punished for it. I tried to hold it down. I did successfully.

Callon said, "Now follow me and I will show you where you will be working until otherwise noted."

I said, "Yes sir" and followed him like his robot. He took me down the main shaft of the cave until we were to the intersection where the Recruit barracks were on our left and the Instructor barracks were on our right.

He went down the right side and into a passageway covered by a curtain.

Inside the path split into two. On the left hung a blue towel nailed to the rock wall and on the right hung a pink towel. I saw these before. These hung outside the boys and girls bathroom by the Recruit barracks on the other side of the main shaft of the cave.

Callon headed into the boy's bathroom stepping carefully to make sure his feet wouldn't get wet. It looked like only the Instructors use this bathroom. If it was anything like the Recruit bathroom there would be many more spots and it would stink more.

He spread out his arms and said, "This is where you will work. You shall clean this boy's lavatory and the boy's lavatory by the Recruit barracks."

"I have to clean?" I said. "That's it? I thought that our abilities would have something to do with what job we get?"

"We have no use for your special ability as of this moment. Until a time arrives when we can use your powers to their full extent, you shall clean the bathrooms."

Callon then reached into a wooden cabinet hanging on the far wall next to a stall. From it, he pulled out a wooden hair brush. He placed it into my hand and said, "You will take water from the sink and mix it with soap from the cabinet in the bucket in the far stall. Scrub the floor, stall doors, sinks, showers and toilets at the end. It should take you all day to do both bathrooms."

"I have to use a brush to clean the floors? Don't you have a mop?" I asked.

"Yes, we do have a mop," Callon said taking the brush from my hand and placing it back in the cabinet. "But if you cleaned with the mop, then you would be finished with both bathrooms in no time at all. Cleaning with the brush will provide you with discipline as well as give you something to do for each and every day you are here."

"This is insane!" I complained and argued. "How can you expect me to crawl around on the dirty floors all day scrubbing with a hair brush? It's almost slavery!"

That was the wrong thing to say. Callon's face morphed into what reminded me of a cheetah just before it pounced on its prey. The corners of his mouth edged up baring his teeth. His eyebrows slanted down towards his nose making his eyes appear fierce.

"How dare you treat me in a manner like that! Have you not learned anything back in my office?" Callon screamed at me to the point that his face was becoming red. "Quick, do thirty push-ups for that."

"Seriously?" I asked. "That's ten more than what I had to do bef-"

"Make it thirty-five and you have two minutes; otherwise you will have an extra ten to do."

I stopped arguing. I dropped to the floor and began to do push-ups. My arms were still on fire from before, but I managed to grit my teeth and push through it. I collapsed on the ground out of breath weary from the day's trials and only half of the day had passed.

Callon watched as I lied on the ground. He stood looming over me and said, "Now, are you going to cooperate and learn to treat people with respect, or shall we keep doing push-ups until you look like my Recruits.

I'm sure you noticed. They are all muscular from hard work. Someday you will be just like them, Ezekiel Laufor."

I stared up into his dark, cold eyes. There was no life there at all. No sense of compassion or understanding. He is being what he thought a leader was; A tough, strong-willed leader that will lead his troops to victory at all costs.

He stepped over me and was about to leave when he said, "One more thing. Clean this bathroom until the dinner bell rings. Don't worry about the Recruit bathroom until tomorrow. I'm going easy on you now. Like I said earlier, appreciate it, because starting tomorrow, you are under my leadership."

That didn't sound like an instruction. No that sounded more of a threat. No more talking back or criticizing Callon or any other Recruits unless I want my head taken off.

He was about to go, but this may be my only chance to ask him. I knew that if I did ask I may be punished, but it's better to ask today than tomorrow.

"Before you go," I said getting up. "I have a question for you, sir." I chose my words carefully making sure to address him correctly with "sir."

"Yes?" He said turning towards me with more anger brewing in his eyes.

"I spoke with Sarah earlier in the cafeteria about her job and she told me that she got her job from Stewart, the Instructor, right after her Test."

Callon focused his gaze more intently at me. Curiously, he said, "Yes? That is true."

My heart rate was off the charts as I said, "How could Stewart know what her job was going to be if you never spoke to him during the Test. It seemed as though you didn't take Sarah's time on the Test into account like all the other new Recruits here, sir."

Callon smiled and gave a menacing chuckle. "Well, what do you know, you do have a little of your father in you."

"What?" I asked.

"You see," Callon began. "Greg was very observant. He could pick out important information from an overload of data very easily. I guess the same is with you. Yes, indeed, how could Stewart know what job Sarah would hold if he never spoke to me after her Test?"

He remained silent as if I was supposed to possibly answer that. "I... I don't know, sir."

"Well the answer is," Callon said. "There is no way Stewart could've known. I gave you your positions before the Test. Sarah had a job like that back in New York, so it wouldn't be a challenge for her to readjust to our way of doing it. She will fit right in."

"Okay then what about me and Trish, sir? How come you are making me clean bathrooms when I could be used for something greater like providing power to the Clade?"

Callon snapped. "We have a generator for that and for all I know, emitting that kind of power may kill you. You are not yet in full control of your ability. How long have you been here? A month? You barely finished Training. That is why you are cleaning floors. Trish on the other hand, will be Trained by Stewart because she has no prior training. If I recall, Marcus informed me of an incident back in New York about a fire in the basement."

"I can handle anything you throw at me," I told him with minor intensity. I didn't want to set Callon off again.

It didn't work out that way. He came to me and put his face directly into mine. He spoke slowly and ominously, "You couldn't handle a pen if I threw it at you. According to that Test, you are nothing more than a new Recruit just like all the others. I noticed that you are befriending Riley and his group."

"What do they have to do with this?" I asked

"Nothing other than they did the worst in the Test among all Recruits. Did you ever hear the phrase, 'birds of a feather flock together?' That is like your group. You did only slightly better than those three and like a moth to a flame, you are attracted to them. Now Bruno, he completed that just under twenty minutes as a new Recruit. That is impressive, so I gave him an easy job. Stand guard outside the tunnel entrance."

"I thought he went on Recruitment missions?" I asked.

"He does, but new Recruits don't just pop up every day. Usually, months go by before another one is found. We just keep an eye out in the local papers and listen to the radio for anything suspicious. That is how all of you are found other than the fact that we know where the Originals' children are placed after birth."

There was a hint at more information I didn't know. How are the babies placed into the arms of "fake" parents? I don't think they could make an ad that read:

"Looking for individuals to raise supernatural babies." How did they find my mom back in New York?

More and more questions swirled inside my head. I completely forgot about asking any more about our jobs, but instead, I got on the subject of children and how that whole process worked.

The more I thought about it now, the more that something didn't add up like most things in the Clade. How come there are so many Recruits, yet only very few Originals. I know there aren't many left because they were killed, but the Clade began with fifty Originals, and with just the New York division alone, there were almost two hundred Recruits and here there are fifty. How can there be so many?

Callon gave me a light shove and said, "No more questions. Get moving. You can stop when the dinner bell rings. I better see this place spotless tonight."

He turned and left the bathroom before I had any chance of asking him about that. Maybe Riley knew. I made a mental note to ask him about that tonight at dinner. Maybe Sarah even knew. She has been here the longest out of all of us.

My head began to ache with all of the different questions that were hurdling through my mind. I thought I knew a lot, but the more I thought about it, the more I realize that I barely knew anything, and the person who would tell me anything, Marcus, was gone. Not dead... just gone.

I found the metal bucket in the stall next to the toilet, wedged in the corner. The thing smelled disgusting after all its uses and not being cleaned itself. I turned on the sink and filled it with warm water. It isn't really warm though, more like lukewarm.

I scrubbed the brush around in the pail while adding soap making suds appear from the goo. I got onto my knees and started to scrub the brush back and forth on the floor underneath the sink in the corner. I planned on moving back until I reach the showers and then after that I would be by the door.

The afternoon passed lazily. It sure took its sweet time to end. My knees began to ache on the solid, rock floor. The bell echoed throughout the tunnel signaling the end of my day. It was only a half day and already I felt like throwing in the towel. How Riley or Conner or McKayla could last here is beyond me.

After all of my supplies were put away, I followed the mad flow of Recruits to the cafeteria. The line was almost out of the curtain by the time I got there. It doesn't help that my job puts me far away from the curtain. The only people further who followed me in line were Riley, Conner, and McKayla and the two guards from outside the cave.

"So, how was your first half day on the job?" Riley asked me as smiley as ever.

"My legs and back hurt and if I see any more soap I'm going to puke," I stretched my back.

Riley laughed and looked at Conner and McKayla. They just sat in their gloom and turned the other way. What was their deal?

"How was another day on the job?" I asked Riley, keeping the small talk moving as the line continued forward.

"Same as usual," he said. "Very boring and very warm. Who knew fires were warm?" He laughed at his joke, but I just smiled.

I saw that Sarah dropped into the back of the line. She would never arrive early in the hopes of getting the full meal time. It's a shame because her job puts her right on the other side of the wall in front of me. I waved and she waved back.

Trish was already eating her food at our usual table. It felt more like high school the more I thought about this cafeteria setup. The same kids sat at the same tables with the same people every day. There is a rush to get food early, and there is a time limit. I can't believe I'm going to say this though... I wish I was back at school.

If I was back in school, though, leading a normal life just like the nerd or geek or jock sitting next to me, then I wouldn't have met so many amazing people. Sarah, Gabe, Marcus, Juliette, Riley... I'm going to leave Callon off the list. I never had this many friends back in school. How come? I had Thomas who is still my best friend and someday, I'm going to try to find him again and tell him what had happened, if we can somehow make it out of this war we are in the middle of.

I took my tray and placed it firmly between my hands. An awkward silence has overcome Riley and I. It's that new friendship silence that everyone gets when they are put into a new friendship. You don't really "know" each other yet, so you don't know what to ask or talk about.

I just grabbed my food and sat down next to Trish who looked like she was ready to fall asleep. "Good morning sunshine," I said trying to smile in a way that didn't hurt my cheek muscles.

"Nuh," she shut her eyes and rested her head on her crossed arms.

I whispered close to her as Riley began to make his way over to us, "I talked to Callon. Found out that he had our jobs picked out before we even started the Test."

Trish peeked open an eye curiously and asked, "What? Why would he do that?"

I said, "He told me that since we had prior experience back in New York for certain jobs, he just gave us those, at least for Sarah. That is why you are being Instructed I'm guessing."

Trish nodded wearily. "It hurts and yeah. What are you doing? I thought you finished Training?"

"I did," I whispered. "Callon decided to give me the fun job of cleaning the bathrooms with a hair brush. It's insanity. My back is killing me and my knees are rubbed to the bone and it's only been a half a day."

"I think he has something against us."

"I wouldn't doubt that, but when I talked to him, he did give me something."

"What is that?" Trish asked.

I watched Riley as he sat down with his food and immediately began to engorge. He looked at me curiously and said, "Is there something on my face? Why are you looking at me like that?"

I said simply, "I have some questions that I think you can answer."

Chapter 18

"Questions?" Riley asked. "What kind of questions and how do you know I can answer them?"

Conner and McKayla just sat down next to Riley as I was about to ask my question. They didn't listen and it wouldn't matter if they did. It's not like they would care anyways.

Sarah rushed herself to her seat next to me and began to eat her grool. "What's happening?" She asked between scoops of the gray sludge.

"I was just about to ask Riley a few questions regarding the Clade," I said. "There are a few things I am still cloudy on and I would like the truth. Callon won't give me answers, but I think you will, Riley," I pointed at him.

He held his cloak by the collar. "Umm... I can try my best but no promises."

Trish bumped her arm into my shoulder and said, "Zeke, what are you thinking?"

"I'm thinking that there were two hundred Recruits in the New York division of the Clade and here there are fifty. Now," I focused my attention back to Riley, "how do you explain that?"

"Well, uhh...." Riley started to stutter. I have only known him for two days, but he doesn't seem like the kind of person who would get nervous. He was always happy and confident in himself. Traits I wish I possessed. I must be getting somewhere with this. "You know, when a mommy and daddy love each other very much-."

"No!" I shouted. I didn't mean to, but I was just so frustrated about everything that has happened. Countless people murdered for reasons possibly unknown to them. They are unknown to me and I think I deserve answers.

The table was quiet. Even Sarah stopped shoveling food into her mouth for a few seconds and stared in silence. I calmed myself down and tried to think of what I would say. My mind ached from the many words floating through it.

"I'm sorry," I said slowly. "I just... I need some answers. My best friend in the Clade was killed by the Agency and for all I know, it was just because he was born with an ability to make fire. It wasn't his fault! He was only killed because of something his parents did and we don't even know what they did, or how they even got their abilities."

Silence surrounded the group like fog. With every deep breath calming me down, it filled in my lungs and eased my tension making me silent along with the rest of the group.

I looked over to Sarah after my rant about Gabe. She just stared blankly into her food tray. She didn't even raise her spoon to her mouth. It hung suspended in the air. I didn't want to vent like that, but it just came out. I hope Sarah can forgive me.

Riley nodded gently and said, "I know, Zeke. I am truly sorry. Nothing like that has ever happened here. I'll try to answer your questions, but I don't really know much either."

"That's fine. I just want to know as much as I can from someone I can trust. Callon will never tell Trish, Sarah and I anything. I couldn't tell you why, but it's true. I tried it earlier."

"Yeah," Riley said finishing off his plate rather quickly. "Callon likes to remind everyone who is in charge. What's worse is that Barbara, the other Head Instructor in this division, doesn't do anything about it. In fact, we hardly ever see her. She just sits in her office until it's late and she goes to bed. At least that is what I heard."

We were starting to get on the right track and I didn't even ask my questions yet, but I wasn't going to stop him. I figure I would hear all I needed to know first and then ask him about the population problem. Barbara is a mystery to all of us including Sarah which is depressing because that is her mom.

Trish said, "I realized that. Barbara never participated in any decisions that involved our entry into this division. Our division was only erased from existence, yet she doesn't even show her face or ask questions. Unless she is with Juliette. We haven't seen her either for the longest time."

Juliette has been gone for a while now. It has been only two days, but Callon separated us from her when he showed us to our barracks. You think that he would let her see us or at least provide us with information to what he and she have been up too.

Riley said, "Barbara just likes to lay low. Ever since Callon was elected as a Head Instructor when another Head Instructor, Samuel Jones, an Original, was killed in a Recruitment mission, he has taken complete control. He believes that the only way to ever defeat the Agency is to build in numbers and train hard like the military. America has one of the toughest armies in the world from hard work and discipline. That is what he thinks will happen if we treat him like a general and he treats us like maggots."

I let that sink in. Callon hasn't always been in control of the Clade here in Colorado. It seems hard to believe, but it has to be true. I believe it, but yet I don't believe it. How can someone have such a powerful influence that he can change all procedures in a division?

"So," Trish began, "Callon is able to do whatever he wants? Back in New York, we had our own ways of doing things. Marcus would treat us like people who were unfairly brought into the world. Yes, we had to go through mandatory training for a month like every other Recruit in the Clade it sounds like, but we didn't have to go through Tests or perform a single push-up."

"I envy your old life back in New York. I wish I could have a stress free life, but unfortunately, that's not the case. I was born in Chicago same as Conner," Riley looked over to Conner who only looked away. "Chicago is sort of between Colorado and New York. If only Marcus decided to Recruit us instead of Callon. Oh well, I guess it doesn't matter now does it?"

"Well, why not?" I asked dumbfounded by Riley's statement. "You know that there are other districts in the Clade that run themselves differently. Yes, there are jobs and training and Recruiting, but those are the concepts acquired by every division. The fact of the matter is you could go to a different division and have a great time there with a Head Instructor or two who treat you right."

"What would be the point? It's not like I could just leave here anyway." Riley shrugged.

For some reason, I began to build rage deep within me. Trish put her hand on my cloak and lightly squeezed it telling me to come back to Earth and control myself. Sarah kept staring at her tray, but she was starting to come around. She noticed what was happening and barely whispered, "No."

My fists were clenched tightly beneath the table. What has gotten into me? Why am I so mad? Is it that Riley could have a better life, but he continues to stay here under the dictatorship of Callon? He may not be able to leave, but how will he know if he doesn't try? If he wanted it badly enough, it could be done.

I came to and lowered my butt back down on to the bench. I didn't even realize I was off it. "I'm… really sorry. I don't know what's happening to me. I just don't see why you wouldn't try leaving. Talk to Barbara or some of the other Instructors. If you want it badly enough, I'm sure there is a way."

Riley just shook his head. "I'm fine here. Yes, it's hard, but it has become my home. I have friends here and I made a life no matter how tough it is. I figure you have to go with the flow. That's my philosophy. You are dealt a hand when you are brought into this world. Mine just happened to lead me here, but now it's what I do with it that will make my life better and it helps that I have friends that are here with me for support." His smile appeared on his face again.

I was going to say more, but that is when the bell rang. Our time together as a group was up, but I may still be able to talk to him once we got back to the barracks. I completely got side-tracked and forgot to get an answer for my question. Typical.

Our group separated as we left the main tunnel and entered our separate barracks. I kept close to Riley in the hopes that I would get the chance to ask him my question again.

I followed Riley through the curtain into our barracks when, suddenly, I was tackled from the side and pushed into the ground. My shoulders were pinned into the rock floor from an intense amount of weight.

I felt the warm, damp breeze of someone's breath near my ear. It came out in a deep, raspy tone. "So, how was your first day in hell, Laufor?"

Bruno pushed the side of my face into the ground. My cheek squished itself up against my teeth causing a cut to form. I could taste the blood beginning to seep out from the gash.

"Ivvv goov," I mumbled out. I could barely open my mouth. How did he expect me to speak?

"What was that, Laufor? 'Ivv goov?'" He laughed and two of his friends standing behind him laughed as well.

Bruno leaned in close to my ear and whispered, "Do you think you are better than us? You are nothing here. Callon knows what he is doing. You deserve to be treated like the scum you are. Remember that, Laufor." He pushed me hard into the floor as he stood up. His friends laughed and gave him high fives and pats on the back as if he was cool.

The group standing around us began to disperse. Riley broke through the retreating viewers and said, "I knew Bruno was a jerk, but what he has against you, I will never know."

I wiped my mouth as Riley pulled me up on my feet. "He is just a bully out looking for more power. Trust me. I've dealt with enough creeps like him to make me an expert."

Concerned, Riley asked, "Did that happen to you back in New York?"

"No, that was before the Clade Recruited me. I was treated like an equal in New York no matter what my ability was, or where I came from, or who I knew. The problem with bullies occurred back in high school where I was the loser. Only one good friend and dreams of dating the homecoming queen." I laughed quietly and said, "Kind of cliché really."

Riley chuckled lightly. "Yeah, it is. You got me thinking for a second."

"Uh-oh," I said sarcastically. "Is that supposed to be bad?"

Riley laughed a little louder this time. He almost caught Bruno's attention. That's just what I need. Another round of "Beating up Laufor."

"No, no," Riley said. "I was just thinking about the fact that you never really revealed your ability to me or anyone else here. Does Callon even know?"

"I think he does, but I never used my ability in front of him. He only knows it from different reports and files that he keeps in his desk."

I began to think about that file that Callon was looking at when I walked into his office. He seemed pretty eager to hide it before I noticed it, and was that a picture of me on the top? What is Callon hiding and planning? I gulped loudly enough for Riley to hear and shivered.

"Is everything alright?" Riley asked as he climbed onto his bunk.

I clamored up into my bunk just a few down from him. We could easily see each other as I rested my aching bones and joints on my firm mattress. Everyone else was standing around the fire or gathered in a corner talking. The cavern echoed voices well. I could hear conversations over the crackling fire just a few bunks down from me. I hoped that they wouldn't hear my question.

"No, not really. You still never answered my question when we were back in the cafeteria," I said.

"Really?" He thought briefly to himself as I watched other people below me beginning to relax on their bunks. A lot of them were on the bottom, only a few were on top.

Riley then said with confidence, "Oh, yeah. I'm sorry. We got side-tracked."

"It's really no problem," I said quickly hoping he would answer it before other people began to eavesdrop.

I didn't know why I was so afraid of other people listening in. Maybe it was because I was afraid of Bruno. If he thought I didn't know something so important about the Clade, he would just call me an idiot or stupid or a stupid idiot knowing him, and then harass me more. I don't need any of that now.

"What was the question again?" Riley asked.

"Why are there so many people in the Clade if there were only fifty Originals? It doesn't make sense to me." I delved deeper into explaining the question. "I know the Clade proposed laws that say that a Recruit can't *be* with a Regular, so that means that they could only *be* with other Recruits. How then could fifty people produce almost three hundred Recruits?"

I began to sweat and my heartbeat easily cleared one hundred and forty beats per minute. My anxiety began to build to uncontrollable levels as Riley debated how he would answer the question. I knew he would know the answer.

"Okay," Riley began slowly. "I will try to explain this to you in a way that you can understand. It's hard to explain especially since an Instructor or Head Instructor never talked to you about this."

"That is fine. I am all ears."

"Alright then," Riley slid to the edge of his bed to get a few inches closer to me, shortening the gap. "You see, it is true that there are laws that state that a Recruit may not be in a relationship with a Regular, or someone who doesn't possess an ability."

"Yes, I know that."

"I'm just confirming what you said. You weren't lied to when you heard that. Anyways, and I don't know why this is exactly, but for some reason, our abilities are contagious."

I thought about that word for a few seconds. Contagious. That made our powers seem as simple as a cold. Could it really be passed around like the flu? If so, then how come everyone doesn't have it?

"That may sound confusing, and the first time I learned about this, I was confused too. For some reason and have no clue as to why, our abilities can be passed on to other people."

"Like how..." I thought out loud. "Is it like our DNA gets in someone else, and it binds with their DNA?"

Riley shook his head. "Again, I don't really know. I can't believe something this amazing can be given to someone else just by eating their hair. There must be some other reason."

"So," I began. "You are telling me that the Originals had children, and those children gave abilities to like three hundred people?"

"Sounds crazy, I know. Like something out of a science fiction novel, but it's true. That's why I think that there must be something special that decides who gets the powers and abilities. I met, bumped into, became friends with easily a thousand people. Maybe more. How come they all don't have abilities? Do only kids get the powers and adults are unaffected? But then, it would still be an extremely high number. I did live in Chicago after all. I went to a big high school."

"You make a good point, Riley," I said. "Do you think the Head Instructors and Instructors know why our powers are passed on?"

"No idea. If anyone would know, it would be the Originals. There is only one here and that is Barbara, but she never appears unless for something important and the Gauntlet."

"The Gauntlet? What's that?"

"You will find out soon enough," he said ominously resting his head down on his pillow staring at the rock ceiling. "Hopefully, if you are lucky, your Instructor that brought you here will take you away before that comes. It's nothing but bad news, but don't worry about it now.

"If you really want to get the answers you are looking for," Riley switched subjects, "talk to Barbara if you can find her, or another Original. However, there aren't many left, just five if I recall."

I began to list them off out loud. "Nathaniel, Barbara, Liam, Greg, and..."

"Stasia," Riley added. "Short for Anastasia. She is one of the two Head Instructors in other division."

"Okay, so there are five Originals left," I said. "Three of them are Head Instructors, one has flown the coop-"

"Haha, yeah," Riley laughed. "Don't talk about him to Callon. He hates that guy. He calls him a traitor and should be killed for abandoning his comrades and what not."

"Nathaniel should be killed if anyone..."

I let that phrase just float out of my mouth and hang in the air. We were both silent, and, unless it was my imagination, the entire barracks became silent. My heart began to race again as I planned my eventual revenge against him. Next time we fight, he will go down.

"Yeah, anyways," Riley said getting back on track once again. "I hope that answers your question more than enough."

"It does, thank you, but I do have one more."

Riley rolled over and looked at me. "What is it?"

The Clade was full of lies and conspiracies and hidden information. How did I know that these people here were telling the truth? I didn't, but maybe Riley would.

"How do you know you are a child of an Original? You know, like someone who actually should have the ability instead of someone who just gets it from someone else? Is there some sort of test?" I asked.

Riley said, "Well, everything you hear here isn't a lie. I'm sure you are really the son of Greg Laufor because, if I remember correctly, he was the only one to be in a relationship with a Regular, and since you won't show me your ability, I'm guessing it's spectacular."

I let the silence drag on a little bit between us before I said, "Compared to everyone else's... sort of."

Riley chuckled a little and said, "Exactly. That has never been done. He must've really loved your mom if he had a child with her and went against the Clade unless they were somehow for it, but I can't imagine why. Anyways, I am a child of an Original as well. We have a lot in common."

I scooted closer to the edge of my bed, now interested even more in what Riley said. "You are too? Who is your mother and father?"

"My mother and father were Jermain and Delilah Forester. My full name is Riley Forester. They aren't around anymore. They were both killed when I was still a baby."

"I'm… so sorry, Riley," I said apologetically.

"Don't worry about it. I'm not sad. Maybe a little just because I wish I had known them, but since I never did know them, I don't have any attachments. You, on the other hand, still have your father alive. If you ever meet him, take advantage of it."

"What do you mean?"

"I mean don't ridicule him and hate him for giving you life. So what, you have an ability and are forced to fight for a secret organization. At least you are alive and exist. It's like what I said earlier. Play with the cards you have been dealt."

It's funny how one person can make you change your entire mind about something. I wanted nothing more than to hate my dad. Granted, I was still confused as to how our first meeting would play out. How can he give me these powers? What was he thinking? But in truth, he couldn't help it. He just wanted a son. He had to do what was best for him to keep him safe and that was to leave him with someone else, away from the dangers of the Clade. I guess I was starting to see the sense in it after all.

My eyes began getting heavy as I watched Riley adjust his head on his pillow trying to get more comfortable. I copied him and rested my head on my pillow and stared up at the ceiling. The voices were beginning to diminish as well. I guess everyone gets so exhausted here that they get sleepy as well.

I shut my eyes and said to Riley, picturing him in my head, "So, do Conner and McKayla have Originals for parents, or are they like the other ninety percent of the Clade, where they gained their powers through someone else?"

Riley said, "They were Regulars who got their powers from me. They are my Bloodlings."

I scrunched my eyes thinking about how that came out so naturally for him. "They are your Bloodlings? What's that?"

"Children who received their powers from the Originals have Bloodlings. Bloodlings are the people who receive their ability from that person. For example, I have two Bloodlings, McKayla and Conner. I met Conner I guess when I was really little at like pre-school, and McKayla I ran into here in Colorado. They are to me as Trish is to you."

My eyes shot open as I heard that. Trish was my Bloodling? That means that she is here... she is going through hell... because of me.

Chapter 19

The next few days passed in a back-breaking blur. Try saying that five times fast. I worked from sunrise to sunset cleaning the bathrooms just to please Callon. I don't mind carrying my own weight, but the fact that he put me on bathroom cleaning duty before he even knew what I was capable of still drove me crazy. Now, I am just whining.

Living in a cave can really cause you to lose track of the days. It didn't help either that Juliette, Trish, Sarah, and I were on the run on the way here and got very little sleep. My internal clock was messed up. I knew a few days have passed, but how many? A week now? For something as well ordered as the Clade, you think someone would know what day it was, but I guess it goes to show that nothing beats actually watching the sun move across the sky. I missed that. It was nature's clock.

Juliette still hasn't reappeared since our arrival here. What was Callon doing with her? Maybe Callon isn't doing anything at all and Juliette went on to warn the other district about the upcoming attacks from the Agency. If so, then why didn't she take us? Callon would probably decide against that and ask her to take an Instructor instead. I hope she turns up soon. I don't want to be here anymore.

Ever since Riley told me that Trish is my Bloodling, I have been wary of her presence. Thankfully, the only time I ever see her or Sarah anymore is during the lunch and dinner breaks. When we are eating though, I hardly ever speak to her let alone look at her. My guilt is taking me over. How could I ever be able to look at her again? All I think about is the life I took from her. She was number one in school, on multiple varsity sports, dated the quarterback (that I actually don't mind taking away), and had a lot of friends.

At lunch yesterday, I sat across from Trish and didn't even look up from my tray other than to talk to Sarah. I felt terrible and a little awkward. Trish must know that something is up. I mean, I always talked to her when we ate, but now, I just can't bear it.

As if on cue, the bell rang. I dumped out the water in the pail and set it beside the sink. The Recruits were already beginning to form the line for food, and I jumped in just before it went out the curtain. The line moved quickly, and before I knew it, I had my food sitting at the usual table.

It didn't take long for the rest of the group to sit around the table. Riley took a spot on my right and Sarah took the spot on my left. Trish, again, sat across from me.

Lunch passed even more awkwardly than it usually did. Riley knew why, but Sarah and Trish had no idea why I was acting so funny. It didn't take them long to catch on.

Lunch was almost over when Sarah said, "Zeke, are you alright?"

"Huh? What?" I sounded confused, but it was faked.

"Yeah, Zeke," Trish chimed in. Not her, I thought. Why did she have to join in the conversation? "Is everything alright? You have been acting funny lately."

"Oh, have I?"

"Yeah, why is that?" Sarah asked.

I didn't have an excuse prepared. Usually, all we do is make small talk to pass the time between us finishing our meal before the bell rings. It's no big deal if you talked or not because it meant nothing. Meaningless, dull conversation.

"Well... I uh.." I didn't know what to say. I definitely didn't want to say anything about Trish and me in front of Sarah. It was personal, and even though she was a friend, this was between only Trish and me.

"You?.." Trish pushed on harder trying to figure out the answer.

I looked around the cafeteria as if looking away from her would give me a good excuse. I found something better than an excuse, and it wasn't even faked. My jaw literally hung open at what I saw.

Coming our way, passing through the curtain with a strong stride, was Juliette. She scoured her gaze over the cafeteria looking for something, most likely us.

I stood up, cutting off Trish and Sarah from their interrogation, and waved to Juliette. "Juliette! Over here!"

Trish and Sarah quickly turned to see Juliette making her way over to us with a big smile on her face. I went to sit back down when I caught a glare from Bruno across the cafeteria.

"Hello everyone," Juliette said joyfully. "How has your stay here been so far?"

I slid over a little to make room for Juliette to sit next to me. The whole group was finally together, except Marcus, but I'm sure he would be here soon enough.

"Juliette, where have you been the last week?!" Trish exclaimed. "We have been worried sick. We thought Callon was torturing you or something."

"As much as I admire that you cared for me during my absence, don't immediately blame Callon. You are all doing fine on your own and I had work to attend to with Callon and Barbara," she answered.

"So, Callon wasn't torturing you?" Sarah asked. "Because, he seems like the kind of person who would torture anyone who didn't blend into his cult."

"Callon may be strict, but he isn't a dictator," Juliette said. "He is a Head Instructor for a reason. The Council at the time found it fit to have him be a Head Instructor based on his skills with his ability, leadership, and experience with the Clade. They don't just let anybody become a Head Instructor."

"I guess you have a point," I said. "They didn't make Nathaniel a Head Instructor for reasons, and that was a smart decision on this 'Council's' part."

Juliette nodded. "It was. They found Marcus more suited to being a Head Instructor than Nathaniel. While Marcus uses his head and comes up with rational plans, Nathaniel gets his emotions involved in any battle. He lets his jealousy, anger, and selfishness guide his life."

We all thought about Nathaniel in silence and wondered about what the consequences would've been if Nathaniel had become a Head Instructor. He could lead his entire division of the Clade into an onslaught with the Agency. Although, he said back in New York that he was angry about the Clade's decision to make Marcus a Head Instructor over an Original like him. He is pretty much the definition of a grumpy, old, man.

"Excuse me, Juliette," Riley began. "My name is Riley Patterson. I have been hanging out with your Recruits for the last week. It is very nice to meet you."

Juliette shook his hand and they both smiled at each other. "Nice to meet you, Riley. I am Juliette Pierce, Head Instructor from the New York division of the Clade."

"You are the Head Instructor?" Riley asked. "I thought Marcus Randalph was?"

"He was," Juliette paused. You could see that she was still in pain from what had happened back at Liam's home in Pennsylvania. They have worked together in the Clade for the last four years.

Incredible that within that time Marcus became a Head Instructor. A person to lead all the others, even Nathaniel, who had been there since the Clade began almost forty years ago.

Juliette snapped back to reality. "Excuse me. He was the Head Instructor, but on the way here, we ran into some trouble with the Agency and he stayed back to fight. Before we left, he told me that I was to be the next Head Instructor to replace him, on the belief that it is Clade law to be able to have the title of Head Instructor passed to an Instructor during battle."

"Yeah, you also said something about having to speak with the Council then too," Sarah said. "What is the Council?"

"The Council," Juliette started, "is the term used to describe all five Head Instructors. You see, there are five Head Instructors in the Clade all together. Marcus was in New York. Callon and Barbara are here, and Greg and Samantha in the final division."

The group looked at me after Greg's name was mentioned. I didn't know if it was supposed to affect me hearing his name, but it didn't. To me, he wasn't my father. I don't even know him.

"You don't have to stare at me just because my father's name was mentioned. Barbara is Sarah's mother, but no one looks at her," I said.

"There is a difference between you and me though, Zeke," Sarah said. "Yes, I don't know my mom at all just like how you don't know your father, but he is kinda a celebrity."

"Not just the Clade. He is also a huge target to the Agency," Juliette said.

"Why the Agency too?" I asked.

Riley answered, "It's because he was the one who came up with the idea of the Clade. A place where people with abilities could live with others like them and learn to control their powers, and the Clade, when it was large enough, would divide into divisions and each become their own entity, kind of like the United States if you think about it."

"He came up with all of that?" I asked.

Juliette nodded. "Riley is correct. Your father came up with most of the ideas about conceiving the Clade, which is one of the reasons why the fifty Originals voted him to be one of the five Head Instructors."

"Well," I said. "That wasn't the brightest plan. A Head Instructor could easily take over their division with brutality and cause chaos and despair. The Recruits would have no power in stopping them."

"The Council has the power to remove any Recruit from their post in the Clade. It is a backup in case a bad decision is made by them," Juliette said.

"Are you on the Council then?" I asked.

Juliette shook her head from left to right. "I'm afraid it's not that simple. The Council is going to gather in a month to decide if Marcus' decision to promote me in the middle of battle was rational. If they feel as though he was not thinking clearly, they can negate his decision. I will continue to be a regular Instructor while someone else is promoted to Head Instructor."

"They can do that!?" Trish exclaimed. "I thought it was a law that a Head Instructor can give their position to an Instructor in the middle of battle in case the worst happens? You just said that a little bit ago."

"Yes," Juliette said. "I did, but the Council will still have to decide if it is right for me to be a Head Instructor. I have barely any experience as an Instructor, and they could promote someone else instead, like Stewart, who has more experience and could help the Clade more than I could. However, the Council respects Marcus. It was Greg's idea to promote him just a little over a year ago. He was the youngest Recruit to be promoted from Instructor to Head Instructor. The Council didn't agree with him, but it's hard to argue with Greg. He did come up with the plans for this place."

I asked Juliette, "Personally, if I may ask," I paused then said, "Do you want to be a Head Instructor? It sounds like a lot more responsibilities."

Juliette said, "I do. I really do. To be entrusted with that kind of power in an organization like this is honorable. I truly believe I will help the Clade and its Recruits as much as possible. I will use every ounce of my ability to make sure I secure this position. Marcus believed in me right? Why can't I believe in myself? Why can't the Council?"

As Juliette finished her speech, the bell rang and the cafeteria began to disperse. I had somehow gotten lucky enough to see Juliette today; otherwise, I would have had to answer to Sarah and Trish. I needed to come up with a logical excuse for my actions.

We followed the group out into the main cavern and watched as they dispersed heading towards their jobs. Conner and McKayla silently passed through us and headed towards the exit to work. I barely noticed them at lunch or dinner.

"See you all later," Riley waved to us as he went off with the rest of the crowd.

We waved to each other and separated. Juliette walked with me as I headed towards the bathroom to grab my brush and bucket to clean the Recruit bathroom.

I turned down the adjoining cave and Juliette followed. Looking around, I realized that we were alone and that most of the main cavern had emptied. I figured I could talk to Juliette privately. She would listen.

"Hey, so where are you off to?" I asked making small talk.

"I am going back to the Instructor barracks as Callon likes to call them. I have been working with Barbara and a few of the other Instructors to try and figure out a strategy for keeping me a Head Instructor. It is what I have been doing for the past week."

"Sounds better than what I have to do every day."

Juliette chuckled. "Yes, I heard Callon had you cleaning the bathrooms. It could be worse I guess."

"I really doubt that. This is the least amount of fun I've had in a long time. I miss being trained."

"I'm sure it could be worse. At least you don't have to empty the tank that holds all of our waste."

I shuddered at the thought of a large metal tank that held our... well, you know what. "Does someone really have to do that?"

Juliette shrugged and said, "I don't know. I have never really spent much time out of the barracks, so there is a lot that I don't know about. Also, I'm not very observant, but don't tell Callon or Barbara that." She smiled and so did I.

I approached the bathroom on my right. Before I entered, I stopped and said, "Juliette, I have a problem."

She stopped walking and turned around. Her face was contorted into features of concern. "Is everything alright?"

226

I told her about what Riley had told me about how seventy-five percent of the Clade is comprised of Bloodlings to a Recruit with a bloodline to the Originals. I then told her about how Riley believed that Trish was my Bloodling.

"Do you think that I am the reason that Trish is here?" I asked.

Juliette thought to herself for a few moments contemplating her answer. "I can't be sure, but it would make sense."

"Is there any way to check and find out? I just want to feel better and no longer guilty about what I did," I said.

She bent over and leaned in close to me. Her hands rested on my shoulders as she said sympathetically, "Don't you feel guilty about that, Zeke. It is not your fault for her being here. It happens to all children of Originals and Bloodlings themselves."

"Bloodlings can have Bloodlings?" I asked

Juliette nodded. "Yes, it is common. Sometimes, one person can have up to six Bloodlings. They were usually football players or wrestlers in high school and were able to pass on their abilities easily if they had an open wound."

I calmed myself down. My heartbeat began to steadily slow itself. I hadn't realized that I was getting worked up over nothing.

"It's hard to even look at her though," I said beginning to shake. "I can't get over the feeling that her perfect life was ruined because of me. I gave her abilities and Recruited her. What have I done?"

"You haven't done anything," Juliette said softly. "If anything, you have saved her life from the Agency. Eventually, they would've found her and killed her or kidnapped her."

"I guess…" I said. After a brief pause, I continued. "Do you think, honestly, that she is my Bloodling?"

Juliette looked away for a short time and then exhaled deeply. "Honestly, I believe so. It would make sense how two people with abilities appeared in the same city. I'm sorry, Zeke. I truly am, but it's not your fault."

I almost began to cry. I guess it was true that Trish is my Bloodling, and; therefore, the reason why she was here. Who else had been affected by my bad blood? Thomas? Brandon? I really hoped he didn't show up here.

"If it helps," Juliette cut into my sorrow. "I am a Bloodling also."

I snapped my head up at her. "Seriously? I figured you were a child of an Original! Who are you a Bloodling to!?"

"Well," Juliette said pulling herself away from me. "I am a Bloodling to Marcus."

"Really!?" I shouted. I pulled myself together and said, "How did he infect you?"

Juliette laughed and said, "We went to high school together in Pennsylvania. When I was a freshman, I had the biggest crush on him then one day, he vanished. I was torn apart, but he came back for me a year later and all my feelings came back."

"So you have feelings for Marcus? Romantic feelings still?"

"Now, that is a little too personal of a question, but yes..." Juliette softened and began to walk away. "I still do."

Juliette walked away down the hall and was about to turn into the Instructor barracks when she said, "The Council is gathering in one month from today. It is one of the biggest events a division can host. I'm sure Callon will work you and everyone else to the bone to make the Clade appealing to the Head Instructors."

I nodded. "Sounds great, and before you go, thank you for the help."

Juliette smiled. "I am here when you need someone to talk to. Don't worry about anything, Zeke. I'm sure Trish would understand that you had no control over her being here."

"Yeah... I hope," I said.

Juliette walked through the curtain and left me to my lonesome. I entered the bathroom and grabbed my bucket, brush and soap and headed to the Recruit bathroom.

Would I even have to tell Trish that I am the reason she was here? If she never found out about Bloodlings, then I wouldn't have to explain how we are connected. Maybe she wouldn't hate me then.

Poor Juliette. Here I am thinking about myself and my worries that is common to all Recruits in the Clade, and she lost one of her best friends and biggest crush. That's similar to if I were to lose Trish. I don't know how I could live with myself if I let her die. Juliette could've stayed behind and helped him out, but she couldn't. She had to protect and lead Trish, Sarah, and I. I feel responsible about that now too.

I began to scrub the boys Recruit bathroom and thought about the Council. The Council is all of the Head Instructors collaborating on one, uniform idea. It seems very prestigious to have to host them. So, the Council is occupied by Callon, Barbara... and my dad, Greg. The other person is unknown to me. I wonder if the others are like Callon. Is my father a dictator like he is? I guess I won't find out until one month passes.

Also, what is the Gauntlet?

Chapter 20

Drama in the Clade had really begun to die down in the past two weeks. Nothing exciting happened that most people could make a remark on other than when Bruno punched me in the shoulder so hard that I flew into the wall, but that is something I would like to forget about.

Telling Trish about her being my Bloodling has left my mind as well. As the days progressed, my guilt began to vanish along with the possibility of ever telling her. I figure, if she isn't curious about what they are, or if she would ever know they exist, then what is the point of bringing it up? She is here and there is nothing I can do about it other than be her friend.

Lunch and dinner in the cafeteria has become a lot less awkward for me also. I feel no pressure to tell Trish the truth, and they just seemed to have forgotten about my time of depression. It has become a foggy time for the entire group.

I keep hearing news about the Gauntlet as the days pass. What is it? Whatever it was, the Recruits, especially Riley, describe it as being something you don't want to be a part of. If it is anything like the Test, then I have good reason to be worried. The Gauntlet, as I hear, is a way for Callon to see if you have improved at all over the course of you being a Recruit, and it occurs every three months. It just so happens that the scheduled date for it lands on the same day as the Council, so I don't know what is going to happen about that. Hopefully, Callon delays it or decides to skip it altogether. Trish, Sarah, and I can't leave this place until Juliette has her meeting with the Council and it is decided whether or not she will remain a Head Instructor.

A lot is riding on that decision for me and the rest of us. If Juliette doesn't remain a Head Instructor, then we can't technically leave this place. We would be stuck here until a Head Instructor allows us to leave, and with Callon being the stubborn, over-bearing ruler he is, and Barbara not even being existent to us, then there is no way we would ever leave.

Perhaps that wouldn't be the end of the world, though. The Recruits here seem to be well trained in using their abilities whenever I see it, and they are a lot more muscular than any other Recruits I have seen in New York. I could use a little more muscle.

The normality did not last for long. For once, I felt as though I could live a somewhat normal life like I once had for a short time in the New York Clade, but that began to change the day the generator short circuited and left the Clade in perpetual darkness.

I was scrubbing the Recruit bathroom floor like I have been doing as part of my regular routine every afternoon. Lunch had just ended and most of the Recruits were already back to their positions. I don't know what had caused the generator to short circuit, but the effects were known by all in the cavern.

Suddenly, a loud booming sound ripped through the deep caverns that made me nearly jump out of my cloak. Then, darkness followed. It began slowly with the light fading away from the bathroom as if it was my hope of escaping slowly fading from existence. The boom continued to ring throughout the cave until the light had completely vanished leaving the Clade blind in its own base.

It felt as though I belonged in a horror movie. There was nothing but pitch black darkness and eerie silence. My hair began to stand on edge as I maneuvered myself into a corner as if someone was going to pounce on me. This could be the work of the Agency after all. Is this it? Are they finally attacking? Or, is this just faulty wiring? I played it safe just in case it was the first possibility.

Feeling like an idiot, I remembered that I can make my own light. I slowly built up a charge into my hand and gave a portion of the bathroom a warm, blue glow. Since I had the ability to continue to work, I grabbed my bucket and kept scrubbing with my other hand. Something told me Callon would be mighty upset if he knew I could work and didn't.

The floor was getting cleaned; although, the darkness made it look as if it was still dirty. The light was oddly comforting. It was as if a part of me was missing and now I feel whole again. The only problem is that my powers are still acting oddly, and the pain from it continues to grow whenever it occurs. Randomly, electricity will spark from my hand, arm, leg, or any other area and shock another part of me. At first, it was just an annoyance, not to mention inconvenient like at the gas station in Missouri. Now, it is really starting to frighten me. I am afraid to use my ability just because it hurts so much and is hurting more and more. Sometimes while I sleep, I feel as though the electricity within my own body is attacking me, as if there is a war waging inside myself within myself.

On cue, the blue electricity radiating from my palm and fingers arced backwards and shocked me in the wrist. I yelled and shook my arm. The light vanished as I clutched my arm. I rubbed it in the darkness feeling for a mark on my skin, but I only found burned hair instead.

Suddenly, a bright light shone on my face. I squinted and moved my burned arm in front of the light to shield my eyes.

"Laufor," said the strong voice. "It appears as though your ability will have some use after all."

As my eyes adjusted to the bright light, I could see the person standing in the entryway with the flashlight. It was Callon. The massive Head Instructor strutted into the bathroom and held out a hand to me. I took it, and he pulled me onto my feet.

"Is this about the generator explosion, sir?" I asked.

I wasn't a fan of calling Callon "sir." I don't think he should be called that because this isn't the army, school, or any other prestigious institution. We are hiding in a cave for crying out loud, but to keep myself from doing more push-ups, I'll just play along. Then again, what is the difference between me acting obediently and

Callon getting what he wants? Nothing. He still gets what he wants no matter how I feel.

"Correct, Laufor," Callon said removing the flashlight's beam from my eyes and onto the ground creating a twilight effect. "I had Stewart take a look at the machine and he found a blown gear. It was old and rusted. Think you could lend a hand?"

Did he just ask for my help? Usually, he just commands me to do whatever it is he wants to be done. This is a weird feeling. I don't know if I should agree or just say "no, you treated me like crap, so you can sit in the dark forever," but then so would my friends.

"Yes, I can help," I said.

"Good. Now follow me to the generator. Stay close in case you get lost. I don't want to have to find our only hope for bringing light to this place lost and scared out of his mind."

He turned and began his trek through the darkness with me sticking close behind. I debated telling Callon about how I can create light by focusing electricity to my hand, but then decided against it after realizing that my ability could backfire and hurt me and possibly him. Hopefully, he didn't see what happened to me in the bathroom. I think he came in a little too late to see it.

Instead, I just said, "Yes, sir."

We walked silently through the main tunnel of the cave towards the cafeteria. Along the way to wherever the generator was, I saw Recruits scurrying back and forth completing their jobs, while keeping their arm on the cavern wall, in the hopes that they don't become lost in the labyrinth. The Clade looked so much different in the dark. Distances seemed longer and the shadows from the flashlight covered some of the accessory tunnels, giving the illusion that there was only one portion to the cave. If you weren't careful, it would be easy to lose yourself.

"Stay close," Callon whispered as if we were supposed to be undercover. It is hard to be undercover when you have the only flashlight available. "I am about to show you a portion of the Clade which you have not seen yet."

"Yes, sir." That sounded interesting. I felt as though I have been in most of the Colorado Clade. Then again, there was a cave hidden in the New York Clade that even Marcus didn't know about.

Then I remembered the passageway that contained a spiral staircase. I wondered what was down there, and maybe now I would finally get to find out, and of course, Callon spun the flashlight and pointed it at the stairway. We let a Recruit walk past us, and then we followed the steps downward.

The staircase was narrow and provided only enough room for one person to walk through at a time. Above our heads, I noticed small, metal bumps that reflected the light of the flashlight and into my eyes. I squinted at their sight. Those must be what light up this portion of the cave.

The steps only circled once and ended. Callon and I stepped into another narrow hallway; although, it was not as narrow as the stone staircase. Callon flashed the flashlight to the left to show a metal door with three bars running parallel over a small opening.

"Only a few more weeks, Laufor," Callon smiled, his teeth glinting off light from the flashlight.

What was behind that door? It looked ominous, and the way Callon smiled in a bloodthirsty glee, I think I should be worried. I gulped loudly as Callon spun around and began to continue down the tunnel in the opposite direction of the metal door.

The tunnel did not continue for long. Soon, we reached a dead end with a tunnel stretching to the left and to the right. Callon turned to the right and walked to the end where it opened up into a small room with a large metal machine in the middle. The entire room, and part of the tunnel prior, smelled like burnt oil and smoke.

Callon circled the machine coming to a rest at the far side of the generator, while avoiding dangling cables, wires and vents. "Over here, Laufor."

I listened and slowly made my way to the far side of the room behind the generator. Callon kept the light on me making it easier to see, but and this is odd, I felt like I was betraying my abilities. As if I was denying a chance for it to come out. Suddenly, the warm, blue glow felt very distant, and I felt empty.

Callon waved his arm in front of me. "Stop there. I have to cut open the generator first, then you will come into play."

"Yes, sir." I stood a few feet behind him. He gave me the flashlight. I held it over him as he worked on opening the hatch...

However, there wasn't a hatch, a door, a gate, nothing. The generator was a solid, metal, box all the way around. The only thing odd about it was the weird, brownish bumps that form a square shape in front of Callon.

Callon dug into his cloak through the head hole and pulled up a pair of goggles that were hung around his neck and put them on his head to cover his eyes. He grabbed his wrist with his palm pointing upwards at the ceiling and said, "Again, stay back, Laufor." I nodded, and Callon continued.

All of a sudden, a tower of flame erupted from his palm and shot into the air. It was an incredibly hot and bright inferno that almost melted some wiring on the ceiling. Slowly, Callon began to use his other hand and squeeze the flaming hand shut causing the inferno to shrink, but focused its power into a small, extremely hot, blue flame that resembled a blowtorch's flame. He moved the concentrated fire over the brown bumps. Sparks erupted from the device. The scene reminded me of a few movies I have seen with my mom back in New Haven when thieves would crack open safes with blowtorches. I stepped back as a few sparks fell short of my feet. The room smelled more like burning metal now than ever before.

After a few minutes, the square piece of metal fell to the rock floor with a clang. Callon grabbed it and set it in the corner of the room. He held his hand out towards me, "Flashlight," he said. I handed the flashlight to him, and he worked inside the generator now.

The inside was as confusing as a newspaper crossword puzzle, at least to me. There were a series of complex wiring each with a different color. I saw reds, blues, greens, blacks, and others. There were also thick, black cables that were connected to a metal box that contained two large gears with an open spot for a third; however, the third was lying inside the small box broken into three pieces. It was terribly rusted and overused for many years. It took the full abuse and demands of the Clade. It reminded me of the Clade in that it took so much stress before it finally broke.

Callon reached for the two thick, black cables and said, "These cables transfer the energy created by these rotating gears to the rest of the Clade where needed. Right now, they are pretty useless, since there is a blown gear. Thankfully we have spares, but it will take time to replace. I want you to hold the ends of the wires and send an electrical charge through them to provide the Clade with light and energy while I replace the gear."

"Yes, sir," I said as he handed the cables to me. I grasped the ends of each cable where round studs jutted out of the insulated wires.

"Now, be careful," Callon said as I was beginning to build up a charge. "These cables can take a lot of energy, but little fluorescent bulbs can't. Make sure you provide enough power to the Clade to give us a temporary light, but not so much that it blows every bulb in the Clade."

I pulled back my electrical build-up and only charged a small amount. "Yes, sir," I repeated for the umpteenth time.

This time, fearful of blowing all the light bulbs in the Clade, I released only a small amount of power. The blue glow and bolts were absorbed by the cables and transferred to all of the different light sources in the mountain. A small buzzing sound arose as the lights began to flicker and give a small amount of light, but it was not enough to walk or even see well. I released some more power, hoping and praying that I didn't get electrocuted by my own ability in front of Callon, and watched as the four, wall-mounted lights in the room began to glow brighter. I used these bulbs to judge what was happening all around the Clade.

Callon had left to go find another gear that would fit the opening in the gear box. I continued to send electricity through the cables until I felt as though the cave was around a decent level of light. I heard a metal door creak open as the hinges had metal rub on metal. I leaned backwards while holding the cables to see down the now lit-up tunnel. I saw Callon going into one of the many metal doors down the opposite tunnel just like the one that I saw when I first exited the stairwell. Intrigued, I kept watching the metal door knowing that if Callon were to emerge and find me watching him, then I would be punished for sure on the count of spying.

All of a sudden, as I watched the metal door shut behind Callon, a mumbling sound echoed in the tunnel. The sound was coming from the room Callon just walked in. I saw a shadow of a head twisting and turning through the light filtering through the metal bars in the door. What was back there?

I heard Callon "sshh" and shut the door as he exited with two, metal, cog gears in his hands. I jumped back towards the generator catching my breath. I'm sure Callon didn't see me. Stress began to form a heavy weight on my shoulders that I couldn't shake off, and suddenly, a loud bang and crackle sounded.

Callon ran into the generator room and looked at me. "You know what that was?" He asked sternly.

I tried to gulp quietly, but I don't think that happened. "No, uh... what was that?"

"That was a bulb shattering down the tunnel. Who knows how many shattered on the main level above?" Callon sighed and said, "Keep the charge going at a steady level now while I put the gears in their positions. When I am done, you will do twenty push-ups for that broken bulb."

My arms groaned silently at the sound of that. All I could say was, "Yes, sir…"

Replacing the broken cog gear didn't take all that long. Callon just rotated the other gears in their place until the new gear slid in perfectly to fit with the others. I handed him the cables, and the machine whirred back to life again creating power for the entire Clade.

Of course, before I could leave and go back to cleaning the bathrooms, I had to perform my twenty push-ups as well as replace the light bulb. Callon wandered into the same room again where I saw the shadow of a human figure, but this time it was quiet. While I stayed put, he came out with an incandescent light bulb and a step stool to reach it. I guess the Clade isn't worried about saving the environment. I screwed in the bulb after removing the old, shattered bulb from its socket, and then went back to the Recruit bathroom to finish up before dinner.

I put a lot of elbow grease, as my mom called hard work back home, into scrubbing the floor, so that I was done with five minutes to spare when the dinner bell rang. I hurried to beat most of the rush and find my usual spot at the usual table. Soon enough, the rest of the group sat down and began to shovel down their food. When the last bite was eaten off of McKayla's plate, not like it mattered though because she never talked anyways, I told them what happened.

"Callon wanted me to help him fix the generator when the power went out, and while I was-"

"You had to help Callon?" Riley said. He made a funny face and said, "That sounds awful."

"Yeah, it kind of was, but, anyways," I said trying to get back on track. "While I was helping Callon with fixing the generator, he went into one of the metal doors at the other end of the hallway and grabbed a bunch of materials to fix it, like gears and light bulbs, but while he was in there, I saw what looked like the shadow of a person's head!"

Everyone at the table looked at me strangely. Even Conner and McKayla looked up from the table for five seconds to give me a strange glance. It did sound completely weird and unbelievable, but I know what I saw, and I heard what I heard. It was like Callon had someone locked up in there.

"Are you sure you saw that, Zeke?" Sarah asked skeptically.

"Yeah, Zeke that sounds really ridiculous," Trish added. "Callon may be tough, strict, and overbearing, but would he really lock up a Recruit?"

Riley said, "I've actually heard rumors that he imprisoned a Recruit a few years ago shortly after he became a Head Instructor. We aren't allowed on that side of the stairwell. In fact, we are only allowed on the lower level if it is time for the Gauntlet."

There that term was again. What was the Gauntlet? If anything Callon said was true, then I would find out shortly, and it wasn't going to be fun.

The bell rang, and we headed back to the barracks in our group. I made small talk with Riley for a little bit then separated away from the group by a few feet to talk to Trish alone.

"You didn't tell Riley or anyone else about your abilities, did you?" She asked.

Surprised, I said, "Actually, yeah, I didn't tell anyone. How did you guess?"

Trish smiled. "I could tell because you seem to be avoiding anything and everything that may connect you with electricity. Like at lunch when you said you helped Callon fix the generator, you didn't say because you can provide power or electricity. Also, you haven't said that or referred to your ability to Sarah or I either in the past few weeks."

"Wow," I said genuinely surprised. "You are observant."

"Why thank you," she laughed. My heart lifted and warmed.

Trish changed the subject as we settled back down to our serious attitude. "Why aren't you telling anyone?"

In truth, I really didn't know why I didn't want other Recruits to know about my abilities. Maybe it's because I didn't want to be the freak among freaks. I hear that enough.

"I really don't know, Trish," I answered. "I just want to be treated like everyone else for once. Even in New York, I got weird looks from Recruits because I had a different ability than anyone else in the history of the Clade. It's not my fault! It's not like I decided to have this power."

Trish nodded. "I can see why then. You make a good point. Is anyone treating you like that, Zeke?" Her facial expression changed to that of worrisome. She truly cared.

Before I answered, I looked across the sea of Recruits to find Bruno staring me down and cracking his knuckles as if we were in some kind of clichéd fighting movie. "Yeah, but don't worry about it. He's nothing I can't handle."

Trish still looked worried. "Okay, I trust you. What now then?"

I was tempted to tell her about the Bloodling dilemma that had been on my mind for the past two weeks. That idea has pretty much faded completely, but I still felt responsible for telling her, but now was not that time, and I wasn't going to worry about it until later.

"I really don't know," I answered truthfully. "I guess we just continue to fit in around here until after Juliette's Council hearing."

"That means we are going to have to participate in the Gauntlet then?" Her voice cracked when she spoke the dreaded word: Gauntlet."

The group began to separate as they entered their correct barracks. I met Trish in the middle as she said, "Was there really a person locked in that room on the lower level?"

I didn't know what to say. I didn't know if I was right, but what I saw seemed to suggest that there was a human locked in that room. "I don't know, but I believe what I saw. You don't have too, but I believe it. Just look at the stuff we can do. It's unbelievable. That just makes me think all the more that something as unbelievable as a prisoner in the basement is true."

"I guess when you put it like that…" Trish said looking at the rock floor. She appeared really depressed, as if she could break into tears at any moment. Then, she said, "Do you think we are ever going to be able to leave this place, Zeke? I can't handle it, and I am only being Instructed."

"Yeah, I think we are," I really didn't know what to say to that either. I'm as lost and confused as everyone else here. It's as though the very air of the Clade, the thing that allowed us to exist here, is a thick fog covering up what was really there. "Be glad you are being Instructed," I said. "When that is over, you get a job that you have to spend every day doing. Instructing, although hard on the body, is cool just because you can control your abilities better. You don't get as exhausted as quickly as you normally would, and you may even discover something you can do that you didn't know you could do before. For instance, during the Test, I somehow wrapped the metal key hanging in the tree in a blanket of electricity and pulled it off."

"Really?" Trish lit up a little, but not by much. "That is really cool, and my abilities are coming around. I can light any appendage I choose on fire and hold it for long periods now, when before I could only light my whole body on fire for a short amount of time."

"You see," I smiled trying to cheer her up. "You should be happy that you are being Instructed, and this may sound morbid, but you will be finishing your Instruction when the Gauntlet starts, whatever that may be. You will have great control of your ability compared to someone who hasn't been Instructed in a while and doesn't use their ability."

Trish nodded with her smile still showing. "I guess that's a good point. Thank you for looking on the bright side."

I smiled back. "It's no problem." Then, she moved closer to me and gave me a big hug. She squeezed tightly, and I squeezed even harder. I never wanted this moment to end, but it must.

I let go and we waved goodbye until tomorrow. I went into the barracks and rested on my bed wondering if we were ever going to be free from this hell. Not just this division, but the entire Clade.

I shut my eyes and felt the sting of my ability ripping my insides.

Chapter 21

The time soon came. The time that all Recruits including Trish, Sarah and I have been on edge about. The time that we have been warned to fear for the past month.

The Gauntlet begins tomorrow.

I still have no idea what it is or what it's purpose is for the Clade. Callon has kept all of his information to himself about this. I only get slight hints about it whenever I ask like, "It's a competition of using abilities," or, "All Recruits participate with Callon and Barbara judging." How is that any different than the Test? Trish and Sarah also have no idea about what it might be, but as the time drew closer, they both became more uptight and stressed. Like a final exam back at school, we didn't know what to expect and that caused a huge amount of pressure on us.

Riley, Conner, and McKayla didn't really talk about it either. It was as if all Recruits who knew about it weren't allowed to speak about it around new Recruits or "freshy's."

For example, at lunch today, Trish, Sarah, and I were talking about the Gauntlet. I said, "Does anyone else find it incredibly difficult to figure out what the Gauntlet is?"

Sarah nodded. "Yeah, I keep asking all the Recruits that I work near, and they just all keep their heads down and stay quiet."

Trish added, "Same with me. I asked my Instructor Stewart what he thought, and he just told me to get back to training even though we were on a little break. It's odd. I feel as though we are supposed to be kept from knowing what it is exactly."

During the entire conversation, I felt Riley shake his feet uncontrollably underneath the table. I looked at him for a few minutes until he finally saw me and caught on that I knew he knew something.

"Is everything okay, Riley?" I said insinuating that he knew something we didn't.

"Yup, couldn't be better," he pushed out quickly.

"We can tell that you know something about whatever the Gauntlet is. For crying out loud, you participated in it a few times, right!?" Sarah said.

Riley just nodded his head fearing Sarah's wrath.

"Then why can't you tell us?" She asked. "We keep questioning what the hell this 'Gauntlet' could be but we have no idea, and no one will help us, and here you are with all the answers about it, and you won't help us in the slightest."

Riley stuttered, "I-I'm… sorry. I'm not allowed to talk about it around new Recruits. We can only give the gist of what it is and what it is for."

Wow, good guess, Laufor.

Trish sighed and slammed her head on the table in frustration, not hard, just enough to make a scene. We were all a little more on edge now that we knew that no one could tell us. Wouldn't that mean it's something sinister, or maybe the Gauntlet is really a good thing like a birthday present? Who am I kidding. I sighed as well and placed my head on my arms.

Riley said, "I'm sorry, guys. I would help if I could, but when the Gauntlet comes, I know you will all do great."

I poked an eye out over my right arm and caught a glimpse of Riley smiling. I shut my eye and groaned. "It's no problem, Riley," I said trying to make him feel a little better as well. "We understand and didn't want you to get in trouble with Callon. Whatever the Gauntlet is, Trish, Sarah, I, and especially you, will beat it with flying colors." Riley perked up while Trish just groaned again. The bell rang, and we dispersed as we have been doing for the past month, keeping schedule with our regular routines.

It was already May. Back home, all the kids would be getting ready for their final exams and procrastinating for those exams. The jitters of summer vacation would keep all of us from focusing on school or any kind of work; although, most of us would have to get a job of some kind since it's summer, but we didn't care. Whatever got us all away from school would be a gift from the heavens.

However, that doesn't happen here. Every day is the same as the last. The generator incident a few weeks ago was godsend for the few Recruits that could not perform their jobs in the darkness. It was a little break from the gruesome reality we live in. Like times during World War II, we all must give up what we want for our own survival, at least, that's what Americans believed at the time, but this was never ending. Would there ever be a light at the end of the tunnel for Recruits of the Clade?

Lights out took a lot longer to arrive tonight mainly due to my anticipation of what would happen at the Gauntlet tomorrow, and how Trish and Sarah were handling it. After that, I spent time with Riley and Conner, although Conner still didn't want either of us to be there. I even got to know a few of the other Recruits like Jeremiah and Blake who were both fifteen and went to the same school together somewhere in Wisconsin and were Bloodlings.

Just before the lights went out signaling time for bed, Bruno and his two bozo friends decided to take me away from talking to Riley. He came up behind me as I sat on an empty bed and wrapped his arm around my head choking me while pulling me backwards onto the floor.

"What's up, Laufor?" Bruno chuckled looking down at me as if his pun was actually funny.

"Not much, just looking at ugly people," I said slyly just trying to agitate him some more.

He didn't like that. His face turned bright red to the point where it could actually explode. He pulled me onto my feet and spun me around to face the monster. I had to look up at him of course due to his height advantage. His fists were clenched and rested just below his chin and out in front of him as he took a fighter's stance.

"You and me," he snorted. "Right here, right now. Why wait until the Gauntlet when I can just crush you right now. Think of the damage I could do with no rules and no holding back." A wide grin formed on his brute face.

I just held up my hands and backed away from him. "I don't want to fight you, Bruno. I don't know what your deal is," my voice rising ever so slightly as I continued on my rant, "but I am sick of it. Just stay away from me and leave me to my peace. I have done nothing to upset you, so once again because I know you aren't the quickest mind here, stay away from me!"

The Clade, not just the barracks, the entire Clade, fell silent. All eyes were pointed at me and Bruno who looked like an idiot now still in his fighting stance. His two buddies behind him even gulped a little and backed off. Bruno scanned the barracks and watched the eager eyes of the twenty other Recruits waiting for a fight. Would he give them one?

Bruno stepped up to me to the point where I could feel his stinky breath on my face. I didn't move. I wasn't intimidated. "What makes you think you can stand up to me, Laufor?"

I didn't even think as I said with confidence, "I have fought for my life against all odds. I have seen things that would make you run scared, and I had to leave one of my best friends as he died. That's why I can stand up to you, Bruno."

He didn't say anything else after that. His eyes never left my gaze, though. Slowly, he backed up with his two, skinny goons behind him following his steps. As he turned away from me, he said loud enough for the entire barracks to hear, "I hope I am in your group tomorrow, Laufor. I can't wait to kill you, and not even Callon is going to stop me."

That was the last thing I saw and heard before the lights clicked off.

The blazing pain increased as the night stretched on, making my forehead sweat and body cringe. I squeezed my eyes shut to try to take the pain and move it to my eyelids. It helped, but when I close my eyes, all I see are little arcs of electricity jumping around inside my body. I don't know if that was real or not, but it made the pain that much worse. I don't know how much more of this I could take. I need to find Juliette as soon as the Council is over.

With only a few pain-filled hours of sleep, the lights clicked to life along with the whir of the generator vibrating beneath our feet. Today was the day that the Gauntlet would start, at least after the lunch break. Our jobs still needed to be completed if the Clade was supposed to keep running, Callon always says. This was also the day where I would find out what was behind that metal door in the basement level that Callon seemed to be so excited to show me in his own sick way.

First things first though. I showered, ate with Trish, Sarah, and the others who all seemed to be a little on edge and alert while they ate. I couldn't help them because I was too. Next, I went off to clean the Instructor bathroom for the next four hours when the bell rang and the Recruits met again for lunch in the cafeteria.

Nobody spoke as we quickly ate expecting something to happen that would assemble us all for the Gauntlet. I still wasn't ready for whatever the Gauntlet held in store for me. Then again, nobody really was. Even Bruno seemed a little on edge last night from the way he shook. Yes, he was ready to kill me today, but he was a lot more temperamental even with his two goons.

As people finished their meals and placed their trays in the correct slot in the wall, they sat in silence as if they were praying. The environment gave me the shivers. Everyone was doing this, even Riley, Conner, and McKayla. These somber people looked as though they were begging for their lives, the way they stared at the cold table beneath them with hollow eyes. Should I be worried for my life? Will that be me after my first Gauntlet, if I survive this one?

I just became a lot more nervous, and as if on cue, Callon walked into the cafeteria throwing the curtain out of his way. Following him were Stewart and another woman I haven't seen before, but I guessed she was another Instructor like Stewart.

Callon said loud and crisp, "Recruits, today is the day the Gauntlet shall begin. For those of you who know the rules, I hope you have prepared accordingly, and for those of you who are new and have the misfortune of participating in your first Gauntlet," he looked over to Sarah, Trish, and I with an icy expression filled with bloodlust, "I hope you are ready to fight for your life."

He turned around and walked out of the cafeteria, leaving Stewart and the other woman in the cafeteria alone with us. After a few seconds pause, Stewart held up a white piece of paper and said, "The following Recruits will gather to the right side of the cafeteria and then follow me down to the arena." Stewart spoke in a very high, kind of nerdy, tone. It made me laugh a little which eased the tension. However, the word arena definitely added to it.

In a smooth succession, Stewart called off names first a boy, then a girl, and so on from there. After a few minutes, twenty kids, ten boys and ten girls, stood in a bundled mass waiting for orders. In that mass of people, Conner and McKayla stood looking as uninterested as ever. A few feet from them stood Bruno flexing to one of his goons. The other still sat at a table by himself.

Stewart commanded again, "Okay, Group One, please follow me to the arena."

Stewart walked out of the cafeteria, the bumbling group of teenagers and young adults followed in his footsteps. They echoed down the tunnel corridors like an army marching towards their battle.

The other woman stood next to the entryway and waited for the final Recruit to leave with Group One. Then, she said, "For the remainder of you still here, you are in Group Two. You will all participate in the Gauntlet once Group One has been divided and finished. There are seating arrangements around the arena for you to watch. Please follow me to the arena."

We all stood just like Group One and followed the woman out into the tunnel and down the steps in a single-file line. The whole process reminded me of the few field trips back in school. All the kids would gather in anxious anticipation and then follow in a single-file line just like this to a big, yellow bus which would then take us to the place we were touring or learning about. However, there was no bright, yellow bus that sparkled gaily in the sun which gave you an overjoyed feeling. Instead, there was just the line that would lead us to our possible torture chambers.

Trish, Sarah, Riley, and I stood back and waited for the group to shrivel down before we made our way to the basement level. Trish spoke up over the echoing stepping sound. "Riley, who is that woman? I've never seen her before."

"That is Lydia," Riley said. "She is the twin of Stewart. Actually, I think they are the only twins in the entire Clade."

"Seriously?" Sarah said surprised. "That is kind of cool." She was speaking in a fake interested tone. It was one of the only ways she could relax a little.

The more I thought about Lydia, the more I thought about how similar her and Stewart look. They both had light brown hair, a few freckles on their face just below their eyes, and both of their front teeth were slightly apart, but not in an unattractive way.

The rest of Group Two had completely moved to the lower level. Riley squeezed into the small passageway and followed a petite looking girl. The rest of us filed in right after with me in the back. I knew where we were going, but Trish and Sarah have never been to the basement level. I didn't want them to get lost even though it would be pretty hard to.

We stayed close as we walked down the spiral staircase. As we exited in a single-file fashion, Lydia pushed and pointed us to go towards the metal door at the end of the long tunnel. She stood with arms out wide, guarding the mysteries that were held in the rooms behind her… one of them being that room with the person locked in.

I walked next to Trish at the back of the long line of people, as the first few had just opened the door and began to move in. Casually, I said, "How are you feeling about this?"

Trish just shrugged her shoulders. "No idea yet. I'm still kind of in my dream state."

I let that sink in and asked, "Dream state? What is that?"

She laughed a little to herself. The door approached slowly as if we were walking to our executions. "I am in the state where I feel as though I am still dreaming and whatever is about to happen to me isn't really happening, and at any point I could just make myself up."

"But… this is really happening, Trish. We really are willingly walking into, what could be, one of the scariest moments of our lives."

"Yeah, I realized that, Zeke. You don't have to remind me," Trish giggled a little and then shivered, her cloak bouncing lightly on her body.

The door was right in front of us now. Bright light streamed through the open archway as if we were going into a sacred and holy place. What was in there? I didn't know, but after a gulp and a small glance at Trish, I entered right after her to see before me…

...a large metal cage surrounded by rows of stone benches that slanted towards the metal cage. I looked around and saw the Recruits sitting next to their friends, spreading themselves out. But, there weren't only Recruits from Group Two sitting down. At least half of Group One sat on the far side of where we stood as well. We followed Riley around to the right side where he said he usually sat. He sat approximately ninety degrees from the door we entered.

To our right another ninety degrees, a rectangular balcony rested with two chairs sitting on the very edge nearest the circular, metal cage. It appears as though very important people were to sit there, and the more I looked around, this place reminded me of the Coliseum in Rome. I just hope the same things don't happen here as they did back during the Roman Empire.

I now focused more on the huge metal cage that surrounded a circular pit which was larger than the cafeteria, the largest area in the Clade. Inside there were six rock cubes which were equally spaced from the other cubes and from the middle which was a pit. The pit resembled all of the pits I encountered during the Test. It appeared as though it was bottomless and the darkness was reaching out trying to use its dark tendrils to pull itself out of the gaping hole. I wouldn't want to fall down there.

All of my thoughts went to dark and dangerous things. Why is this down here? What purpose could this possibly have? People could die.

Sarah knew it too. She said, "Riley... why does this not look like a good thing?"

Riley just said simply, "Because it's not."

Chapter 22

Before long, when the very last Recruit had found their seat next to their friend, the curtain on the balcony swayed. A hand had pulled it open, and the two hooded figures behind the curtain moved to the seats in front of the cage. During this time, the arena fell to no more than a hush as we watched these figures sit.

After sitting, the figure on my left lifted their hands and slid down their hood revealing his true identity: Callon. The other did the same revealing the face of a middle aged woman, most likely an Original, with short, curly, blonde hair and deep, blue eyes. A few wrinkles appeared under her eyes as she scanned the arena and then finally rested her eyes on our group... mainly Sarah. That must be Barbara, the other Head Instructor and more importantly, Sarah's real mother. After a few moments of intense stares between Sarah and Barbara, the

Head Instructor moved her gaze back to the arena where they rested.

I turned to Sarah, and was about to ask if that was her mother, but I didn't have to. As I turned, Sarah said, "Yeah, I know everyone is thinking it. Yes, that is my mom." The words came out like ice on a frigid, winter night. There was no love in her sentence, just anger and hate. Sarah told me during our midnight meeting at her home she didn't want to meet her mom just because she didn't want to hate her. Well, here she is, right in front of her, and she is completely filled with anger. Again, I think to myself, will I no matter what hate my father even if I tell myself to like him and understand?

Slowly, Callon stood and spread his arms out wide covering the entire arena and Clade resembling some sort of pariah. With brute force, he said, "Recruits, this is what is known as the Gauntlet. Many of you know what occurs in this arena, but for the select few who do not, this is what will happen." He paused as he thought over the instructions and scanned the crowd for dramatic effect.

Suddenly, he echoed, "In a few moments, I will call off the names of ten Recruits selected in Group One. They will enter through the curtain directly below this balcony and enter the arena. They will have ten seconds to prepare themselves after the last Recruit crossed into the arena. Once those ten seconds have come to an end," he paused again feeling the emotions of his audience. We all wanted to know the final words in his speech, and he knew it. "Then," he said. "A battle shall commence between the ten in a free for all competition."

My eyes grew wide. Yes, I had a good feeling that that was what this was all about. Otherwise, why have a metal cage around a circular pit? At least there were no lions.

Callon continued, "As you can see, there is a perfectly square pit in the center of the arena. If a Recruit were to fall into the pit, then they would be out. If a Recruit was knocked out, then they are out of the Gauntlet. This is not a battle to the death. Stewart and Laura will be in the arena as well, making the calls like referees, who are in and who are out, but don't be fooled. The Recruits who take this as a battle to the death, anything goes fighters, are usually the victors. I expect each and every one of you to perform your hardest and try to succeed in overcoming your opponents."

Callon took another pause and then slightly changed gears. "There are a few reasons why we do this. I believe it is important that every Recruit has experience in life threatening combat, so they are ready when the real thing comes, and if my information is correct," he looked over to our group then said, "then this is vitally important to your survival. Also, and maybe more importantly for you, depending on how one does in the Gauntlet, their job may be changed. For example, as many of you know, Bruno assists Stewart and Laura in Recruitment missions when one occurs; otherwise, he has the comfortable job of standing guard outside the cave."

That explains why the guard when we first arrived was so rude and offensive to us. Bruno was the guy that shoved us around and held the guns to our heads. We even proved to him that we were friends, yet he still acted like a complete jerk. I guess it's true that too much power can go to someone's head. If the Gauntlet has the ability to take power and rank away from someone, then I am going to take advantage of that. I don't really care what happens to me; although, I really would like a job more specified to my ability, but more importantly, Bruno needs to be taken down.

Stewart moved behind Callon and gave him a folded piece of paper. When he opened it, I caught a glimpse of a bunch of little squiggles that ran the length of the page. Those must be the names of the Recruits fighting.

"There will be five rounds with the last two remaining from each round moving on to the final Gauntlet battle two days from today. There is a one day break for the ten victors due to Council taking place tomorrow."

Callon began to announce the ten names written on the piece of paper. As each name was announced, a Recruit walked through the curtain beneath the balcony and entered the arena. The names were being called off rapidly, and the Recruits ran to a good starting position either behind a large block or against the cage wall. I took mental notes to prepare for my round.

I wasn't paying much attention to the names that Callon was reading off. I was too absorbed in the strategies that some of the more veteran Recruits were using to hear Conner's name get called off. He walked through the passageway in a cool, calm, and collected poise. His facial expressions were the same as they always were at the lunch table, blank and dense. As if he never really cared about what was happening, or he hated whatever he was involved in. Either way, he took his position in the arena behind a large rock closest to us.

Callon finished reading off the ten names, folded the piece of paper, and handed it back to Stewart who ran behind the curtain, and a few seconds later, appeared in the arena with Laura. Callon stood and said, "Recruits, you have ten seconds until the first round begins. Use it wisely." Nobody really moved from their original positions except for the two Recruits who had just entered, a boy and a girl.

The seconds ticked away in my mind. 10...9...8. Sarah then interrupted by asking, "How are the round matchups decided?

Riley said, "They are completely random. When Stewart walks out from behind the curtain, he has just written down who will be in the next round. They do that also with Group matchups as well. All of the names are selected randomly from a hat."

7...6...5... Everyone was in their position waiting for the ten seconds to drop to zero. I felt the anticipation of all the Recruits in the arena. I began to get goosebumps wondering what it would be like to watch a group of people with abilities duke it out. I've seen one on one, but never a whole group in a battle royale type setting. I would soon find out in 4...3...2...1...

Callon shouted, "Begin!"

Suddenly, every Recruit in the arena began to move and spread out. Some stayed hidden behind their barriers like Conner, while others like a bigger built girl in the far corner, immediately dove for the closest Recruit to her, a small boy. She picked him up and put her palm to his chest, and before he knew it, a concentrated blast of air punched him in the chest sending him flying across the arena. His back snapped against the solid, rock edge of the floor, and he fell into the depths of the pit. His screams could be heard well after he disappeared out of sight.

Across the arena, three Recruits were in a brawl against the cage. One Recruit, a boy, had pinned another younger boy up against the cage while the girl continuously punched and kicked him in the face and chest. Bruises began to appear on the poor boy's face while tears welled up in his young eyes. After a few minutes of beating, Laura ran over and called off the assault. After all of that, all the young Recruit would get for participating in the Gauntlet was a few welts and bruises.

Immediately after he was removed, the boy and girl started to fight. The girl punched, but the boy ducked under and swept her feet out from under her. She fell hard to the ground. The boy then stuck his index finger in the dirt next to the girl, and with a sudden blast, the ground the girl had been laying on blasted straight out of the earth. It was amazing and terrible at the same time. The chunk of earth flew into the metal cage shattering it into a million little bits of earth and dust while the girl tossed and turned in the air. Her trajectory ended with a high speed assault on one of the rock blocks. She hit and fell to the ground limp and unconscious. Stewart called off the assault on her. Out goes number three.

My mouth hung wide open as I watched the brutal onslaught of our own people, our allies. Bodies were being flung from one end to the other in the arena. People exploded, burned, flew, and broke with each attack. The sounds were ghastly. Rocks crumbled when Recruits were sent into them, screams were echoing in the open cavern which made them never ending, and a few cracking sounds were heard that could only be bones breaking. How could Callon do this to his own kind? How was this supposed to help us survive when the Agency attacked?

I looked up to Callon who held a sickening grin across his face as if he was really enjoying the brutal carnage of his Recruits. My hatred for him grew even more. Barbara, on the other hand, looked indifferent, as if whatever was happening in front of her eyes did not matter. How can she sit there and watch what was happening? Have all morals and sense disappeared and replaced with savagery?

Sarah said holding her hand over her mouth, "How can he do this to us? This is disgusting! Callon has gone way over the edge here!"

Riley shook his head. "I know… it's terrible, but Callon is the Head Instructor, and he can make whatever rules he wants here. We just have to go along with it."

"Why don't the Recruits just not fight? It's not like Callon can punish the entire Clade, right? Then, no one will have to suffer," Trish asked just as disgusted as Sarah.

Riley said, "We thought of that, but only a few of us were actually for not fighting. The incentive to fight is far greater than not, as in, the chance to have a better job for three months is more appetizing to Recruits than being on Callon's bad side and have a bad job."

Riley paused to watch another person, a girl, get blasted straight into the air and fall into the black abyss. "I don't really blame Callon for making the Gauntlet, though."

My eyes held wide open. "What!? How can you not blame him or hate him for this?"

Riley just shrugged. "I guess, when you think about it, he is really trying to help us all. This will make us better fighters than most of the other Recruits in other divisions of the Clade. Also, it gives us the opportunity to work hard and then earn our reward at the end."

I watched the carnage some more as Riley spoke. Conner kept hidden behind a rock. Every so often, he would take a peek to see who was all left and would make a move towards a different rock. At all costs, Conner avoided battle and moved to a safer area if it was necessary.

Another Recruit was called out by Laura, followed by another called out by Stewart. They were starting to drop like flies due to exhaustion. Using an ability for prolonged periods of time can really take a lot out of you. Before I knew it, only four Recruits remained with Conner being one of them.

Conner kept moving around the arena as the other three Recruits began to circle each other in locked combat. Riley cheered for Conner, but he just ignored it. The other Recruits were beginning to cheer and holler as well for their friends in the arena.

A moan erupted from a small group of Recruits on the opposite side of the arena as the person they were cheering for was blown across the arena. A Recruit, the same one as earlier, stuck his finger in the ground and blew the girl into the metal cage. She dropped holding her face while blood trickled out of her forehead. The girl wasn't done fighting yet, though. She stood as quickly as she could, wobbling slightly when she got on her feet.

This was when Conner made his move. He picked up a small chunk of rock from one of the larger blocks that was hit hard with a Recruit earlier and carefully stalked the girl as she started to move towards the other two fighting Recruits. Once she got close enough, the girl began to hold her hands out.

Amazingly, out of thin air, a small cloud appeared over her head, and water began to trickle out of it. Soon, it was down pouring on her. The ground beneath her had turned into mud so sticky it almost sucked the shoes right out of her feet. Then, she raised her hands over her head and pushed them forward which caused the cloud to be pushed over the heads of the other two Recruits in hand-to-hand combat. They were drenched with the rain water as they fought each other, and just like the girl, the Recruit's feet were beginning to stick to the muddy ground.

Conner crept closer to the unsuspecting girl. His plan, if he even had one, was working extremely well. The rain would eventually eat away at the ground causing a kind of quicksand where the feet of the two male Recruits would get stuck or at least slow them down. The girl would then be occupied with them, like she is now, and would be easy pickings.

The bigger male Recruit realized something was happening to their feet too soon; however, he tried to swat the cloud away but to no avail. He tried to lift his feet as the girl moved closer laughing as their feet became trapped in the goo. Thinking quickly, he stuck his index finger in the ground once again. Conner realized what he was doing. We had all seen what this Recruit was capable of doing to the earth.

He was going to blow them all up.

Conner realized this, and began to backpedal away from him. But, he was too late. An explosion ripped through the arena floor causing the ground to shatter beneath all of their feet. Conner was far enough away from the blast to not get lifted up on the piece of earth like the other three, but he was still thrown into the arena wall. He groaned as he fell backwards holding his arm and rolling over onto his side screaming.

Riley stood up looking extremely worried. "Conner!" He yelled down to him. I looked over to Callon who seemed to not even care that his Recruit was in agony. I ground my teeth together in pure anger. Not realizing it, I calmed down defusing the building charge in my body.

Conner's screams distracted me from what happened to the other three combatants. I looked around where the hole in the ground was across the arena and found three bodies lying on the ground. The Recruit that caused the explosion struggled to get onto his feet while the girl moaned and rolled on her back.

Stewart and Laura ran into action. Stewart ran over to Conner who was still screaming and holding his now swollen, black-and-blue, arm. It didn't look good. Stewart looked over at Laura, and she waved him over. Stewart quickly ran over to Laura and checked the other three Recruits.

They talked and mumbled to themselves while soaking in the surroundings. Everyone in the crowd, including my group, waited silently for the decision. I was more worried about Conner, even though he had never really spoken to me.

Finally, Stewart stepped away from Laura and into the middle of the arena. He looked up to Callon and Barbara and said, "These Recruits are in no shape for fighting. They are all in bad or terrible conditions. Since one blast has caused all of this damage to the final four, Laura and I have decided, based on their ability to keep fighting in battle, that Luke Roland should take fourth," he pointed to the unconscious Recruit, "and Conner Mitchells," he pointed to Conner still holding his arm but now only wincing at the pain, "should take third. Therefore, Ruby Adams and Rafael Butros should move onto the final round."

A mix of cheers and moans roared in the seats. A few Recruits stood and clapped while others were red in the face with rage that their friend lost or won. I didn't cheer or moan. I just kept looking at Callon who appeared to not care at all. I was angry all right, but not at the results. I was angry with Callon.

"Why didn't he use his ability?" Trish asked frustrated. Her eyebrows were almost digging into her eyes they were pushed down so hard.

"Not much you can do with the ability to turn snow or ice into liquid water. That is why his job takes place on top of the mountain. He melts the snow so we can drink it," Riley said.

I do hope that Conner isn't too badly injured, though. He took a hard hit into the arena wall and barely moved his arm after. I'm not a doctor, but I have seen kids break arms before, and that definitely looked like a broken arm. Poor guy. All of that for nothing.

Stewart and Laura helped Conner, Ruby, and Rafael out of the arena carefully making sure not to injure them anymore than they already were. For the unconscious Luke, he was rolled onto a poorly made, makeshift stretcher and carried out of the arena.

That was only round one. There were still four more rounds left. I didn't even think about my fight at all and what would happen to me. Instead, I thought of Trish. I couldn't get her out of my head. There was a possibility that we could end up in the same round together. What then? Do I fight hard and try to win even if that includes taking her out? No, I wouldn't do that. She is my friend, and I still felt slightly guilty for giving her abilities to begin with. Then, I would fight to try to get us both to the finals without either of us getting hurt too badly.

What about Sarah then? I shouldn't have to worry about Riley. He has done this a few times already and probably has a pretty good idea at how to win at this. Sarah, on the other hand, like me, doesn't have any prior experience in fighting other than the night the Agents attacked in New York, but there was no hand-to-hand combat. Overall, though, I would hope to be with Trish because she would need more help than Sarah. She has been here two years longer than either Trish and I, and she is pretty tough too.

All of this went through my head as the arena was cleared of the remaining bodies and all of the holes were fixed. Instructors I have never seen filled some of the holes caused by the explosions using abilities and elbow grease. The rock blocks weren't fixed. Instead, the larger pieces that may have broken off a few of the rocks were just placed on top of them. Before long, the arena was looking brand spanking new as if a battle hadn't ended in there just ten minutes ago.

"What happens now?" Trish asked Riley.

He said, "The whole entire process happens again. Stewart will give Callon the list of remaining Recruits who have not fought yet in Group One," he pointed up to Callon who had just received the folded up piece of paper. He continued, "and then the Recruits whose names were called off will enter and fight just like last time. Once that is over, we will go in the waiting area until our name is called off to fight."

"McKayla is fighting in this round, then," I said. I turned away from them and looked at the curtain waiting for her to emerge. "Hopefully, she does a little better than Conner."

"Yeah, hopefully," Riley said worried, his voice shaking.

Sarah said, "What is McKayla's ability, Riley? I don't believe any of us have seen it."

Riley answered, "You're right. You guys haven't seen it. It's a pretty cool ability if you ask me. She can use the air and make it spin."

"You mean she can create tornadoes and whirlwinds?" Sarah asked.

"In a way," Riley said. "Yes, she can. Of course, the faster and stronger the whirlwind is, the more energy it takes to make it. She could probably make a tornado the size of the arena if she stood in the middle, but it wouldn't be that strong. It would be like a strong breeze at most." As Riley spoke, McKayla walked out from behind the curtain and into the arena. She was the fourth Recruit to be called out by Callon for this round. "Now, if she stood in the middle of the arena and created a whirlwind that stretched just a few inches beyond her, then it could be strong enough to lift a Recruit and put them right into the pit."

Her ability did sound cool, but it wouldn't be very effective in a free-for-all fight. The area was too large and too many people could strike her from any side while she concentrated on the whirlwind. What would she do then if she couldn't use her ability? Conner seemed to do a decent job, but he couldn't win.

McKayla took a position up against the metal cage nearest me and the others. The remaining Recruits entered the arena one after the other when their names were called. Each one caught a glimpse of McKayla as they entered, savoring the possibility to attack her. She could be easily outnumbered and surrounded from where she was, and every Recruit knew that.

Maybe… that is what she wanted.

Chapter 23

"3...2...1... Begin!" Callon shouted, and the Recruits sprang into action.

Four Recruits on the far side of the arena immediately began to fight. The two male Recruits of the four were using fire abilities from their hands to create a wildfire on the ground like napalm. It looked as though they were working together. They avoided the flames themselves and just sprayed the ground between them. The girl Recruits between them tried to escape but not quick enough. The bottoms of their cloaks caught fire and burned bright orange and red. The flames moved its way up the cloak burning more of their skin. The girls cried out in pain as the two other Recruits left to take down everyone else. One of the girls tried ripping off the bottom of her cloak below the knees to stop the fire while the other girl just screamed for help.

Laura ran in and put out the fire with a fire extinguisher by spraying the lower half of her body. The girl walked out of the arena limping while Laura stood by the other girl who was still screaming, not giving up. However, Laura called her out before the fire spread above her waste and sprayed the extinguisher on the fire. The girl fell to the ground still screaming, her legs bright red with dry blood stuck to her calves. It was disgusting. That would take months to fully heal if it ever did. Laura called for Stewart, and he quickly ran over with the stretcher. They carefully placed the thrashing girl on it and carried her behind the curtain, out of the arena. Two down.

McKayla kept quiet against the wall of the arena waiting to strike. She watched what had happened to the two girls before, and the two boys were on their way over to her. She stretched out both of her arms to her right and held them there preparing for them.

"What is she doing!?" Trish exclaimed. "It's two against one, and if those two Recruits get their hands on her, she will be finished not to mention badly injured."

Riley just chuckled to himself lightly. "Then, her plan is working perfectly."

"What?" I asked. It didn't look like McKayla had anything up her sleeves. She just held her awkward position as the two boys stalked her getting ready to strike.

Riley nodded at McKayla. "Just watch, and you will see what I mean."

So, I watched as the two Recruits approached McKayla, their hands blazing with a well-controlled fire. They were only a few feet from McKayla now, and she just held her position. She had to do something now; otherwise, she would be burned!

She did do something. Just a second before the boys released the fire from their palms, McKayla flung her arms in a semicircle around her body and held her hands to her right. For a moment, nothing happened, other than the two boys laughing almost hysterically. They shrugged and began to move into range for their attack.

Suddenly, a strong, circular breeze picked up in the isolated arena. My hair was whipping around in the hurricane like a storm as I gripped the bottom of the bench to make sure I wouldn't be taken away with it.

"What's happening!?" Sarah yelled.

The wind ripped past our ears creating a wind tunnel sound blocking out all other noises. Riley shouted over the strong wind, "This is what McKayla is capable of if she has enough time to charge and focus. This whirlwind is at its strongest just outside its center."

"We are only getting the weak part of it?" Trish asked gripping her seat so tightly her knuckles were turning white.

"Yup," Riley said smiling. "Unfortunately, for those two boys, they are right in the strong spot."

I quickly turned back to the fight to see the two Recruits trying to get away from McKayla. They pushed hard making every step count. Each step took a lot of energy to move just a few inches. They weren't going to escape. McKayla wouldn't allow it.

I turned my attention to McKayla who had her arms crossed and smiled. She did plan this right from the beginning. The wind appeared to have no effect on her either. She stood tall and confident with only her hair blowing around in the hurricane.

All of the other Recruits in heated competition halted their fighting and waited for the wind to die down. To them, McKayla's breeze was nothing more than a strong wind, but it was still strong enough to stop all fighting.

We all watched as one of the two cocky Recruits lost his footing and was lifted into the air holding onto the other Recruit for dear life. But, the other Recruit couldn't hold both of them and they were thrown into the metal cage hard and were held there as the wind kept going. Blood began to pour out of one of their eyebrows covering the dark bars of the cage with a red tint.

Then, McKayla finished the job. She flung her arms back over to her right. The wind stopped, releasing the two Recruits off of the cage only to be picked up by the wind that had begun spinning in the opposite direction. They were lifted and slammed into a rock block knocking off a small chunk that rested on top of the block. The boys flipped over the rock and were blown across the ground until they fell into the pit below.

"That was incredible!" Sarah yelled, her face frozen in an ecstatic expression.

Riley nodded. "She is something else. The only downside is that her ability needs time to recharge now, but since she didn't do a very large attack, it shouldn't take too long."

"That wasn't a very big attack?" I asked. "She just blew two big Recruits in every direction and then finally down the pit."

"Yeah, like I said, she is something else," Riley said. He kept his eyes locked on her now moving behind a rock barrier. There was a sparkle to his gaze that screamed only one thing: He liked her. I just smiled a little and turned back to the action.

McKayla remained hidden for the next few minutes as she recharged her power. She went down onto one knee and held her forehead. The exhaustion of using such a force must be catching up to her giving her a head ache. Luckily for her, most of the fighting occurred on the other side of the barrier near the pit. The Recruits couldn't care less about one attack that wasn't even focused on them. I guess they assumed that she couldn't pull off another attack like that and will be easy prey later.

Since the rest of the quarrel didn't involve McKayla, I talked to Riley. "Hey, Riley," I said casually. "Mind if I ask you some personal questions?"

He looked at me funny and said, "Sure, I guess. Depends on what they might be."

Sarah and Trish overheard and began to listen in as well. I said, "They aren't about you. They are about McKayla. I was just wondering some things."

Again, he looked at me strangely and said, "Umm… okay, I guess, but I will only tell you things that can be said. Things that if I were to tell you would cause McKayla to blow my head off are off limits."

"That's completely okay with me. I was just wondering a few things since she is so quiet at lunch and stuff."

"Okay then. Shoot."

Okay, in truth, I did have a few questions about McKayla. Some of them did seem unfit to ask about like, "Why does she hate us so much?" or "Does she care about anything?" But, I think I could get the answers to those questions if I asked Riley some other one's closely related to those questions.

I began. "Do you know what McKayla was like before she came into the Clade?"

Riley just shrugged his shoulders as another Recruit was called out of the arena. "Not really. I didn't know her at all."

I became instantly confused. If my memory served me correct, McKayla and Conner were both of Riley's Bloodlings. How could McKayla be if he never really met her before? I understood why Conner would be because they were from the same area. At some point, they could've gone to the same playground or rode the same bus or even went to the same daycare, but if McKayla is originally from Colorado, then how could she get abilities.

"Wait," I said still thinking about what to say. I couldn't use the term Bloodling because Trish was sitting right behind me listening to my every word, so I tried to fill it in with something closely related that he would understand. "If you and McKayla are so close," I winked slightly hoping he would catch what I meant. His eyes opened slowly and nodded acknowledging that he knew what I meant. "Then, how come you never knew her that well before the Clade?"

"Now, that is a good question," Riley said still smiling as yet another Recruit was sent to her untimely end in the Gauntlet. "I'd like to say destiny was at work here."

"Really?" I asked. "Why do you suppose that?"

"Because," he looked back at McKayla with that same twinkle and aspiration in his eyes. "It was a million to one chance that I would have run into her. I was Recruited by an old Instructor named Cissi and Bruno roughly a year ago. They came in the night breaking into my apartment in Chicago and telling me that I had to go with them because of an impending attempt at possibly my life. I ran into my dad's bedroom only to find it empty except for a man dressed in a suit."

This all sounded far too familiar to me. Neither Sarah nor Trish could understand exactly what he was feeling here except for me. It was almost exactly like how I was Recruited except that I was Recruited by a Head Instructor (which is just because I have unusual abilities), and he had only a father. It's uncanny how similar we truly are other than he is perpetually happy and I am a mixture of emotions depending on what else is happening here.

I kept listening to Riley as he recounted the events of his Recruitment a year ago. "I ran from the man in the suit only to wind up into Bruno's arms. He squeezed me hard and dragged me to the door while Cissi fought off the Agent. Bruno finally got me out on the street when the apartment exploded. A pillar of black smoke came from the huge gash in the building. Thankfully, no one was hurt, and officials blamed the explosion on a gas leak. However, in reality, the explosion was far to concentrated to have been a random gas leak. I found out when I was taken here that Cissi had the ability to literally blow herself up and other things close enough to her. This time, though, instead of blowing up something around her, she took her own life to save mine."

Riley's eyes began to fill with tears. He shut them and rubbed them quickly to conceal his sorrow for the late Cissi. Sarah and Trish noticed the tears but just remained silent like I did. It wasn't our place to say anything, and he knew that we were sorry for what had happened.

He wiped his nose with the sleeve of his cloak and continued, "Cops concluded that I was either not home, or I was incinerated. They waited on my block for a few days finally deciding that I must've completely been vaporized in the explosion since no bodies were found."

Sarah cut into the story. "So, at least to the world, you are dead?"

Riley just nodded his head slowly. That was a lot to take in all at once. That was something else we didn't have in common. That one part to his story, that one key part, makes his situation way worse than mine. The world thought he was dead. I tried imagining what my world would be like if Tom thought I was dead... sure, I didn't know that many people, but it would still hurt not too even be cared for anymore by any outside friends.

My mind grabbed hold of the steering wheel of thought and dragged me to Thomas. What does he think of me now? Is he angry that I left with no reason why? Marcus said that all relatives in some way receive letters or messages that say that I had to leave urgently. Will he understand, or will he be mad that I haven't contacted him in two months? I hate to admit it, but if I was his shoes I would be angry.

Riley kept going with his story that was really about McKayla, "Anyways, Bruno took me back to the Clade here in Colorado, but before we got here, we had to pass through a town called Matheson. On the way through, the bus we were riding in broke down. The driver pulled over and tried to fix the problem, so in the mean time, Bruno and I got out and walked towards the mountain the Clade was situated in. He said it wasn't too far from where we were."

Riley looked back at McKayla who was now moving back to the metal cage slowly hoping that the other one… two… three people wouldn't see her. "I was walking out of Matheson when a girl with bleach blonde hair, except for a small strip of pink at the time, wasn't watching where she was running and ran into me with a sharp piece of cardboard. It just sliced my arm enough to draw blood. I pulled my arm back and saw the blood dripping out. She turned to face Bruno and I and saw the blood as well. Quickly, as if her life mission was to cure all the problems in the world, she rubbed her hand over the cut gently smearing the blood across. It was amazing. I haven't seen anyone do that in my life and now here was this pret-, I mean, this girl wiping blood off my arm."

"She said, 'Sorry about that! I really am! I'm on my way to school, and I have a project to present in a few minutes, and I can't be late.'"

"I raised my hand and said, 'It's okay. I completely understand. I can handle this. You go to class and get an A for me, will ya?'"

"She smiled wide and said, 'Thanks, I'll try. Maybe, I'll see you around school sometime? Unless, you are a tourist, of course.'"

"'Yeah,' I said. 'I'm a tourist, but maybe I'll see you at some point in the future?'"

"'Sounds great, but I really got to get going, see you later... Actually, I don't know your name?'"

"She jogged in place waiting for me to answer so she could take off and head to school, so I answered quickly, 'Riley.'"

"She smiled again and said, 'Nice to meet you, Riley. My name is McKayla.'"

"And she took off for class. I never expected to see her again, but wouldn't you know it, just a month later, she appeared in the cafeteria. I didn't know it at the time that we were so close," Riley nodded slightly to me. I looked back to Sarah and Trish who didn't seem to pick up on it. "After that day, we became really close, and then Conner showed up, and we immediately let him become a part of our two person brigade."

There was a pause from Riley. I quickly turned to see that the field was dropped to just McKayla and two other Recruits. I knew both of the other Recruits still in the arena with McKayla. His name was Jim, but a lot of people called him Jimbo. After talking to him for a few minutes, he seemed like a nice guy, expect all he talked about were walruses and how they could be super heroes. It was really odd, so I just nodded my head and walked away slowly, but he was a decent guy, so I hoped he and McKayla would move onto the final round together.

Unfortunately, that didn't happen. The other Recruit, who just happened to be Bruno, ran up to McKayla faster than she could react. He didn't use any kind of abilities; instead, he used what he was good at, brute force. He rammed into McKayla which sent her flying into Jim who was standing just behind her. She hit him hard enough to hear something crack. McKayla stopped in her tracks, but Jim flew through the air eventually hitting a rock block knocking him out. Stewart and Laura ran out to check on him and called him out.

Stewart, once again, talked to Laura, and then moved towards the center of the arena watching his footing around the pit. He directed his attention to Callon and Barbara and said, "After Jim was knocked out, the round came to an end with Bruno Jaggers and McKayla Forwing moving onto the final round."

An intense amount of cheers and boos erupted from the bandstands. I couldn't blame the other Recruits. I was cheering for McKayla, screaming as loud as possible, but Riley was by far the loudest. She looked up to us after shakily standing on her feet, and for the first time, I saw a small smile poke through her concrete expression.

I looked over to Riley and saw the biggest smile he has ever given to us to witness. I was happy for him. Something had broken through to McKayla. The girl he described in his story did that a lot it sounded like. She smiled and talked and was a very cheerful person, but the person that Trish, Sarah, and I have been around wasn't even close to that. Maybe there is hope for her after all.

I was just happy that Bruno didn't completely destroy her. If he were to, then I would just have to hurt him even more.

The arena was cleared almost immediately and then Callon stood and made an announcement. "For all of Group Two spectating the fights, it is now your turn to engage in the Gauntlet. Please walk around the viewing area and enter through the doorway at the end," he pointed in the general area where it was; although, he couldn't see it. A pink curtain hung to the floor covering another hole, like all of the other passageways in the Clade, directly across from me and the others. "Good luck to you all."

His voice cut out but the words echoed in my mind as if he had signed my death sentence. I looked over to the curtain which had been pushed up against the cavern wall to allow the few Recruits who could still walk into the viewing area. Among the Recruits in Group One walking to their seats, McKayla and Conner came out towards the end.

We all stood as if we were about to march into Auschwitz. We kept our heads low as we followed the others around the cage getting ready to face the worst. I swear I even saw a few Recruits silently praying to themselves. After what I had seen, the brutality and the carnage, I may need to also.

Conner and McKayla passed us by. Riley waved and said, "Great job, guys. Wish us luck."

Conner didn't say anything. If he felt anything at all, he probably took that as an insult, but McKayla, on the other hand, smiled just a bit more again. She was beginning to break out of her shell. That was the confidence Riley needed. I could tell that he would fight hard now, for her.

We passed through the curtain as Conner and McKayla took the seats that we had previously sat in. The tunnel was dark and dank. It looked like a place that you would see in a horror movie filled with skulls and corpses. Thankfully, none of those were found here. The crypt-like atmosphere made me want to reach out and hold on to

Trish for support, but I couldn't show weakness, not now. Also, I would just be too big of a chicken too.

Group Two funneled into a small room with stone benches all around the outside of the room. The middle was completely open to anyone willing to stand which most of the Recruits were. As I followed Riley to the far side of the room, I listened to a few of the conversations. A lot of them were Recruits trying to either hype themselves up with their friends, or they were trying to calm themselves before their inevitable fight. I felt the same way as all of them. I thought that I should be a part of their group.

Instead, Riley led Sarah, Trish, and I to the far side of the room where he sat on the stone benches. "This is where Conner, McKayla, and I usually sit. Before each round, it's best to stretch in case you were called in for the next round."

I looked around the room and saw Stewart shut the curtain and stand in front of it acting as a bodyguard, so that none of us could leave, only adding to the feeling of a death sentence.

The lights were dim in this area of the Clade. I guess I could see why. They only used this place every three or four months, so no point in wasting the precious energy they have in lighting it. I didn't like it. I felt as though my heart would soon pump out of my chest if something didn't happen soon.

Then, something did, Stewart nodded over to Laura who stood beside a curtain to our left. She moved through it and went up the steep flight of steps that were on the other side carrying a note in her right hand. Those were the people up to fight next. Soon, ten of us would be in heated competition to destroy each other.

Riley stood up and said, "I guess we'd better stretch now since the third round will be beginning soon. Just follow along with what I do and we should hopefully be ready to go if we are called."

We listened and followed along with what Riley was doing. He would stick out his arms and try kicking them, then he would do arm circles like I used to do in gym and other sitting stretches. It felt great to give my muscles a stretch after being in the same position for the last month cleaning bathrooms.

All of a sudden, Bruno appeared at the bottom of the steps that led to the viewing section. He looked around until he found his lackey who would be fighting in these last few rounds. They conversed and laughed while glancing around the room, taking in the competition.

I asked Riley, "Can Bruno be down here? He has already fought."

"Yeah, unfortunately, he can be," Riley said. "You get a lot of perks winning the Gauntlet especially four times in a row like him. Besides just being able to go on Recruitment missions and get out of the Clade for a while, the winner also has some immunity to a few of the rules, at least minor ones. He can come down here and converse with the competitors in Group 2."

It seems as though the winner of the Gauntlet is treated like a god around here. It reminded me a little of the Coliseum in Rome. I turned away and stopped thinking about Bruno.

Then, the time came. Round three was upon us. Immediately, Riley stopped stretching when he heard Callon's voice.

"We are now ready for round three of the Gauntlet. Would the following Recruit's please step into the arena when called."

He began to call off names one right after the other like before. I watched as other Recruits walked out into the Gauntlet where Recruits cheered and booed for them. It was intense and nerve-racking. A part of me just wanted to get called right away before my heart and head explode from anticipation of what will happen.

…I got my wish. About halfway through the list of Recruits, I heard Callon shout, "Ezekiel Laufor!" I caught my breath and stared down at the floor. I didn't think about what was happening around me or who else was being called out to face me. I just began walking.

I heard a few good lucks from Trish and Sarah which helped create a spark of hope and fight inside of me. I lifted my head and walked towards the curtain with confidence in myself. I have the advantage of surprise on my side. These Recruits have no idea what I am capable of. I hid it from them since day one. I'm glad I did that.

Just before I was about to step into the Gauntlet, Riley ran up beside me, "Good luck, dude." He sat and pat me on the back. "There is no pressure. Do what you want and fight the way you want. No one will stop you."

I nodded. "Thanks for the pep talk, but before I go, I have one quick question."

He looked at me curiously and said, "What is it?"

The question had been bouncing around in my head ever since Riley had told his story about McKayla. It was open and honest and I respect him for that, but there was something I needed to figure out. Something I didn't quite understand.

Just as the seventh or eighth name was called off, I asked, "What made McKayla and Conner become so quiet towards you? What made them so shut in?"

He looked at me intently for a brief moment and then finally answered, "I told them that they were my Bloodlings."

And after that last statement, I walked into the Gauntlet getting ready to possibly fight for my life.

Chapter 24

The crowd went silent when I stepped out onto the arena floor. All I got was a mixture of confusion, awe, and intrigue. I'm sure they were all thinking about what the new Recruits from New York were capable of. Little did they know, I was capable of more than they could ever imagine. I just had to stay on top of my game if I was going to show them that.

Callon kept calling off names as I sprinted to the metal cage barrier near Conner and McKayla. I pushed myself up against it tightly making sure that I had a good view of the entire arena in front of me. If anyone tried to attack me, I would blast them without thinking...

...But could I? My thoughts jumped back to the night when the Agents attacked in New York. The soldiers fell to the ground at the power of my attacks. Did they die? Was I a murderer, or did they survive? My heart sank into a deep pit and the room became incredibly warm. What if I killed one of the Recruits here by accident? I couldn't live with myself then.

And, what about the pain and irregularities I have been feeling. The pain would die down during the day, but when I slept, it came back out like a monster hidden in the closet. It would wait until I am most vulnerable and then give me piercing shocks of pain and agony. Will I hurt myself more if I were to use my abilities? Will Callon notice? I couldn't let that happen. I just had to hope that if I needed to use my abilities that it wouldn't spark back at me.

This is exactly what I didn't want to happen. I began to sweat before the round even began. All eyes were locked on me now even though the last Recruit was just called out. In only ten seconds, the fight would begin. I needed to get my act together quickly if I was going to fight well.

I looked up to Callon as the clock ticked away in my mind. I felt as though I could actually hear the clicks of the imaginary second hand as it moved closer to the top of the clock. Surprisingly, Callon wasn't looking at me. He was so interested in my abilities and comparing me to my father that I would have bet that he would be interested in me.

Instead, it wasn't Callon watching me, it was Barbara. Our eyes locked on each other's. Why was she interested in me? Did I just catch her randomly glancing at all the Recruits before the fight, or was there something more there? I felt an odd connection to her as if I could hear her thoughts. I swear I felt a sensation deep in my gut that told me that she was only watching me because I was so close to Sarah. She wasn't worried about me. She was worried about Sarah.

Time was almost out. I cleared my head with a few deep breaths and shook off my nerves. I kept telling myself that I can handle this. If I can survive an attack from the Agency, then I can surely survive this, and maybe even win if I tried hard enough. I really needed to concentrate and want a victory.

Callon stood from his seat and looked out across the arena. He raised his arms like an emperor commanding his soldiers to battle. He said, "Round three begins now!"

It was go time. I didn't move right away. I remained stationary as all of the other Recruits moved to a Recruit near them. I watched different Recruits of all shapes and sizes go at each other with a bone-chilling lust for pain. These people were friends. How could they do this?

I didn't have time to think anymore. Coming from my left was a girl a little smaller than I was but not by much. She swung at me with a left hook, but my reflexes kicked in, and I ducked underneath the swing. She was ready for that, though, and she sent her knee up hard hitting me in the chest right on the sternum. I fell backwards a few feet shaking off the small amount of pain that came from that attack, but now she was on the offensive as I sat on my butt looking up at her.

She came at me again in an artificial fury. I pushed off the ground with my hands and dodged an incoming kick that almost swept me off my feet. Now, she was vulnerable facing a different direction. I moved fast ducking under her arms and wrapping mine around her torso. She grunted as I flung her onto her back. I pinned her to the ground with my knees and threw a few quick punches. She caught them with ease but wasn't ready for my elbow counter across her nose. Her face jolted to the side as my hit landed. A little blood dripped out of her nose.

All of a sudden, a quick, repeating, thumping sound came from behind me. I didn't look to see what it was. I jumped off of the girl and dove over her. As I dove through the air, I contorted my body to turn around and see a Recruit charging. I've seen him a few times before in the barracks. If I recall, his name was Wallace, and he has a great ability. Good thing I got out of the way in time.

The girl wasn't so lucky. She couldn't get up in time when Wallace dove on top of her. She struggled to get him off of her, but Wallace was just too big to push off. He gripped her left wrist hard and held it in place. It didn't look like he was doing much when, suddenly, the girl screamed bloody murder. She writhed in pain from Wallace gripping her wrist. I looked at her wrist where Wallace held his hand tight to see steam coming up from the cracks between their hands.

The girl kept screaming and shaking, and I just froze solid watching as she struggled to get free. How could I not help her? I had the perfect shot at Wallace, but instead, I just stood and stared at the girl being tortured. How was I supposed to win with a fighting will like mine? I needed to get angrier and not care who I hurt.

Stewart ran up quickly and through his arms in the air. "Enough, enough! She is done."

Wallace grinned wide and stood. I looked at the girl's wrist and saw icicles and frost on her wrist. He was freezing her solid. I wondered if that was frost bite. I always heard my mom say that if the tips of your ears had frost bite, then they would fall off. I just wondered if she would lose a hand because of the second degree freezer burn Wallace gave her.

Stewart escorted the girl quickly out of the arena. I looked back to see Wallace moving for me. I didn't know what to do. I didn't want to use my abilities right away, but I felt as though I had no choice. I wanted to save it until the number of Recruits still competing was lessened.

I turned to try to get a look at who was still competing. As far as I could see, only three other Recruits were left other than Wallace and myself, but the large rocks blocked a lot of the view of the opposite side of the arena.

My time to think was up. Wallace jumped at me with his right arm extended grasping at the air. I fell backwards keeping my distance from his grasping hand. I successfully dodged it and watched as he soared over my head. I rolled onto my chest and jumped to my feet. I tried to run in the opposite direction, but a cold hand gripped my ankle.

Almost instantly, a searing pain shot through my ankle that spread to my entire leg. I yelled trying to kick him away, but he was getting to his feet now. If he were to jump at me, he would easily be able to get a hold of me and freeze me until Stewart came to call me out. I kept kicking as I thought, but it was to no avail.

He was on his feet now, and the eyes of the entire audience were on me. Even Sarah's and Trish's eyes were locked on me although they couldn't see me, but they could hear my cries of pain. I couldn't go down like this. Not when I know I could beat him, and everyone expects so much from me.

When the time came, I didn't think, I just acted. Wallace pulled hard on my leg as he stood flipping me over and onto my back. He let go of my leg briefly to use both hands to grasp my arms, but I didn't let that happen. As if everything that was happening was in slow motion, I lifted my hands and stuck them to his chest. I dug deep within and released a big blast of electricity sending him straight up into the metal cage touching the rock ceiling through the bars. He fell twenty feet landing face first into the ground. Dust lifted around his unconscious body.

I twisted rapidly and held my hands out in front of me, electricity surging through my veins giving my hands the warm feeling that comforts me; although, lately it has been more of a pain to me. Speak of the devil, a bolt of electricity arced backwards and onto my arm which caused me to cringe and fall on a knee. I looked up and hoped that nobody saw that. I stood back up quickly shaking the pain off and got ready for whoever was left, but no one was coming at me...

...Nobody was left. I looked around the arena and saw no one left to battle against. I ran around the perimeter to find Stewart calling out a Recruit who was getting beaten up pretty badly. The person doing it was one of the goons that hung around with Bruno a lot. His little lackey rose with pride in what he had done and immediately looked up to Bruno for gratification in his work, but he didn't give him any. He stared coldly at something else, something that made him uneasy but wouldn't let anyone know that.

He was staring at me. In fact, the entire cheering section of Recruits was staring at me. A few were wide-eyed, and a few had their mouths agape, but all were stunned by what had happened. I blasted Wallace straight into the ceiling with enough energy to know him out.

Nobody clapped or cheered as Stewart ran to the center of the arena and said, "Round three has come to an end. The winners are Ezekiel Laufor and Shane Thurman. They will move onto the final round of the Gauntlet."

Still no cheers as the final words were spoken by Stewart and the cleanup crew came onto the arena floor. Wallace was placed carefully onto a stretcher and moved behind the curtain. I should've gone with them. My time out here was done for now, but I couldn't get over the stares pouring in. I felt like a freak as I slowly walked out of the arena. Were people really that dumbfounded?

I opened the curtain and stepped into the waiting area to find most of the Recruits doing the same as the Recruits in the cheering section. All of them were giving me stares of awe and bewilderment... well, almost all of them. Sarah, Trish, and Riley barreled through the zombie-like crowd and met me as I entered the waiting area.

Trish ran up and threw her arms around me embracing me in a big hug. "I knew you could do it! Congrats, Zeke!"

I would cheer and smile and dance and hug back if I could breathe. Trish was squeezing me way too tightly, and even if she was only near me, I wouldn't be able to breathe anyways.

Sarah tapped Trish's shoulder, and she released her grasp. Sarah moved in and gave me a hug as well and said, "Great job out there, Zeke. Wallace didn't know what hit him."

I smiled now and cheered with my friends. "He really didn't. I didn't tell anybody about my abilities. Wallace was probably knocked out when the electricity hit his body, so when he wakes up, he won't know what happened."

The group looked around the room to the people, glaring at us probably jealous of how I won the Gauntlet in my first time through. Perhaps, they are worried that Trish and Sarah would be as powerful and unique as I was. Maybe they were fearful of us. I don't know, but something has got all of the local Recruits on edge about our group.

We turned back to face each other all a little shaken from the awkwardness. Riley patted me on the back as Trish and Sarah stepped away from us. He said quietly just above a whisper, "Congrats, dude. You did well out there. Way to keep away from Wallace's hands. You saw what he could do and immediately found a way around it. I don't know if anyone told you this, but you have the instincts of a born leader, kind of like your father."

I didn't know whether it was fate or random chance that Riley would compare me to my father, but it definitely struck a chord in my brain. It was ironic that I was thinking about Callon comparing my father to me and thinking of me as a possible leader, and now Riley said it. Should I start to believe now that maybe I am like my father, maybe I am a leader?

I just shook my head and said, "I wouldn't go that far. It was only my first fight in the Gauntlet, but thank you for the compliment."

I began to walk away, back towards the benches where I could rest and hope that Trish, Sarah, and Riley do well in the final two rounds, but I stopped. Slowly, I turned to my side to look at Riley standing next to me.

Confused, he asked, "What's wrong?"

My eyes and mouth drooped down as if gravity had suddenly multiplied by a thousand. I had a flashback to before I went into the arena, and what Riley had said to me.

"I… I don't know. It's just… what you said before," I said stammering on, the flashback still repeating in my mind.

"Yeah?" Riley asked. "I remember what I said. What about it? Are you thinking about telling Trish that she is your Bloodling?"

"Well, not anymore." I began to whisper as we carefully approached Sarah and Trish who were beginning to stretch for the next round that would start soon. "I don't know if you know this, but I kinda have a crush on Trish."

Riley chuckled a little and said, slowing our pace as we got closer to Trish and Sarah, "Yeah, I noticed. The way you look at her is gorgeous. It's pretty obvious that you have liked her for a long time."

I really hoped that wasn't the case, and everyone didn't know that I liked Trish. I was hoping to keep it a secret from her until I gained enough courage to tell her, after this whole ordeal with the Clade and the Agency is over, no matter how long that would take.

I stopped, and Riley stopped with me. "Yeah, I'm bad at hiding it, but I can tell that you like McKayla."

He looked at me through torn eyes. His eyebrows lifted up until they almost reached his hairline. Sorrow overcame me as I saw what happened to him. He said, "Is it that obvious too? I guess I'm no better than you then. I do like her… a lot. I regret everyday telling McKayla and Conner about them being my Bloodlings. All I wanted was to be open and honest with them so we could have a great friendship. I figured it would be hard to be close friends with someone who you were keeping a huge secret from, so I told them, and ever since then, they don't speak to me that often. Conner just gives me cold looks and McKayla shrugs off everything I say. At one point, I really thought they liked me. It made being in the Clade all the more bearable. I felt like I had real friends again like I had in high school, but that all changed when I told them that. I thought that they could see my point of view and realize that it wasn't my fault that they have abilities. I didn't know other people could catch them like a cold, but they didn't care. McKayla instantly ignored me and Conner shut me down. They stayed at the cafeteria table because I was the only other person they really knew here, but they didn't say anything."

I listened as Riley told me his sob story. It truly was sad and I could relate to it. I would never have been close to Trish if I knew that she could become a Bloodling of mine. I didn't even know it was possible, and I didn't even know I had abilities until the day before I was Recruited. The longer I talked to Riley, the more and more not telling Trish about Bloodlings became more appealing.

"I can't believe you had to go through all of that pain and suffering alone, Riley," I said somberly and apologetically. "I really am sorry."

He looked down at the cavern floor and said, "Yeah, it's okay. It's not your fault or anyone else's but my own-"

"No, no," I quickly cut in. "It's not your fault either. You didn't know what was going to happen. All you wanted to do was be a good friend to Conner and McKayla. You couldn't help that they gained abilities and were Recruited as well. If you thought that they were going to be accepting of how they came to have abilities, then you did what you thought was right. How could you know that this was going to happen?"

"I guess…"

I looked to my left to see Stewart with a folded piece of paper in his hands heading for the stairwell that leads to Barbara and Callon. The next round would begin shortly. This conversation had to end quickly if Riley was going to be ready possibly for the next round.

"The next round is going to begin soon," I said. "Don't worry about what happened. I think that she is finally beginning to see that it wasn't your fault about what happened to her and Conner. She looked at you differently today than she did since the first time I met her."

Riley perked up. "You really think so?"

I put my hand on his shoulder this time. "Yes, I really do. I think it is amazing that you have taken all of this stress by yourself, yet you still are this very cheerful, happy-go-lucky guy."

He just shrugged, smiled, and said, "I just didn't want what happened to me, McKayla, and Conner to change who I am. I love being the guy that makes everyone smile and stays on the cheerful side. It makes the world a brighter place." He laughed to himself a little bit. I laughed along with him.

"Good," I said releasing my hand from his shoulder. "Don't ever let that change."

It was then that we heard Callon's voice echo over the entire arena. "Round four will now begin! Will the following Recruit's please enter the arena!"

Callon began to call off names loudly, his voice bouncing off the walls in the cave creating an echo. I followed Riley over to the girls who were finishing up their mini-stretches. Riley started to do a few stretches in the arms and legs and torso. About four names were called off when I heard, "Sarah Irving!"

An ache in my gut began to form. Sarah had been called out. I knew eventually that we were all going to have to fight, and if I can be truly honest, I was kind of glad it wasn't Trish whose name was called out. I didn't know if I was ready for that yet.

Sarah began her march towards the arena when I lightly spun her with one hand on her shoulder and embraced her in a deep hug. "Good luck, you will kick butt." I smiled warmly hoping to cheer her up, but her face was hard. She wasn't going to be intimidated. She was in the zone and wasn't going to be moved out of it. I relinquished my grip on her shoulder and let Riley and Trish say their good lucks and best wishes.

As Sarah grasped onto the curtain edge and lifted upwards creating an opening wide enough for herself to fit through, Stewart stomped down the stairs. He passed through other groups of standing Recruits and moved towards us.

Sarah let the curtain fall behind her, and she disappeared from sight. My forehead began to sweat, and my heart pumped rapidly for her. The stress was unbearable. I was glad I wasn't able to watch, yet I wanted to just because I believed in her… and if I needed to, I could jump in and protect her.

Stewart was right by us now as Callon called off the last few names on the list. He said, "Laufor."

I turned to face him and so did Riley and Sarah. "Yes, sir?" I asked in my speaking to Callon voice.

"Callon would like to have a few words with you up on the balcony level immediately." He quickly marched out into the arena getting ready for the fight to begin. Callon had silenced, so the fight would begin in ten seconds.

I asked Riley walking to the benches, "Does this sound like trouble?"

"Callon wanting to talk to you while the Gauntlet is in progress never happens. Whatever he wants from you must be because of something he saw out in the arena while you were fighting," he said sitting down.

I remained standing. "Well, hopefully he doesn't kill me in front of everyone who already hates my guts."

Chapter 25

I walked to the curtain covering the staircase that led to Callon and Barbara's ringside balcony. The stairway was narrow and steep with a few cobwebs sticking to the corners of the ceiling and wall. My legs began to burn the higher I got on the steps because they were so tall.

Those were the only parts of me hurting though on this climb. This new lifestyle of work and push-ups has really given me a more rugged body. My chest and core have become fairly solid for the first time in my life, and my arms have almost doubled in size. Sometimes, I think that this will help Trish like me, but then again, I don't know if I would like that. If I would ever get out of here with Trish and the others, then this body will most likely not last long. I don't see myself keeping it up for the rest of my life.

I stood on the final step and stared at the ragged piece of red carpeting that hung down allowing no light to escape from the arena. Using a firm tug on the heavy rug, not curtain, I pulled it open and looked upon the arena with a bird's eye view.

The Recruits had begun fighting. A few of them were beating on a skinny boy with black hair in the nearest corner. I wasn't worried about him, though. I kept scanning the arena for Sarah to see how well she was doing.

Callon poked his head out from around his seat as I slowly approached the balcony edge. "Looking for Ms. Irving, Laufor?"

I kept looking at the arena floor. No matter how hard I tried, I couldn't find Sarah. Could she be out already? No, Sarah is too strong. Then again… I never saw her in hand to hand combat, and there was no water around for her to use her ability on. What would she do?

Callon coughed obnoxiously in a very, "You should look at me when I speak to you, Laufor," way. I turned to face him. He sat across from Barbara. I glanced at her from my peripherals, but she just kept staring at the battlefield below her completely ignoring my new presence.

"Yes," I said to Callon. "Yes, I am looking for Sarah, sir." Callon chuckled quietly but heavily. I could imagine his cough being a physical object that would plummet straight into the ground below breaking through the metal cage of the arena.

Callon said, "She is down there in this corner near me." He pointed down below him. I looked back and forth between Callon and Barbara and then moved behind them towards Callon's side of the balcony.

I looked down to find Sarah fending off two other female Recruits. The girl with short, black hair was pinned to the cage while Sarah and the other girl fought each other with their fists while trying to keep the other girl pinned.

"Go Sarah! Kick her butt!" I exclaimed right into Callon's ear.

He leaned back slowly glaring at me. I just leaned back awkwardly hoping that Sarah could finish off those two girls without me watching. My face felt red hot from the embarrassment. I even think a few people in the crowd were gawking at me. I didn't know if that was for me shouting or for me being up by Callon.

Callon rested back into his seat and kept looking down at the arena as if my presence there was meaningless. "There is a reason why I called you up here, Laufor."

I stepped up again and stood next to him while he kept sitting in the stone chair. "And, what would that reason be, sir?"

He looked up to me and grimaced, "I think you have been hiding something from me since you arrived here. We don't keep secrets from the Instructor's here, Laufor. You remember that."

I felt lightheaded. I didn't know what I was hiding. Did he know about something I did that I don't even remember doing? That couldn't be it. Perhaps, I am forgetting something. Wait... could it be that...

"Yes," he said reading my mind. "I know that you have Overload, and it is a serious matter, Laufor."

I gulped. Overload? What was that? "Come again, sir?"

Callon stood and turned his back to the arena just as Stewart called someone out. I hope it wasn't Sarah. He strode to the carpet covering the tunnel and stepped behind it wagging a finger for me to follow. I did as he directed.

We stood in the dark cavern so close that we were almost touching faces. It was a very cramped space. He said, "This is a private matter. We don't need the other Recruits watching us. They are already envious of you winning your round of the Gauntlet. As a matter of fact, not only were they surprised about your victory, but so was I. I had no idea that you had such great control of your ability."

"T-Thank you, sir," I stuttered. "I learned from the best."

He nodded and twisted his head towards the bottom of the staircase. His eyes grew dark like black marbles that were from an evil beast. "Marcus was the best. He was a better Instructor and man than I will ever be, and yes, for once you are correct. He did teach you well."

I agreed and waited for him to respond, but he just kept staring at the empty abyss below. It was odd standing so close to him and not having a feeling of dread. Those feelings subsided when I realized the worst thing he ever did to any of his Recruits was make them do push-ups or even crunches. Never once did he try to physically harm someone, which was good because he could do some serious damage with his flame throwing hands.

After a few silent moments, not accounting for the shouts of Stewart emanating from the arena, I said, "What is an Overload, sir?"

He looked back at me with his dark eyes and explained, "An Overload is what happened to you, Laufor. Tell me, and be honest," he said with force, "have you been experiencing pain whenever you use your ability? At times, does it seem that it is controlling you instead of you controlling it?"

He does know about my problem. Every time I used my ability the past month I hurt, and sometimes, it would strike back at me giving me red, burn marks. I am able to take tasers set to kill, but I can't take a blast from my own ability. I'm my own worst enemy.

"Yes, sir," I said not getting overly excited; although, I felt incredibly excited. For once, I knew what was causing my pain. Well, I didn't know what it was exactly, but at least it had a name now.

Callon put his hand under his chin as if in deep thought. "Have you felt like that if you get a good night's sleep, you would explode from the agony."

Again, he got it right. "Yes, sir," I said a little more excitedly.

"Then, it has progressed rather rapidly. The Overload is damaging your body from the inside out. If we don't do something soon, then you may never be able to use your ability again and that is the best case scenario."

Not what I wanted to hear. "What!? I may not be able to use my ability anymore? How do you even know that this is an *Overload*. Maybe you are wrong."

He shook his head. "I am not wrong. I saw what you did to Wallace in the arena. You blasted him straight into the metal cage, and while he fell, you grabbed your arm. It hurt you didn't it?"

I gulped. "Yes... yes, it did. It has been for a while now."

"When did it start? I need to know everything about when it started and how it progressed. We may have a chance to cure you of it."

He made it sound like it was a disease, but I told him anyway. I started with the lightning strike in Pennsylvania followed by the convenience store failure when I tried to blast the camera with electricity. I continued on with my story until I got to the point where we were now.

Callon thought to himself for a little bit and said, "That makes sense then. From what the Clade knows about Overload, it is caused by a huge increase in your supply of power."

"What?" I asked confused.

"Let me elaborate for you, Laufor," Callon said using his hands as speaking devices to help describe what he wanted me to see. "An Overload occurs when a Recruit has a drastic increase in power. For you, it was the lightning strike. You survived because your body uses electricity, and then it got a sudden surge in electricity. Think of your body as a box that is filled with electricity and continuously fills with electricity for every little bit that you use, so it's always full until you become exhausted."

"Okay..." I tried to grasp the mental image he was describing for me. All I thought about was a cardboard box that radiated blue energy. Suddenly, I felt as though I wanted to be near that box even though it doesn't exist. Maybe my ability is taking me over.

Callon continued, "An Overload occurs when that box is overfilled. That lightning bolt added a lot more electricity to that cardboard box that is you. Now, it hurts you because you are overflowing with electricity, and it hurts when you use your ability because you are releasing a great pressure that has built up."

It began to make a lot more sense now. The lightning bolt caused my ability to short-circuit. There is a huge amount of electricity built up inside me and my body keeps naturally producing more.

I said, "If I just release electricity for a large amount of time, do you think it would deplete back to normal levels?"

Callon shook his head in dismay. "Unfortunately for you, Laufor, that doesn't seem to work. Your body only uses the electricity that it produces. That lightning bolt will forever rest on top of the naturally produced electricity inside yourself until it eventually kills you from the inside out."

My eyes grew wide open. Die? I could die from this? I never really thought that this was a big deal. Juliette didn't know what was wrong with me. She thought it would just go away by itself. I guess that is what the difference between a Head Instructor and a regular Instructor is. Shame, I really want Juliette to become a Head Instructor.

"This could… kill me?" I asked.

Callon just shook his head and looked at the rock floor. "To be honest, I don't know, Laufor. This is only the second case of Overload since the Clade first formed roughly forty years ago."

"What happened to the other person who had Overload?"

Callon didn't answer right away, and when he did, he gave a very cryptic answer. "He's around, but in incredible pain. No matter how much of the drug that suppresses abilities, it still hurts like hell. Sure, the drug helps, but not that much. It's kind of like taking Advil when you lose an arm."

The room got suddenly very hot. I wondered if someone in the arena missed their target and their flame shot into the cave Callon and I were in. This was the worst news I could get about this problem of mine other than I would be dead in two minutes. I didn't want to think that, though. With my luck, I would probably die in two minutes.

"Who was the Recruit that had an Overload before me?" I asked.

"His name was Shiloh Webber. He is roughly a few years older than you and your friends. He was recruited when he was thirteen, and then when he was sixteen, he was pushed into an incinerator on a Recruitment mission. Thankfully for him, he had a fire ability, a good one too. The Agents believed that he would be killed, burned alive, but he didn't. Instead, he had an Overload and the Agency captured the possible Recruit."

"What happened to him after that?"

Callon leaned back against the wall and folded his arms across his chest. "The same exact thing that you are going through happened to him. At first nothing, then whenever he would use his ability, it would burn him.

Soon, it came to the point where if he didn't use his ability it burned him on the inside like an oven."

"Is he still alive?" I asked keeping the interrogation going.

"Yes, he is still alive. Perhaps, you two should talk sometime. Then again, I'm sure talking to him won't give you any hope for the future. Overloads are extremely rare, but when they appear, they can destroy the life of the Recruit afflicted by it."

We stood in silence letting that sink in. My life in the Clade could soon be over. Unfortunately, it's not the way I would like to go out. My freedom from the Clade's missions and trials would be filled with pain and suffering beyond measure. There has to be a way to cure it. If the Clade can come up with a drug that suppresses the abilities of Recruits, then they can figure out how to cure an Overload.

Laura screamed out from the arena calling another person out. Callon stepped forward and said, "Now that that conversation is over, we should go back to watching the Gauntlet. You are a victor, Laufor. You should see who you will be battling against in two days. It could be your friend Ms. Irving for all we know."

That's right. I had completely forgotten about Sarah. I began to step down the stairwell when I thought about something else that I had never asked Callon or figured out on my own. I stopped, turned around, and raced back to the top catching Callon just before he went back out to the balcony.

"What is it, Laufor?" He asked.

"I just have a quick question to ask and then I'll be on my way, sir," I said trying to sound polite.

"You have my attention, Laufor, but be quick. I should be in attendance of the Gauntlet at all times. Your case was an exception."

"I was wondering how come Barbara never speaks to us, or more importantly, how come she never speaks to Sarah. She is her daughter, but she just stares out at the battlefield below."

Callon removed his clenched hand from the curtain and let it drop. "That is a difficult question for me to answer, Laufor. I am not Barbara. If it helps at all, she barely ever speaks to me either. She just agrees with any idea that comes to me. One of the only times she ever spoke to me was when I first became a Head Instructor. The Coucil decided that I should work with her here in Colorado. Immediately after the other Head Instructors left, your father was one, she said, 'I am tired of this. You have shown the Council that you are worthy of their attention; therefore, you shall take lead here in this division of the Clade. I will agree to whatever you need, but don't expect me to make life-altering decisions. I need a break from this life.'"

"She has been this quiet and unnoticeable since you became a Head Instructor?"

He nodded. "I'm afraid so. Sometimes, I even catch myself wondering what goes on through her head. Maybe she is depressed about Sarah."

"How so?" I asked.

"It's really simple, Laufor. She had to give up her only baby to two strangers. Yes, they were wealthy and nice people, but Barbara didn't know if they could be trusted. She really blames herself for all of the deaths in the flood of the Irving mansion. She thought that if she had never given Sarah up; they would all still be alive. Who knows?"

I thought it over about what Sarah had said back at her home in Missouri. I reminisced about the scene between Sarah and me in her destroyed living room. We had a deep conversation that night. That's also the night I learned about her feelings for Gabe.

"If Barbara's and Sarah's last name is both Irving, then how come I saw Irving on the door knocker at her mansion? It couldn't be a coincidence."

"Actually, Laufor, Sarah's fake parents actually had the last name Irving. They were descendants of Washington Irving, the person who wrote Sleepy Hollow. Their family still made a fortune off that which allowed them to start their own company that later became a Fortune 500 firm. It just goes to show that some people are born luckier than others."

I looked around the dark cave and thought to myself, "You got that right." I said, "That's all I was wondering. Thank you, sir."

"No problem Laufor, now get back to your holding area." Callon looked, stepped beyond the carpet and walked back into the stairwell. "Well, what do you know; Ms. Irving is in the final four."

Suddenly realizing how important this was, I took off down the steps going as quickly as possible. A few times, I had to stop and catch myself before I tumbled down on the jagged, stone steps. Then an Overload wouldn't be that bad compared to the broken bones I would have. I hit the bottom and ran through the curtain.

I saw a group of Recruits squeezed together near the arena opening all trying to get a view of what was going on. I found Riley and Trish in the nearest corner trying to look over people to see. Riley held Trish by her waist and hoisted her up into the air to get a view. He was a strong guy thanks to the work Callon puts him through. That goes for all of us though.

I walked up behind them. "What's happening with Sarah? How is she doing?"

Trish kept her focus on the small slit that was formed by someone holding the edge of the curtain open. Riley said, "Sarah is one of the last four. She and the others are just circling the arena waiting for someone to make their move. It's getting pretty intense, and the fight is making all the Recruits in here go nuts."

"Who is left to go up against her?" I asked looking around the holding area to find Bruno shoving Recruits out of the way to get a good look. That's when I noticed that his lackey wasn't at his side. I knew one was in Group 1 and therefore wasn't down here, but where was the other.

I asked, "Is Sarah going up against one of Bruno's guys?"

Riley nodded. "I'm afraid so, and he is tough. He and Sarah are right next to each other circling the arena. Something has to happen soon."

Trish didn't take her eyes off of the arena as we waited for something to unfold. Suddenly, she threw her arms up and screamed, "Bruno's weasel faced friend is going after Sarah!"

Bruno heard that, of course, and didn't like that she called his friend a jerk face, but it was true. The weasel faced boy charged at Sarah heading for the curtain we were all standing behind. He dove at her flying through the air as if he was levitating. Sarah held up her arms as the boy collided into her. He wrapped his arms around her tightly and tried to stand while Sarah repeatedly threw fists down on his back and shoulders.

Just then, all hell broke loose. The other two Recruits took this chance to go after each other, another boy and girl duo. That fight quickly dissipated as the girl flicked her wrist at the boy. Suddenly, a huge gust of wind that even blew the curtain open protecting us spectators from the carnage sent the boy flying a few yards, eventually sliding into the dark pit.

Fans cheered as the girl put her back against the metal cage and slid down it, exhausted. She wasn't going to be participating in the last battle. It was a waste of time and energy. She would be moving onto the next fight, and, like the rest of us I'm sure, we all wanted to see what Sarah was capable of. She was a new girl as well.

Weasel Face, as I was calling him now, stood squeezing Sarah tightly against his body. He walked, staggering with every step towards the pit.

"Sarah!" Trish called out still being lifted by Riley, "He is going to throw you at the pit. Do something before he throws you in!"

It was loud and she might not have heard us over the roar of the crowd. All of the Recruits wanted Sarah to go into the pit. No way was a freshy, in their eyes, going to win the Gauntlet. We were at the bottom of the totem pole, and we had to be taught why.

It was too late for Sarah. She struggled but couldn't break free from Weasel Face's massive biceps. He lunged forward, towards the pit, releasing Sarah. Trish and I both gasped as she tumbled through the air. Riley was holding up Trish and therefore, couldn't see anything that was happening.

She hit the ground hard and rolled to the edge of the pit. Sarah didn't stop quickly enough. She rolled over the edge, out of sight from the spectators behind the curtain.

"Sarah!" Trish and I called out. We didn't know what had happened. Stewart hadn't called her out yet, but she appeared to have fallen into the abyss. What was happening?

Just then, I noticed a pale hand clutching to the side of the pit gripping for dear life. Sarah clung to the arena floor trying to pull herself up, but she was too weak. Weasel-face stalked the pit laughing out loud; the rest of the Clade chimed in. They all pointed and ridiculed Sarah who desperately clung to the edge of the pit. If she didn't do something soon, it would be over for her, and she would end up like most of the other Recruits who happened to fall into the pit.

He approached her, his head cocked back grinning at the metal cage roof. "Look at you down there. That's exactly where you and your pathetic friends from New York belong, at the bottom. You are in our world. Whatever happened back in New York doesn't matter here. Soon, your girl friend back there will feel the wrath of Bruno, and soon, so will Laufor."

Then, he stepped forward and held his foot over Sarah's hand hanging onto the edge of the pit. "Any last words before you fall, Irving?"

Sarah pulled her head up over the edge far enough for us to see her. Her forehead began to form little beads of sweat that slowly ran down her face which plummeted into the dark below. She looked above the waiting room curtain and at the balcony staring at the side that Barbara sat on. Her eyes were full of pain, anger and sorrow. If it was possible to have all of those emotions at the same time, Sarah showed them.

She looked back over to Weasel Face and said, "I do have a few last words." She paused to pull herself up a little more and rested, taking in a deep breath. "You and your little gang are nothing more than bullies. You think you... scare me. What I encountered is what fear is made of. It breathes it in and courses threw the veins of those to... full of cowardice to handle it. It would kill you."

She struggled and slipped a little. She caught herself and held for a little longer when she said, "Hate me. Fine. I can live with that, but if you think you can hate me because I'm expected to run this place, you are wrong. You have no right to hate me for that. Hate me for this."

All of a sudden, Sarah flung her dangling arm up from out of the pit and onto the surface. Weasel Face just laughed and brought down his foot on Sarah's hand. He pushed hard, and Sarah screamed in response.

That didn't last long. Just then, a wall of water shot out of the pit like a geyser picking up Sarah in the process. Weasel Face was swept up as well into the current which defied gravity. Together, they swirled in the liquid until they collided with the metal cage above them. They hit with a loud clang, and along with the water which fell now like rain, they fell to the surface.

Sarah hit the ground first followed by Weasel Face who landed right on top of her. He groaned and rested there. Minutes passed as the crowd remained silent waiting for something to happen. Stewart glanced at his twin and then approached slowly. He got close and looked for any signs of fight left in them. He got up and approached the balcony.

"Ariella Gibbs has made it too the final round of the Gauntlet. For Sarah Irving and Isaac Parker, they are both unconscious. Since Sarah was the first one to hit the ground, however, I feel that she was knocked out first and therefore loses, allowing Isaac Parker access to the final round."

Chapter 26

Cheers erupted from the crowd and waiting area as if it were a pressure building up waiting to be unleashed. The Recruits bunched together and rooted for Weasel Face who remained on the ground unconscious next to Sarah. Bruno didn't cheer and holler. He kept his arms folded across his chest and looked at his lackey lying face down in the dirt. He held an expression of, "How could he be knocked out by her!?"

It was priceless, but not very satisfying because Sarah had been taken out of the Gauntlet. Out of everyone cheering, only Trish, Riley, and I were silent. My rage built up even more. The things Weasel Face said to Sarah were unforgivable. I hoped he would face me in the finals. I would destroy him.

Suddenly, a burning pain shot up my left side. I gasped and gripped my left hip trying to squeeze out the pain; although, that never really worked. My ability burned me because I got worked up. I needed to relax; otherwise, the pain would just increase, the Overload would spread faster.

Callon had made it clear to me earlier what this thing was that was killing me from the inside out. He made it seem as if it was cancer for Recruits. Out of the entire conversation with Callon, I found it overall very ironic. It was ironic because the thing that gives us power, the element we control, is our greatest weakness in high dosage. I don't know if it applies to all abilities, though.

Although I didn't get all of the answers I wanted from speaking with Callon, I still felt like I had enough to paint a clear picture of what I was dealing with. At least my condition had a name now, but a new question arose. Should I tell the others? They know I have been suffering from this for a long time now, since the beginning of our escape from the New York Clade, but would it be wrong to tell them something this dire at a time like this? Juliette has Council tomorrow and the Gauntlet is still taking place with Trish still left to fight. No, it would be better to wait to tell them. Maybe, if I was extremely lucky, Callon will find some sort of cure or medication to prolong the disorder so I wouldn't have to tell them.

Stewart and Laura took a stretcher that was leaning against the back wall of the waiting room and hurried onto the arena floor. They took Weasel Face first, since he was on top. They carried him out of the arena, his adoring fans still cheering as his unconscious body passed by, and up the stairs to a healing area. Shortly after, Arianna walked out of the arena grasping her right arm covering a large cut which was inflicted when she smashed her arm into the metal cage. The edges are sharp, and a small red stain was left on the bar that did the job.

Sarah remained unconscious on the arena floor for a few minutes until Stewart and Laura returned to pick her up and carry her off on the stretcher. Carefully, they lifted her and set her gently on the stretcher. It was horrible. I never thought I would see someone as tough as Sarah be taken down like that.

As Stewart and Laura passed by, the crowd stepped aside creating a path for them. They didn't say anything, no cheering, booing, ridiculing remarks. Nothing. I ran up to Stewart with Trish and Riley right behind me to get one more look at Sarah.

I asked him just as he was about to go up the steps, "Where will she be taken? Is she alright?"

"Ms. Irving will be taken to a special waiting room for occasions such as these. She is overall fine, just a small bruise on her head when she collided into the metal cage." He turned the stretcher to show us a black and blue lump just above her right eye. "A few days will be needed however for her to be fully recovered. I wouldn't be surprised though if she is up and about tomorrow for the Council meeting. I was honestly surprised by her amazing talents. She has mastered her ability well."

I didn't say anything. I just waved to Stewart, and he and Laura continued to bring Sarah to her resting area. We regrouped back in our normal meeting place at the far end of the waiting room by the benches. Trish didn't waste any time stretching and getting prepped for her fight. She was next no matter what. She did arm circles, mountain climbers, and hemi stretches. I only knew that thanks to my Phy. Ed. class.

I sat slouched up against the rock wall staring at the floor. Riley sat close to me, and he put a hand on my shoulder. He leaned in and said, "I'm sorry about Sarah, dude. It probably doesn't help, but she put up one hell of a fight. I was even surprised by her power, and I know Isaac was surprised."

A smile crept along my face, but my depression pushed it away. Riley was trying to cheer me up, but it wasn't working all that well. I kept picturing Sarah hitting the metal cage and falling the thirty feet only to be knocked unconscious. Watching Trish stretch made me think of that happening to her. Her body substituted Sarah's in the horrible memory. I couldn't let her go in there, but she had to, or Callon would destroy us all.

Riley got up and began to stretch as well. Stewart and Laura were still cleaning up the arena for the final match, so they had all the time in the world to get ready. What would Riley do when he faced Trish in the Gauntlet? Would Trish go after Riley? This round seemed more important than mine and Sarah's put together.

Riley asked lunging forward on his left leg, "So, what did Callon want with you? I have never seen him ask anybody to speak with him during the Gauntlet. It must have been really important."

"Oh… yeah, it kind of was," I said quickly trying to think of a good answer to that question without revealing the truth. After deciding that I wouldn't tell them the truth about Overload until the Gauntlet is over, it will be tough to keep it from them, but I must.

The two kept stretching. Trish joined in the conversation saying, "So, what did Callon want?"

"He… uh… he," I stumbled over my words trying to speak and think at the same time. "He wanted to tell me about how surprised he was about me winning my round."

"Really? That was nice of him. Just wait until you win the whole thing," Trish said shaking her arms to get them lose, finishing her stretching.

Riley continued to stretch, but while he did, he glared at me quizzically as if he knew I was hiding something. I would suspect that he knew I was hiding something. I came up with a terrible lie (not completely, Callon did say I performed well), and Riley knew Callon better than I did. He didn't take a break from the Gauntlet to give compliments to Recruits. He told me that a hundred times.

Before Riley could say anything, Stewart ran up the stairs to give Callon the final note with the Recruits battling in the last round. Stewart reappeared at the bottom of the steps a few seconds later while Callon called off the final names.

"This is the final round of the Gauntlet preliminaries. Would the following ten Recruits please enter the arena when called upon? Patricia Dawson!"

Trish began to approach the arena when I ran up behind her and wrapped her in a warm embrace. "Good luck," I whispered. She just nodded and continued towards the curtain with a look that said, "Don't mess with me." If intimidation was what she was going for, she got me.

A few more Recruits entered the arena when Callon called out, "Daniel Durdek!" Just then, a huge man, easily in his mid-twenties, built like a rock, approached the arena floor. The crowd cheered loudly for him. What was so special about him? I have seen him a few times in the barracks, but I never really worried about him. I spent all of my time worrying about Bruno.

Right after Daniel was called to fight, Callon screamed, "Riley Patterson!" He wrapped his arm around my neck and said, "Wish me luck out there, dude." He smiled.

I smiled back at him and said, "Good luck. You and Trish make it to the finals then we will be in control of the Gauntlet."

"Sounds like a plan," he said. Before he left, he leaned in close and whispered, "I want to know what really happened when you spoke with Callon." He looked at me with intense eyes and then walked off into the arena, a few Recruits parting making a path for him.

I knew Riley suspected that I lied to him and Trish earlier. Maybe it wouldn't be so bad if Riley knew, though. He kept secrets well. He never told Trish that she was my Bloodling, and it would be nice to tell someone. There is an intense pressure building in my throat, and the only way to release it is to give away the secret. If I tell anyone, it would be Riley. Hopefully, Sarah and Trish wouldn't find out from him though. That could be devastating to our friendship.

Callon finished calling out the names of the Recruits competing. I quickly moved forward, shoving my shoulder into the ravenous group of Recruits, a few taller, a few smaller than me. A girl up front held the curtain a pinch allowing us adequate viewing of the arena; however, it was nothing like watching from the stands. The large blocks covered most of the far end of the arena.

I saw Trish with her sleeves rolled up and folded over so they would stay in the middle circle of the arena up against a rock block. What was she doing there? She could be swarmed and taken out almost immediately. Unless, that is what she wanted. Maybe she doesn't want to fight and wants to be out.

I couldn't see Riley anywhere, but I saw Bruno standing between the metal cage and a rock block on the far right. Three Recruits were around him before the round started. He would be too occupied with them to go after Trish which is always a plus, but there was a Recruit, a man in his mid-twenties, that could be seen between two blocks just behind Trish against the cage. I hoped Trish knew what she was doing.

8...9...10... "Begin!" Callon shouted from directly above me. In an instant, the Recruits sprang from their positions strategically maneuvering themselves in the arena to get the best opportunity at eliminating the other Recruits. Trish, however, didn't move. She remained still on the pit side of the rock only moving to poke her head around the corner to see if anyone was coming.

Daniel was completely swarmed by the three Recruits as if they had planned on attacking him early and taking him out of the Gauntlet. Perhaps, they are fed up with him always winning.

They sprinted at him at full speed. I saw one of the Recruit's, a girl, slam her fist into the ground watching as an icy path formed over the rock floor. Meanwhile, the two other Recruits, both boys, jumped for Bruno. Bruno was easily six-foot-five, so they really needed to jump high to get at his face.

Daniel grabbed one by the collar in mid-air, his biceps bulging to fight gravity, while he slammed his knee into the other one. The boy gasped, the wind being knocked out of his lungs, and he fell to the ground. Bruno wound up and kicked him across the face sending the boy sailing into the metal cage. A huge cut from his lip to lower eye formed. He wouldn't feel it for a while though because he was knocked out.

Quickly, the icy trail approached Daniel. He knew it was coming, though. He has been in the Clade long enough to know everyone's abilities. He could have even helped recruit that girl. He threw the boy down at the ground as he dove out of the way. The ice continued until it collided with the boy. His cloak was trapped into the ice, his skin embedded in its crystalline structure. He was trapped there.

Suddenly, Daniel bent over and clenched his fists tightly. He groaned loudly and threw his fists outward from his body with surreal force. A loud creaking and grinding sound came shortly after as two rock blocks, the two nearest to them, slid in a blur. The girl couldn't escape quickly enough and she was pinned against the arena wall by the rock. The side of her cloak was damp with blood. The other rock pinned the boy's foot who was against the arena cage already.

He cried out and begged for it to stop. Laura ran over and told Daniel to pull the rocks off. He did, and the boy and girl fell to the ground clutching their aching body parts. Laura helped them off the arena floor as all of the spectators in the waiting room, including me, stepped aside for them. They quickly rushed up the steps to go get treatment right away.

I looked back out to see the crusted dirt and rock break apart and melt back into water. The boy quickly tried to get up, but Daniel just picked him up easily, and cockily. He walked up to the pit and dropped him. Another Recruit bit the dust.

Daniel sprinted across to the other corner of the arena, where the stone wall met with the Gauntlet cage, and battled with two Recruits who were already in a heated fight. Trish, in the meantime, kept still behind the rock block, her sleeves still rolled up.

"What is she doing?" I whispered conversing with myself.

Trish remained calm as Daniel ran through the arena eliminating anyone who wasn't paying attention to him. He single handedly eliminated four of the Recruits in the arena, and he was working on number five. I couldn't see some of the Recruits that Daniel eliminated other than the one's right at the beginning of the round. I hoped Riley wasn't one of them. I didn't see him yet.

Something began to move behind the rock that Trish was hiding behind. A black cloak sleeve fluttered in the air behind the rock. What is going on? I thought the worst almost immediately. Someone was back there and knew Trish was hiding behind the rock. They were just waiting for a good time to move in.

The person moved. A teenage girl ran from the left side of the rock and was ready to jump out at Trish. Little did she know, Trish was waiting for that. Trish's fist and forearm burst into bright orange and red flames. She pivoted and threw her fist into the small crevice between the two rocks.

The girl wasn't going to be able to react fast enough. Trish had trapped her. Her flaming fist smashed into the girl's cheek. Her head spun to the right. The force threw her into the side of the stone knocking her hard then dropping her to the ground.

Then, from behind the other rock that made up that small passage, Riley stepped out holding his hands over the girls face. The girl instantly began to scream as small flames flickered between her fingers covering her cheek. Her face was on fire and was being burned to a crisp.

Riley held his position while Trish moved back to her original spot behind the rock. The girl began to cry out, tears rolling down her red and burned face, "Stop! Stop! I'm done! I'M OUT!"

Riley quickly dropped his hands to his sides and knelt down by the girl. Stewart sprinted over to her while Riley comforted her.

"I'm sorry!" He said. "I didn't want to do it, but I had no choice! I hope it gets better."

Stewart held out his hand to the girl who stopped screaming and helped her onto her feet. She ceased crying while she trudged off the arena floor; the Recruits moved aside to allow her through.

If I recalled correctly, Riley said that her name was Bethany from a lunch time in the cafeteria. I haven't gotten to know many of the Recruits, but I did learn a few names and everyone had begun to look familiar to me.

So, Riley and Trish were working together! That was great! Trish would use her ability to burn the enemy, and then Riley would use his ability to keep the burn burning. Maybe there was a chance for them to both make it to the final round then. Trish, Riley, McKayla, and I could all work together to take down Bruno and Weasel Face. I didn't even care about winning that much. If it came down to it, I would throw myself down the pit and end up in the water bath that rested at the bottom if it meant that Bruno and Weasel Face were defeated.

Only four Recruits remained. Trish, Riley, Daniel, and a girl named Lilly. Lilly was very passive out in the arena. She kept away from Bruno the entire time, thus she avoided all conflict. He single handedly took down almost the entire arena by himself. I began to sweat a little under my cloak thinking about taking him on.

The cheering section shouted in an uproar. Something was happening that I couldn't quite see. Trish was still in the same position, so there was no reason to worry about her wellbeing. Was Riley okay? I didn't watch him go back behind the rock. I'm guessing that is where he was. What was happening?

All of a sudden, the block next to Trish, the one that Riley hid behind, slid into the wall at high speeds revealing Riley shocked and frozen in place. Daniel suddenly appeared from behind the rock Trish was hiding behind and punched Riley so hard he flew ten feet through the air.

"Riley!" Trish called out stepping out from behind her cover.

Daniel was ready for her, though. He swung his right fist forward and then towards Trish. Another grinding sound resonated through the arena when the block Trish was hiding behind slid across the ground colliding into Trish.

"Trish!" I called out. The Recruits in the waiting room that remained, the fifteen or so, all looked at me awkwardly only to go back to watching Bruno ravage the arena.

And Trish was the next person on his list.

Trish's helpless body tossed and tumbled across the ground being scraped, cut, and bruised along the way. She rolled a few more feet, slowing down as she went, until she fell into the pit.

"NO! Trish!" I screamed out loud. The Recruits stopped their cheering and looked at me again, but I didn't care. I didn't even think about them. I wanted to get out there and blast Daniel to the next dimension.

Trish was out. She fell into the cold, black pit that resembled a black hole. I could picture so clearly her body falling into the water bath waiting for her at the bottom. How would she get out? There must be some sort of mechanism or person waiting down there to help them out, but I couldn't see that. I just saw her helpless at the bottom of the well-like structure.

I looked over to Riley who was shakily getting to his feet after being punched to the ground by Daniel. He successfully stood upright before Daniel got to him. He ducked under Daniel's first fist and dove out of the way before Daniel's roundhouse kick got to him. Quickly, Riley turned and ran in the opposite direction realizing that he couldn't fight Daniel alone.

A few Recruits laughed in the audience, but they weren't the ones going up against Bruno. I thought Riley was being smart in avoiding him. He may see the other girl still in the arena and go after her instead.

Or, he could just do both. Riley ran as fast as he could, but Daniel was just too fast. Riley successfully got across the center of the arena, jumping over the pit which Trish had fallen into and to the other corner of the cage where the girl hid. Riley tried to pry the girl from the corner of the cage and throw her in front of him, so that Bruno would take her down before Riley. It was his only chance left.

Daniel didn't care which Recruit was eliminated, though. To him, all of the Recruits would have to be eliminated some way. He ran forward and grabbed the small girl and Riley around the waste and hoisted them into the air. He brought them close to his chest as he approached the pit. They kicked and screamed. Riley tried elbowing him in the face, but Daniel took it like an MMA champ.

Daniel reached the pit with Riley clutched tightly in one arm and Lilly in the other. He held out his arms over the pit preparing to drop the two Recruits. Riley and Lilly tried to cling onto Daniel's massive arms, but they couldn't do it. Riley slipped and fell with Lilly right behind him.

The crowd erupted in a cheer. Daniel didn't falter. He just stood staring down at the hole with a very content expression as if he succeeded in his life mission. Before Stewart called out the winners, he slowly trudged off the arena floor and silently walked up the staircase.

People fear Bruno and not him? All of a sudden, Bruno didn't seem like that big of an issue to me. Daniel took down almost all of the Recruit's in that round. Bruno only took out a few Recruits. Daniel was easily stronger than Bruno, but then what gave Bruno the edge over Daniel? Is Bruno's ability even more powerful than Daniel's?

I began to walk away from the arena and towards the bench when a deep voice called out my name. "Zeke!"

I turned around knowing immediately who it was. Bruno stepped out from the middle of the crowd and said, "What do you think of the Gauntlet?"

I just shrugged. "It's alright I guess. Not much to really comment on other than it's a brutal way to decide who is the fastest, strongest, and most in control of their ability."

"It's great I know," Bruno said smugly. "I don't know how you made it to the final round, Laufor, but I hope you are ready to face the consequences for that. It was unfortunate that we didn't end up in the same group, but I promise you I will give you one hell of a final round."

He trudged off slowly giving me a death stare while he went. He disappeared behind the curtain when Stewart made his move towards the middle of the arena.

Stewart called out to Callon and Barbara, "The final round of the Gauntlet preliminaries have come to a conclusion. The winners are Daniel Durvak and Kristie Bonveck. These two as well as the other eight winners: Ruby Adams, Rafael Butros, Bruno Jaggers, McKayla Forwing, Ezekiel Laufor, Shane Thurman, Ariella Gibbs, and Isaac Parker."

I followed the rest of the Recruits left in the waiting area up the staircase and into the audience. It was weird to think about as I walked the dark staircase that Riley, Trish, and I all walked down here together. This time, it was only me. I hope they were okay. I wonder where they went and will reappear?

As I circled the stone bleachers with Recruits still sitting on them spread out around the semicircle, Callon stood and announced, "The final round of the Gauntlet will take place two days from now. The Council will be gathering in the cafeteria tomorrow to discuss the unapproved promotion of Juliette Dean. I feel as though this is an occasion that rarely occurs, and therefore, all should be in attendance. It will take place shortly after lunch period tomorrow."

Callon took another breath and continued. "All Recruits who were incapacitated or have taken injury during the Gauntlet will be in the medical center of the Clade. Please, go to Stewart or Laura if you wish to visit any Recruits of your choosing. We can only allow two at a time to go and visit due to limited space. Also, all of those who were eliminated by the pit will be back before dinner period which will be here within the hour. Barbara and I have to unlock the trapdoor to the pit in seclusion. Overall, it was a great preliminary round, and I look forward to seeing all of the finalist's battle in the final round."

The crowd quickly dispersed and exited the arena in a one-by-one fashion. I kept my eyes on Callon and Barbara for a bit longer watching their movements as they conversed for a few moments and then exited through the carpet.

I waited for McKayla and Conner to come to the exit before I left. They didn't say anything as they passed me by. The only form of acknowledgement I got was from McKayla who looked at me cautiously and then followed Conner. I followed right behind them looking for Stewart and Laura to meet up with Sarah. Hopefully, Trish and Riley will be out of that pit soon and be right behind me.

Chapter 27

Stewart and Laura were found shortly after reaching the first floor. They waited with their arms folded across their chests talking about the Gauntlet results and the upcoming Council. Most of the Recruits had gone back to the barracks. For some reason beyond my knowing, the other Recruits didn't really care about what happened to their friends. Maybe I was overreacting, and I shouldn't care either, but Sarah was a friend and unless I'm told not to, I'm going to go check up on her.

I approached them confused as to wondering why nobody else was in line before me. "Excuse me, Stewart, may I go check up on Sarah, or am I not allowed to? I don't know because nobody else is in line before me."

Stewart said, "No, nobody else really goes to check up on the other Recruits after the Gauntlet. Callon still provides them with the option, though, just in case someone is seriously injured. Every once in a while, a

Recruit will decide to visit a Recruit who suffered second degree burns or something just as serious."

"So, they just don't care at all? Aren't their friends down there waiting to be visited?" I asked.

"Sarah will be surprised, and I'm sure, very happy to see you. However, the other Recruits have become used to the lack of visits. They just sleep and rest up, so they can leave as soon as possible. Most go in a day usually."

I thought to myself a little and then asked, "Why in the world would they not want to visit their friends and see how they are? For all they know, they could be really hurt."

"You are correct, Ezekiel, but they get pretty competitive during the Gauntlet. As far as the other Recruit's are concerned, their friends are dead during the Gauntlet. It's a dog-eat-dog competition, no room for friends, only enemies, but the Gauntlet will come to an end and then everyone will be close and friendly to each other again."

I can't believe that the Recruits here get so caught up in the Gauntlet that they forget who their friends are. Does that mean they aren't really friends at all? I never stopped caring about my friends while they were in the arena. Even Conner, who never speaks to me, was on my watch list. I wanted him to win, but unfortunately, he was beat. Good for him for not getting crushed to the point where he couldn't move anymore.

Stewart asked, "So, do you want to go visit Sarah? There is no one down there now."

I just nodded, still absorbed in my deep thoughts. He waved his arm as a sign to follow him, and I did. He went back down the spiral staircase, and instead of heading towards the arena, he turned towards the generator room. I followed him silently as we approached the intersection between the generator room and the other rooms on the other side of the hall.

To my surprise, we turned left towards the room where I saw the shadow of the boy through the window slits. I looked at the metal door as we passed it and noticed that there was a board nailed over the slits in the window. That wasn't there last time. Who put that there and why? There was something back there that wasn't supposed to be found, and Callon knew the answer.

We continued to walk down the hallway a little bit futher and stopped at the next metal door on the left. Stewart stuck the key in the lock and gave it a twist to the right making an echoing click sound.

I asked Stewart, "Why are you locking the Recruits in?"

He said, "There are two reasons. One, it's in the best interests of the Recruits who we believe are in need of rest to get that rest. Some feel as though they are tougher than nails and will leave right when they get in. This forces them to rest up in case of an attack; although, that has never occurred here in the mountains. Two, Callon made orders clear that no one is allowed in this area of the Clade, and he doesn't want any Recruits snooping around down here without his permission."

It sure sounded like something was hidden down there. Perhaps, a human prisoner. The problem is that there was no real way of knowing for sure short of breaking into that room shortly down the hall from us.

Stewart opened the door. A loud, creaking sound came from the hinges as the heavy door swung open. Inside, three rows of tables with blankets draped over them held the unconscious or weak bodies of the fallen Recruits. There were boys and girls of all ages. Some moaned as I stepped into the room, while some were completely unconscious and unresponsive.

I walked down the first row looking tentatively at the Recruits. A few glared at me, mostly the conscious boys, while the other Recruits just took one look at me and then rolled to their side. I noticed that a few of the Recruits had slings on their arms and bandages on their legs, chest, arms and head. All over really depending on where they got hit.

Slowly, I turned and kept a close eye on the Recruits in the bed. Someone croaked out, "Hey…Zeke."

I looked over to see Wallace spread out on a wooden table. The blankets have become uneven and almost fell off the table altogether from Wallace's stirring around.

"Hey, Wallace, how are you feeling?" I said trying to sound sympathetic. I felt a little awkward standing by Wallace, the guy I blasted into the ceiling of the cage. It never occurred to me that this guy may want revenge, but he didn't seem to care.

He tried to sit up but fell back down. "I've felt better," he laughed a little. "How are you doing? I can't believe your even walking. Usually, my ability gives a nasty freezer burn that leaves that part of the victim's body useless until it heals."

"I have a special knack for healing quickly," I said not giving away the full extent of my abilities.

"I wish I had that kind of ability. It would come in handy right about now."

Then, a girl's voice intruded in our conversation. "Zeke?"

I looked beyond Wallace and a few tables down. There, surrounded by two other unconscious Recruits, rested Sarah. Her head slightly elevated by a bundle of blankets at one end of the table.

Wallace untwisted his neck and focused on me. "I think she wants you. Besides, I'm sure you came here for her anyways."

I didn't say anything. I just smiled and treaded over towards the table Sarah rested on. A few more Recruits gave me looks that said, "Why are you here? Nobody visits us." I just kept on walking towards Sarah, my friend.

I stood next to her table. She continued to lie down on the table, unmoving. I rested my hand on hers and said, "How are you feeling, Sarah?"

She turned her head towards me and forced her eyes open. "I am hurting... in a lot of places. My head especially. It feels as though someone is banging on a drum set inside my head. What happened after the Gauntlet? Did Trish or Riley win?"

I told Sarah everything about what happened in the last round with Riley and Trish being defeated by Daniel. I told her about his sheer size. She didn't wiggle or even acknowledge my existence, but I could tell she was listening even through closed eyes. I told her about Daniel's ability, and how Trish and Riley were defeated by the pit.

"...And that was all that happened," I finished.

Without opening her eyes, Sarah said, "Dang, I thought for sure Riley and Trish could get to the finals, at least one of them. Did they return yet?"

"No, not yet, but Callon said it would take a little bit to get them out of the pit. I figure he is telling the truth. No point in him lying about that just because we are here."

"You have a good point." Sarah stirred a little. "What happened between you and Callon? If I remember correctly, he wanted to speak to you."

"Yeah, we talked during your round." I considered whether I should tell her about the Overload, and what Callon told me about it. If I didn't tell Trish or Riley, then I didn't think I would tell Sarah. She would keep the secret well, I am sure of it, but it wouldn't make any sense for me to tell Sarah if I didn't tell Trish and Riley. What if Trish was to find out that Sarah knew? Think of how furious she would be.

I said, "We just talked about my round. He complimented me a lot about it. I was kind of surprised."

"That is odd of him from what I have seen," Sarah said. "What are you going to do now?"

"Truthfully, I don't know. Bruno has pretty much called me out in front of the entire Clade. The only thing I can do is ready myself for the upcoming fight in two days."

"Don't forget about the Coucil tomorrow," Sarah said. "Then, it will be decided if Juliette will keep her position as Head Instructor. She will have the authority to lead us out of here then and away from this hell."

"Yeah, there is that." I thought about Marcus and Juliette and the scene in the forest where Marcus left Juliette to take care of us. What happened to him? It had been over a month since we left Marcus in Pennsylvania. I guess it was safe to say that he... No, I couldn't accept that.

Ever since I had to leave Gabe in the forest back in New York to deal with his bullet wound, and the fire spreading rampant across the forest, I couldn't wrap my head around any more of my friends dying. I wouldn't let that happen again. I'd do whatever it took to make sure that that didn't happen again.

I didn't want to bring up anything about dead friends to Sarah. She was still hurting from Gabe's death. How could I let anything happen to her? I cared about her too much and everyone else for that matter. Hopefully, Juliette becomes a Head Instructor and gets us out of here before the Agency attacks. I was surprised we're still here to begin with.

Something came to my mind as I spoke to Sarah, "Remember when I told you about the shadow of the person I saw when I helped Callon fix the generator?"

"Yeah, that was a few weeks ago. What about it?"

"This room that you are in is right next to the room where I saw the shadow of the boy through the window grates in the door. However, while Stewart led me back here, I noticed that the window panel was boarded up. I think Callon saw me watch him go into that room where the shadow was. Then, the next day, he boarded up the window so I couldn't see it again."

This time, Sarah forced herself up onto her elbows. She groaned a little in the process to ease the pain. "Are you sure you are not over-exaggerating this just a little bit? Maybe you saw something else? Maybe it was Callon's shadow all along?"

"No, I'm sure it wasn't his," I said as I tried to be quiet so that no one else heard me. "He was moving around the room while the shadow stayed in the same place. Also, he left the room and shut the door and the shadow was still there. That's when he noticed that I saw the shadow."

Sarah groaned again. "Okay, then, if there really was a person locked in that room, what would we do about it? There is no way we could sneak down there without getting caught. This isn't New York. Callon has this place on lock down. If we got caught, do you realize how severe our punishment will be?"

"Trust me… I have been letting my thoughts stew for a long time now. I am confident in what I saw and I really do think that we should try to get him out."

Sarah stared at me for a long while. Her eyes were tinted a faint red. Exhaustion had begun to set in, and soon, she would be asleep again. What would she say? Would she want to help me? If she did, then Trish and Riley might want to help as well. The more Recruits the better. McKayla may even want to join in now that she was feeling more like the person Riley used to know.

Sarah answered, "Fine, I'll help. I don't know how, but if you need anything, just let me know."

I nodded. "Thank you, Sarah. The only question that still remains is when are we going to go after him?"

Sarah said almost immediately, "The Council is tomorrow and then the final round of the Gauntlet the next day. Most of the Recruits will be overtired from all of the events happening so close together. If we go tomorrow night after the Council, we may have a good shot at getting back down here unnoticed."

"That's a great idea, Sarah," I said through a wide grin.

"It's nothing." she couldn't help but to smile back. "Just make sure you at least talk to Trish before going tomorrow night. I'm sure she will want to be a part of this."

"That was my plan."

The door creaked open again and Stewart stood in the doorway waving me over to him. Immediately, my face got red hot and sweat began to run down my back. Did he hear anything? Is that why he wants me?

He then said, "Laufor, I'm afraid time is up. You have to come with me and let the Recruits sleep now."

I eased a little and said bye to Sarah who fell back asleep. I walked out being wary of the tables with the Recruits napping on them. Stewart gently shut the door and locked it in case of any escapees. He led us through the winding passage and up the staircase. He went back and stood next to Laura while I went back to the barracks until dinner time would come around.

I crashed on the lower bed below my bunk and stared at the wooden boards separated by portions of a dark blue mattress. Hopefully, I wasn't wrong about what I saw in that shadow. If I was, then our mission would be for nothing, and we would be risking getting our butts kicked from Callon. Why do I always have to get myself into these situations? Why am I so darn curious?

Suddenly, my daydreamy thoughts were interrupted by a pair of big, hairy hands. At first, I thought a gorilla grabbed me. Instead, it was just Bruno with only one of his lackeys behind him.

He pulled me off my bed with a hard yank and said, "You got lucky today, Laufor. We weren't even in the same group. What a shame, but luck won't save you two days from now. I will make sure that I destroy you in the Gauntlet, then, everyone will see what a weakling I know you are."

He turned and began laughing with Weasel Face. "What is he doing awake? Sarah knocked him out. He should be down on a table on the basement level."

"Stewart and Laura, a pathetic bunch they are, were carrying me off to the makeshift infirmary," Weasel Face, Isaac, said, "but I woke up just before they got there. They said they would let me go if I felt well enough. Pff, of course I did. I'm Isaac Parker!" He and Bruno laughed again.

For some reason, I never got any of their jokes. Why else would I not be laughing with them? Bruno threw me down on the bed, my head scraping the wooden frame of the bunk, and I bounced onto my side. I rolled back around and saw Bruno was gone. What is that guy's problem anyways?

I rested back down on the bed and got lost in thought again. My mind drifted around and around in a foggy haze. I think the exhaustion was starting to creep up on me. Just then, a sharp, blinding pain shot up my leg and into my gut. I cringed and held my stomach tightly. Overload was having its effect on me. If I get too comfortable, I get zapped. It was going to be a long night, I thought. The dinner bell rang shortly after.

I followed the lessened crowd to the cafeteria and took my spot at the usual table. Conner and McKayla joined shortly after doing their usual thing, being dead quiet. Thankfully, Riley and Trish entered a few minutes later rushing to grab their trays and slop. They sat down, and after shoveling it down, we talked.

I began, "About time you guys showed up. How long were you down in the pit?"

Riley scraped a few dried spots of food off around his mouth. "About an hour. All the pit really is is a large hole filled with water. That is why Sarah could shoot a geyser out of it during her round."

Trish carried on. "There is also a small cave that connects to the pit that you wait in until the Gauntlet is over. It bites because you miss the other rounds, but it could be worse. We could be by Sarah in the makeshift infirmary."

"Yeah," I said. "I went to go check up on her and see how she was doing. Speaking of which, I have to talk to you about what Sarah and I discussed just about an hour ago while I visited her. It's important, and we need to be alone."

They both nodded and looked over to Conner and McKayla who just remained staring at the table; however, McKayla did sneak a peek at us as if she was curious about what was happening. Maybe I will fill her in as well.

Dinner ended and we headed off to our separate barracks, but not before whispering to Riley and Trish about our plan to break out the person in the cell on the basement level. Riley wondered if McKayla could be informed about the plan of ours, and I didn't see why not. The more people helping, the better, and it's not as if she speaks a lot. Our secret should be safe with her.

They all agreed that they would help in our plan in some way or another. No solid plan had been fully made, though. Instead, we all just decided that we would do something to help the person locked in the cell downstairs tomorrow night. Sarah will be out of the infirmary by Council tomorrow, so we could come up with something then.

After that, we separated and headed to our barracks where Riley and I talked about the Gauntlet and other things happening in the Clade, like the Council, for instance. Turns out that the Council is a rare event that hardly ever occurs unless something drastic happened. I guess a division of the Clade being destroyed by the Agency army and being betrayed by an Original is something drastic.

I climbed up onto my bunk shortly after and continued to talk to Riley while resting my head on my hard pillow. We talked for a few more minutes and then the lights clicked off, the generator powering down for the night.

I lay there in bed with my eyes shut. They were so heavy and tired from fighting and cheering and watching in horror that my eyes could no longer maintain open. I stayed awake, however, thinking about Juliette and her impossible task at hand tomorrow. She will have to impress the other Head Instructors in order to maintain her rank as a Head Instructor. Will they understand why Marcus did what he did?

My thoughts whirred through my head like the generator whirrs in the basement below the barracks until they slowed and eventually died out, leaving me to my much needed sleep.

Chapter 28

I had a dream that night. A most painful dream that made me scream out in my mind. My voice echoed throughout my entire being. The sound bounced off my toes and off my chest, ears, hands, all over. I dreamt that I was floating in space. I didn't know if it was space exactly, but it was an empty blackness that ate all things of life.

I was alone in this blackness. I spun in circles finding it surprisingly easy that I was able to move so freely in this space, so naturally. Time did not seem to exist inside this universe. The only thing that existed was myself… and the bright light illuminating itself in the far reaches of the black.

The light zoomed in closer moving faster than anything could ever move in the normal universe. Suddenly, it leapt all around me and I could see that it was a bolt of electricity. It hopped, skipped and pranced all around me as if it was under my control. I thought it was. Electricity has always been under my control.

I held out my hand, and little sparks branched off of the main stream sticking into my fingers. I watched the sparks wrap around my fingers and my hand. I held my hand up close to my face and watched it while the large bolt kept circling me. My hand began to fill with energy, and I released it causing a blue glow to cut through the darkness. It was amazing, spectacular, and even a little frightening for those who are not used to this kind of power. For me, it was all too normal.

All of a sudden, the large bolt, as if it had eyes and was watching me, launched at me like a snake cocking back readying itself to strike. The bolt shot out and collided into my side. The pain was intense. The light cut out from my hand, and I grasped at my side screaming at the pain.

The bolt then recoiled, circled me, and struck again on my other side. I screamed in agony once again and held that side. The bolt continued to follow that pattern of jumping back and forth striking me on all the possible sides it could hit. Eventually, I just collapsed but continued to scream. The electricity had taken me over. It was in control now, and soon, it would destroy me...

I shot upright in a cold sweat. Carefully, I lifted my cloak up and looked down at my sides which were burning. There, looking back at me, were two dark blue bruises which hadn't been there when I went to sleep. What was happening to me? I thought to myself. This was getting out of hand. Something had to be done, or the Overload would destroy me from the inside out.

The lights were still out in the entire Clade. I sat folded over my body clutching my sides as if that would make the bruises go away. I thought my ability healed me as well. If that was so, then why did that happen? I guess it can't heal me if it was the cause of the injury.

A loud, vibrating, whirring noise sparked beneath the floor of the barracks, and the lights gently rose to life. The other Recruits began to stir and moan as I threw my cloak down over my legs to hide the bruises.

Riley rolled over on his bunk to face me. He rubbed his eyes and yawned. "Ugh... good morning, Zeke. What are you doing up already?"

I didn't know how to respond, so I just said, "A bad dream woke me up a little early, but it's nothing to worry about. Honestly."

Riley just nodded slightly and tried to sit up. He still didn't believe that Callon congratulated me in the Gauntlet. He knows that I am hiding something, but he has no idea what it is exactly. No one has heard of Overload other than the Head Instructors. Juliette didn't even know what was plaguing me when I asked her.

Juliette! I had almost forgotten. Today was the day of the Coucil meeting. I wondered how Juliette was feeling. She was probably extremely nervous. The Head Instructors were intimidating. Even Marcus was intimidating the first time I met him. Callon... well, that was obvious. Also, I will get my first glimpse at the two other Head Instructors in the last division of the Clade. Were they both like Callon? Was there any escape from this army base Callon is running?

I found the ladder for the bunk bed with my feet and crawled to it. Still in a daze, I carefully stepped down the rungs on the ladder until my foot hit the bottom.

Suddenly, the curtain to the barracks flung open. All of the Recruits watched as Callon walked briskly into the room with an air of confidence and a bit of concern. He looked worried about something. What could it be that was bothering him?

He passed all of the other Recruits, even his so-called favorite, Bruno, as he made his way towards me. He stopped in front of me just as I stepped off the ladder. All of the Recruits kept watching as he spoke to me.

"Laufor, I have some business to talk to you about. Be in my office in ten minutes with Ms. Dawson and Ms. Irving," he said in all seriousness. "This does not give you the authority to enter the girl's barracks; however, you will wait outside until they are ready as well. I expect you to hurry and shower."

"Yes, sir," I said.

He nodded back at me and then exited the barracks with the Recruits still watching and then back to me when he left.

Riley ran up to me. "What was that all about?"

I shrugged my shoulders. "No idea. Whatever it was, though, it sounded important."

"Yeah, it did. Callon hardly ever comes to speak with us in the morning. If anything, he waits until we are on lunch or dinner break."

I didn't respond right away. I thought about what Callon might want since he sounded so desperate to speak with me. Could it be information about the Overload?

Then, if that was the case, why would he tell me to bring Trish and Sarah along? Does he not know that I didn't tell them anything? This could be really bad if that was what Callon wanted to talk to us all about. It could blow my secret in front of Trish. She may never forgive me if she found out like that.

I stopped thinking and quickly took a shower before the other Recruits had a chance to get to the bathrooms. I changed cloaks and waited outside the girls barracks just as Callon instructed me to do.

After a few minutes of waiting, Trish and Sarah exited their barracks. I took a good look at Sarah and noticed a huge black and blue bump and small cut on her forehead. If only she had the power to heal herself, then again, it hadn't really been helping me much.

Trish said, "Good morning, Zeke. You ready to speak with Callon?"

"As ready as I'll ever be," I said. "Anyone have any idea what it is about?"

They both shook their heads. Sarah then said, "Callon seemed to be in a rush to tell us, though. We better hurry and meet him in his office before we are late. If he gets furious when a Recruit breaks a small rule when he is happy, we really don't want to upset him now."

So, we began to walk down the hall, took a right, and continued to walk down the cave. While on our way, we talked about the Council coming up after lunch break.

"Do you think we will be allowed to watch?" Trish asked.

"I think we will be," I said. "Callon made it seem like it was a very important moment in Clade history, so I would guess that we should witness it."

"But," Sarah chimed in. "If everyone is there, then none of the Recruits would be doing their job. Isn't that something Callon always is adamant about? Isn't that why he spends so much time testing Recruits to see where they would fit in well."

"I have no idea what is going to go down exactly, but I'm assuming that we will at least be a part of it. Callon and Juliette made it sound like a court case. I'm guessing witnesses will be needed," I said.

"Who knows?" Trish finished. "I guess we will just have to wait and see."

We were silent the rest of the way as we walked towards Callon's office. We were right on time and had nothing to worry about as we approached the small hallway.

I stopped before entering the cramped office and said, "By the way, I'm glad you are feeling better, Sarah."

She smiled. "Thank you, Zeke. I got back to the barracks last night. Stewart let me out cause he said I was looking too well for someone to be in the infirmary. My head is killing me, though."

We all laughed gently, hoping Callon wouldn't hear it in his office just in front of us, and then, we entered. Callon was seated behind his desk, his chair pushed all the way up against the wall. Juliette was to his left watching us as we entered. On the desk sat a radio which was tuned into a local news station, but it was breaking in and out as Sarah, Trish, and I entered.

Callon slid up his cloak sleeve to reveal a silver watch that reflected light off of the three lamps situated in the corners of the room. "Right on time. Perfect, we can now begin."

Juliette reached for the radio and turned the black dial. It was a really old model of a radio. It had a metal handle and two, big, black speakers on the front of it. There was no input for a CD, only a cassette tape.

The radio grew louder as Juliette turned the knob more. The static kept cracking in and out while a reporter was giving his news story.

"What is this about?" I asked starting to get a little agitated to the fact that Callon rushed us all down here to here a fuzzy radio station.

He glared at me. "What was that, Laufor? You will address me as 'sir.' How many times do I need to tell you that? I expect thirty push-ups when we are done here, but we need to focus on the job at hand."

Sarah and Trish looked at me like an entire class of students gawking at the kid who was yelled at by the teacher. I hated that feeling.

Callon continued, "I was listening to the radio last night and heard an unusual report from Pennsylvania. Rumor has it that this story was all over the national news making it a very important case for us here in the Clade."

Pennsylvania? What happened in Pennsylvania? Does it have anything to do with Juliette, Trish, Sarah, and I when we landed there? It must, but we didn't leave any sign of us being there.

Callon said, "The story intrigued me and gave me insight in the possibility of a fresh, new, Recruit. The reporter said there was going to be a story on it in a few minutes. When I heard this, I thought that it could have something to do with you four because you were travelling through there on the way here."

The reporter finally came in clearly, and the rest of us hushed up to listen to him. There were still a few spots where the speakers crackled and whined, but it didn't impede on us from hearing the story. I think the real story didn't start right away. Instead, we caught the end of another news report.

He said, "...*the three were professional clowns in the McDuby Brothers Travelling Circus. An eyewitness of the accident repeated what he saw that day. Paraphrasing, he said, 'One clown got into the cannon and shot himself across the arena into a net being held open by two other clowns. I figured it was a trained stunt that would entertain the kids, but the result wasn't entertaining at all. It was disasterous.'"*

"*The clowns,*" the reporter continued, "*were killed in the accident. Wade Osterberg, the clown launched in the cannon, flew at an unprecedented and unpredicted speed head first at the net. The clown hit the net so hard that he broke through the wall behind him pulling along the other two clowns, Jake Van Hecke and Craig Schommer. The flying bodies collided into an SUV in the parking lot outside the arena causing an explosion. Investigators believe that they died on impact with the truck and that there was no foul-play involved in the accident.*"

That was... odd. Why did those names sound so familiar to me? Oh well, It was nothing to concern myself with. The important part of the radio broadcast approached as the reporter signed off and a new one went on the air. Trish was still snickering a little bit when the broadcast changed.

"Good morning, state of Colorado. This is Weston Layell. We have breaking news today happening across the nation. In Pennsylvania, an odd phenomenon occurred just outside the town of Wellsboro. Twenty people mysteriously died of asphyxiation at a Middle School parent teacher conference. Investigators have been searching to see if someone had done something to the water or put something in the ventilation to make the individuals choke, but they found nothing."

"However," the reporter continued sounding intrigued himself. *"Investigators have found a digital recording of the surveillance cameras planted around different parts of the school. At the time of the sudden death of the people there, one boy, Theodore Clemson, was at the school as well. While the others, including his parents, were choking all around him, he ran, unaffected by the things happening around him. A search has been going on for the past two days for the boy now, but he hasn't turned up. If anyone has any information, please call-"*

Juliette clicked off the radio after Callon's signal. We all sat and listened to the nothingness occurring around us. The static hummed thick in the air as if it could crush us with its impossible weight.

Trish spoke up first. "What does this have to do with us? It sounds like this kid, Theodore, has an ability, but we can't be expected to be blamed for all of those peoples' deaths? Can we?"

After Trish spoke the boy's name, it snapped in my head. At first, I was confused as well. How could a boy with abilities be our fault? But, then I remembered. I ran into a boy who was being picked on by bullies in Wellsboro. He wiped the blood off of my face before it healed itself.

I began to sweat thinking about Theodore when Callon said, "This has everything to do with you. The deaths, not so much. Disasters like this are how most Recruits are first identified. This boy fits the description quite nicely of a possible Recruit mainly because his family died while he survived, and you four passed through that town on the way here if I recall correctly."

Juliette nodded. "Yes, we did. But, we didn't run into a boy while we were there. Something must've happened after we left."

Trish spoke up again. "I really don't see how this could be our fault still! Let's say that we did run into this boy, how can just speaking to this kid give him abilities?"

Callon groaned and leaned back in his seat. "Clearly, Marcus did not instruct you about Bloodlings before his passing."

I lit up. Oh no, he was going to give away that Trish was my Bloodling. Maybe, I can play dumb and be just as surprised as her that she was my Bloodling. Would she buy it? Juliette knew that, though. I spoke to her about it shortly after Riley told me about Bloodlings. She would know I was lying. Would she rat me out to her?

I was overreacting. After a few deep breaths, I calmed myself down. Callon may not even reveal the fact that Trish is my Bloodling. Instead, he may just give her a quick overview of what Bloodlings were. The question is now, would that be enough information for Trish to infer herself as my Bloodling.

Callon began, "Bloodlings are Recruits that aren't direct descendants of the Originals in the Clade. There are over four hundred and fifty Recruits in the Clade including the Originals, and only a very small fraction of them are true children of Originals. All of the rest have gained their abilities through some sort of contact with a person with abilities. That is one of the reasons why we isolate ourselves from the rest of society. Like a plague, we spread fast, but we only infect certain people."

Sarah said, "If only certain people are infected with this, what allows those people to gain abilities? Isn't this a genetic power?"

Callon shook his head. "That is what the Originals thought as well, but then they realized that people were gaining abilities with whom they came in contact with. However, even the Originals don't know what causes our abilities. They thought it was genetic as well. That is really the only logical explanation for such an unusual trait like ours, but if that was the case, then it wouldn't spread. There has to be something else at work."

Trish looked down at the floor. I could tell her mind was racing trying to figure everything out. Soon, she would realize that I gave her abilities and ruined her life. She would never forgive me, and she would hate me like Conner and McKayla hate Riley; although, he is one of the nicest guys ever.

There was a short pause then Callon said, "Therefore, I believe that we need to go to Pennsylvania when we get the chance and Recruit Theodore Clemson before the Agency gets their hands on him. Unfortunately, I think we are already too late."

Juliette said, "You think the Agency had something to do with this boy's disappearance? You don't think he just ran away afraid of what might happen to him if he stayed around?"

"I really don't know," Callon said entranced in deep thought. "This occurred two days ago. That is plenty of time for the Agency to get there. Plus, we have the Council today and the final round of the Gauntlet tomorrow. It will be hard for any of us, including Stewart and Laura, to Recruit him if he is still around."

"Can't you just postpone the final round of the Gauntlet one day until you find him?" I asked beginning to sweat profusely thinking about Teddy's death on my hands. It was my fault that he had abilities, but I didn't know at the time. I hope he can forgive me as well if he is watching down upon us from a cloud up in the heavens somewhere. This is horrible, a nightmare that I can't wake from.

"He may already be captured or dead, Laufor," Callon said. "Might as well finish what we started if there is a chance that he is already dead. We missed the golden opportunity window. If he is still alive, he can make it another day."

I kept my eyes on Trish waiting to see if she would figure out the terrible truth. I began to tremble as time passed. Would she find out? She had to be close. All of the information was given to her other than just flat out saying that I gave her abilities.

Suddenly, someone spoke out in the silence causing Trish and I to both jump. A hooded Recruit stood in the doorway of the office and the mini-hallway, his hands at his sides, showing his obedience to Callon.

"Sir," the Recruit said in a deep voice. "A guest just appeared at the cave entrance. She says she is a Head Instructor from the other division."

"Just one?" Callon asked intently.

The Recruit just nodded with his hands holding each other at his waist.

That broke all thoughts about Bloodlings and who is connected to whom in the room. Callon jumped out of his seat and headed for the exit.

"Okay then, I will go down and make sure they are who they say they are," he said. "I would hate to have Nathaniel at the entrance pretending to be a Head Instructor." He laughed out loud, alone, to himself. "He would never be Head Instructor material. It's almost drop dead funny. If he was there, though, I would kill him before he could say one word."

Callon's joke wasn't that funny to anyone in the office who remained. He wasn't in New York to see the betrayal. He didn't understand why that wasn't funny.

He popped back in front of us before we left the office and said, "Before I forget, you three," he pointed to Trish, Sarah, and I, "should be at the Council meeting, since you were with Juliette and can testify for her. Be warned, the Council is intimidating."

He left, his footsteps echoing off of the cavern walls. After a few moments, Juliette followed right behind him. She turned and said, "I will see you in the cafeteria after lunch period. Hopefully, this all goes well."

Sarah smiled at her. "You are going to do great, Juliette. We believe in you, and we have your back if you need it."

Trish and I said at the same time, "Yup."

Juliette lit up. "Thank you so much. Hopefully, I keep my position as Head Instructor, and then finally, I will have some say in what occurs around here."

She walked away down the cavern away from us. We followed close behind in a group like we always do when all three of us were together.

Sarah said, "Amazing, don't you think? I had no idea that we could give abilities to someone else."

Trish said, "Me either. It's pretty shocking to say the least. It's really sad to hear about that Theodore kid, but we didn't give him any abilities. If I recall, we didn't run into anybody, did we Sarah?"

She shook her head, "No, I don't think so."

I just said, "Yeah, same here."

I didn't know what to say. I didn't want to say anything that would reveal that I knew something about Bloodlings prior to that meeting with Callon. First, Trish, and now, Teddy. He was such a nice kid. I hope he was okay. Tomorrow, after the Gauntlet, his life would become a living hell. That is, if he was still alive.

Chapter 29

Sarah, Trish, and I left to do what we would do on any normal day. Sprawled out on the bathroom floor, I scrubbed the grime and mildew that began to build up after an overnight passing on the rock floor. This job was getting old really quickly. My back and knees always seemed to be on fire. The Overload didn't help much either. Greedy, I began to think about what I would get if I won the Gauntlet, but that would mean defeating McKayla at all costs, and I didn't know if I could do that.

The time seemed to pass by a lot quicker today than any other day, though mainly because I wasn't all there, mentally at least. I kept thinking about Trish. My anxiety kept telling me that she figured out by now that she was my Bloodling. I just hoped that she would see reason behind what happened. It wasn't my fault, and I didn't know that I even had abilities. How could she possibly know that, though? We never spoke enough after elementary school. She never met my mom who wasn't really my mom, just someone standing in as a mother figure until I reached my reaping age.

The bell then rang its hypnotic chimes which pulled me out of the deep recesses of my mind and back to the real world. I put away the bucket and sponge after dumping out the water in the sink and headed for the cafeteria. I followed the usual crowd of people into the cafeteria, grabbed my food, and sat down to eat.

Trish and Sarah followed shortly after as they usually did. They grabbed their food as well and sat down beside me and began to eat. We munched away at our gray, spongy slop until every crumb was gone. After replacing the trays, we sat back down next to Riley, Conner, and McKayla who were still finishing up.

Not a lot was said during the lunch period. Instead, we all just watched Stewart and Laura take tables that had only one or two people on it, and, after asking them to move, rearranged the tables. The cafeteria was beginning to look like a court room before long. One table sat in the middle up against the wall with just enough room for a few people to slide in. Then, there were two tables placed a short distance away from the head table spaced apart nicely. All of the other tables, including ours, were pushed back giving the area in front of me its own separate entity.

"This appears to be a big deal," Trish said.

I didn't say anything. I just kept hoping that she wouldn't bring up the Bloodling thing again. Unless she wasn't going to because she already knew that she was my Bloodling. My anxiety rose once again.

Riley answered, "It is a very big deal. A Council hardly ever occurs. The last one to happen was in New

York before I was even recruited and before Callon was a Head Instructor. At least, that was what I was told."

Callon was taking a lot of pride in this. He was allowing two of the strongest and wisest individuals into his home, and he wants to make a good impression. Sure, Head Instructors travel and communicate almost every day, but never in such a formal way before. I was starting to feel the magnitude of the event.

Then, the lunch bell rang signaling the end of our free period. For the rest of the Recruits, it was back to work. For Trish, Sarah, and I, we were to stay.

While the Recruits were preparing to leave, Callon showed up blocking the exit with Juliette at his side. He said, "The Council will now be taking place. I request that you all stay and watch this. Recruits hardly ever have the chance to witness history such as this. However, for the two guards covering the cavern entrance, they will have to perform their duties."

Two large Recruits groaned, one of them being Daniel from the Gauntlet, stood and walked past Callon who stepped aside for them to leave. Everyone else stayed where they were on the small half of the cafeteria.

Callon walked down the center aisle until he reached one of the two tables up front. He held his hand to the one on the left, and Juliette sat down. Callon then stood behind the head table situated against the far wall.

"Everyone," he said. "I would like you all to welcome one of the Head Instructors of the Florida division, Layona Vesicore."

All of the Recruits watched as a beautiful woman, probably in her low thirties, walked down the center aisle towards the head table where Callon stood. She had long blonde hair and deep blue eyes. She walked with an air of godliness surrounding her. Maybe she believed she was a goddess in human form. She certainly looked like one. Her legs must stretch on forever underneath her cloak. She had to be at least five-foot-ten. Maybe a little taller.

She held her hand out to Callon who shook it. "Thank you for having the Council here, Callon. I have been eagerly awaiting this for quite some time now."

"As have I," Callon said very politely. He sounded like a suck-up, then again, he had to be. She helped give him his position here.

She sat down, "Juliette, it's very nice to see you again, my dear. I am interested in hearing about your case."

Juliette nodded sternly and sat down while Barbara walked in shortly after, taking her place next to Callon. In this room there were four Head Instructors at once. One more would be on the way... my father, but where was he, I wondered. I kept watching the entrance, but he never showed.

Callon said, "Let the Council hearing begin." Everyone sat down in unison as if this was church.

Sarah whispered to me, "Zeke, wasn't your father a Head Instructor? Shouldn't he be here?"

I just shrugged. I thought he was too, but it must've been a lie if he wasn't here. Then again, what if he was killed on the way here like Marcus... or Gabe? That still stung like a needle deep in my chest. I still hadn't gotten over Gabe's death. How would I react if I found out that my dad was dead?

Callon announced, "Before we begin, I would like Ezekiel Laufor, Sarah Irving, and Patricia Dawson to please take a seat in front of the Council to be witnesses for Juliette's case."

We stood, took a deep breath, and walked up to the front of the large group of Recruits. They all gave us hurtful looks as if they were jealous about us being called to participate in this. I didn't feel so lucky, though.

We took our seats across from Juliette at the table to the right of her. "Thank you," Callon said. He was getting ready to begin when I noticed Barbara watching Sarah through her dark eyes. Sarah noticed, and quickly turned in the other direction.

Layona stood, "Juliette, you have been an Instructor for the New York division of the Clade for the past five years. Recently, the Clade was destroyed by an Agency attack; at least, that is what you say."

"What do you mean 'that is what you say?" That is what happened. Trust me, if the Agency hadn't attacked, I wouldn't be here right now, and Marcus would still be alive!"

Layona held her hand up to Juliette signaling her to be silenced. "There is no proof that the Agency attacked the New York Clade division. The only thing that we know is that there was a large fire that burned down the hospital and most of the forest. Also, almost three hundred Recruits, three quarters of the Clade, disappeared. Now, these Recruits could've been killed by the fire, but investigators found no bodies."

"That's because the Agency killed them and took them!" Juliette yelled. "I can't believe you are accusing me of killing all of my Recruits! I recruited a lot of them.

How dare you tell me that I was responsible for their deaths."

"Juliette, could you please restrain yourself?" Layona said annoyingly.

I couldn't believe she was doing this. Sarah, Trish, and I all sat with dumbfounded expressions, mouths open, and eyes wide, at what we were hearing. Layona was accusing Trish of killing all of the Recruits in New York! We all thought that was madness.

"Excuse me, Layona," Sarah interjected. "On what grounds do you believe that Juliette was responsible for all of those deaths?"

"Excuse me, Ms. Irving," she spat right back. "Last I checked, you were only a Recruit. You will address me as Ms. Vesicore or not at all. Is that understood? Next time you rudely become a part of this hearing without being told to join in; I will make sure you never do it again."

She glared intently at Sarah who shivered and sat down. I have never seen anyone make Sarah just back down like that. Who was this girl? How can she be such a tyrant? All of a sudden, Callon started looking like a pretty good leader, and Marcus was amazing.

"As I was saying, I believe that you, Juliette, started the forest fire, told Marcus that you believed the Agency was attacking, and led the Recruits to their demise. It would be the perfect plan to attain Head Instructor status with Marcus dead."

After hearing that, even Callon shook his head at her. I truly thought that he believed our story that the Agency attacked. He was still hurting from Marcus' death, but he still didn't think that Juliette was responsible. I still didn't believe that Marcus was dead.

Callon stood up and said quietly, "Layona, don't you think that this sounds a little ridiculous?"

"Sit down, Callon," she said through gritted teeth. "I know what I am doing. I really think that this monster killed all of those Recruits including Marcus. If we don't do something, she will kill us all to. She wants the Agency to win."

"Layona… I miss Marcus too, but accusing his Instructor, the Recruit he went to for advice and help when he needed it, of killing him is ridiculous."

"How do you know it's so ridiculous, Callon? Do you have any proof that the Agency actually attacked the New York division?" She laughed quietly to herself. "That has never happened before. It's completely absurd."

"I know you are scared, Layona," Callon whispered trying to be comforting and actually succeeding. "I am scared as well, but we need to see the truth. The Agency destroyed and killed everyone back in New York. These are the only survivors, but Marcus put up one hell of a fight if I heard the story correctly."

Suddenly, Layona's eyes began to well up with tears. She choked and coughed before she spoke. "I thought I would be stronger than this. I really did… He was just so amazing, Callon."

"I know that, Layona. He was important and valued by us all, but we need to focus on the matter at hand. Making random accusations and criticizing the person that Marcus appointed as his replacement won't get us anywhere," Callon whispered over the insane silence given off by all of the Recruits.

"I guess you're right…" Layona admitted and slowly sat down.

I looked over to Juliette who seemed genuinely concerned about how Layona was. She was stronger than me that's for sure. I would still be infuriated with what Layona accused me of. If it wasn't for the forty Recruits standing behind me, I would've jumped over the table and started beating her up.

After a short break, Callon stood, "I'm sorry about that. Now, back to the matter at hand. Juliette, on your journey here, the Clade lost a valued member and Head Instructor, Marcus Randalph. Before his untimely demise, it was rumored that he appointed you, Juliette, as Head Instructor. Is this true?"

Juliette swallowed loudly. "Yes, that is true."

The pressure was beginning to get to Juliette and the little outburst from Layona didn't help either. How did Layona ever become a Head Instructor? She isn't old enough to be an Original, and she isn't very level headed. Some things you just can't explain.

"This is just going to be an evaluation to see if you are capable of being a Head Instructor. Usually, a lot of thought and work goes into selecting the correct replacement. It helps if a Head Instructor could give the Council some comments about your performance; however, Marcus was the only Head Instructor in New York, so we have no information about your performance.

"I understand," Juliette said exasperated. She was beginning to feel the weight of what was happening to her. We all were.

"Thankfully, we have three Recruits at our disposal that were in your company at the New York Clade. If you may, the Council would like to ask the three Recruits a few questions concerning your status as an Instructor, your character, skills, and any other information the Council may find relevant."

Juliette looked over to us for an answer. We all nodded at her. She smiled a little and said, "They will be willing to answer any questions."

"Perfect," Layona said wiping away the last few tears dripping from her eyes. "I shall begin then. I would like to ask Patricia Dawson a few questions."

Trish took a deep breath and stood, "I am ready, Ms. Vesicore."

"Excellent," she looked down at a piece of paper on the table, and then said, "How long have you been a part of the Clade before arriving here in Colorado, Ms. Dawson?"

"I was a part of the Clade for about a week before it was attacked. I really got to know Juliette well while we travelled together. That is really when I got to spend time with her; otherwise, I wasn't around much in New York."

"Okay, next question," Layona said. "Can you please describe the last time you saw Marcus?"

"Alright," Trish thought for a moment, and then said, "We were in Pennsylvania in the middle of a huge forest. Liam, Marcus' father, found us after our helicopter crashed. Somehow, still cloudy to me, we all survived. He took us to his home and warned us about the Agency. He warned us we have been playing this game of who-catches-who first for too long, and now, they were preparing their endgame. The end of the Clade, and the end of their problems. Then, the Agency attacked the house after following the smoke of the damaged helicopter. We escaped, but Liam stayed back. Marcus did as well, speaking to Juliette before we left."

Layona listened carefully and nodded at the end of her story. Trish triggered the memory in my mind too. A part of me missed Liam as well. He was kind of silly and fun to be around for an old guy at least. I would still want Marcus to show up before him, though. None of this would have even happened if it wasn't for… what? How did we survive the crash?

Before I finished my thought, Layona said, "Thank you. Those are all the questions I have for you, Patricia. I will take your answers to heart as well as Mr. Laufor's and Ms. Irving's before I make a decision regarding Juliette."

Trish sat back down slouching in her seat. She can finally relax. Her time for being grilled was over, but now it would be time for Sarah or myself.

Chapter 30

Callon stood, "Mr. Laufor, I have a few questions for you as well."

I stood up just like Trish. "I am ready and willing to answer, sir."

"Very well," Callon said looking down at his paper. "According to your report, which I have studied numerous times, you were Recruited on your birthday at your apartment in Connecticut. Marcus was the one who Recruited you, correct?"

"Yes, he Recruited me at my apartment in New Haven after my mom disappeared."

"Alright, after that, he also Instructed you. Is this correct?"

"Yes, sir. That is also correct."

"Then," Callon said not looking down at his sheet. "Would you say that you know him quite well? Just as well as your Instructor Juliette, Mr. Laufor?"

I gazed at the entire Council before answering. I noticed that Layona was staring at me intently as if there was something special about me. How come all of the Head Instructor's do that? Marcus was the only one not too. I wished he was here right now. If he had Gabe with him, that would be even more amazing.

I answered, "I guess… but not as much as Juliette, and probably not even as much as you, sir."

"Okay," Callon grabbed a pencil on the table and made a few scribbles on his paper. After a few moments of staring at his paper and appearing to be in deep thought, he said, "Are you familiar with Operation: Zeke Laufor?"

The Recruits in the audience began to mumble amongst themselves wondering what that was. Callon slammed his palm down onto the table and said, "Quiet! Please."

I did hear that before, but I kind of forgot about it. Operation: Zeke Laufor was flashing on the computer screen 241F. I looked at Trish and Sarah to my right who looked just as surprised as me. Trish didn't know what that meant any more than I did, and she wasn't even around when Sarah, Gabe, and I stumbled upon it. Wow, that seemed like an eternity ago, but here it was coming back up once again. Now, the real question at hand, should I answer it truthfully? It seemed to be a secret, but Marcus and Nathaniel knew we snuck down into Room 241F and saw that, and they weren't angry or anything.

I answered, "Yes, I have heard of it, but I don't know what it means."

The eyes of Layona, Callon, and even Barbara, perked open a little. Callon made a few more scribbles down on his paper while I told myself to remember to ask someone what Operation: Zeke Laufor was.

"I have one more question for you, then. If you could rate Juliette's performance while she was Head Instructor on your journey here, what would you rate it between one and ten. Ten being Marcus level work."

I didn't even think about my answer, "Ten, no doubt about it."

"Really?" Callon sounded a little surprised. He looked at Juliette and then back to me. "Why do you say that? You are saying that she is as great as Marcus, you know."

"I know, sir. When she was promoted to Head Instructor, it was a shock. Yes, it hurt to let go of Marcus. It was hard to think about him not being the leader anymore, but he trusted Juliette, so I trusted Juliette. She fought off Agents single-handedly to help us get here. She made all of the same decisions that Marcus would've made. She had worked with Marcus for so long; they kind of have the same brain. If you allow Juliette to maintain her status as Head Instructor, it doesn't matter what happened to Marcus because you will have someone who makes all the same decisions as him."

As I stood there, I realized how powerful my answer was. I wiped a few beads of sweat that formed on my forehead as I waited for Callon to speak.

He said, "Thank you, Mr. Laufor. You may sit and finish wiping off your sweat with your cloak."

I groaned a little when I sat down listening to a few chuckles from the audience behind me. Juliette even got a small giggle out. I'm happy she did. It's a lot easier to handle this much stress when you are happy and laughing. For the other Recruits, they could shut up anytime now.

Barbara then stood from her seat. This was even more intense than the entire Council itself, just this one moment. It would be one of the first times we hear Barbara speak, other than through Callon, and it would be to Sarah. I looked over to Sarah, Trish and I both did, and we saw her stare at her mother with sorrow-filled eyes. Poor Sarah. The first time she would have her mother speak to her would be during a Council meeting.

Barbara said in a very smooth, but dense tone, "Ms. Irving, could you please stand and answer a question for me?"

Just *a* question, that's it, I thought. Sarah stood, exhaling shakily, and, nevertheless, said, "Yes, *ma'am*. I will answer *a* question." She really put emphasis on the ma'am.

Barbara, in a shaky voice, said, "Sarah, I know you know I am your mother. Marcus told you a long time ago, and it was wrong for me never to see you. Sixteen years ago, I gave you to a family that would raise you well, and look at you." Barbara's eyes began to fill with tears. "You are beautiful. It was wrong of me to do the things I did, Sarah. I was just so scared to ever visit you or see you even when you were Recruited. I asked Marcus, back when he was only an Instructor, to have someone Recruit you for the New York division because I didn't know what I would do if I was ever around you. What would I say to my daughter whom I was forced to give up to a random family?"

There was a silence. I didn't know if that was the question Sarah had to answer, but she didn't say anything. She just kept staring at her mom, emotionless. It was amazing. Here was Barbara Irving, the silent woman of the Clade, who was spilling her heart for her daughter. How can Sarah be mad at her after this?

"Finally," Barbara continued. "Your path and mine crossed here. Unfortunately, it had to be at the cost of a great man, but we have a chance to have a real relationship here, Sarah. Did anyone ever tell you that you got the name Sarah because it meant 'princess?' It was ironic that the family you were given to was rich and powerful, so in some ways, you were a princess. In short, words can't describe how sorry I am, Sarah." Barbara truly began to sob now. I looked up to Sarah who was beginning to crack as well. "I am so sorry for everything that had to be done to keep you safe. I never wanted this life to be yours as well. I love you with all my heart and I hope you realize that I would do anything for you. Someday, I will prove it. I swear if you can just promise me that you will, someday, give me some of your time to possibly get to know you. I want to know everything about you. Favorite color. Favorite movie. Which boys do you find cute. All of those things that mothers and daughters are supposed to talk about. Could you give me that? Maybe, someday Sarah? Could you forgive me?"

There was a huge silence. Sarah just stood in shock after everything she had heard. I couldn't blame her. It was a lot to take in, but her mother was waiting for an answer, and she would have to give one. What would she say? The suspense was killing me and everyone else in the room. Even the Recruits behind me appeared to be just as anxious to hear Sarah's response as well.

Then, Sarah replied, "That was three questions." Barbara seemed a little hurt, but then Sarah finished, "And, someday, maybe even starting today, we can do all those things you want to do. I missed having a mom."

Barbara smiled wide and began to sob a lot. Sarah did the same. No matter how much they wiped their eyes, the tears just kept pouring down like a dam with a huge hole in. There was no way to stop the magic that was happening. It would only continue until they ran out of tears, and, when they talked they would cry some more.

Barbara sat back down, and so did Sarah. Callon then stood after a short break and said, "Good for you, Barbara." They both smiled warmly. Maybe he has a heart after all?

"Now, back to the subject at hand. We have all gathered enough information to decide on whether or not you should keep your Head Instructor status. Like I said earlier, it is a huge decision that the Council makes together. There are rules that allow your position change to be permanent, but those are for extreme conditions. Since we have time to appoint a possible replacement ourselves, we will decide on whether or not you are fit for the position. Before we deliberate, do you have anything to say?"

Juliette stood up and said, "I do. I just want to let the Council know that I feel pain as well for Marcus and Liam-"

Callon interjected, "I really don't care for Liam, but Marcus, okay."

Juliette rolled her eyes without the Council seeing and said, "There is not a moment that passes that I don't wish that Marcus was still alive and with us today during these hard times that war brings upon us, but he isn't. Therefore, plans had to be made before anything could happen, so he chose me to be his replacement. He could have told me to tell anyone else in the Clade to replace him, but he chose me. I think that stands for something. You respect Marcus as much as I do. You know he wouldn't intentionally lead the Clade in the wrong direction. He wanted nothing but the best for all of us in this room." Juliette waved her arms out wide.

I felt chills crawl up my back and into my neck as Juliette finished. "I will be a great Head Instructor if you give me the chance. You won't be disappointed. If you trusted Marcus' decisions and intentions, then you will trust me."

Juliette then sat down and let her fate be decided by the Council. Callon sat down as well, and the Council moved together and whispered to each other. What were they saying? Would they accept Juliette as their equal, or replace her with someone they feel more suited to uphold the reins we all thought.

I swear I could hear Juliette's heart beat from across the gap. She sat, alone, no one to help her in case of the worst scenario. I wanted to be over by her. I wanted to be there for my friend. No one should have to go through this kind of torture by themselves.

The Council's uniform voice then perked up and quieted down. Maybe it was my heart I was hearing? It pounded against the inside of my chest shaking me gently back and forth. I swayed with every second that the Council talked. Sarah noticed and just gave me worried eyes. I was wearing those same eyes as well. My whole being was full of worry. My fingers bounced and jittered on the table creating a light tapping sound.

Finally, the Council stopped talking and Callon stood up to announce their decision to the cafeteria audience. "Juliette, it was a hard decision to make," Callon paused.

That is never a good thing to hear first. Callon continued on no matter how tense the situation. "The Council and I do agree, though, that it was appropriate for Marcus to promote you during your battle with the Agency if he knew he may not make it back."

Juliette's face began to glow. The corners of her mouth began to turn upward. She was going to be a Head Instructor... but then, Callon said, "However, that was only appropriate for your situation. Now that you are back in the confines of the Clade walls, the Council feels that they have the right to select their own replacement to fill Marcus Randalph's position."

Her smile faded immediately. All of ours did. We were crushed. We had been hoping for two months that Juliette would keep her Head Instructor position, but the Council didn't feel as though it would be right if they made a uniform decision. I got angry. I wanted to beat on all three of the Council members until they made Juliette Head Instructor. There was no one better.

Callon finished, "I'm sorry, Juliette. You are truly a talented Recruit and a terrific Instructor, but I'm afraid-"

He was cut off by a hooded Recruit, the same one that told him that Layona was here in his office, running into the cafeteria.

The Recruit said, "Sir, there are three people outside of the cavern entrance. Daniel is keeping them on close watch. They say they are a part of the Clade. What should I do? It could be a trap by the Agency."

Callon became unsettled quickly at the Recruit. "Thank you for the information; however, the Council meeting is coming to a close. You could've handled the situation for a few more minutes and then come seen me."

"Umm…" The Recruit stuttered. "This couldn't wait. One of the individuals knew that the Council was happening and needed to get here and see it end."

Confused, Callon said, "What?"

Barbara stood next to him, put a hand on Callon's back, and said, "Let them in. Keep them surrounded though in case they really are intruders."

"Yes, ma'am," the Recruit bent over as if bowing to the Council and ran out of the room.

The audience began to stir and talk about the possible intruders. I heard people begin rumors about how the Agency had followed us, and now they were going to kill us, or how Nathaniel may be outside wanting to apologize for what he did. Some were just plain ridiculous.

The Nathaniel idea stuck in my mind. It could very well be that Nathaniel and two of his Agents were here to distract us while the Agency bombed the mountain or something. He did know where the divisions were. This was what I was afraid of. He was going to destroy the entire Clade and all of the Recruits. Could he be stopped surrounded by a division worth of Recruits?

That is what didn't make sense to me. Nathaniel wouldn't walk head first into a fight that he knew he would lose. He was terribly arrogant and brags about his ability, but he still wouldn't be dumb enough to walk into a losing battle. He would make sure there was nothing that his opposition could do to save themselves before he went in. Then, what was happening I thought.

Callon stood up and yelled to the audience, "Quiet! This is not an attack! Quit spreading dumb rumors. We will find out who these people are and take care of the situation accordingly. I expect not a single word coming from the viewing area."

The audience mumbled, their volume lowering until they were completely silent. Callon sat back down and resumed talking to Layona and Barbara. Juliette kept watching the entrance to see who it was. A lot of the Recruits were. I was as well including Trish and Sarah.

For a few moments, nobody came. We just sat and waited for something to happen. Callon stood and said, "We are just going to continue until our guests arrive. I'm sure my two guards can handle the situation. They were selected for that job after all."

The tension and stress refilled the room and soon, we were all on the edge of our seats again. "Juliette," Callon began. "As I was saying, the Council believes that they should have the right to decide who replaces Marcus Randalph's position as Head Instructor. No matter how great of a leader we all know he was, a decision of this magnitude should be left up to the Council to decide and not just one person."

Juliette swallowed hard, her face beginning to swell with sorrow. "I…understand."

"Okay," Callon said softly trying to make it genuinely easy for Juliette to take. "This is nothing personal, but we believe that you should be moved down to Instructor level, but remain here and help train our new

Recruits on how to use their abilities along with Stewart and Laura."

Juliette just nodded, eyes sealed shut, and forced out, "Yes, sir."

"You don't have to call me 'sir,' Juliette," Callon said. He focused on the entire audience now and said, "Now, the Council will discuss who will replace Juliette as Head Instructor. This may take a while, so you should all go back to your jobs. I want to thank you all for witnessing this historic event, but this is the part where the Council needs to be alone and talk. Picking a new Head Instructor is an important matter."

Suddenly, just as everyone was getting ready to go back to their jobs, including Trish, Sarah, and I, a man ran down the aisle up to the front table. We all watched in spectacular awe as this person ran right up to the front and stopped, facing the Council.

"I...I don't believe it," Callon said.

The mystery man said, "What's so wrong with the Head Instructor I chose, Callon? I thought you trusted my judgment more than that?"

Everyone's mouth hung agape as the figure slowly spun around, making sure to keep his right arm elevated in the sling he was wearing, and faced Juliette. Juliette's eyes began to fill slowly with tears, but not of sadness, of joy.

There, standing in front of us, wearing a Wintry Slope Diner sweatshirt was Marcus looking more alive than ever!

Chapter 31

Immediately, I sprang from my seat, hurdled the table, and ran up to Marcus. I squeezed him tightly, but he was ready for it. He joined in the hug. Soon, Sarah, Trish, and Juliette all ran up behind me and began to surround him. It was spectacular. I knew he wasn't dead... I just knew it.

"Ow! Ow!" Marcus said trying to wiggle free. "Remember, my arm is kind of broken!"

We eased our grip, and we all backed off. His right arm was in a blue sling. It hung lifeless out of Marcus' control. What happened that caused that? Who cares. At least, he was still alive to be here. My head was reeling which, I'm sure, I can say for everyone else as well. There wasn't one frown or unhappy face in the room.

"Sorry!" Juliette said. "I just can't believe it. You are alive. You are okay!"

Marcus laughed a little. "Of course, I am okay. Do you really think that a few Agents could take me and Liam? Nah, we are just too tough to handle." He flexed his left arm and then made a weird face showing the pain in his right arm when he tried to do that. We all laughed at him.

"It's great to have you back, Marcus. It's been pretty rough without you," I said.

"Really?" He said. "I thought I trained you better than that," he laughed again. It cheered us all up. "It appears as though Juliette got you all here safely. Trish, Sarah, I'm glad you are both okay as well."

Callon jumped from his seat behind the Council table. "Marcus… I don't believe it. We all thought you were killed by the Agency, you and your father. You didn't show up for two months. What took you so long?"

Sarah asked quizzically, "Yeah, Marcus, what did take you so long?"

Marcus rubbed the shoulder of his broken arm. "This happened to be the problem. Liam and I beat the Agents alright, but I got shot in the arm which broke the bone inside. After we finished the Agents off, Liam took my inside to pull out the bullet and heal my arm. It was pretty bad. The broken arm hanging in the sling you see now is beautiful looking compared to the disaster it looked like two months ago. That is why it took so long for Liam and me to get here. Also, we picked up a peculiar traveler along the way."

"Huh?" Everyone asked at once. Callon then took over. "You mean your father lived?"

"Yes, he did. If it wasn't for him, I may not be here right now. The things he can do with pliers," he rubbed his arm. "It was like magic, very painful magic."

Callon said, "I'm glad your okay, Marcus, but where is your father? Shouldn't he be here, or did he just abandon us again?"

Then, two people walked into the cafeteria. One was Liam, the other was a small boy. It was Theodore! They picked him up on the way because they knew he had abilities. That's why he disappeared! Marcus and Liam Recruited Teddy!

"I didn't abandon you, cry baby!" Liam said in his older, cranky tone that is all his own. "I was doing what I was supposed to do to help the Clade. Lucky I was there; otherwise, these five would be dead." He waved his hand at us. "How are you all doing? I haven't seen any of you in a while."

Juliette said, "It's nice seeing you are well, Liam, but I think living in the woods of the country has started to affect your speech."

"Blah!" Liam waved her hand at her. "You are just jealous of my dialect. What do you think, sonny?" He looked down at me.

"I find it very… you," I said. I had no real answer.

"See," Liam said. "Like I said, it's cool and you are just jealous."

In the meantime during this joyous reunion, Teddy hid behind Liam trying to take in his surroundings. He peered from one corner of the cafeteria to the next. His eyes grew huge when he set them on some of the Recruits. A few of them were at least two-and-a-half feet taller than he was. Then again, he was only in middle school and most Recruits are Recruited during their early high school years. Why did he develop abilities so quickly?

I walked away from the group and talked to Teddy a few feet behind Liam. "Hi, Teddy, if I may still call you that. Remember me?"

He looked me up and down. "Yeah... you are Zeke. You saved me from McMan and his friends a while ago. What are you doing here?"

I looked over to my group of friends, laughing and smiling, poking at Marcus' cast, and figured we were out of hearing range. I said, "Listen, it's hard to explain, but you have an ability that no one, at least that I know of, can do in the universe."

He stared down at the floor. "I know... I saw what I did to those people... my mom... my dad..."

He began to cry. I rushed over and wrapped him up in my arms. "I know this may not mean much right now, but you need to know it's not your fault. If anything," I said, "it's mine. You are surrounded by people who will help you and teach you how to control your ability and want you to succeed."

"I don't know..." He said still whimpering. "How is it not my fault? My parents saw my grades, and they got angry at me for having one B. I tried... I really did."

I bent over to be at eye level. My mom would always do this to me, and it always made me feel good, like I was in control. Hopefully, I will be able to duplicate that effect.

Softly, I said, "You got mad, and then that awful thing happened?"

He nodded very slightly, tears still dripping from his soaked face. I continued, "That is exactly what happened to me three months ago." Has it really been three months already? Wow, I guess things change quickly in the Clade. "It is very hard. I lost my mom and never really had a dad just like you lost your mom and dad, but it isn't the end of the world. Yes, right now, it hurts like hell, but you will see that what happened wasn't your fault. Things happen. I'm sure your parents would forgive you for what happened someday wherever they are now."

I smiled hoping he would cheer up, at least a little. To my surprise, it actually worked. He didn't smile, but he did slow the flow of tears. It wasn't going to be easy to make him feel better, but I was determined to make it my job. It was my fault after all that he was here. He was my Bloodling after all. Just like Trish, I will take care of him too.

"Thank you, Zeke…" He inhaled deeply through his nose. The sound of mucous being sucked up rang out. "So… all of these people can do what I do?"

"Sort of, but each person can do something just slightly different. They all have abilities to control air, water, fire, or earth." I didn't tell him that I was the exception. I didn't think I had to make things any more confusing for him than they already were. "Why? Well, I haven't answered that question myself yet, but I will find out someday. That's for sure."

"We are superheroes then?" He asked pleadingly.

"Yeah, you can say that." I pointed over to Trish. "See that girl? That girl went to school with me my whole life, and luck would have it, that we both have abilities. She can turn any appendage or her whole self, on fire."

His eyes grew wide. He asked, astonished, "Really?"

"Mhmm, and my friend Sarah, right there, she can move water around with her mind. Juliette, she can create little missiles out of thin air that pierce through any armor. Marcus, he can move through the air kind of like a ghost. He can even move so quickly that it looks like there is a million of him. Liam... well, I don't know what he does, but I'm sure it's just as cool."

His eyes remained wide open. He took quick, short, breaths as if he were still trying to absorb everything that was thrown at him. "Amazing..."

"Yeah, it is amazing," I said.

"What can you do?" He asked me staring me down.

"What can I do? Well, it's kind of confusing. I can use electricity from within my body to do whatever it is I want."

"I thought you said that people only had powers over fire, air, water, and earth?"

"I did say that," I said trying to explain things as easily and as clearly as possible. "But, I am the only exception. I don't really know why."

I spent the next few minutes describing to Theodore everything about the Clade including its hierarchy system and some of the people I've met while I had been a Recruit. I tried to make things sound less horrible than they really were. It was weird describing these things to him because they sounded so natural to me. It was as if I have fully accepted my life as a Recruit.

Just two months ago, I was trying to break out with Sarah, Gabe, and Trish, and now I know I'm here for life.

I told Theodore about the Originals and how there were only a few left, Barbara, Liam, Nathaniel, and Greg, my father. I have met them all except for my father who was supposed to be here if he was a Head Instructor like everyone said. It worried me; although, I had never met my father, and I thought I should hate him. Callon seemed surprised that only Layona showed up for the Council. Did something happen to my father I wondered. Why do I care again?

"Wow, that is a lot of stuff to know," Teddy said.

"Yeah, it is, but soon, it will become a second language to you. I was just as confused and as scared as you were, but with the help of my friends," I waved my hand crossing over the entire group of amazing people still chatting, even Callon joining in, "it was easy."

We talked for a bit longer and then rejoined the group. I listened as Marcus and Liam described their journey back to the Clade. Marcus' version sounded very truthful, while Liam's sounded a lot like an action movie. I thought the part where he took down the entire Agency and Nathaniel with only one hand and not using his ability was the part that got me. It was still funny, and I enjoyed every second of listening to the two of them talk and bicker like father and son.

That didn't last long, though. As soon as the audience was beginning to chat amongst themselves, Callon slammed his fist into the table with enough force to make his whole hand go white.

He yelled, "This is great! I mean it… but we need to finish this meeting before we waste the entire day. If we may continue where we left off, that would be most appreciated."

"And," Marcus said. "Where did you leave off?"

Callon said, "The Council had just decided to elect their own Head Instructor and keep Juliette in her former position as Instructor here in this division."

Marcus approached the table, remaining just a few feet away from Callon and the others. "Now, why would you do that? Do you not think that Juliette is capable of fulfilling the duties needed to be done by a Head Instructor?"

"We feel," Layona stepped in, "that she is very talented; however, she has not proven to us that she is capable of holding the position. Important decisions must be made in order to keep the Clade aloft in these hard times we face ahead of us, and the Council feels that it would be best if it selected its own Head Instructor."

Marcus nodded. "I understand what you are saying."

Juliette immediately began to run up to Marcus to tell him wrong, or complain to him, or argue, but she didn't get that far. Liam grabbed her by the shoulder and said, "Trust the boy. He knows what he is doing." Grudgingly, Juliette listened and eased off.

Callon then said, "So, you agree with our decision? I say it's a valid decision with a lot of merit behind it. In fact," he looked at Barbara and Layona, "I think we know who would be her replacement."

Marcus looked at him questioningly, "Really, and who might that be?"

"Well, obviously, Marcus, it would be yourself," Callon said smiling.

The next thing I heard come out of Marcus' mouth had enough weight to shake the entire mountain. In my mind, it was, and I'm sure it was for the others as well.

He said, "Thank you, but I am not interested in reclaiming my old title as Head Instructor."

The Council's mouths, all of three of them, nearly hit the table. Marcus being a Head Instructor was just so natural. How could he not take it back? You'd think that this would've been a blessing, but instead, it's nothing. What was he thinking?

After silencing the crowd once more, Callon said, "What? Why not Marcus? You were an excellent Head Instructor. You could continue that here or in Florida. It's up to you, really."

"Again, thank you for all of your kind compliments," he said. "But, I feel as though I did not do well under pressure. The Agency was going to attack and I believed that my division could hold them off even though we were grossly outnumbered. We lost a lot of Recruits that night. A lot of good people died because of one decision made solely by me, and why? Because, I felt that that place was my home, and you need to defend your home from intruders. I was a fool."

"It was just a mistake, Marcus," Callon pleaded. "Don't put all of that on yourself alone."

He shook his head unwilling to listen. "I'm afraid it was a mistake that cost the lives of almost three hundred Recruits. In order to escape in the tunnel, one Recruit, Trevor, I believe, turned around and collapsed the hospital taking down most of the Agents. I have not heard from him since. His death, as well as all of the others, hung over my head for the past two months while I healed at Liam's. This is the right decision. I will step down and take an Instructor role. Therefore, I find it fitting that Juliette take over in my place as Head Instructor."

"Why do you think that Juliette is so fit to take your place?" Barbara asked.

Marcus turned around and faced the group, primarily Juliette. "She is strong, intelligent, and trustworthy. Any task needed to be completed; she will accomplish it without a single word between the start and the finish. Everything I am, she is and more."

He smiled at her, and Juliette blushed bright red. She looked very cute and human. Marcus and Juliette... why aren't they dating yet!?

Marcus faced the Council. "If you believe I am as great as you think I am, then you will have no problem listening to what I am saying and understanding what I am telling you. Juliette is perfect for Head Instructor. Also, I'll be here, and if she really needed any help, I would not hesitate to help. That is what she did for me when I was Head Instructor."

The Council sat in silence, stunned by what they heard. Juliette, on the other hand, wanted to scream at the top of her lungs and launch herself at Marcus. Trish, Sarah, and I watched her as she tried to contain herself and laughed quietly.

Juliette couldn't do it. She ran and attacked Marcus with a big hug and many "thank you's." It was really cute and it was about time they started revealing how they felt about each other.

Liam folded his arms and said sarcastically, "That's my boy. Like father, like son."

The Council let the two be together until they separated just a minute later. Then, Callon stood up and addressed the audience. "The Council will now re-deliberate our previous decision regarding the fate of Juliette."

Once again, just like before, Callon and the others grouped together and whispered to each other. This time, they seemed to delve deeper into the subject. With Marcus alive, and his proposition of switching Juliette and himself, they had a lot to talk about. This decision would be hard and could play an important role in the future of the Clade if they didn't know it.

None of us moved or even twitched as if just a slight tremor would ruin Juliette's chances. Marcus appeared to be confident like his rant had total control over the Council. I still couldn't believe that Marcus was really preparing to throw away all that he worked for, but, like Liam said, we needed to trust him.

I stood, fingers and toes crossed in every which way, as the Council remained talking. I caught a few words that travelled the distance to me like "Juliette" and "Council," but that was to be expected. Sarah and Trish stood close, and they moved towards me, and Trish held my hand for support. The moment was so tense that my heart didn't even skip a beat.

Teddy stood beside me as well. However, he just watched everyone. He was fine himself, well, as fine as anyone who just murdered his parents could be. That will always haunt me from now on including Gabe's death...

I shook the image out of my head by physically swinging my head left to right. Trish looked up at me, "You okay, Zeke?"

I said, "Yeah... I'm fine. Just some thoughts flooded my head."

Sarah choked on her words as she said, "Yeah... me too. I can't stop thinking about him. He should be here..."

She was almost about to cry as well. Suddenly, this happy reunion became anything but happy. It was filled with tears for the ones lost because of the costs of the Clade, the costs of war.

Everyone ceased their aching memories when the Council dispersed back to their original positions. Callon stood, staring down at Juliette like her executioner or savior, and said, "Juliette, the Council has reached its verdict."

Juliette held onto Liam tighter while Marcus stood in front of the Council, unfaltering. Callon continued, "We said, just earlier, that the main reason why we couldn't promote you was because you had no one on the Council to represent you, and now that has changed. Marcus has stepped forward and spoke wonderful things about your character, skill, and loyalty. You can probably tell as well that we on the Council respect Marcus highly for all that he has done."

Callon took a pause, building suspense until it practically crushed everyone in the room. He finished, "Therefore, the Council has decided to accept Marcus' offer. You will be promoted to Head Instructor and Marcus will become an Instructor."

We all jumped, Juliette the highest, and came together. Juliette has done it. She was promoted to Head Instructor status officially. We all gathered in a large circle with Juliette in the middle. We rushed her like a bunch a kids rushing the basketball court after a big win. If you think about it, this was a big win, for all of us.

Now Juliette had the power to choose where she wanted to be stationed. Either here or with Layona in Florida. If my opinion mattered, I would love to be down from this mountain and see some sun. I had never been down south, either. It would be a neat experience I thought.

Juliette was nothing but cheeks, eyes, and teeth. They were all so big I thought her face was going to be sucked up by them, but she had every right to be happy. We all cheered for her and complemented her on the great victory; however, none of this would be possible if it weren't for Marcus.

I looked over to Marcus briefly to see him talking to Callon. I didn't know what they were saying, but what I saw confused me. Shortly after I saw Marcus' lips form the word "Juliette," Callon switched the subject to… at least what I thought was "Zeke." I focused my attention and curiosity a little longer on Marcus and Callon. Again, it looked as though my name appeared. I wondered what they talking about?

All of a sudden, a pair of large, slightly wrinkled hands grabbed my arms and spun me around in the air. It was Liam holding me slightly off the ground, just enough that my toes were barely touching the floor.

He said, "Hey, sonny, did your brains go soft? The screaming girls are over here."

"Yeah…" I said slowly slipping back to reality. "I'm fine. Don't worry about it."

Liam then disconnected our gaze and peered at Marcus and Callon. He looked back down and said, "Don't worry about them. Everything worked out fine."

He was right. Everything was fine. I should have been happy, but I was sick and tired of having people talk about me behind my back. What in the HELL is Operation: Zeke Laufor? Why do Callon and Marcus continuously talk about me behind my back either between themselves or someone else? I found files of myself back in New York, and that file that Callon was looking through could've been me as well; although, the more I think about it, the more I think that for once it wasn't.

Marcus then left the table of Head Instructors and joined in our celebration. The audience of Recruits just looked around trying to go unnoticed. Maybe then they wouldn't have to go back and continue their jobs for the rest of the day. Riley, Conner, and McKayla all sat in the back also trying to look inconspicuous; although, that is hard for Riley since he was always so happy and outgoing. He seemed to stick out no matter where he was. I thought I even saw McKayla talk to Riley a little bit, and I may have seen a smile.

It was a momentous day, for everyone. Marcus, Juliette, Liam, and Riley. Might as well throw in Sarah, Trish, and Callon for having their friends back. I felt bad for Teddy for all of the bad stuff that happened to him, but this place will definitely help, for now. If something wasn't done soon, this place will be in ashes like the hospital in New York… like Gabe.

Ah! Why was he coming to mind then? Suddenly, a sharp shock pierced up my leg and into my torso causing me to stagger. I cringed and hoped that no one saw. I quickly reorganized myself within the group.

It was indeed a great day, at least in some way, for all of us, but then why didn't I feel so great?

Chapter 32

The rest of the exciting day was spent cleaning the Recruit bathroom. Hopefully, the Gauntlet will change my current job to something more of my liking and talents.

Shortly after the announcement was given that Juliette was to become Head Instructor, the audience dissipated down to just two. Only McKayla and Riley decided to stay and congratulate Juliette on her accomplishment even though they have never truly met her before. It was a kind gesture, and Juliette accepted it. They left and the rest of us followed, going back to do what we usually do on any other day here. Our jobs would have one less hour though because of how long the Council took.

Layona didn't stay much longer after the Council meeting. There were a few words passed between each Head Instructor and others like Marcus and Liam.

However, it was all business. They didn't speak about anything that didn't involve the Clade. They didn't even talk to each other about what they were planning on doing this weekend like normal friends would.

With all of the talk about the Clade and future plans, my mind jumped to my plan. I didn't forget the plan. No one did. If there was a plan, that is. Even with all of the joy and adulation for Juliette, Marcus, and Liam, we were still going to sneak out and try to get at that Recruit locked in the basement.

Dinner came quickly, and that was when Sarah, Trish, and I talked about how this would work. We only had ten minutes to figure a solid plan out before we were to head back to the barracks. We would have to be fast.

After quickly shoveling down the little food I had, I said to Sarah and Trish on my left, "The plan is still on tonight, right?"

Sarah nodded, "I guess so. I just hope you are right about all of this, Zeke. If you are wrong and then get caught, Callon will actually destroy you. No point in worrying about the final round of the Gauntlet tomorrow. You will already be dead."

"Sarah is right," Trish said. "You better be one hundred percent sure about this. I heard stories of what you did back in New York, but that was with Marcus as Head Instructor. You have Callon and his Instructors roaming the tunnels here. If you are found, you will be punished severely."

"I realize this isn't probably the smartest thing to do especially now that Juliette has been promoted to Head Instructor, and we represent her, but I am confident about this. Callon is hiding a person in the basement. The way he hides his files, and how he doesn't let anyone go back there without supervision appears odd.

Sarah twirled her fork on her tray. "Okay, Zeke. Whatever you say. What do you want us to do?"

I shrugged. "I don't really know. I don't have a real plan."

"Then," Trish began. "How can you do this tonight if you have no plan?"

She had a real point. All we have done so far was decide that something was going to happen tonight, there are way too many variables to take into account. Callon may have guards prowling the caverns watching for Recruits. He may have people stand right outside the entrance to the barracks. Overprotection and order were Callon's forte.

"What do you think, Zeke?" Trish asked.

I looked up from my tray. I didn't realize that my head sank down in the first place. "I don't know now. Maybe it would be the best if we didn't do anything."

The words just left my lungs. I didn't want to put my friends in danger of being torn to shreds for something that may be there. It could be my imagination just playing tricks on me. My subconscious may just want Callon to be hiding something, so then, we had an excuse to hate him even more. Maybe, I wasn't even that sure anymore.

"Are you sure?" Trish looked genuinely surprised. "I thought for sure you would hold onto this idea until you discovered if it was true or not."

"Well... I guess you were wrong," I laughed lightly.

Sarah said, "I think you are making a smart decision, and besides, if there really was someone locked in a room downstairs, then there must be a good reason as to why that is. A Recruit who went insane and tried to kill everyone, but Callon felt a little sincerity and decided to lock him up instead of throwing him to the Agency."

"That is the most ridiculous thing I've ever heard, even after everything I've said."

We all laughed again when the bell rang. I walked with the girls until we split to go to our own, separate barracks. After that, I spent time talking to Riley before lights out. It turns out that he overheard Sarah, Trish, and I at dinner. I told him about the plan we originally had to see what was down in that room.

He said, "Shame that you decided to drop the idea. I would believe that Callon had hid something, or maybe even someone, down there. It makes sense to me."

"You really think so?" I asked a little surprised.

"Yeah, I do. Callon has always been on edge about being downstairs alone. At least, since I've been here."

The conversation ended when the lights turned off. I lay in bed and stared at the ceiling for what seemed like an hour. Who really knew, though? Time seemed to pass in random moments instead of steady increments like outside the cave. One second could've lasted ten minutes there.

What should I have done? If I do anything, Trish and Sarah wouldn't be involved in it. That's for sure. If I got caught outside of the barracks during lights out, and was found in the girl's barracks, I would be past destroyed.

I closed my eyes, finally deciding on what I should do, and fell asleep. However, sleep didn't last as long as it was supposed to. I woke up sometime later, hoping that at least a few hours passed, and slowly climbed down from my bunk trying not to wake anyone or cause them to stir. I am going to see who is locked in that room downstairs.

I didn't bother changing cloaks. It wasn't a new day, and it didn't matter if I stank. No one would catch me if everything worked out the way it was supposed to.

It was hard to navigate the barracks without the use of light. I didn't want to use my ability yet in case the light woke anyone up. I needed to be as sneaky as possible if this was to work out.

After a few times of running into empty bunk beds, I found the curtain. I pulled it open slowly, a few peeps sounded out as the curtain creased over itself. Then, I released it letting it fall.

The tunnel was pitch-black. Literally, I couldn't see two inches in front of me let alone two feet. With the curtain down, I took a risk and let energy flow into my right palm. The warmth crawled down my arm, hopping over the elbow, and pooled in my palm. The cavern filled with a very dim, blue light. It was so dim that hardly any shadows were created. I pushed a little harder trying to brighten the tunnel a little bit more, but I stung quite badly by the Overload. I covered my mouth to keep my scream in. Eventually the pain won out, and I let the electricity weaken causing the light to dim.

It would be hard, but I had to traverse the cave with barely any light. I kept my hand against the wall and made my way towards the intersection. When I did reach it, I turned left and followed it down towards the steps.

The cave looked a lot different at night. Distances seemed to change in response to light. When illuminated, the cave was long, but you could be down to the other end in just under five minutes. In the dark, it took me quite a while to reach the steps. Then again, I was being super cautious making sure that no one was following me.

I took a chance and crossed the tunnel to the other wall and continued towards the steps. If I would happen upon it, I was on the correct side now. My chances only improved the further I went.

Suddenly, a sound peeped out from the darkness behind me. Instantly, my thoughts jumped to an image of Nathaniel stalking me in the darkness, waiting to strike me down. That was ridiculous, though. Callon had guards at the entrance at all times. Didn't he? And, if he did, those guards wouldn't stand a chance against Nathaniel. He's too strong. He took down Marcus and me at the same time.

My head started to race as the noise approached. I hurried my way down the dark tunnel hoping I wouldn't run into any Instructors or Callon on the way. The sound continued to make its way towards me no matter how quickly I moved. I dimmed the light until it no longer existed and walked briskly in the darkness.

Then, just as the pitter-pattering sound was a few short feet from me, I found the corner of the doorway to the staircase. My hopes lifted as I turned the corner...

...And into the chest of a large figure. I jumped back and turned the light on from my hand. It was dim, but I could make out who it was. It was Marcus. At first, I thought it was Callon. They were both so similar looking.

I can't believe I didn't notice it before. Their beliefs were incredibly different, though.

He stepped forward, out of the passageway, and said, "It's a little late to be out of bed, don't you think?"

"Uh…" I stumbled. I didn't know what to say. All I thought about was the unending punishment and grief I would get once Callon found out I was out.

Marcus raised his hand and calmly said, "Easy. Calm down, Zeke. Just tell me why you are out of bed."

"Ah, okay, yeah," I said still not completely calmed down. "I was out… um… just to go to the bathroom?"

No way was Marcus going to believe that. He could see through my lies, and it didn't help that I stuttered on almost every word.

"Really? Did you know that the bathrooms are right next to the barracks?"

"Oh," I said. Crap. "I must've gotten lost. It is a pretty dark cave."

Marcus nodded. "Did you just see me agree with you?"

"Yeah…" I answered.

"Then I guess it is not that dark."

He caught me. I should've seen that coming. Now, since he was an Instructor, he would have to rat on me, and then Callon would make sure my punishment was so severe that my arms would hurt for months.

I said, lowering my head due to cowardice, "What are you going to do?"

He rubbed his chin and said, "Hmm… well, I could tell Callon." My skin began to shiver. Would

Marcus really turn me in? Then again, did he have a choice? He wasn't in charge anymore. I was done for. "But, I think if you go back to your barracks right now, we will pretend like this never happened."

"Really?" I said genuinely surprised. "You are going to let me off the hook? Just like that?"

"Oh no, you aren't getting off that easy. I say, for punishment, I walk back with you to your barracks and you can tell me everything that has happened since I have been gone. Also, tell me why you were out so late," he said.

That sounded like a trap, but it was better than getting the snot beat out of me by Callon. If this is what Marcus wanted, I guess I would give it to him. A friend to a friend perhaps.

We began to walk down the hallway. I held out my hand and let the dim light guide us both, but Marcus held his hand out in front of me and pulled out a flashlight. He led the way with the light shining the caverns ahead of us.

"So… where do you want to start?" I whispered.

He thought for a second. "How about we start with the matter at hand? Why were you out of bed past curfew, Zeke?"

I didn't know how to respond. Should I lie, or should I be honest? Different excuses floated through my mind bumping into one another, each one not making any sense to me. I looked up at Marcus and decided to tell the truth. Hopefully, he would understand. I told him about what had happened while I helped Callon fix the generator and that I was on my way to see if someone was really down there, and if there was, find out why he was there.

"Interesting," Marcus said. "However, you can't just sneak out of your room. This isn't New York." He glared at me. It wasn't allowed in New York either.

"I know… and I'm sorry." I wasn't really sorry. I was just sorry that I happened to be caught.

"Ezekiel." He used my full name. That was something my mother used to do when I was in serious trouble, and I didn't like it. I sound like an old person. He said, "You are just going to have to trust Callon on this one. Talk to him. Maybe he will give you the answers you seek without having to break any rules, and if by chance someone is locked in that room, you will just have to trust Callon's instincts. He isn't that bad of a guy, really. He would take a bullet for you if he could I bet."

"You are not the first person to tell me that, Marcus. I was debating this for a long time, and I got mixed reactions from my idea."

"Well… yeah, and you always will if it's a dumb idea," he laughed a little. "I'm sorry if I'm being hard on you, but you need to just let things be. You can't be sneaking around and trying to fix things that may not be broken. We are on your side. We are just trying to help."

I said, "I don't need this little 'team' talk, Marcus. Callon has made it clear that I need to step up and show the Clade that I am really my father's son. That is unfair. I don't even know the guy and he never even bothered to come see me once. Why should I care about him? If anything, I should try to not be like him. I would love my children."

Marcus stepped in front of me. The light from the flashlight burned bright in my eyes. His face looked like a silhouette in the darkness.

He said, "How dare you. Don't say that about your father. He did what he had to do, and for all you know, he was there with you the entire time while you grew up. He just couldn't be there because he was always on the run from the Agency."

I stepped back. "Easy, Marcus. What has gotten into you? Didn't you say that you hated Liam for all the stuff he did to you?"

Marcus eased back and took a few deep breaths and thought to himself. He said, "Yes… I did say that, but I was wrong to. I now understand the sacrifices Liam had to make and I finally accepted that. Now look at us. We are a perfect pair. I'm excited to see where our relationship will go."

"Good for you, Marcus, but you aren't me," I said. "Is my father even that great of a guy?"

Dead serious, Marcus said, "Your father is the reason why we are all still alive today. You should be honored that you are his child."

"Really?" I said. "Because, it seems like everyone here wants to just pick on me and beat on me for being different." I released a lot of energy and let it flow rapidly into my palm. A bright light formed. I felt the pain of the Overload. I was absorbed in the heat of the moment. "This power I have. It's not a gift. It's a curse. How come I'm different than everyone else? I'm sick and tired of being talked about behind my back as if I'm some kind of object or tool at the Clade's disposal."

Marcus didn't say anything as I simmered down to just a frustrated smolder. There was just too much going on in my life right now. I can't handle the stress. The Gauntlet was tomorrow, and I was stuck working a job day after day that does nothing to help the Clade be free from the war. I had so much power to donate to the Clade that I would happily give it if it would mean freeing us all someday, but nobody gave me any answers. I wondered why I had electric powers and no one else did? What is Operation: Zeke Laufor I wondered. There were just so many things that didn't make sense to me that I wanted to explode.

Marcus said after a short break, "I'm sorry you feel that way, but do you feel any better now?"

I kept breathing deeply and said, "A little, but not much. There is just too much going on right now to even think."

Marcus stepped out of my way, and we began to walk towards the barracks again. He said soothingly, "It's alright, really. I was in your position before. I was young and hated every second that I spent here in the Clade, but I promise you, Zeke. Someday, you will be told everything, and you will see why everything had to be done the way they were. You are in the dark now, literally and figuratively, but soon, you will be in the light."

I said, "I can't wait for that to happen. It'll be the day pigs fly."

He laughed to himself. I didn't. I was dead serious. I didn't think any of us were going to get out of here, and I didn't think that I would get all of the information I am supposed to have.

Marcus said, "Trust me. I know you will learn everything you need to before the Clade is over with. However long that may be."

There was a short silence as we thought about the deepness of that statement. Until now, it has only been me talking about the end of the Clade, but Marcus thought about it too. Did he think it was close, or were we just the beginning of something that would last for generations? More importantly, could we stop the Agency from ending it prematurely?

We made the turn towards the barracks when Marcus said, "What do you think of this place? What about the Test and the Gauntlet? Callon told me some things about your performance in the Test and Gauntlet. I have to say I'm impressed."

I laughed a little. "Callon didn't seem so impressed."

Marcus shrugged. "Don't worry about what Callon thinks all of the time. Sure, he is a Head Instructor and is very important to how this division of the Clade runs, but he is still just a person. He can be killed no matter how powerful he is. Nobody is a god. Even the strongest can die if you believe in your abilities."

I wasn't sure, I thought. Callon seemed like the kind of person who had no weaknesses. He had every aspect thought out. He probably was the one who put Marcus on the steps to guard the basement level. Then again, maybe Marcus knew I was going to go down there. He did talk to Callon about me today after the Council meeting. So much has been happening these past few days that my head began to spin. I hoped it would all be over tomorrow…

…in the final round of the Gauntlet.

I told Marcus about everything that had happened to me in the Test and the Gauntlet. I told him about my job cleaning bathrooms and my performance in the Gauntlet as well as Sarah's and Trish's. He seemed impressed by their performance as well, but truly happy that I won my round. We connected really well probably because he Instructed me back in New York. Does everyone have that kind of bond with their Instructor, or is there something more between Marcus and I that I haven't found out about yet?

He stopped in front of the entrance to the boy's barracks and said, "Callon did tell me one thing today before the Council ended."

I knew it. "What was that?" I asked.

Marcus looked down upon me with grave eyes. They seemed truly frightened, but for what reason? "Callon informed me about the incident that occurred while Juliette escorted you, Sarah, and Trish here. He told me about your Overload."

"Oh," I said. "No need to worry about it though. It's not that big of a deal. I have control of my abilities. Anyways, have a good night."

I tried to rush through this part of our conversation. Somehow, I knew that he knew about the Overload. I rushed towards the curtain, but he grabbed me and pushed me backwards. I stumbled but caught myself before I fell.

He said, "This is no joking matter, Zeke. I'm afraid this is actually a serious problem. Only one other Recruit had ever had an Overload, Shiloh Webber, a Bloodling, a term I can use now that you know about them, and he was in serious danger. His life was filled with pain after that… just don't push yourself tomorrow, okay?"

His face looked as if it was being scrunched together by an outside force. Marcus looked truly in pain.

I said, "Relax. I will take it easy. I just don't want you to worry about me. That's all."

Marcus smiled a little. "I always worry about you. Now, get to bed and rest up for the Gauntlet tomorrow. You are going up against some pretty tough competition. I know. I read some of their files."

I said, my hand placed on the curtain, "You don't have to remind me. Have a good night, Marcus."

"You too," he said to me. "And, if you ever need anything, tell me. If your Overload begins to tear you apart, tell me. I can help treat it."

"Okay, thank you," I whispered as the curtain fell silently behind me.

I stood in the completely dead and dark space waiting for anyone to move. Slowly, I made my way back to my bunk, fatigue starting to set in. I counted down the number of bunks in the middle row until I found mine, at least I hoped. I crawled up and tucked myself back in without making a peep and closed my eyes.

Tomorrow was going to be the last big day for another three months until the Gauntlet starts up again. Then again, Juliette was Head Instructor now. Perhaps, she could get Sarah, Trish, and I out of here, maybe even Teddy.

I couldn't see him, I couldn't see anyone, but I knew Teddy was just a few bunks away from me. He requested that he would be close to me. That meant, unfortunately, that he would have a bottom bunk. The poor guy wanted the top one so badly. Even I wanted the top bunk more than anything when I got the chance to sleep in a bunk bed when I was younger.

He would be okay here, I thought. His ability is amazing. I don't know how he would use it in the Gauntlet three months from now. Although, he still had a lot of Instructing to go through before he had to worry about controlling it. It was powerful, alright. It could kill anyone he so chose.

Eventually, sleep overtook me. I didn't dream. I was too exhausted to. Instead, my subconscious floated through limbo inside my brain with thoughts of the Gauntlet and Bruno ravaging the interior. He has been a bully since he first won the Gauntlet over a year ago, and it was up to me too stop him. Would I risk pushing the Overload further to beat him? I told myself at the beginning of this tournament that I wouldn't succumb to Callon's ways of testing the strengths and weaknesses of Recruits, but it was too late now. I have to fight.

And I will win.

Chapter 33

Morning came way too fast for my own good. I guess staying up half of the night doesn't help keep you awake and ready to fight. My muscles and bones ached. I don't think they completely healed from the first rounds of the Gauntlet, or Overload was wreaking its havoc on me again in my sleep.

I forced myself up and out of bed shortly after everyone else was getting ready. I slid down the ladder and got ready to take a shower when Bruno and his lackeys walked up behind me giving me a shove onto the lower bed of the bunk.

"Today is finally the day, Laufor," Bruno said his face directly over mine as I lay on my back. "Today is the day I get to pound you into the arena dirt." He sneered loudly, his lackeys laughing behind him.

"We'll just see about that, Bruno," I said forcing myself up onto my elbows and then on my feet. Bruno stepped backwards, intimidated by my retort.

Bruno didn't respond. Instead, he pointed at me and walked away. Weasel-Face and his other follower laughed until they left the barracks.

I groaned and dug in the garbage bag underneath my bunk bed for a clean cloak. They were always wrinkled, but at least they were clean. I felt bad for the person whose job it was to clean these.

I felt a finger begin to poke me in the back as I pulled out a clean cloak. I thought it was Bruno, so I spun around quickly and grabbed their finger, growling as I did it. It wasn't Bruno or any of his lackeys. It was Teddy. He seemed really frightened about what I did.

"Oh, I'm sorry, Teddy," I apologized. "I thought you were someone else."

He rubbed his finger gently. Looking down at the floor, he said, "It's okay. Who is Bruno? Was he the guy giving you a hard time before?"

"Yeah," I said wrapping my cloak around my arm. "He likes to give everyone a hard time but especially me. I don't know why, but it doesn't matter. I think he is just afraid of my power."

"Ah," Teddy said. "Well, if you do to Bruno what you did to McMan, I think you will be fine."

I laughed. "I'll try my best, but he has abilities too."

Teddy asked, "So, if you don't mind my asking, what is the Gauntlet? People are going crazy over it. It's the last round of it whatever it is."

I said, "It's hard to explain. It's kind of like a tournament to see who is the strongest fighter is here. The stronger you are, the better job you get. That's why so many people take the Gauntlet seriously and just want to win. Bruno has won it the past four times. I am one of the final ten fighting today. I have to stop him."

Teddy said, "Okay, I think I get what you are saying. So, you are going to beat up on your friends just for a dumb job?"

"Yes, I guess that is the simplest way to put it."

Teddy thought to himself. "Huh, that's the dumbest thing I've ever heard, and I'm not even a teenager yet."

"You're telling me, Teddy."

I went to the bathrooms and got ready. I tried to keep my energy up all day by putting hardly any effort into cleaning the bathroom floors. I figure the toilets could last one day without me scrubbing every square inch of the bowl.

An idea could tell you if it's brilliant or not if a child says it sounds dumb. The Gauntlet would be one of those ideas. Callon should have discussed this with Barbara and a few others before implementing a device like the Gauntlet. I understood the idea behind it, but pitting Recruit against Recruit, friend against friend, is silly. It was hard to form solid friendships and relationships in the Clade when Callon was destroying them. He wanted us to be soldiers, not friends. It was truly sad. Everyone there was divided and on their own. In New York, everyone was equal. Everyone got along and worked together, even when the Agency attacked. What would happen in that case here? Would certain

Recruits, Bruno specifically, throw other Recruits into battle to protect his sorry self? That is how civil wars started. Different ideas cause a division between supposed allies. These old allies then fight until only one was left standing, and in the end, you just wanted your friend back, but it was too late. Their blood was on your hands.

I still felt terrible for what I did to Wallace. I never spoke a word to the guy except for when I was in the infirmary visiting Sarah. He said he was okay with all that had happened, but his body expressions said something different. It doesn't matter the situation, you don't hurt your partners. Now, I don't think we could ever be friends. Any hopes for a possible friendship have been destroyed because of Callon and the Gauntlet.

There were no real relationships in the Colorado Clade. In the lunch room, everyone is silent. Recruits will sit with other Recruits they are familiar with, but my table is the only one that would speak. It was eerie. I kept feeling as though people were giving us annoyed stares. After that began, I started to whisper most of what I say during lunch and dinner time in the cafeteria.

All of this built up inside of me as I scrubbed the bathroom. The more and more I pushed my hand across the wet floor, the more I didn't want to fight, but there was no getting around it. First of all, people were counting on me. I had to stop Bruno. Nobody told me that other than my true friends, but I could tell that people were relying on me by the way they made odd looks and hopeful stares at me. Second, I fought my way to the finals. I only took down one person myself, but I still put up a fight to stay in the game. I could've let Wallace take me down, or I could've just jumped in the pit and gave up, but then Callon would have had my head for sure.

This particular Gauntlet was especially important for him because he wants to see what I am made of, and lastly, if I just quit, that would bring huge amounts of shame to Marcus. How would it look if his star Recruit just gave up when a fight approached? No, I knew I would have to fight...

...but, maybe I wouldn't have to be the one to hurt the others? A plan began to formulate in my head as the bell for lunch rang. I threw my supplies back to where they were supposed to go and quickly walked to the cafeteria and ate as much as possible before the others showed up. I saw Teddy walk in with Sarah and Trish. He sat down with us as well. He made a disgusted look at the off-color goop he was expected to eat, so we gave him some tips on how to eat it.

"If you keep your tongue away from the little green bits, it's not that bad," I said.

He said, "Yuck!" as a spoonful of goop slithered off the utensil and onto the tray.

I helped him eat a portion of it just so I could have enough energy for the Gauntlet. I may have formulated a plan where I wouldn't directly hurt anyone, but I still needed energy to do it.

Lunch was just a few minutes away from being over. After that short period of time, the Clade would gather and watch the final round of the Gauntlet unfold. If I was going to come out close to the top, I would need McKayla's help. She and I were both in the final round, and with her ability combined with mine, we had a strong chance of winning.

"Hey, McKayla," I said casually. "Could I talk to you for a minute?"

Confused, she said, "Sure."

I got up and walked to a table where we could be alone to talk about the upcoming finale of the Gauntlet. It wasn't a secret to the others, but they would just be a distraction, and we didn't have all the time in the world. Now that McKayla was being open and friendly, she was easy to talk to.

She sat down across from me and asked, "What's on your mind?"

"I have a plan for the finals of the Gauntlet. I was wondering if you would hear me out and help," I said.

"I will here you out. I was actually hoping that we would work together. With Daniel and Bruno in the finals, it will be hard for us to win individually. Riley and Trish worked together just on Daniel and got defeated without Daniel even breaking a sweat."

"Exactly what I was thinking," I said. "Okay, here is my plan. I'm sure you know by now that my ability is... slightly different from any other Recruit."

"Yes, I did notice that when you blasted Wallace into the arena ceiling."

"Okay, good. You see, McKayla, my ability is very versatile. When I was in New York, there was a terrible fire that nearly destroyed the entire basement level of the building we hid in. The only way to get to the source of the fire was for Sarah and me to use our abilities in unison."

"And, how did you do that?" She asked me.

"It was confusing at first. I found out that it requires a certain amount of energy usage by me. I put my hands up in the air and released energy into a ball of water she made around us. After I did that, Sarah said she had an easier time controlling her ability."

Puzzled, McKayla asked, "How so? That sounds really complicated."

I shook my head. "I really don't know. I had the easy part. Sarah just told me to keep releasing electricity into the water. It didn't electrocute her because the water didn't touch us, but she said it was easier. I asked her what she meant by that as well and she said that it was as if she could control the single water molecules and arrange them in any way she wanted."

"Do you think it will have the same effect on me?"

I just shrugged. "I have no idea. It was just a guess, but I saw what you can do. I figured if we stand close together and use our abilities at the same time, we could do some real damage. Possibly place us as the last two left in the Gauntlet."

"It's worth a shot, but best case scenario, we are both left standing. What do we do then? Should we actually fight to win?"

I didn't know an answer to that yet, but my only goal was to take down Bruno. I guess McKayla could win, and I could take second, which was fine by me. Granted, that could mean my position as bathroom scrubber may stay a little bit longer.

"I don't know yet," I answered. "We will cross that bridge when we come to it."

She nodded keeping eye contact with me. "Sounds like a plan."

On cue, the bell rang. The Recruits began to shuffle and mumble around. I watched them all move as one uniform group towards the cafeteria exit while Bruno passed me by and gave me a death stare. The showdown would soon begin.

Before any of the Recruits escaped the cafeteria, Callon walked in. The Recruits backed up and silenced immediately like Callon's trained pets. It made me sick, but I wanted to hear what he had to say.

He said, "Recruits, the last few days have been long and stressful for us all. From the Gauntlet to the Council meeting yesterday, it seemed as though these days would never pass, and the sheer weight of the tasks ahead would bury us, but this is not the case! Today, the final round of the Gauntlet will take place. I would like everyone to follow myself, Barbara, and Juliette down to the arena except for the ten finalists. You should remain here until Stewart and Laura take you down themselves."

Callon turned and nodded to Stewart who was at his side as usual. He ran to the far corner of the cafeteria and said, "All Recruits participating in the finals please come by me. Everyone else, please go with Callon to the viewing area."

The Recruits immediately began to move towards their host. McKayla and I rose from the table and began to walk towards Stewart, but not without stopping to get some inspirational words, hugs, and other kind gestures from our friends. Through those few moments, all I thought about was how I was going to defeat Bruno for them. If Bruno was knocked off his high horse, the Clade would be a much more peaceful place. At least, that's what I hoped.

We relinquished each other and headed towards our Instructors. McKayla and I were the last two to arrive by Stewart. Even Bruno beat us to my own amazement.

Once all of the other Recruits were grouped together, he nodded in Stewart's direction and said, "Good. Now, follow me, and keep together."

He left with all of the other Recruits following. It took a minute for all of the Recruits to squeeze out single file through the small opening in the wall, but, eventually, they were gone. Suddenly, my nerves began to take control of me. I was so calm a few moments ago, but my head must be realizing that I would be in a fight soon.

The footsteps of the Recruit horde echoed down the cavern. After that vanished and all of the Recruits had made it down the steps, Stewart said, "Alright. Now, we may go over the rules of the final round."

Bruno sneered and said, "There is no point, Stewart. You might as well save your breath. These nubs aren't going to beat me."

What a cocky thing. He said that even in front of Daniel who actually seemed a little scared, but he was bigger than him!? What could Bruno have been hiding?

Stewart said, as he glared slightly at the four time consecutive champion, "Thank you for that, Bruno, but there are some Recruits here who have never been in the finals."

Ruby then joined in, "Yeah, Bruno. How about you just be quiet for a few minutes? I'm sure it wouldn't kill you, and, if it by some miracle it did, then the world would be a much better place anyways."

Bruno created a gruesome grin. "Ruby, I'll make sure you are the first one I eliminate."

She gulped. Suddenly, she wished she hadn't said that. Good thing McKayla and I were being silent, but Bruno still gave us death stares, mostly to me.

There were no words spoken for a short period of time when Stewart continued. "Okay, now that you have all said what needed to be said, here are the rules. Unlike the previous rounds of the Gauntlet, there will be only one victor and that victor, therefore, will be the Gauntlet champion. Again, it's an anything goes match. Don't expect to win if you aren't expecting to kill your opponent. If someone is in life threatening danger, Laura and I will call it off and escort the victim off of the arena floor. Safety is our number one priority."

Yeah, that made perfect sense. Safety was the most important thing here that was why we wanted us to fight each other almost to the death. Callon was ridiculous, I thought. This was only going to get people seriously injured. A few Recruits still limped or wore bandages covering up bloodied wounds from the first round two days ago, and being in the same round as Bruno will only make things worse.

Stewart finished, "Are there any last questions before we begin?"

Nobody spoke. I wanted to raise my hand ask if I could leave, but that probably would not have worked out. I'm going to take a wild guess.

Clapping his hands together, Stewart said, "Excellent. Follow me then to the waiting area. There, Callon will call out your names again. However, you will be given a full thirty seconds while Callon announces the opening to get ready to fight."

Callon's ego was starting to intrude on my happiness. It was typical that he would need to give a big speech to pump up the Recruits watching. I thought this was only to see who worked the hardest and deserved to have a better job, to be a better leader. If that was the case, then why do these fights have to be viewed by the entire Clade? It was a mandatory event. Callon had made it clear that he wanted everyone to view this. Juliette better get me out of here soon, or I will snap!

Stewart led the ten of us out of the cafeteria and to the steps. We went down in a single-file line with McKayla and me in the back. We reached the basement level and turned towards the daunting metal door that faced us at the end of the corridor. As a group, we moved swiftly to the end of the Gauntlet. However, I didn't enter without having one last glimpse behind us to see the intersection in the cavern where a person was locked in.

The Recruits watched as we, the ten champions, made our way to the portal at the end of the viewing section. One by one, we disappeared behind the curtain and down the dark descent. McKayla and I reached the bottom and entered the waiting room that had become all too familiar to me in the most horrible way imaginable.

We gathered in a semicircle around the covered opening to the arena. There were no words spoken, only harsh looks. Friends didn't exist down here. All relationships died when you descended the stairwell. Only enemies existed in the waiting room of the arena, and only winners and losers exist in the arena. I gave back all of the hateful and disgusted stares except to McKayla and gave them especially to Bruno.

Then, over the incredible loudness of the silence, Callon's voice rose. "Hello, Recruits! Thank you for joining me in this final round of the Gauntlet! It has been entertaining and the ten Recruits fighting soon have shown that they have worked hard to improve their strength to where it is now. All of you should watch and take mental notes. These are the Recruits that you should aspire to be. With hard work and dedication, even you can become an Instructor. That is how I started, Stewart, Laura, and even Juliette."

A few Recruits applauded the speech and one shouted out, "Go Ariella!" He was silenced shortly after.

"Now," Callon continued. "I would like to introduce to you the final ten Recruits!"

There was a short pause, probably because he had to unfold the slip of paper Stewart usually gave Callon. Then, he began, "First, Ruby Adams!" There was a short applause. Then, Callon shouted, "Rafael Butros!"

The names were called off in the order in which the Recruits won. After each name was called, there was a short applause and a few cheers for that person. The Recruit would then break the semicircle of Recruits and enter the arena.

Bruno was called out next. The audience grew louder and more rowdy when he walked into the arena, not without punching his fist into his hand at me. I growled to myself and thought about all of the things I would do to him in the arena. I pictured his body being vaporized by lightning. That cheered me up as well as surged my body with adrenaline. I'd never felt more alive than I did then.

"McKayla Forwing!" Callon shouted.

I turned to her and gave her an encouraging thumbs up. She nodded back and said, "Remember the plan. Look for me out there."

"Will do. I'll be out shortly," I said back.

She stepped out into the arena with only a few audible claps except for a few loud cheerers in the corner. I knew immediately, without looking at their faces, that it was Riley, Trish, and Sarah. I laughed to myself a little and got ready for my name to be called.

There was a pause, and then, "Ezekiel Laufor!"

I took a deep breath in and out, and made my way for the arena. I didn't make eye contact with any of the other Recruits waiting to be called out, but Daniel was hard not to notice. He appeared as a boulder in the corner of my eye. I felt slightly intimidated, but then shook it off when I heard the crowd cheer for me. It wasn't much, a few claps here and there, but the one's that mattered most to me came from my friends in the corner like I predicted.

I pushed away the curtain and stepped into the arena looking just the same as it did before. Trish, Riley, Teddy, Liam, and Sarah kept clapping as I approached them. They appeared to be happy, but none of them were. They were all worried for our safety, especially Teddy, but Liam talked to him until he was soothed. Those two were really close. It was like Teddy was the son Liam never had the chance to have.

McKayla hid near the corner of the cage just beneath our friends. I gave a wink up to them and put my game face back on.

Stepping next to McKayla and putting my back to the fence, I said, "You ready?"

"Yeah, I am even beginning to charge up as we speak. This will give us a head start while the other Recruits are called out."

And, they were. The other Recruits were called out in the same order that they won their rounds. For each one, there was a slight pause for adoration from the audience, and then they took their position. Most of the Recruits stood next to another Recruit that was already in position to fight. It looked as though the other Recruits thought the same as McKayla and I. There is safety in numbers, and instead of a free-for-all, it appeared as though the fight would be between five groups of two.

Things got seriously bad when Daniel was called out. There was a loud cheer for him from his supporters and he took his position… next to Bruno! They shook hands and grinned. What was going on? They were partners?

"Umm… McKayla?" I pushed out noticing what was going on.

"Bruno and Daniel are always together, but Bruno always beats out Daniel for the victory when they are the only ones left. It makes sense that the two powerhouses teamed up together. Bruno may be a jerk, but he isn't an idiot. He knew after his first Gauntlet that Daniel would be an asset to him so he befriended him just for the Gauntlet. Little does Daniel know, but he could probably take us all out himself," she said still focusing her will into one huge attack when the fight begins.

Finally, after Kristie was called out, Callon stood again. While he was standing up and getting ready to speak, I saw Juliette and Barbara at his sides. It was odd to see Juliette up there. I always pictured Callon and Barbara as my enemies, but with her up there, they looked more friendly; however, they were the one's putting me through this. Before Callon spoke, I caught a glimpse of Juliette nodding at me. She believed in me, and I believed in myself. I wasn't going to lose. Not to Bruno, at least.

Callon said, "The time is almost here. I will give you a few moments to prepare your strategies and battle tactics. When the start is nearing, I will count down from ten. Good luck to you all!"

A few of the Recruits spoke to their unofficial partner discussing about who they would go after first. I didn't know that for sure, but by the way they looked at the other pairs, it appeared as though they were sizing each other up. A couple groups gave McKayla and me a glance and nodded or shook their heads at us. Bruno was one that nodded his head.

I asked McKayla quietly, "What do you think?"

She shook her head and groaned, "I don't know. If anything, the two behind the rock in front of us will be a problem as well as the two to the left. Bruno and Daniel are all the way across the arena, so they shouldn't be a problem, but watch out for Daniel's ability. It's a killer."

"Okay, good plan," I said. After a few more moments, I said, "Are you okay? You sounded in pain?"

Gritting her teeth, she said, "I'm almost at a full power blast, but it hurts to hold it in for so long. Also, it takes a lot out of me. I hope your idea works."

"It should. Don't worry," I said; although, I was incredibly worried. What if my ability decided not to work or blow back in our faces? What would we do then? If it does, hopefully it knocks us both out. Then, the others, especially Bruno, can't get an easy knock out.

Then, Callon began the countdown. "Recruits, you have 10 seconds…"

He began to count down from there. My heart beat loudly as each second was counted eventually speeding up as he got closer to one. My nerves began to emerge, and I wanted to fight now. My body surged with sheer power. I kept thinking of inspirational moments in movies like "Remember the Titans" and "Never Back Down."

I took a quick look at the now, three Instructors stationed at different positions around the arena. Stewart and Laura were close to each other while Marcus was between McKayla and I and the group to our left. Something tells me he chose that position after McKayla got here. He looked over to me and winked without breaking facial pose.

"5…4…3…" Callon counted.

The audience went silent. Callon went silent. The entire world went silent in my mind. Then, like an alarm clock cutting through peaceful sleep, "Begin!"

Chapter 34

All of the Recruits bolted to whomever they wanted to battle. Bruno and Daniel fought against Ariella and Shane. They came at them so quickly that Shane was immediately knocked to the ground hard by Bruno's fist while a large, stone block shifted from its place and slid at Ariella clipping her in the side. She tumbled until she hit the metal cage.

Bruno ran up to Ariella and grabbed her by the neck. Falling on top of her, he squeezed her neck tightly until her face grew red and she began to choke. She tried to get him off, but he was just too large.

Suddenly, Shane ran up from behind and flung himself at Bruno with one fist cocked back, but it failed. Bruno was ready for his attack and quickly swung one arm backwards hard smashing into his face. He flew and skidded across the ground and into a block surrounding the center of the arena. A bloodied cheek was all that remained of his attempt at knocking Bruno off of his ally. Instead of trying to fight, he struggled to get up, but only fell back down to the ground while Ariella struggled to be freed.

Laura ran in rapidly and immediately called off Bruno before Ariella passed out. He got off of her and stood with his arms held high in the air celebrating her early exit from the Gauntlet.

He didn't forget about Shane, though. He sprinted over to Shane before Daniel could get to him and lifted him high over his head. How is he that strong!? Bruno squeezed Shane's leg in one hand and his neck in the other. Lifting him high above his head, Bruno chuckled to Daniel and spiked Shane's weak body at the rock floor.

The sight was sickening. Blood splattered the tan floor like paint on a wall. Shane's body cracked and rolled over itself. Laura called Shane out shortly after not even checking to see if he could still fight. No one could've still been conscious after that brutal hit. It was disgusting how much power Bruno had.

It appeared as though McKayla and I were the only one's not to move from our original position besides one other group hidden behind the rock in front of us. I kept my focus on them and waited in case one of them were to attack us. McKayla was almost at full power and ready to unleash her deadly wind with my help. We just needed a little more time.

Suddenly, McKayla screamed, "Zeke, look left!"

I turned to the left and saw two Recruits, Isaac, Bruno's weasel-faced friend, and Kristie. Bruno must've wanted Isaac to go first to see if we were even worth his time. I almost completely forgot about them. I was too focused on the group in front of us.

Isaac came quickly sprinting hard in front of Kristie. I didn't think. My only job was to protect McKayla until her ability was ready to be used. I ran at him as well with my hand folded into a fist behind my back. As he approached, I let my hand fill with a small charge that should do a good amount of damage without tiring me out.

He swung first from his right. I caught it with my left hand sending a small amount of pain down my arm. Then, I unleashed my electrified right hand at his chest straight on as a jab. Even if he did block it, he would be in for a world of hurt.

He wasn't quick enough to block it. I punched him straight in the chest causing him to only stumble back a few feet, but that wasn't where the damage came from. He caught himself from falling and immediately dropped to the ground convulsing as the electricity coursed through him.

The sight didn't make me forget about Kristie behind him. She kept her distance after seeing what a punch from me can do. A standoff was formed between her and me around Isaac still recuperating on the ground.

Slowly, she put her hand behind her back and waited. I did the same and charged up another electrified punch. What was she hiding behind her back, I wondered. I kept on my toes in case the worst happened.

It did. She pulled out her hand and revealed a deep red and orange flame in her hand. Suddenly, she cocked back and through it at me fast. The fireball was travelling rapidly towards my body. I didn't think. I only acted. If I were to dive out of the way, the fireball would collide with McKayla behind me. The damage would cause her to lose her focus, and it might knock her out.

I had to hold my ground and stop the fireball from reaching me. I dug deep and pulled out a little more energy and fired a bolt of electricity at the ball. Hoping to repel it, I used a little more energy than needed. The bolt collided with the fireball piercing through it as if it wasn't there. The fireball exploded causing bits of fire and sparks to rain down on Isaac as he was finally getting up from my attack. The fire floated down like snow on a winter morning and stuck to his skin. He cried out and tried covering every bit of exposed skin including his face.

The lightning bolt continued to travel until it collided with Kristie a few yards away from Isaac. The jolt knocked her back off her feet and onto the ground. She convulsed and rolled onto her side where she bent into the fetal position trying to fight off the jitters.

Since those two would be down for a few moments, I ran back to McKayla. "Are you ready to go, yet?"

"In about five seconds I will be," she said.

I looked around the arena to the remaining six Recruits that would have to be taken down by the coming storm. Isaac and Kristie were still shaken, burned, and electrified. Bruno and Daniel were in the middle around the pit fighting off Ruby and Rafael.

They were all on a different side of the pit slowly walking in a circle keeping their eyes locked on their target. Ruby had her back to me when Daniel clasped his hand around the air and pulled it towards him as though he was pulling an invisible cord. Confused, Ruby didn't think anything of it. Maybe it was just a weird reflex to something, but I knew it wasn't.

Then, the rock in front of me began to move back and forth slightly. I knew what was coming, and I don't think Ruby did. I was about to call out, but it was too late. The big boulder left its position and slid slowly towards Ruby's back.

I was about to run in and get her away from the rock, but Isaac and Kristie were getting back on their feet. She was going to have to be on her own.

Isaac got back on his feet with a few burns along his cheek and his right hand. He touched his burned cheek and cringed in pain. "You... How *dare* you! No more playing around!"

He stood in place and took a deep breath. I braced myself for whatever was coming while charging up another weak blast. I have been using my ability too much, and now the Overload was beginning to hurt me.

He formed an O with his mouth and blew. At first, nothing happened, but then, a strong blast of wind lifted me off my feet and hurled me into the rock wall behind me. I smacked it hard enough to get the Head Instructor's attention. They looked down at me while the strong wind continued to hold me in place. No way could Isaac hold his attack for much longer, then I would blast him with another bolt.

I forced my head to the right to see what had become of Ruby. I saw Bruno, Daniel, and Rafael, but Ruby was gone. Instead, a large boulder had replaced her spot around the pit. She must've been forced into the pit by the boulder. Now, Rafael was fighting alone against all six of us. It could be four if I didn't do something quickly.

It was Kristie's turn now. While I was pinned to the wall, she came to and raised her hand in the air. A loud, rumbling, sound rose from deep within the mountain. It sounded like a train approaching a stop too fast. The rumbling and moaning silenced as soon as a geyser of water erupted from the pit like what Sarah did in her round.

While the geyser blasted water into the metal ceiling, Kristie used her other hand and pulled a stream off of the main cylinder. It was like she was pulling a strand of string cheese. The water circled her like a snake and halted besides her float-ing in the air.

Isaac said, "Are you going to finish him?" How did he say that without the wind dying down?

Kristie nodded, "Yeah, just give me a minute. It takes a lot of energy to change states."

That didn't sound good. I tried to force myself off the rock, but the wind was too powerful. If my feet were on the ground, I could push my way through the turbulent gust. Even if my hand could wiggle, I would be able to shock Isaac and stop the wind. He was stronger than I previously conceived. I guess that goes to show never underestimate your opponent even if he is a Weasel Faced scumbag.

No matter how much I forced my body to move free from the wall, it wouldn't budge. Kristie had been gathering a lot of her energy into this one attack. I watched the water slowly twirl and spin through the air beside her as if it was her pet.

Suddenly, the snake-like stream of water began to freeze solid from the tail moving towards the now spiked head. The water flowed slower and slower until the icy mist overtook it leaving only a spear of ice when the entire stream was frozen.

Kristie took a deep breath, "Alright, it's ready."

Weasel Face nodded not risking saying anything in the case the wind would lose contact with me, and I'd be free. Unfortunately, he wasn't taking any chances.

I yelled, "McKayla, a little help here!"

She said, "I'm almost done... just hold on, Zeke!"

Kristie grunted and said smugly, "You aren't getting out of this one, Laufor. It's time to meet your maker."

The ice spear hovered over her hand while she pulled back. The ice spear followed the track of her hand getting itself ready to be launched at me.

That's when I heard shouts from the audience besides me. "Zeke! Do something!" Trish called out. All of a sudden, all of my friends began to shout and cry out for me to do something. Even Liam got on his feet and started screaming at me in his backwoods English.

Weasel Face was getting blue in the face when McKayla called out, "I'm done! Hold on, Zeke!"

With that, she flung her arms around her body in a semicircle from left to right. At first, nothing immediately happened. I thought that her ability had failed her, or maybe she didn't gather enough energy.

Kristie just laughed and said, "Wow, all of that prepping for nothing? Too bad, now you have to be taken down."

I shut my eyes tightly and braced myself for the ice spear to make an impact, but that never came. Instead, a strong wind, the strongest I have ever experienced, blew from an invisible source. Actually, it was the air already in the room that McKayla used. She charged her energy and successfully released her cyclonic attack.

The wind was even stronger than Weasel-Face's ability. If I couldn't move off the wall before, there was no way I would be able to get off of it now, but I wouldn't be alone. I tried to open my eyes and watched as Weasel Face and Kristie were lifted off of the ground and flung at the wall with such force that the rock actually cracked a little. Blood began to drip from their bodies only to get sucked up by the double hurricane force winds.

They weren't the only ones affected by the wind. Everyone in the audience gripped onto each other and the benches they sat on to keep themselves in place. For some, they weren't strong enough and were thrown into other Recruits knocking them off of their seats.

Bruno and Daniel were being pushed furiously by the prevailing winds. However, Bruno was able to get behind a boulder before the wind swept him away. For Daniel, he wasn't as lucky. The wind picked him up and threw him at the Recruit absorbing wall like the rest of us. McKayla kept her feet planted on the ground and made sure they didn't move. She was in the center of the vortex and would be safe there minus the bad hair day she would have after this.

A scream was heard over the whipping wind. The audience and I turned our heads towards the pit and saw Rafael tumbling on the ground only to end up plummeting into the pit. His screams were shortly muffled out by the storm.

McKayla kept her arms to her side trying her best to hold the strength of the wind while she said, "Zeke! I can't hold this much longer! You have to do something quick! Use your ability!"

I knew I had to use my ability and it was up to me to put an end to anyone stuck to the wall. I just hoped that my ability wouldn't fry me in the process. Normally, electricity striking me wouldn't hurt, but now, things were different. I could be injured easily by myself.

Twisting my head, I saw Stewart, Laura, and Marcus huddled in the far corner trying to keep away from the strongest part of the current which has gotten everyone else. It was safe to take the risk. My hands were pushed up against the rock wall so tightly it felt as though they were nailed to the mountain. I inhaled deeply, the wind taking some of my air from me, and felt energy coarse to my palms which were facing out towards the center of the arena.

A few seconds passed, and then I released my electricity in thin bolts from my finger tips. The threadlike streams branched off into many tiny bolts moving across the arena disregarding the brutal winds. That didn't last forever, though. As soon as they reached the furthest block, the wind was too great, and they were forced back at the Recruits glued to the wall like a boomerang.

The Recruits yelled and thrashed, but they couldn't get free. McKayla had them pinned solid to the wall. They could only watch as the electricity twirled and danced through the air until they connected with them. Daniel, Weasel Face, and Ruby were hit with the small bolts. They convulsed back and forth while still being completely pinned to the wall. A few of the bolts came back and hit me, but it was nothing more than a tingle to me.

"Zeke!" McKayla screamed. "Finish them! I am going to lose it!"

There wasn't much time left. I didn't want to have to do it, but since they were all still conscious, I would have to use a little more power. I was afraid, though. I didn't want to overdue and permanently harm them. In the end, the Gauntlet was just a fight and we could still be friends after.

With the bolts still coursing from my palms, I released a little more energy. The bolts thickened and continued to follow the same path as the other bolts. They boomeranged, and then came back to connect with their human lightning rod.

This time, the Recruits were affected much more severely. They convulsed to the point that their arms actually broke loose from the wind pressure colliding into them. Their limbs flailed wildly in all directions including Daniel. Drool began to pool in the corner of Weasel Face's mouth. He already took a shot to the head, how would he handle this?

I actually felt pain myself this time. Not from the electricity colliding with my chest, I wish that was the case. It was something much worse. The Overload had returned and was beginning to burn away at my insides. They ached and scorched the longer I held the electricity. Soon, I would have to stop too.

But, it wasn't me that crapped out. The wind halted almost immediately dropping Daniel, Ruby, Weasel Face, and myself off of the wall to the ground below. We all landed with a thud, but some hit harder than others. Weasel Face landed on his unconscious head while I was able to contort my body to land on my feet.

I didn't bother to take in all the carnage that McKayla and I created. I ran over to her almost as soon as my feet hit the ground. She was laying face first on the rock, a little bit of the dirt rubbing on her cheek.

I crouched beside her and rubbed her back gently trying to get a reaction. "McKayla? Are you there? Please, be okay. You did amazing."

She scrunched her eyes and opened them. She looked at me through her bright blue eyes that were almost hypnotizing. I could see why Riley cared for her so much. She was very beautiful. My face grew warm when I thought that. I felt as though I was cheating on Trish, and we weren't even dating.

"Zeke? What happened? I blacked out," she said weakly.

I smiled. "You did everything that you needed to. You caused a giant storm which threw everyone up against the wall including myself I might add," I laughed slightly and then said, "I used my ability then and electrocuted the other Recruits. I'm sorry you had to use so much energy. I shouldn't have waited so long to use mine."

She struggled to shake her head at me, but I got the message none the less. She said, "No, it was fine. I'm just glad that the other Recruits succumbed to your lightning. That is quite the gift you have, Zeke. It comes in handy."

I laughed a little. "Yeah, I guess it does."

All of the eyes of the Recruits in the audience were locked on us. I looked up to my friends above McKayla and smiled to them showing that we were all okay. They cheered back chanting our names even though they stood out amongst all of the other Recruits. Riley looked especially pleased that we were okay. I'm sure he thought McKayla overdid it.

I looked back down to McKayla when she said, "So, is it over then? Is everyone down?"

I rolled her onto her back and into my arms. They were still aching from exerting so much electricity while the Overload took its toll on me, but I was still able to pick her up. Carefully, I lifted her a few inches in the air and spun her to face the line of unconscious Recruits. It was Weasel Face, Ruby, and Daniel at the far end. The Instructors were just getting out of the corner to see the damage.

"No way," McKayla whispered in a half gasp. "I can't believe we did it."

I nodded. "We really did do it, McKayla. Congrats to you and me, I say!"

She smiled and cheered lightly with me. Then, while the Instructors were calling Daniel, Ruby, and Weasel Face incapacitated and unable to fight to the Head Instructors, she said, "Now, what? You said we would cross this bridge when we came to it. Who wins?"

To be honest, I didn't think we would make it this far in the Gauntlet. Our plan was ridiculous, and, with the Overload, I thought for sure that we would be in over our heads, but we pulled it off. As I looked at Weasel Face, blood dripping from his forehead and drool pooling from his mouth, I felt as though I had accomplished everything that needed to be accomplished. I set out a goal for myself and completed it, but, for some odd reason, I felt like I was forgetting something...

...and then it hit me. I immediately set McKayla down on the rock floor and crouched over her, my hands held in front of me in case of an attack.

McKayla looked up, scared, "What's wrong?"

As the Instructors were helping each other move the unconscious bodies out of the arena, she got her answer. Behind the nearest rock, Bruno came stepping over Weasel Face, his lackey, while Marcus was picking him up.

"I think your friend forgot about me."

Things were about to get ugly, and McKayla was, unfortunately, in the middle of it.

Chapter 35

We kept our eyes on the circling beast. He held his head high above his prey, McKayla and I. I swear I saw saliva dripping off his teeth, but that had to be my imagination.

He was just trying to psych us out. He had to know he was physically stronger, but my ability may give me the upper hand. However, his ability is still a mystery to me. I will need to keep my guard up no matter what I do and watch out for surprise attacks from him.

This is what I asked for. I wanted to take him on and defeat him in front of his peers, his followers. For not being an Instructor, he had an incredible amount of power. He controlled the Recruits like a dictator by using his power to frighten others. I wouldn't be like them. I would put a stop to him once and for all, but as I looked up at him still crouched next to McKayla, I began to doubt myself.

Bruno walked back and forth in front of me. The audience was glued to the friction building between him and me. Who did they want to win? Did they want someone to take down their four time champion, or did they want Bruno just so they didn't get beat up later?

My mind raced about the surroundings. The arena seemed a lot smaller now that it was just me and him. McKayla would be of no help. She was too exhausted, and I would much rather take a beating than have her potentially harm herself further. I would have to do this alone, and trust the instincts I didn't have, at least not like Marcus, Liam, and Juliette.

Bruno stopped and raised his hand. "C'mon, Laufor, get on your feet! I am sick of all the things you have been saying. You wanted me? Well, here I am, just like you wanted. Unless, you are afraid now, of course," he began to laugh to himself. "I wouldn't blame you if you were afraid. I admit, honestly, that little move you and the quiet girl played was good. You got Daniel, but then again, I'm not Daniel. I'm better."

I rose up and stood over McKayla facing Bruno intently. "Thank you, I guess. That's what happens when you work as a team, but you wouldn't know that."

"Really?" He said. "How wouldn't I know that? Daniel and I were partners, and I had Isaac test you out, and you performed better than I expected, better than three quarters of the weaklings here."

He threw his fists in the air and made a circle, facing the audience. I couldn't believe what I saw. He insulted all of the Recruits here, and none of them even stood up for themselves. What were their problems?

"See that, Laufor?" Bruno said circling me again. "I can get away with whatever I want. That's true power, when everyone knows you are the strongest and wouldn't dare mess with you. All I have left to prove to is you, and your little friend up there."

He made an evil grin up at Teddy who then hid behind Liam for support. Bruno laughed at his cowardice.

I stepped in. "You only carry that kind of power because the Recruits fear you. After watching you destroy and blast their friends in the arena for the past year, you have become a symbol of power here, and I am going to put an end to that because I'm not afraid of you." I lied.

He scoffed. "You think you can stop me, Laufor? I have been here years before you were Recruited, and I was Instructed by Callon. There is no way a first timer in the Gauntlet can stop me."

"You will just have to watch and see then," I said back.

There was a moment of silence as we stared at each other trying to anticipate what the other would do. The audience remained silent as well. They knew that this was coming, Bruno and I. It was time to see who the stronger of us was.

I slowly sidestepped away from McKayla hoping Bruno would follow me, and he did. She was far too weak to help fight and needed to be kept at a safe distance. I didn't know what Bruno was capable of other than he was fast and strong; two very deadly attributes. I would need to be on my A game like the time I faced Nathaniel, but win.

When I felt a good distance away, I stopped and took in my surroundings. The pit was directly behind

Bruno, but a large rock rested between the two. The pit was probably my best chance at eliminating him, but I wouldn't be able to force him in. I would have to use my ability, but with only so much left until the Overload ravaged my body to shreds, I only had a few chances.

Bruno struck first. He launched from his standing position and came at me quickly with his fists held high. He threw a left hook followed by a right jab. I ducked under the hook, but the jab go me in the chin and knocked me off my feet.

This fight was going to be over quickly if I didn't do something soon. I looked up and saw Bruno ready to jump on top of me, but I reacted swiftly. I held my hands in front of me when Bruno launched down at me. I unleashed a blast of hot electricity which hit Bruno right in the chest. He sailed through the air and hit the boulder behind him.

Suddenly, my arms felt like they were on fire. I yelled and squeezed them tightly hoping to keep the pain down, but that didn't help much. The Overload was rooted deep in me now, and any ability use would result in a painful backlash on my body. What would I do?

I forced myself up onto my feet and looked around the arena. The audience all kept their mouths open amazed that I was able to knock Bruno off his feet. The Head Instructors, especially Callon, all looked down at me. I don't think they were surprised. They looked more worried than anything. Callon gave me a "watch yourself" look. I couldn't, though. If I did, I would surely lose to Bruno. I would have to risk allowing the Overload to progress further if I wanted to win.

I took a few deep breaths and watched as Bruno pushed himself off of the ground and back onto his feet. He brushed some of the dirt off of his cloak and jerked his head to the side, cracking his neck in the process. There was a scorched hole in his cloak over his chest where the blast hit him. The sight made me feel good.

He laughed a little. That wasn't a good sign. He said, "That was a good shot, Laufor. For anyone else, that would've knocked them down for quite some time, but you are going to have to do much more than that."

I went back into a fighting stance and said, "Good thing I barely used any of my strength on that shot."

He replied. "Good! Very good! I expect nothing less from the son of the great Greg Laufor, but let's see what you can do against my ability."

I braced myself as Bruno stayed in place. He didn't even build up energy to use his ability. He just stood there and stared at me. Suddenly, a smile broke across his face when he launched himself at me at impossible speeds! He came in a blur and knocked me off of my feet with his elbow to my face. I soared through the air and landed just shy of the metal cage. I felt my forehead as I lay on the ground and found a lot of blood pouring from my head.

Bruno snickered. "I guess that's the end of that. No one could take a blow to the head at that speed."

He stopped snickering to himself when he saw me struggle to stand. I slowly turned my head towards him as my ability sealed the gash shut on my head; the Overload stinging my skin as the wound sealed shut. I forced myself up onto my feet; although, I staggered back and forth as I did it.

"You would… be right," I pushed out trying to stabilize myself, "but, I'm not no one." I grinned at him wildly.

"You think I am intimidated by you, Laufor?" He said. "I give you props for knocking me to the ground and still being able to fight after a blow to your head, but you wouldn't be anything without that nifty effect of your ability. You see, one of the beauties of winning the Gauntlet so many times is that you get to go on Recruitment missions, which also means that you get to read the files on all of the other Recruits."

I looked at him quizzically. "What are you getting at, Bruno? If you knew I could heal myself, then why are you so surprised that I am up again?"

"First of all, I only brought that up because I was surprised by how quickly your ability fixes yourself up," Bruno said slowly sidestepping towards McKayla. "Secondly, I only brought up the files because I was looking through yours just yesterday and noticed something kind of interesting that I think someone might want to hear."

I kept a careful eye on Bruno as he moved closer to McKayla. "What did you read? Who wants to know about it?" I was actually interested in what he had to say. I always wanted to know what the files the Head Instructors kept said about me, about all of us, unless he was going to lie about it.

"Not so fast now, Laufor. Everything will be revealed shortly," he said moving ever closer to McKayla. I began to follow his steps and prepared myself for a possible attack on McKayla, but if he used his ability to use the air as a springboard, I won't be able to catch him.

He continued, "There is a reason why Daniel always wants to team up with me. It's simple. I. Always. Win. He may be bigger than me, but I am still strong, and my ability gives me an edge over him. It gives me an edge over all of you including your little lightning powers, and, if I feel threatened because of my position, I can just look at some files in Callon's office and find out what the Recruit's weakness is. This time, and you may not know this Laufor, but I know yours."

Confused, surprised, and a little scared, I asked, "What are you talking about, Bruno? Just spit it out already, so we can get back to the battle."

"This is very important to our fight, Laufor, so shut it. I'll get back to destroying you in a second, but first, I need to say this," he said stopping just in front of McKayla.

I stopped across from him. McKayla rested now between us trying to get out of the way, but she was too weak. I wished she would just call herself out. I don't want her to be hurt.

I didn't reply to Bruno. I just stared at him, and so did everyone in the audience, when he continued to speak. "You said you were holding back your power. If that is the case, then I'm afraid the only way to bring out your true power is for you too want to kill me in an angry rage. If that is the case, then listen up, Laufor."

I remained silent and let Bruno speak. If it was going to give me the power to destroy him, then so be it. Make me stronger. I dared him.

"In your file," Bruno said, "I found something quite odd. How could it be that two people were

Recruited only weeks apart from the same area? Then, it hit me."

He knew my secret. He was going to spill the beans and Trish would hate me forever. I had to do something, but I couldn't move! I was frozen solid and helpless to stop that blabbing mouth.

He looked up to Trish and said, "Trish, you have abilities, but like most Recruits, you aren't really a descendant of an Original in the Clade."

She looked at him, confused, and let him go on. "For some reason, the offspring of the Originals have the burden of watching their step. They can give their abilities to a Regular if their blood ever comes in contact with a child of an Original. These Recruits are called Bloodlings, and you, my gorgeous little rose, are the Bloodling of Ezekiel Laufor." He pointed a thick finger at me.

There it was. She now knew. Everything I worked so hard to conceal was revealed in a matter of seconds. Not only Trish knew, but I'm sure Teddy could piece together that him being here was my doing.

If Bruno wanted rage, he got it. I felt my strength increase what seemed like ten-fold. I pictured the electricity jumping around in my body hitting every bone and muscle on its way from my core to my hands. Each jump caused a sharp pain in my gut. The Overload wasn't going to stop me. How *dare* Bruno reveal that! I am going to kill him!

He smiled at me, "There, now, don't you feel stronger?"

I grinded my teeth and tried to control myself, but there was no hope. "Why would you do that!? Are you *heartless!?*"

"No, Laufor," he said. "I just enjoy power and truth, and the truth is that you can't stop me no matter how powerful you are because I am just that much stronger than you."

He looked back up to Trish. "Now, you know. He must've been keeping that from you for a long time. What kind of friend is he to do this to you? You seem like the kind of girl that had a great life. Cute, witty, you were probably top of your class too, no doubt. I can only imagine what your parents must think. One day, they have a beautiful daughter, and the next, she disappears, never to be heard from again."

She looked at Bruno with a dazed and shocked look about her. The audience watched as she slowly turned her head at me and said, "Zeke... is this true?"

As I looked at her dumbfounded and hurt eyes, I weakened. I felt like dying in that one second of having to look at her in hell. "I'm sorry, Trish. I am so so so sorry."

She just kept staring at me and then said, "And... my parents? I thought I had fake parents, like you, who knew I was going to be Recruited?"

"I... I don't know what to say, Trish. I only found out a few weeks ago myself."

"And, you never told me?"

"I wanted to!" I yelled, the prequel of crying starting to hurt my eyes. "If I told you though, then you would hate me forever!"

She was silent as if she was thinking about what would've happened if I did talk to her and told her about her being my Bloodling. She looked up and said, "I would've understood, but now, I don't know if I can forgive you." She unfocused her attention from me and said to herself, "My parents... what are they thinking right now? Do they hate me?"

Sarah put her arms on Trish's shoulders and tried to comfort her, but Trish just shook them off and went back into her misery cocoon. My friends looked down at me like my mom did when I did something wrong. Suddenly, I flashed back to a time when my mom was yelling at me for over feeding the goldfish and killing it. The images flashing before me tore at my insides. Overload was nothing compared to the excruciating pain I felt in those few seconds.

That sadness reemerged as rage. The electrical storm building up inside me increased, and it was directed at Bruno. Of all the things he has done to hurt me, tease me, this was the lowest.

He raised his arms in the air like a televangelist and said, "Now, do you feel the power? If so, bring it! And, quickly too, otherwise, your friend here will be more than unconscious."

He crouched down by McKayla and pulled back an arm. I needed to do something quickly, or she would be crushed by his fists! I didn't think. I acted. The storm that was building up inside me was instantly released and aimed for Bruno.

He was ready and launched himself out of the way, the rock behind him taking the blast almost disintegrating. I needed to control myself. That would've killed him, and I didn't want to kill him. Do I, I wondered.

Suddenly, a fist smashed me in the left cheek which twisted my head fiercely. I managed to stay on my feet though, but I wasn't ready for the barrage of punches and kicks to the gut that came. Each punch came right after the other and each one should've left a huge bruise, but thanks to the Overload, they didn't. I just felt really weak and in torment from the Overload.

To end his combo, Bruno unleashed a roundhouse kick to my ribs which connected with a loud crack. The pain was immense, and this time, as I sailed through the air to the ground, it wasn't the Overload.

At the same time Bruno's foot connected to my chest, a blast of electricity erupted from my side like when I protected Teddy from those bullies. My body is too full and unleashed itself at the nearest person it could find, Bruno. He groaned and squealed as he was dropped to the ground almost in an instant.

As I lay on the ground, I looked down, blood trickling from a cut in my mouth and running over my lip, the bulge I saw was a broken rib. Bruno had fractured a rib with his last kick. I didn't think my ability would be able to fix that. I tried to touch it with my left arm, but it hurt too much to even move. I think Bruno had me down for the count.

But then, as I looked over my broken rib at the immense body lying on the ground, I knew it was Bruno. This time, the entire top half of his cloak was shredded and burned by the electrical blast that was released when he kicked me. I guess Overload's can come in handy after all.

As I thought that, a strong wave of electricity was unleashed beyond my control and wrapped me up in a web of pain. The bolts stung me brutally, and I wanted to die right there. Tears were even beginning to form in my eyes as the electricity continued to electrocute me. I then noticed, that at the same time, my rib was healing itself. I wondered how that was possible. I thought that my power only healed skin?

Then, as the intense electrical pain subsided, I looked at the final masterpiece, and it wasn't perfectly healed. A large bump still remained. The bone was regenerated, but it wasn't set in place. It didn't hurt at all, but it was a nuisance and unappealing to say the least.

I struggled to get up. The audience was in shock by everything they had seen. Their eyes wandered between Bruno, McKayla, who was still struggling to push herself up, and me, whose broken rib healed in a minute. I looked around at them and the Instructors and Head Instructors. They all looked shocked, confused, and impressed. Little did they know that what just happened was an accident, and, on any other day, Bruno would've crushed me. The only two who didn't seem to be in shock was Callon, Marcus, and Juliette. They all seemed worried, and it looked as though Callon was giving Marcus a sign to take me out before the Overload killed me.

I said, limping to Bruno who was lying face first on the ground, "I'm… fine! Don't… don't take me out!"

I took a few deep breaths and grabbed onto Bruno's hand. His head slowly rotated and looked up at me, a few cuts and burns on his face from the burst of electricity. "What… what are you doing?" He asked.

I said, "I'm… I'm stronger than you. Admit it. You are too weak… to fight. Give up, or I'll send electricity to you until you are forced to quit."

He looked up at me with only one eye open, the other being blinded by the spot light shining down on me from above. He said, "I don't think so, Laufor. You... haven't won! I won't let you!"

Just then, he launched himself into the air and landed behind me. He wasn't done just yet, and I was too weak to react to his move. I turned around just in time to see Bruno's fist connect with the side of my chest. The pain was intense, but I managed to stay on my feet while more attacks collided with my chest and face.

His punches were quick. He must've been using his ability to make his punches and kicks faster. That's why he could beat Daniel and everyone else. He was too fast and his super speedy punches and kicks packed a lot of weight behind them.

Then, with one a loud "huff," Bruno launched his entire body at me. I was too dazed and hurt to even wiggle. He connected into my ribs at high speeds which launched me halfway across the arena and into the metal cage. I felt limp the moment I hit the cage and fell lifelessly to the ground amazed that I was still conscious, but everything ached. I think my rib re-broke itself, and then immediately healed.

The audience gasped and mumbled as I laid on the ground. I forced my head to turn up at Bruno, but it hurt so much I could barely do it.

He limped over to me holding his shoulder where a large burn was from my attack. "How... How can you still... be conscious? You... you should be out if not dead."

I willed my body to move, but it was to no avail. I watched as Bruno stalked closer kicking McKayla out of the way in the process.

I croaked, "You... will never... win, Bruno. I... won't let you."

He fell on his knees next to me while I was still unable to move. He said, between deep puffs of air, "Wrong... Laufor. I am stronger... than... you. What makes... you think I will lose to you?"

"Because," I said accepting the fact that I will soon be pummeled with fists, "I believe... that goodness... will always beat evil... no matter what the odds."

He coughed and laughed a little. I could tell that it hurt him. "You put up a good fight, but... you are wrong. It's time to... grow up. Goodness doesn't always prevail. Look at the battle... between the Clade and the Agency. We're screwed."

I said in one last push, "If... you believe that... then you are the weakest Recruit here."

His face morphed to one of rage. He didn't say anymore. He wanted this to be over. Bruno stabilized himself by keeping one hand on the ground while pulling back for a punch. His eyes went cross-eyed when he tried to charge up an attack, then he stopped and took in a deep breath. He was too winded to use his ability, so was I. This would be settled the old fashioned way.

Angrier than ever, Bruno raised his fist and dropped it down on the side of my face hard. With each swing of his hammer fist, the pain shot through my body, but the Overload healed the bruise that formed before Bruno could strike again. The pain was so intense I just wanted to be knocked out there and have it all end.

Suddenly, another blast of electricity erupted from the side of my face that sent Bruno across the arena and left me in agony. I screamed out loud as lightning surrounded my body burning and shocking me with every jump of the bolt.

` I thought it would go away, but it never did. It kept getting stronger and more painful. I could hear the audience shrieking from their stands. I even heard Sarah yell out my name.

I screamed, not caring about Bruno or the Gauntlet anymore, "HELP! PLEASE! MAKE IT STOP!"

Just then, another strong burst of energy radiated from my body frying me and anyone that happened to be too close. I couldn't control it anymore. The Overload had won, and it had taken me over. I forced open my eyes just enough to see Callon and Marcus running towards me wearing a pair of rubber gloves when the pain caused everything to go black once and for all.

Chapter 36

Falling into black... it was kind of nice. Not too many people have probably had the pleasure of slowly being absorbed by the darkness.

The pain immediately subsided. I barely remember what pain felt like floating in the empty jar. My soul felt as though it had left my body. For the first few moments, I felt as though I actually did die, and the Overload did kill me. I was warned to be careful and not overdo it, but I didn't care? In this place, the Overload was not a problem. Nothing was a problem.

However, there was something that kept my mind wandering back to reality. I couldn't help but think about the Gauntlet, and the thing that was said during the battle. I barely remember the moment, but I know it happened.

Trish knew.

She knew everything about Bloodlings, and she hated me for it what I did. It was my entire fault that she was in the Clade. I couldn't let it go and neither will she. Even though I couldn't feel pain in the infinite abyss, I was being tortured by the thought of her, and what ever happened to Bruno and McKayla, I wondered.

Carefully approaching was a bright light at the bottom of the abyss. It came rapidly growing ever brighter as it engulfed me whole. Then, I began to hear voices. I heard Marcus, Callon, Barbara... all of the Instructors. It was as if the light was the portal back to reality, and it was taking me no matter what I wanted. As much as I longed to stay in the darkness a little bit longer, the light wouldn't let me. It grew brighter and brighter until...

...I opened my eyes slowly to a bright light shining down from above me. I glanced around the blurry room and saw all of the Instructors talking to one another near a metal door with bars covering a small window near the top.

My body felt completely numb. It was as if I wasn't really in my body at all. Instead, I was just watching from outside of it. I forced myself to stay awake and not drift back off into the comfort of the blackness no matter how appealing it was.

Juliette then noticed I was beginning to come around and told the others. Like a cult from a horror movie, they all turned their attention towards me. It gave me the creeps. They all gawked at me like I was their ridiculous pet or something.

Marcus knelt down next to me and asked, "Zeke, thank god, how are you feeling?"

"Not that bad," I lied. I didn't tell him that I could see three of him, but that would hopefully pass soon.

Callon said, leading the rest of the Instructors over to me, "What were you doing? I specifically told you not to overdo it, or the Overload would kill you. Now look who was right."

Barbara smacked him in the chest, "Easy, if it wasn't for your dumb little Gauntlet, he wouldn't even have to risk it. Let's just be glad that we got him some treatment in time."

Wow, go Barbara, I thought. I guess knowing your daughter still loved you and wanted to spend some time with you will give a mother her strength back. Also, it was pretty funny watching Callon get smacked like a child. I smiled, but it really hurt. I cringed at the pain.

I was sitting in a metal chair that was rather uncomfortable, and the Instructors surrounding me didn't help make me feel any more comfortable either. I tried to stand, but I couldn't. I tilted my head down and saw two belts strapped tightly around each of my arms to the arm rests of the chair.

I sprang fully awake and said, "What the hell is going on? Why am I strapped to this chair?"

Marcus and Juliette looked at each other with sorrowful eyes and then to Callon who wouldn't care if I was strapped to a chair or cannon.

Barbara, her wrinkled arms folded across her chest, said, "Why don't you tell him, Callon? This is your doing after all."

Callon said, "Are you telling me that this is my fault, Barbara? What makes you think you can speak up now after being silent for so long?"

"I only need to speak when I see something terribly wrong at work," she said. "The Gauntlet was pushing it, but this? It's not the boy's fault that he has an Overload, but to strap him to a chair is inhumane!"

Callon turned away from her and faced the wall. "These are the tough decisions I am forced to make! You haven't spoken in the last four years, and now you think you can give me advice after everything I have done alone?"

Marcus stepped in between them and said, "Both of you keep yourselves under control. You two are Head Instructors and are supposed to be representatives of what every Recruit should hope to be. If you can't get along and continue to bicker like small children, how will anything get done?"

There was a heavy silence in the room that normally followed a disciplinary action. It was as if Marcus just scolded his two kids Callon and Barbara. I laughed in my head, but I would never show my feelings. I remained quiet and still while the tension was dissolved.

Marcus said, "Yes, it is difficult to deal with a situation like this. An Overload has only occurred once before in the short history of the Clade, and we all know how that turned out. Let's try to reverse that and save Zeke before the Overload spreads further. The drugs won't keep it at bay forever."

What was Marcus talking about when he mentioned drugs? I tugged my arm on the belts only able to wiggle them, but in that small wiggle, I felt a light tug in the middle of my arm. I looked down to see what was there when I saw a thin, plastic, tube sticking out of my arm like an IV. Off colored, yellow fluid flowed down the tube, and with every drip, my body felt numb.

I struggled and moaned attracting the attention of the bickering Instructors. "What the-!? What are you pumping into me!?"

Callon said, "Relax yourself. It isn't dangerous at all. In fact, you have had it in your body before. It's Dopaphine. It suppresses abilities for a few hours, but since you have an Overload, we are keeping it on IV for you."

I remembered about what Dopaphine was and what it was capable of doing. I watched Nathaniel inject Trish with the drug that made her body twitch and shake violently. The image of the small foam bubbles dripping out of her mouth was stained in my memory. How come I wasn't convulsing? Did Nathaniel inject her with something else? No, that would be silly, I assured myself.

"Why am I not foaming at the mouth, or shaking, or freaking out?" I asked.

Marcus stepped forward and said, "This is a better version of the Dopaphine drug. It is more advanced and all convulsing has ceased with this development. It is unfortunate that we didn't have any when you were first Recruited. At least you were asleep when that happened, right?"

"That doesn't make up for the fact that you injected all of the Recruits in the Clade with a drug beyond their knowledge," I said. "I'm sorry, Marcus, but it's hard to be okay with something like that."

He nodded and said, "I understand what you are saying, Zeke, but it is important that we inject them when they are first Recruited-"

"-Otherwise," Callon said, "Their abilities could destroy an entire division. When a Recruit first gains their abilities, they are out of control. Without the injection, they could bring harm to themselves and others."

"Because of the Overload coursing through your veins, you have become that again. It has developed to such a severe state that your ability burns you on the inside, and don't lie about it. I could tell when you were fighting in the Gauntlet."

There was a silence. I continued to watch the yellow fluid flow into my arm numbing my powers. I tried to call upon the warm electricity to move into my hand, but it just wouldn't. Suddenly, I felt lost. Without the warmth of the familiar electricity moving through me, I didn't know what to do. My mind went into a lock and it felt as though I was about to hyperventilate. I was as much as my power as it was to me.

I said, still thinking about never having my ability again, "What... what will happen now?"

Nobody spoke. Juliette began to inch herself towards the door to remove herself from the tense situation. I knew the answer wouldn't be good, but I still had to know.

Callon said, "You will remain here and be treated until a cure is found."

"How long will that be?" I asked.

He didn't say anything. Marcus spoke for him instead. "There is no exact time. If there is a cure, it is doing a very good job at hiding itself from us. I know Callon has been looking through the files of the only previous Recruit to have an Overload, Shiloh Webber, and has been trying to find a solution. It's unfortunate, but now, we can compare your Overload with that of Shiloh Webber and see if there is a correlation."

They tried to give me words of encouragement, but they didn't help much. I was still depressed as ever. At least, I now know that Callon was looking at Shiloh's files in his office and not mine; Trish's, Sarah's, or anyone else's that I care about.

"So, there is no hope," I said confidently staring down at the floor beneath Marcus' feet.

"Don't say that," Juliette said stepping back into the group. "There is always hope. No matter what the circumstance, there is always a fighting chance, but you have to believe." She glanced back at Marcus and Callon. "Isn't that right?"

Marcus nodded, "Mhmm, Juliette is absolutely correct, Zeke. There is always hope. Don't say something like that."

Callon began to move towards the door. He placed his hand on the knob and said, "We will be working hard to cure you before your Overload worsens further. Until the time that a cure is discovered, you will remain here. All necessities will be given to you, so do not worry about that."

The others began to follow his lead. Callon held the door open while Barbara left. Juliette and Marcus stayed a bit longer to give me a few words of encouragement, but, again, they didn't help much. They walked out of the door and left Callon and I to an awkward stare.

Before he left, I said, "Callon, before you go, could you tell me what happened in the Gauntlet? I only remember intense pain and blacking out."

He was slowly shutting the door while he said, "Yes, Bruno beat on you pretty hard, but your Overload caused a backlash of energy that sent him across the arena. He was knocked out after that, and since you blacked out, McKayla won."

I smiled a little, lifting my spirits. "Good, she is tough and deserves it."

"Yes, she is tough, and so are you. Much stronger than I expected at first," he said. "I saw your rib. It broke and healed itself before it could be set. When a cure is discovered, we will fix that too."

I shook my head. "I guess I'll just wait here until that happens, alone." I put emphasis on the alone part to hopefully make him realize that he should come visit me at times, or let my friends come see me.

Especially Trish…

He smiled a little bit and said, "You won't be alone for long, Laufor. Get some rest, you are weak from the Gauntlet and that will only hasten the spread of the Overload. I will see you soon."

He shut the door leaving behind the echoing metal clang. As the ringing slowly faded from existence, I felt more and more alone. Would that be the last sound I was going to hear? Would I be in that place forever, and what did Callon mean when he said that I won't be alone for long? Maybe he would let Sarah or Trish come visit me.

Still, my thoughts were swarmed with thoughts of Trish. I kept picturing her face, her smile, and everything that I care so much about that you can't see, like her personality. A part of me doesn't even see her as a person anymore. My inner self, the deep romantic, sees her as a beautiful ball of light. It's so warm and bright that you just wanted to be by it all the time. Sometimes, I forget that she is even a person. No mortal can be anything that amazing.

And, I lost her. She hated me for what I have done, but I have no right to be angry at her for that. I would be mad at the person who gave me these powers too. I guess that meant I hated my father. My heart ached with the sheer drifting memory of her. If I could move my arms, I would rip out my heart and end the pain now while I was still capable of doing so. It would kill two birds with one stone. I would no longer care for Trish, and the Overload would have no effect on me anymore... because I would be dead.

What's going on with me, I wondered. How can I be having these thoughts? I am not that depressed. Then again, now that I think about it, I guess I am. All I have done since Gabe's death was blame me for not being able to save him. After that, I let myself become hollow. I was convinced that the Agency would destroy this division just as easily as they destroyed the other division. The massacre...

Stop, I screamed to myself! I shook my head fiercely back and forth, my hair becoming a tangled mess in the process. I needed to stop thinking. I was going to be in this room, strapped to this uncomfortable, metal chair, for a long time. I can't start going crazy now. Perhaps, Trish is really okay with everything that had happened. I'm sure she will understand eventually. What I saw in the arena was just the shock of her finally realizing why she is here. Although, Bruno could've been a little gentler when telling her that her parents are probably crying over her missing.

Bruno, I thought… he deserved what he had coming. Maybe, now that he was defeated, Recruits will finally start standing up to him. That's all I can hope. My job was done. Now, it was up to the Clade to take control and stand up for themselves. It is their fault that they let him get all this power. They cowered in fear and did nothing while he let all of this power go to his head. Losing the Gauntlet might finally make him realize that he needed us just as much as we needed him and that it didn't matter how strong you were because there was always someone who would be stronger than you. You could run one hundred miles an hour, but then you would find someone with a truck that can just run you over. There was never going to be an omnipotent human that can win every fight in every different scenario. I truly hope (which is odd) that he came to this realization.

I took in a deep breath and blew it out slowly. My mind was finally relaxing; therefore, so was I. For once, I didn't have to worry about anything. No work, no Callon, no problems. Having an Overload may be a blessing in disguise. I have the time to rest up now and get ready for when Nathaniel and the Agency strike because it will happen. I still haven't gotten over that yet. Even if they don't, I will make Nathaniel pay for what he did to Gabe and everyone else in New York!

"I will kill him," I said out loud not realizing that I said it out loud at first.

I sat in silence. It was weird to be able to say what I want knowing that no one will ever respond. I was in pure isolation, away from all people, Recruits, and enemies for a while.

I was wrong. As I was getting used to being alone, a voice cut over the silence that seemed to be distant whisper and said, "Who are you going to kill?"

I was in a trance like state. I should have realized that it wasn't a trick that my mind was playing on me, but I answered it as though it was a part of my subconscious.

"I will kill Nathaniel... for everything he's done," I said.

The whisper groaned oddly and then said, "What has he done?"

"He has killed my best friend, Gabe, and countless others in his betrayal. He turned away from his friends for power and control. I will stop him before he hurts anyone else," I said, my voice growing louder with each sentence.

"That sounds very noble... aahh... of you. You hold your friends very highly in your life."

The whisper was becoming more real to me. It was as if I was pulled from my depressive coma and back into reality. I looked around the room as much as I could, but found no one that could produce any sounds especially words. I wondered if the figure was behind me, but the whisper didn't sound like it was coming from behind me, but from my right side by the wall.

The wall was complete rock, jagged and solid. I couldn't see anyone whispering. For a short time, I truly thought that these first few moments of isolation were already driving me insane, but then, I heard the whisper again coming from a small metal vent on the top of the wall.

"Who is that?" I asked.

The whisper responded, "My name is Shiloh Webber."

Chapter 37

The name was all too familiar to me. Shiloh Webber. He was the only other person in the short history of the Clade to ever have an Overload, but I thought he was dead. Callon sure made it seem like he was dead, but then again, if you aren't of use to Callon, you might as well be.

Things were beginning to make sense to me now. There really was a boy locked in the storage room Callon went into while we fixed the generator. It wasn't my mind playing tricks on me! It was Shiloh, the boy with Overload, and now, here I am to join him in this prison. I wonder how long he has been down here. Would I be here for that long?

While I was busy thinking, Shiloh said, "Hello? Are you still there… aahh, or did the Overload get you to? I'm guessing that is why Callon put you here like me."

"Uh… yeah, I have an Overload too," I said.

"Hmm...," Shiloh responded. He groaned loudly and said, "Sorry about that. Eventually, when you have had an Overload for as long as I have, the pain gets pretty intense no matter how many drugs Callon pumps into you."

The realization must've still not hit me yet. I asked, "Shiloh Webber?"

"Yes, that is my name, and may I ask who I am speaking to?" He said.

"My name is Ezekiel Laufor, but my friends call me Zeke."

"Laufor?" Shiloh asked sounding a little surprised. "Are you the son of Greg Laufor?"

"Yes," I said a little annoyed that everyone knows me through my father, and I don't even know my father. "I am more than just his son, though."

"Of course," Shiloh said. "I was just making the connection between you and your father. I hope you didn't find anything wrong with that."

To be honest, I did, but I didn't tell him that. I didn't even know who this guy really was other than having an Overload. I guess that gives us something in common. Only, we won't last long enough to find out what more we have in common. The Overload will most likely kill us by then. I thought I already felt a slight tingle of energy burning at my insides even with the medicine dripping into my arm.

"So, tell me, Shiloh," I said. "Do you know anything about an Overload? I've had mine since I was blasted by a bolt of lightning, and since then, all I know about it is that it hurts like hell and will eventually be the death of me provided the Agency doesn't come here and kill me first."

He said, "That is all I really know about it too…ugh, aahh… At least you aren't as bad as me yet."

"What do you mean?" I asked. "What is all that groaning?"

He laughed a little and cried out a tiny bit, and then he said, "Sorry, my Overload has reached the point where it flares up every few minutes and really burns me. No matter what the strength of the Dopaphine is, I still ache and burn. Sometimes, I feel as though this is God torturing me for having abilities that no other mortal should have, but it's not my fault."

He paused and said, "Oh yeah, about how I got my Overload. I was thrown into a furnace while I was on a Recruitment mission. Little did I know that the Agency was following me for a few hours and when I reached the freshy, I was surrounded and thrown into a furnace. I didn't die. I have an ability to control fire, you see. I can breathe fire. I may have survived, but I was left with an Overload. That happened almost… three years ago. I can't believe I have been here for that long."

Three years, I thought!? He has been locked in that storage room for three years. How can Callon do that to him!? It's inhumane. That sounds like something the Agency would do if they ever got their hands on us. Would I be here that long?

"How could you last three years locked in a room alone?" I asked. "That's insane. Haven't you ever been out?"

"Unfortunately, no," he said somberly. "Callon comes to visit me every day to bring me food and water and allow me to use a bed pan to go to the bathroom in, but otherwise, I'm strapped to this chair. I won't lie to you, Zeke. It's horrible. My muscles have deteriorated to almost nothing and I'm extremely pale. I have a beard that annoys me all day and night, and speaking of night, it's hard to sleep or tell time for that matter. I just try to sleep whenever I hear the dinner bell. I'm used to that schedule even still."

I let myself sit and think before I responded to Shiloh. There was no way I was going to be kept locked in a basement room. I have too many good things in my life to let Callon take it all away from me. I have great friends that have my back even in the toughest of situations like in New York. I smiled to myself thinking about them. I couldn't believe I actually thought of ending it all earlier. I have too much to live and fight for.

I tried thrashing around in the chair, but the belts were too tight on my legs and wrists. I couldn't use my ability no matter how much I forced it out. The Dopaphine was too strong to overcome. I had to overcome the weariness that the drug was causing me to begin with.

Pulling hard on the leather belts, my arms became chaffed and started to bleed a little. My forehead was starting to produce sweat that ran down my temples and chin eventually dripping on my cloak.

"Are you okay, Zeke? It sounds like you are struggling with something," Shiloh said.

"Yeah..." I said puffing deeply. "I'm going to get out of here."

"What?" Shiloh asked in shock. "How are you going to do that!?"

"I... don't really know yet," I said honestly. "I will find a way, though. I'll get out of here, and then I'll get you out too. There is no way I am going to be stuck in here for three years!"

I began to struggle again at the belts hoping that one would give a little my way, but that never happened. My wrists only got bloodier, and I got sweatier.

Then, a plan came to my mind. I could break out of this chair if I could use my ability, but in order to use my ability, I would have to pull the needle out of my arm. The question is, how would I do that if I couldn't use my hands or even legs?

That's when I began to swing my torso from left to right. If I could tip the chair over, maybe that would pull the IV out; otherwise, I would be in a very uncomfortable position. It was a risk I was willing to take if I knew I could get free from this prison. I continued to toss myself back and forth. The chair was starting to tip on two of its legs after a few minutes, but my head was beginning to ache, and the chair was just too heavy to flip over. I gave up, and the chair fell back down with a clang.

"Any luck?" Shiloh asked tentatively.

"No," I said angrily. I groaned and tried to kick the air in front of me, but my leg was stuck tight to the legs of the chair. It made me even angrier that I couldn't express myself.

"Just relax," Shiloh said. "It's hard at first, but Callon will come back down when the dinner bell rings and feed us. You can talk to him then and see if there is any chance that... grraaaahhh... ugh, you can get out."

"And, what if he says no? What then? He will know that I will be trying to escape," I said still upset.

"If so, then you stay here. It's really not as bad as you might think especially now that you have someone to go through it with you. Try going through all of this torture alone. It's hard," he said.

"Sorry, Shiloh…" I said. "You sound like a really nice guy and a good person, but I will not be stuck down here. I don't care if I have an Overload. I won't be an animal in a cage."

I kept struggling, wriggling myself back and forth furiously trying to break the binds on my wrists and legs. The cuts grew deeper allowing more blood to pour out the wounds and onto the floor and bands. I relaxed to regain my strength and my cuts healed themselves immediately, searing pain torturing my wrists and ankles. My blood glistened on the dark belts.

Shiloh didn't respond after I told him off. I didn't really expect him too. I just said that I didn't want to be an animal like him. He gave up, but I won't. There are people that need me upstairs before it was too late. I just had a really bad feeling about something to come.

The hours passed on with no luck in escaping. The belts were just too tight, and I couldn't unhook the tube from my arm to blast them off. No matter how much I struggled, I was stuck in my position. There may not be a way out of here. I would have to think of something else instead of just brute force.

I didn't have a lot of time, though. I felt the Overload beginning to dominate over the Dopaphine. There was a small flicker of pain deep inside me like a match in a completely dark room, and it was going to spread. The cure would not come fast enough. I needed to accept that, so using all of my energy to try to break out and be with my friends doesn't sound like that bad of a plan, but I just couldn't get free.

Shiloh remained silent for most of the time after my last comment about him. Every few minutes, he would groan and ache that gave me chills and haunted my thoughts even more than the Agency. Was that going to happen to me? Is there no escape from our painful fates? All of this happened because I was trying to protect my friends. Am I being punished for being a nice person?

The dinner bell rang loudly in the room. There must've been a speaker in every room of the Clade. That way, there was no excuse for someone missing their small break. Callon kept his pets trained well.

Speak of the devil, a few minutes after the dinner bell rang, an echoing clank came from Shiloh's room. It was the door being unlocked. From what I heard, it sounded like someone was walking around in there, but it could have been Shiloh.

Then, I heard Callon say, "Hello, Shiloh. I hope you are having a good day."

Shiloh said, "As good as I can have down here. How has your day been?"

They spoke to each other like they were best friends. There sounded to be no awkwardness between the captive Recruit and his captor Instructor.

"My day," Callon said, "has been the same as every other day. I keep these Recruits organized and under control while trying to find a cure to your problem."

Shiloh laughed a little then wheezed from the pain. "I know. You say that every day."

No one spoke for a few moments. I wondered what was happening that made them both go silent for such a long period of time especially since they were having a decent conversation. The groaning and aching was still present, but words were not.

Then Callon said, "And you say that every day, Shiloh."

"Can't help it," he said. "You can only let your mind wander so much until it gets trapped like me in this room. I don't know if that is the Overload causing it or just because I daydream all day."

"I am truly sorry," Callon said. "I don't want to have to do this, but-"

"- but, you have to for the safety of the rest of the Clade. I know, Callon. You say that all the time too."

"That's because I have nothing more to say about it," Callon said.

Shiloh cackled a little and said, "For being an intellectual mind, you really can't think of anything better to say than the usual stuff?"

I heard the door creak open. Callon was about to leave when he said, "Wise men are considered wise because what they speak is true and allows the listener to think as well, not because they make multiple guesses for one problem."

"I guess that is true," Shiloh said. "Still that doesn't mean you have to *always* give me the same answers."

Callon laughed lightly and said, "We'll see if that changes tomorrow. Goodnight, Shiloh."

The door clanked shut, and the lock was reset.

Just then, my door began to wiggle as someone tried to undo the lock. The tumbler turned and clicked open. The door swung, and there stood Callon with a tray of grool in one arm.

I didn't say anything to him as he walked back to the far wall and came back with a folding chair. He plopped down next to me and said, "Not going to speak to me?"

I kept quiet and remained focused on the open doorway. I was going to give him no recognition and pretend that he didn't even exist. That way, he won't catch on that I was going to escape, somehow.

"I'm going to take that as a 'no,'" Callon said. "I'm not worried, though. Shiloh acted the same way, but he turned around after a month."

I said, "I'm not him."

Callon shook his head. "Indeed, you are not him. You are just a stubborn Recruit that doesn't seem content with the decisions his Head Instructor makes."

"This stubborn Recruit would if your rules made any sense. The Gaunlet. That's a terrible system for seeing who is the strongest," I said scowling still not giving him eye contact.

"It was hard for me to decide to do that," he said pulling out a spoon and sticking it in the grool, "but it had to be done."

"Why do you say that?"

"Because," Callon began, "the Gauntlet is a way of determining who will fight the hardest against all odds even if their opponents have abilities instead of guns. This important because now that Nathaniel has switched sides, we will have to take him down. The winner proves to me that they have battle smarts as well as a strong control of their ability. Bruno has this; however, it appears as though you and Ms. Forwing have shown that you are more apt to battle than Bruno."

"You think hurting our own is a good way of showing strength in battle?" I asked.

"I really do. Believe me. If I could throw Agents into the arena against my Recruits, I would, but unfortunately, I don't have that luxury," he said. "Now, have some food." He raised the spoon into the air, the grool dripping off it and back onto the tray.

"I'm not that hungry," I said disgusted.

"You should really eat," he said moving the spoon closer to my mouth. "It's the only food you are going to get until tomorrow."

As much as I hated to do it, I took a bite. The disgusting goo slid down my throat slowly causing me more pain than the Overload. This was the only food I was going to get for a while, so I might as well eat it no matter how much I hated Callon.

"That's better," he said giving me another spoonful. "When you are done eating, I will release you from your binds so you may use the bathroom with my supervision."

I just nodded and kept eating the goo. He looked down at my wrists and smiled a little.

"Trying to escape were you?" He asked.

"What do you think?" I responded harshly back.

He laughed a little and kept feeding me until the tray was completely empty of even the smallest scraps. Callon set the tray down and stood up, moving the chair back to its regular position on the wall. He walked back towards me and pulled out an IV bag filled with pale yellow fluid.

"Here's a refill for you," he said. He unhooked the old bag, which was now almost empty, and clipped the tube onto the new IV. The yellow liquid flowed into my veins numbing the Overload slightly, but not completely extinguishing the pain.

"Thanks," I said turning away still angry.

"You are welcome, Laufor. I am going to release you now so you may use-"

Suddenly, Callon was cut off by loud booming sounds coming from overhead. The force was so great that the boom echoed throughout the entire cave causing pieces of rock from the ceiling to fall, creating a very dusty atmosphere.

I coughed a few times while Callon covered his mouth. The booming sounds continued to resonate through the mountain. Each one seemed more powerful than the last shaking the mountain creating small cracks in the rock walls.

"What's going on!?" Shiloh shouted from the other room, his voice barely making it through the loud booming sounds.

"I don't know, but I'm going to find out!" Callon shouted, and he sprinted out of the room shutting the door behind him.

The booming shook me left and right in the chair reopening the cuts in my arms as they moved across the belts. It wasn't smart for Callon to leave me stuck in place. What if a chunk of the ceiling fell on me, I wondered. Then, I wouldn't have to worry about the Overload because I would be dead already.

I heard Shiloh shout, "You okay, Zeke!?"

"Yeah!" I shouted back as the biggest boom yet shook the Clade even harder creating a larger crack in the rock wall between Shiloh and I. "I'm alright! A little dizzy, though!"

He laughed, "Tell me about it!"

The shaking finally stopped and the loud booming sounds faded away leaving behind an annoying ringing in my ears followed by a headache. What was that, I thought. I had a terrible feeling…

Faintly, I could hear the pitter patter of feet upstairs through the rock ceiling. Either there were a lot of people running around above me, or the cracks in the ceiling were allowing the sound through, or both. What was going on up there?

Just then, I saw Callon sprint down the hallway through the slits in the door. I heard him open the door to the room on my left and talk to some people in there. I could barely make out what he was saying over the different concoctions of noises coming at me.

"He… attack… need to mobilize…help…" I made out an attack. I needed to break out and help with whatever was going on. My friends may need me… Trish may need me, I thought.

"Callon!" I screamed at the top of my lungs to the point where my throat was sore.

He stopped in front of my door and said, "What is it, Laufor? I don't have time."

I asked while watching Isaac, Rafael, Daniel, and all of the others from the last round of the Gaunlet with bandages all over their bodies run past him, "What's going on? Let me out! I can help."

He shook his head. "Sorry, Laufor. You would be helpful, but with the Overload, I can't take that risk. You would be endangering all of the Recruits in the Clade including yourself."

He ran from the door following the mass of Recruits heading towards the steps. I growled and threw myself into a tantrum in my seat. My wrists were cut deeply again, but I didn't feel it in my rage.

How could Callon not let me help? I may be a ticking time bomb, but I can still help until the Overload gets to that level of severity. I screamed out in agony and slouched in my seat, helpless.

While I sat helplessly, Shiloh said, "He is probably right. We are far better off here."

"Are you insane?" I snapped at him, adrenaline rushing through every vein in my body.

"I guess so," he said calmly. He wouldn't be so calm, cool, and collected if he was on the same side of the wall as me. "Callon is usually right about decisions as extreme as these. If it was a serious problem, he would take us out and... aaahh... guhh... let us fight."

I refused to listen to Shiloh. He was naïve and needed to stand up for himself. He shouldn't believe and listen to everything that his superiors told him. I learned that by being on the bottom rung of the social hierarchy. The only way to make it by is to listen to yourself and your friends. Otherwise, trust no one. That may sound a little extreme, but these were extreme circumstances.

I said, "I'm sure Callon wouldn't have let all the Recruits in the infirmary out if it was a minor problem."

Shiloh didn't respond for a few moments, and then he said, "I still don't think-"

He was cut off by a loud, high pitched, piercing ring. It bounced and reverberated off the walls of the cave carrying the noise all the way down to Shiloh and I. It was so painful that I wished I could cover my ears, but my hands were strapped to the chair.

Just then, the noise suddenly stopped. An eerie calm rested over the Clade, but that didn't last for long. A voice spoke up through some sort of sound amplification device. That is the only way a human could speak with us from… wherever the hell they were.

"Hello, Callon!" The voice bellowed. "You and your Recruits are under arrest for treason against your country and for the murder of government soldiers! Come out with your hands up, or we will go in there and kill you all with no mercy!"

The demonic voice gave me the deepest chills I ever had. I knew the voice. It was all too familiar to me. My body grew incredibly warm, and I felt weak all over like my muscles were removed.

The voice finished in a tremendous uproar. "It's the end of the Clade, and your extinction, Recruits!"

It was Nathaniel.

The Agency was on our doorstep.

Chapter 38

Nathaniel was back and was ready to blast the Clade into oblivion. His voice sent me back to the Clade in New York and the deaths of all of the other Recruits...

...including Gabe.

I began to hyperventilate. I truly felt as though my life was going to end strapped to that metal chair, helpless against the Agency. I could picture their destructive paths in my mind. They would kill everyone including my friends. Then, when everyone was gone, they would check out the cave and find Shiloh and I strapped in our chairs and simply put a bullet between our eyes, or Nathaniel would split me in half with a mountain.

I began to form tears in the pits of my eyes. Was this what happened to Gabe when he knew he was about to die, did he panic, I feared? I couldn't get him out of my head. I wish he was here now... he could come up with a good plan of getting out of here and helping our friends.

I couldn't let anything happen to Trish. Not now… not ever, but no matter how much I tried to break free, I couldn't. The bands were too tightly strapped around my wrists and ankles. If I could use my ability, I could get free, but as long as the IV was pumping Dopaphine into me, I have no choice but to wait until someone got me out, like that would ever happen.

Nothing could be more insulting than keeping me locked up in here. I helped save a few Recruits by risking my life in New York against Nathaniel. They were my friends, but I would still fight for the others as well. I mean, while I am fighting for them I will be fighting for the other Recruits. Did I really not care about the others? Was I selecting favorites?

All of this doubt was driving me crazy. It didn't matter if I was selfish or not fighting for only my friends if I couldn't get out of this room.

Then, a thumping of many footsteps closed in on our rooms. I tensed up. Could it be the Agents, I wondered. Suddenly, I felt at peace like all my worries and troubles would be taken away if it was the Agency. I actually started to hope it was them until I heard Callon's voice from outside of Shiloh's room.

He said, "You three stay here. I'll toss the weapons on the floor. You pick them up and distribute them to Recruits who can't fight with their own ability. Whatever you do, do not go in this room. Understood?"

I heard, "Mhmm," from the three Recruits in unison shortly before the sound of Shiloh's door being opened.

I could hear Callon's hurried footsteps from the entrance to the back of Shiloh's cell. There was another door being opened and a bunch of different things being tossed around. If what Callon said was true, then those were guns. They were about to go to war with the Agency. Round two.

Shiloh said, "What's happening, Callon? Who was that on the microphone?"

Callon didn't stop working when he said, "It was Nathaniel. It is true. He has joined forces with the Agency, and I'm afraid they found our hideout. We're going to battle. I'll come back and tell you when we are victorious."

Shiloh said, "Okay," while Callon was finishing throwing his weaponry together. I could hear the other Recruits grunting as they heaved, what I could only imagine as heavy weapons, in their arms.

The door slammed shut again. I could sense the anxiety driving Callon to hurry him which is good because he should be worried. The Agency would kill us all if they got in here. How was he supposed to defend a cave in a mountain?

"Let me OUT!" I shouted before Callon and the other Recruits left. I didn't get a response other than a painful jolt up the side of my body from the Overload.

A few minutes later, I heard more steps, but it wasn't just one person, this was multiple coming from above me. I looked up and saw Recruits through the cracks in the ceiling. Then, more and more Recruits continued to mobilize in that location. It appeared as though something important was going to happen like a speech or battle strategy. The only thing they should talk about is how to get out of here without getting murdered. They were wasting time.

The cracks were small and didn't allow me to see how many Recruits were there, but there was some chatter between them which made it seem as though everyone was there except for Shiloh and I. I must be locked beneath the cafeteria. That is the only room large enough to hold all of the Recruits in the Clade.

At once, all of the Recruits went silent. The something I was wondering about was about to start. I remained as quiet as the other Recruits and listened.

Callon's voice was heard first. "Recruits, as you are aware, the Agency has found us. Unfortunately, for them they don't know what they are getting into!"

There were cheers from the Recruits. This was like a pre-game warm up, but this wasn't a game. This was life they were gambling. Callon needed to do the smart thing and just run away from this.

"This is what we have trained for for countless hours. This is why we have Gauntlet's and Tests and work hard! The Agency is trying to take away our god given freedoms! The freedom to live!"

The Recruits cheered even louder this time. I even was starting to get chills listening to Callon, but that's not a good thing. If he gets the Recruits pumped up enough, they would want to fight. They weren't immortal, and the Agency would murder them!

Callon continued, "For those of you whose ability will not cause severe damage to heavily armored Agent troops, grab a gun up front by the Instructors. They will give you a quick run through with how to use them if you are unaware. Everyone else, move towards the cavern entrance, and I'll mobilize you from there. We will win today, Recruits!"

Everyone cheered and began to move towards where they were directed. They had no idea they were like cattle waiting to be slaughtered. There were only fifty Recruits and a few Instructors against the Agency's army. They had no chance. I hoped Marcus was trying to talk some sense into him considering he went through the same dilemma.

The Recruits kept moving about above me preparing for battle. It was surprising that the Agents didn't bolt into the cavern and kill everyone already. Were they toying with us, or did they want to see what we were made of? Nathaniel seems to be a leader among the Agent ranks, but he can't be the top even if he does contain a lot of power. If he was in charge of this group of Agents, then it would make sense that his arrogance was the controlling factor, and the reason why the Agents would be waiting for a fight.

Eventually, the Recruits vanished and headed towards the battle waiting outside the cavern entrance. I began to think about how many of the Recruits were going to their imminent deaths and were going to see the sun for the first time in years. The Recruits here really were like animals, I thought.

Time passed by and nothing happened that led me to any conclusions about the fate of the Recruits and most importantly, my friends. I could only imagine what Teddy was going through considering this was his first fight and he didn't even know the full extent of his abilities yet. Heck, even I didn't.

Shiloh and I continued to be silent. I never felt more helpless in my life. As each precious second ticked away, I imagined another Recruit being shot, another friend being murdered, another Instructor betraying us. If there were a way to get out, I would take it, but I couldn't find anything that would help. Even with the new extension to my power that I discovered while taking the Test, I couldn't use it because there was no metal in the room. Also, my hands were strapped too tightly for them to even wiggle.

During my deepest moments of depression, faint rings of bullet fire began. I knew it was the sound of guns firing bullets. Once you hear it, you never forget. My body ached and felt lifeless. My mind grew dim as my thoughts died out. That was it... I couldn't help them now other than hope that their end is quick. Maybe I'd see Trish, Sarah, and the other's when this is all over wherever we end up if there really is an After. Maybe Gabe would be waiting for us...

Almost a half hour passed while I was strapped to the chair listening to the quiet but excruciatingly loud bullets. A few screams were heard as well that made me shiver. Shiloh continued to gasp and moan like usual, but he must've been having the same feelings as me.

Suddenly, more footsteps were approaching from down the hallway, but these weren't the footsteps of Recruits. No, instead, I could audibly discern a difference between their sound and these. These feet contained some sort of metal tips in their shoes or boot. I could tell by a small clicking, and there was more than one person.

From what I could hear, there were two. Who were they, I feared?

I got my answer soon enough when one of the mysterious men spoke in a husky tone. "How long do you think this cavern stretches on?"

The other one said in a deep, masculine, voice, "Does it matter? Chairman Harwell wanted the tunnels cleared out of all subjects before Nathaniel was finished with the ones fighting."

They were Agents I realized. They must've snuck in while the other Recruits were being distracted by the Agency's army. They were closing in on Shiloh and me, and soon, they would have us... and destroy us.

I began to panic. It was weird. I felt comfortable with dying a few minutes ago, but now, that I knew my grim reaper was approaching with guns at the ready, I wanted to get out of there as quickly as possible.

Shiloh was beginning to struggle to break free for the first time since he was probably taken down here. I could hear his chair wiggle back and forth, but without abilities, Callon has signed our death certificate.

Shiloh was still moaning from the Overload tearing his body apart. I whispered, "Keep quiet if you can. The Agents may pass us."

"Ahhh..." he said. "I'm trying... but, grraahh, it hurts so much. I can't keep quiet. It's just too painful."

The Agents were rapidly approaching. It sounded as though they were picking up speed. Did they hear Shiloh aching, I wondered. If so, then the Overload would be our downfall after all.

My heart stopped as the Agents stopped just outside Shiloh's door. I could hear the two conversing while Shiloh and I sat as still as possible trying our best to not make even a peep. That was incredibly hard for Shiloh to do, though.

The Agent with the deeper voice said, "This room has its window slits boarded up. I wonder what Subject Alton has hidden in there."

"It must be something important like that hi-tech computer system we found in New York," the other Agent said.

"Yeah, that was useless. Not even Nathaniel wanted that hunk of junk back. Think of how advanced that was twenty years ago when the subjects first escaped."

First escaped? What are they talking about, and why do all of the Agents call us subjects? We're people aren't we?

"There is probably nothing in there we are to be concerned with," one Agent said. "We found no subjects upstairs, and, if what Nathaniel told us was true, then there is no reason for subjects to be down here. It is off limits to them except for subject Alton and subject Irving."

I could hear them approaching my window, which had open, exposed, window slits. Sweat dripped off my face, the anxiety creating a furnace inside my body. The Agents stopped just before my door and stood in place for a few moments.

"What was that noise Agent 56?" The deeper voiced Agent asked.

"I have no idea. It sounded like someone was in pain. Do you think it is a subject?" The other Agent asked.

"Only one way to find out," the Agent said as he approached Shiloh's door.

There were a few clicks with the turn of the knob on the locked door. A few pounds and shoves shook the door on its metallic hinges. Shiloh must've been in pure terror. I could only imagine the horror he must be going through. How could I help him, though? With no abilities and the state I was in, I couldn't help anyone.

One of the Agents said, "56, take out the mini-explosive and rig it to the door. That will take down this door."

"Right, sir," the other Agent said. He sounded like he was a lower ranking Agent than the deeper sounding voice Agent.

There were a few shuffling sounds and clicking of bolts while the device was being applied to the frame of the door. It sounded electronic because there were bleeps and bloops of buttons being pushed, then, an electronic ticking sound.

After the Agents sprinted towards the generator room, there was a distinct moment of tension. The only thing heard was the ticking sound of the bomb waiting to blow open Shiloh's cover and most likely mine soon enough. Shiloh struggled more to break free while he ached and groaned, but it wasn't enough. There was not enough time.

He was too late.

The device rang three times like a phone and exploded. I rocked slightly in my chair and saw pieces of rock and metallic debris soar through the hallway across my window slits. There was a rattling sound coming from Shiloh's room.

I could barely hear him over the ringing sensation happening in my ears, but I'm pretty sure he yelled, "No! My Dopaphine!"

Shiloh's Dopaphine must've been knocked over from the blast. It's a shame it didn't knock mine over. He began to scream even louder now. The pain must've been incredible. If he groaned and ached with painkillers flowing through him, I couldn't imagine the pain he must be feeling now.

There was a bright red light that would fade and then return with each scream and inhalation Shiloh would take. The light passing through the vent created demonic shadows of cabinets and other things, like myself, in my room. What was happening to him, I wondered.

The Agents didn't waste time. Shortly after the device detonated, they began to walk down the hallway until they finally reached Shiloh's door.

I heard one gasp and the other chuckled lightly. "What do you know," the deeper voiced Agent said. "There appears to be a subject tied up just for us like a little present."

"AAAHHH!" Shiloh belted out followed by a bright reddish orange light and a slight tinge of heat.

"Oooh," the lesser Agent said. "He is giving off some intense energy. What do you think we should do to help, 32?"

Agent 32 bellowed like evil itself and said, "Put him out of his misery."

"NOO!" Shiloh cried out. "Please... aahh! No!"

That's when I heard a gun being taken out of its sheath. Another blast of heat irradiated from Shiloh's body. He was about to be killed and there was nothing I could do.

I didn't think. I just acted. "No! Leave him alone you jerks!"

There was a pause and Agent 32 said, loud enough for me to hear, "Well, it appears we have another subject in the other room. Don't worry. We will be over soon enough to end your tyranny, but first, this boy has to die."

"No! Please! Aahh!" Shiloh cried out again. I could hear him choke up on the last word as if he was about to sob. I didn't blame him.

Agent 56 said, "Sorry, boy, but that's what you get for having stupid powers. Look where it's got you. Is it really worth it?"

Shiloh choked up, said, "I... didn't want these powers..."

Agent 32 said, "Just hurry up so we can get the other guy. It's getting warm in here."

There was a silence. Shiloh didn't even say anything. In that moment, it was like the planet stopped spinning. Everything that was happening around the world, the pain, the hunger, the wars, that didn't matter. Only this moment seemed to decide the fate of everything that existed, and I was strapped to a chair. Helpless.

Just like I was with Gabe...

Suddenly, there was a loud bang. The trigger had been pulled and Shiloh was silent. The light faded abruptly, and the heat no longer continued to fume. He was in a better place now I can only hope. Hopefully, his pain didn't follow him. I closed my eyes and took a moment of silence for Shiloh. He was trapped in here the last three years of his life. What a terrible end to such a kind soul.

Agent 32 then pulled me out of my trance. "One down. One to go."

Just then, the light reappeared from Shiloh's room, and this time it was brighter and hotter than ever! I began to sweat almost immediately after the first wave hit me.

The Agents began to freak out. "What is happening to the boy's body!?" Agent 56 screamed.

"I don't know, but-"

There was a huge explosion from Shiloh's room. It was so powerful it blew open the wall and tore my seat from its bolts in the floor. My chair blew sideways while a wave of intense heat and flame shot over my head nearly burning my face. I have never felt something that intense before in my life.

The flames stopped shortly after the eruption. I slowly opened my eyes to see a pile of rubble and ash from the wall that separated Shiloh and I. Even the wall to the hallway had been blown to pieces leaving behind only a mound of dust and rock debris.

Tentatively, afraid of the massacre I may have had to look into, I glanced to see what was left of the Agents. On a first look, there was nothing. No bodies were left other than a few scraps of armor and stained blood. It must have been an incredibly intense explosion for the bodies and blood itself to be almost completely vaporized.

I looked over to where Shiloh's chair should have rested, but there was no chair left. However, lying on the floor facedown was the boy I have been talking to for the last few hours, his final few hours of life. How did he survive the explosion if the other two instantly disintegrated into nothingness, I asked myself?

There was a huge gash in Shiloh's neck where the bullet went through. Those Agents were monsters. They didn't want him just to die. They wanted him to suffer as well. My rage built up. If I wasn't connected to the Dopaphine, I would be feeling an excruciating amount of pain right now from the Overload. Instead, there was only a touch of it.

Suddenly, Shiloh's body began to twitch and stir. I watched carefully as Shiloh opened his eyes slowly, blood still pouring out of the hole in his neck. He was still alive but not for long.

He coughed, spitting up blood, and said, "I... feel... great."

"What?" I asked shocked. "How can that be, Shiloh? You are bleeding an enormous amount. I need to get you help."

It was at that moment that I was able to finally get a picture of whom I was talking to the last few hours. He was tall, probably six and a half feet tall. He had black hair and a beard from the lack of shaving over the last few years. His eyes were bright blue, but tainted with red splotches of blood and imminent death. Looking at him, I never felt more useless and terrible in my life, even counting Gabe's death.

"Yeah..." he coughed some more. "The... Overload. I don't... feel it."

"How can that be?" I asked realizing what he was saying.

He shook his head from left to right. "Don't... know, but... if I'm going to die, at least I'm human for it."

A tear rolled out of my eye and off of my cheek. I nodded. "Of course, I'm sorry I can't help you Shiloh."

He said, "Don't...be. It's not your... fault. Just, do one thing... for me."

I listened intently, "Yes, anything."

"Save your...friends. They're all you have... in hell," he said, and with his final words, he shut his eyes and exhaled a deep breath never to take in another one.

Chapter 39

There was a somber period for me as I lay strapped to the metal chair. Shiloh's body rested on the rocky debris only a few yards in front of me. Thankfully, his eyes were closed to make it look as though he was sleeping. I don't know if I could've handled staring into his empty eyes. It would've torn me apart, and reminded me of...

The gunshots could still be heard outside the cave. It was amazing to me how well I could hear all that was happening. The cave must've taken quite a beating and created many cracks in its foundation in order for me to hear the sounds so well. I was worried that it was probably close to collapsing then. If that was so, I needed to get out as soon as possible. The explosions and gunfire weren't helping my situation.

How was I supposed to escape, I wondered. My arms and legs were belted tightly, and the yellow goo continued to ooze into my arm. Now, it was only helping a little. The Overload was taking its toll on me. I could feel the pain ready to burst out at any moment and wreak havoc on my body.

My face was just beginning to dry from the tears that fell for Shiloh. There were only a few, but they were large. No person should live and die like he did... no one.

Then, more footsteps could be heard hurrying their way down the tunnel. I tensed up and quieted myself. I didn't see the point, though. The explosion was immense. I'm sure all of the Agents in the cave could hear it, and they are on their way to finish the job the other Agent's couldn't complete, and that was killing me.

The footsteps grew louder as the mysterious figure approached. The stress on my body made it feel like the entire world was crushing me. My breathing became sporadic, and I began to sweat even more. My nerves wouldn't rest. They kept my body twitching and jumping trying to keep itself alive, but my brain knew that there was no way I could get out of this mess.

The figure turned to the hallway I was down. Soon, it would all be over. I would be just like Shiloh, a Recruit lost in tragedy and misfortune in the Clade, which would soon be forgotten as well. The Clade would fall just like all of the other Recruits. Sarah, Trish, Teddy, Liam, Marcus, Juliette, Riley, McKayla... they needed me.

I whispered to myself, "I'm sorry... I failed you guys."

The figure appeared in the exposed portion of wall that was blown away by Shiloh. The person didn't wear black armor or metal boots. Instead, he wore a long, black, cloak and carried a gun at his side.

It was Conner of all people.

"Conner?" I asked shocked.

He turned my way and trampled over the fallen debris. "Laufor, what happened here? Who is this?" He pointed to Shiloh's body.

I didn't know what to say, so, I said, "A friend who lived a terrible life and died a terrible way."

Conner just shrugged and said, "Okay, whatever you say."

He approached and began to undo the belts on my wrist and legs. I rubbed them gently making sure I wouldn't reopen any wounds that my ability didn't heal especially since it was being slowed by the Dopaphine.

I stood and pulled out the IV from my arm. Slowly, I could feel my power rising back inside me. Along with that came intense pain from the Overload. I cringed and bent over my chest. My vision went blurry for a few moments and then it subsided.

Conner said unsympathetically, "You okay?"

"Yeah…" I said with my eyes squeezed shut. "I'm fine. Don't worry."

He helped me stand up straight and said, "How are you feeling? All of the Recruits saw what happened in the Gauntlet. I'll be honest. At the time, I didn't care that you could have potentially died."

I didn't look at him. With no emotion, I said, "Gee, thanks."

"Don't mention it," he replied. "Anyways, I did like what happened to Bruno." He didn't laugh. His words had no feeling behind them like he was holding his emotions in like a rock. "He took a huge spill after kicking the hell out of you. It kinda sucks now that we need him to help defend us all, and he is all beat up. Good goin,' Laufor."

I said, "I try."

His presence down here was confusing to me. He never spoke, and he never dared show a hint of compassion or a will to make friends. Why does he go against Callon's demands to save me now, I wondered.

"Why are you doing this, Conner? You never seemed to care about me before this battle. Why are you here to save me?" I asked.

Conner began to walk towards the exit. Climbing over the rubble, he said, "Don't think of me as an idiot, Laufor. I never did like you, nor do I like any of the other nimrods I have lunch with. I only do because everyone needs a place and mine is there. I know Riley is my Bloodling, and because of that, I feel as though we have a connection, but that doesn't mean I like him."

He crossed the rubble and stood in front of the gaping hole in the wall, arms crossed. "I don't care for anyone here especially that Bruno. He is a pompous, arrogant, jerk that deserved the defeat he was handed. However, I do rely on them for my survival. My ability is weak in comparison to them, so I focused all of my efforts in building strength and practicing my martial arts on top of the mountain which I have been on for the last year and a half. The problem is that martial arts can only go so far. Guns and abilities can easily stop me. That's why I'm silent and observe. If I am just around and develop no friendships, then the people believe I am on their side, and then when they are killed on a mission or when I face them in the Gauntlet, I feel no sympathy for hurting them."

Conner's entire world unraveled in front of me. His words spoke wisdom that would be great for those who had a cold heart like his. He was so detached from everyone that it made him strong, at least in his eyes.

Was survival all that mattered in a place like this? Were friendships and relationships even possible when at any moment you could be attacked by the Agency? My father could do it, and so could all of the children of the Originals. How come we couldn't? Marcus once told me that the Agency has finally unleashed its endgame. They never attacked the Clade until just recently. Maybe they needed Nathaniel to help them before they could attack, but even with his power, they are still stronger than all of us, I thought. It confused me more than Conner's mentality.

I said, approaching him by tediously stepping over the debris, "I don't think you need to live that way. It just seems so cold. How can you not care for anyone?"

Conner looked down at the floor, "That's not entirely true. I do care for someone, but that's not important. I will never be with her because, like me, she will eventually be killed off."

So, Conner does have strong feelings for someone. Who could it be, I wondered. He has been here a lot longer than I have, and considering the small number of Recruits, I still have no idea who half of the women are. It could be a girl I never met.

No matter, I shouldn't worry about it now. The gunfire was still echoing in the distance reminding me of the chaos and death occurring above. If I didn't hurry, my friends would be gone.

I didn't realize I had been staring at the base of his shoes on top of the rubble. I was lost in thought when Conner said, "You there? C'mon. Your friends are up there, and they need you."

I locked eyes with him. They were cold just like him. I never took the time to really get to know Conner, but I get his entire outlook on life when I stare at his eyes. However, there is a small sparkle in the far corner for that girl he cares for.

Stepping off the rubble and standing beside him, I said, "Right, show me the way."

He nodded and took off down the dark hallway. I was about to follow him when I caught a glimpse of something on the back wall. I turned and saw a large monitor of a super computer. It was completely destroyed. Burned wires and broken glass clung to the screen and control panel beneath it. My mind kept flashing to the super computer in the New York Clade before that was destroyed as well. What do these things do?

As of now, it didn't matter as I chased behind him as quickly as I could. All of the lights were out where areas of immense structural damage could be found. One area had completely collapsed in from the top level of the cave. Everything after that was bright with light still being powered by the generator. As we approached the fallen piece of rock, the light behind it shone on Conner and I like a guardian angel guiding us to our fate. Whatever fate we had, it would be found outside the Clade.

We squeezed through the small gap between the rock wall and the fallen floor one at a time. After I pushed my way through, Conner turned and ran up the slope of the rock. He placed each foot carefully on a jagged piece of rock and climbed his way up. I followed him in suit doing the exact same thing as he did and put my feet in the same positions his were. It was steep and holding on was difficult, but I made it shortly after Conner.

He stood casually next to me as if nothing was wrong. When I got on my feet, he said, "About time. The battle is going on outside. The Agents have dispersed themselves in the forest and are approaching the cavern. All of the Recruits have been placed between them and here. I don't know how many are still alive, but if they are, they won't be for long. I did see your group of New Yorkers when I ran inside, even Teddy."

Those words had sparked some hope for me. If they were still alive, I could still get them out of here in one piece, but how? I don't really have the answer to that yet, but that would be my first priority, I know.

"Good," I said. "I'll do what I can. It sounds like you are putting a lot of hope in me, though. If anything, I can give you all some time to get out of here safely."

"Do you really believe running is the only solution?" He asked.

"I do," I said delving back into the repressed portions of my memory banks. "I have faced them before, and the Agency wasn't something to toy with. They will kill us all like they did the Recruits back in New York. I am only one Recruit that has been here for a few months. I am no Instructor. I couldn't even beat Nathaniel. One bullet and I would be killed just like anyone else."

"Fine," he said heading towards the dull light at the end of the tunnel. "I didn't have high hopes anyway. At least I bought myself some more time."

He started for the exit and I followed. We didn't sprint this time. Instead, we walked at a normal pace. It was a moment that was filled with somber and peace. We both knew that our ends could be waiting for us the second we step out into the dark, gray light, but we couldn't run. The Agency would find us, and my friends needed me.

I wouldn't let what happened to Gabe happen to them!

Adrenaline rushed through my body. Every cell of my body accelerated to one hundred times its speed. My body felt like it could block bullets, and the Agency couldn't defeat me no matter what they threw at me, but shortly after that, my body exploded in pain. The Overload sparked my every pore and blasted every vein. I dropped to one knee and held my abdomen with one arm. I groaned and cackled like Shiloh had done so many times before his death.

Conner stopped beside me, "You okay?"

I said, "Yeah... ahhh... I'm... fine." I stood up to prove it to him and that he shouldn't be worried; although, I didn't think he was.

"Okay, then. Get up and get moving. You are no help to the other Recruits in here," Conner said.

The pain subsided to just an awful annoyance. "I'm fine. Let's go, and the Recruits need you out there as well."

He lifted his gun in front of himself and said, "Yeah, I'm so much help. Guns are not power here. Abilities are, and I was given a terrible one. I can transform ice into water. Unless the entire Agency was standing on a frozen lake, and they couldn't swim, I'm useless."

"If you think like that, then you are useless," I said.

He shrugged his shoulders and kept his eyes focused on the opening. Shouts of different commands became more audible the closer we moved to the opening. My heart raced. I had to make sure that if I was going to die that my friends were safe. I hate to point out favorites, but Trish for sure even if she hated me to the core of her being. I hoped that wasn't the case, but I would still make sure she was safe and away from any danger that may come her way.

Conner and I continued to walk until we reached the very edge of the cave. We stopped. A few Recruits were outside of the edge of the forest. The guards that were being stationed outside the entrance left to go fight. I couldn't find any of my friends or the Instructors. They must've been deep in the forest fighting for their lives or conceiving a plan to get us all out of here.

The sky was filled with massive, gray clouds that blotted out the sky from atop of the mountain all the way to the horizon in every direction. Rain drizzled down upon the mountain making the soil wet and muddy beneath my shoes. Darker clouds rested further out in the distance. It would pour rain later. Whether we would all be alive to experience it was still a mystery to me.

I stepped out slowly into the rain, being the first time since I had seen nature in months, and let the rain fall down on my body. I thought it would feel nice and cool, but instead, I got an immediate and painful shock through my body. I cried out and dropped to the ground again. It didn't stop there. With every drop of rain water that hit me, another blast of Overload coursed through my body. The pain was intense but I could take it. I gritted my teeth and fought through the pain. Working as hard as I could, I stood on my feet.

Conner stepped next to me, "Is that because of the thing that happened in the Gauntlet?"

I nodded trying to deal with the pain. "It is also the reason why I was locked in that room in the basement."

Conner said, "What is it?"

I said, "It's called an Overload. I don't know much about it other than there is no cure and only Recruits get it."

Conner said, again with little emotion, "Interesting."

A cry was heard in the middle of the forest followed by more gunfire. Another person, a woman, lost her life. Was she an Agent or Recruit, I wondered. We needed to hurry. I could barely deal with the pain to begin with, and if the heavy part of the storm hit us, then there would be no way I could help. I would probably kill myself to take away the pain.

"Let's go," I said.

Then, Conner and I took off down the slope towards the battle in the woods just like in New York praying that the results would turn out differently. I could begin to see glimpses of black cloaks in the green backdrop of the forest. It appeared as though they were slowly moving forward, a few with guns, a few with just their abilities to defend themselves. More screams and cries could be heard from the middle of the forest.

We hit the bottom and ran into the forest as quickly as we could run. The brush flattened and the sticks crunched under my feet. Mud began to cling to my black shoes slowing me down slightly. The rain continued to fall making the problem worse and giving me a severe beating. Every few drops, I could catch a glimpse of a bolt of electricity jumping on my skin and then having pain follow it.

The forest swallowed Conner and I. I didn't know why he was keeping up with me. He didn't seem to care about anyone. If that was the case, then why did he want to rush in and help them? My thoughts switched from him to the girl that we almost ran into when we weren't looking ahead.

I stopped abruptly creating a little spray of mud and dead grass. It was Ruby Adams from the Gauntlet. "Hey, Ruby!" I shouted.

She crouched low. "Ssshhh!" She whispered loudly. "Get down. The Agents are ahead of us. I don't know where, though."

She stood behind a tree, and Conner and I hid behind two other trees beside her. Her gun was held across her chest, and every once in a while, she would peek out her head to see if anyone was coming. No one ever came.

After a few moments, she said, "I think we are okay."

We stepped out from behind the trees and grouped together in a small opening. She said, "Laufor? I thought you were dead after what I heard about the ending of the Gauntlet."

"Nope," I said fighting the pain. "I'm still here just a little late. What's happening?"

She filled us in on what had occurred since the Agency first arrived. The shaking we felt before were bombs being dropped from planes. They guessed it was only a scare tactic. Portions of the cave collapsed, but they weren't powerful enough to destroy it. It was as if the Agency were trying to scare everyone out. When they did get out, Nathaniel had his men quickly retreat back into the forest. Callon had teams stick together and head into the forest and kill them, but there were too many Agents.

"So many people were killed," she said. "Ariella, Isaac, even Daniel were killed by gunfire."

Hearing that Daniel was killed gave me the shivers. He was a tough guy with a great ability, but that couldn't stop a reign of bullets. None of our abilities could.

"I'm sorry," I said genuinely.

She shrugged. "It's okay. I just want to get out of this alive. I don't know how many of the other Recruits are left. I think the people you two are always with are still alive, though. I saw them while I retreated after Daniel was shot."

"How long ago was this?" I perked up.

"About ten minutes, maybe. I would hurry, though. I think this was all planned," she said.

"What do you mean?" Conner said at my side, his arms crossed. I swear they were always in that position.

"I'm just saying. I think they are after someone, and not to kill them. Otherwise, they would've just leveled the entire mountain and been on their merry way," she said.

"Who do you think they're after?" I asked.

She shook her head. "No idea, but I wouldn't want to be them. Then again, at least they will be kept alive. Everyone else is as good as dead. That's why I'm getting out of here, only the Agency has blocked the path down."

So, the Agency has blocked the path down to the diner at the base of the mountain. Now, we were all trapped like rats in a cage. If they continued their march forward, they would kill us all. Something had to be done quickly, or there would be no hope for any of us.

Chapter 40

Conner and I took off for the deeper parts of the forest. If I was going to find my friends, they would be somewhere in there. Ruby remained at her post on the outskirts of the forest. Callon most likely told her to be the last line of defense in case the Agency broke through. I didn't see the point. If the Agency got to the cave, there would be nothing and no one left there. She would be just one of the last ones to die.

We ran as quickly as we could into the heart of the forest. It was difficult to move very quickly. Branches of low growing trees smacked us across the legs or scratched our face. Bushes and shrubs tangled our feet together. Fallen logs were in our path that needed to be overcome. It doesn't sound all that difficult, but when there is something on the line, and there is no sun to light your way, it's hard. I tripped and fell a few times into the mud myself, but I just wiped it off, dealt with the overwhelming pain of the Overload, and kept on going.

Guns could be more easily heard the more we pushed ourselves into the forest. I'm not going to lie. I was terrified. At any moment, we could've been ambushed by Agent troops and killed. I tried to move as silently as possible, but with all of the brush, my legs kept colliding into them making swishing noises. Conner, on the other hand, was like a ninja. He was agile and dodged all of the small brush in our way. Not a sound was made from the vigilante behind me.

It wasn't long before I heard Juliette's voice over the rustling of the plants. "Their grouping on our right! Take cover and protect our flank!"

I stopped and whispered to Conner, "Juliette! It sounds like she is to our right. We should head over and help. My friends might be there."

Conner just nodded and stayed behind me as I took off for Juliette's location. We needed to be more careful than ever now. I heard her say that there were Agents attacking them. I slowed my pace a little, and Conner reacted the same way. We didn't want to give away our position. We could be what Juliette needs at a moment like this, and if the Agents heard us coming, we would lose the advantage of surprise.

We passed a few trees and hurdled a few logs when we saw a group of Recruits hiding around a large boulder. Juliette was behind a tree slightly in front of the boulder. She was still giving out commands over the sound of gunfire. Bullets whizzed by and collided with the rocks. I think one even flew between Conner and me. We jumped out of the way and hid behind separate trees just in case they spotted us. That bullet was too close for comfort.

Juliette must've noticed us behind the trees. She said, "Ezekiel? Is that you?"

I didn't move; I just answered, "Yes, Conner and I are here."

"You aren't supposed to be here!" She shouted over incoming bullet fire. She lifted her open palm in front of her to gather energy. "If Callon finds out that you are out of your holding room, he will kill you!"

"I'm willing to take that risk, Juliette. We need to get everyone out of here."

Gunfire continued to pelt the trees and the large boulder. Chips and splinters of bark showered down from the trees. A Recruit hiding behind the boulder was a bit too far out and was hit with a shot in the arm. He fell to the ground and held his left shoulder tightly screaming in pain. The rain water covered his face and removed any signs that he was crying.

Juliette panicked. Her face contorted to one of fear and disgust. What kind of cruel person would shoot a kid, I thought. With a rage of determination, she turned from her cover and spun her arms like a windmill. Tiny shimmers of air over her head launched themselves at an incredible speed. Two of the air darts collided with trees, exploding on the spot. One blasted off a leg of an Agent who was hiding behind a tree trunk, and two others blasted two Agents to nothingness, literally. Nothing remained of them.

She quickly tucked herself back behind the tree. The wounded Recruit was getting help from a girl who was also hiding behind the rock with him. Her machine gun was propped against the large boulder. Rain water dripped down its metallic edges.

Juliette shouted. "Is he okay?"

The girl nodded. "He will be, but the bullet is still in his shoulder! It needs to be taken out before it gets infected!"

Juliette scowled. They were in a pinch. Agent troops were still moving in from the back. Before long, they would have enough troops to surround us and take us out. The problem was that she only had a few Recruits at her disposal.

She shouted, "Zeke, Conner, can you get up to me!?"

"We can try!" I replied.

Conner made a funny look at me. "Seriously?"

"Yes, seriously. C'mon, follow me," I said as I began to move from tree to tree.

Conner stayed close by me as we moved. Bullets continued to pelt the trees. A few were extremely close to hitting Conner and me. We would drop to the ground when we heard the bullets riddle the trees beside us or if they flew by near us. We had to be extremely careful. One wrong move and we would be done, I feared

Carefully, we army crawled on the ground breaking twigs and crushing worms along the way. Juliette was only a few feet ahead of us, but it would be a hard crawl to get to her. I put my right hand down on a broken branch, the end snapped to a fine point. I gasped and pulled it up. Blood trickled from the opening. My brain has been trained to associate blood with a brutal pain shortly after, and it did. Electricity rushed through my arm bringing scorching pain followed by visible bolts sealing the hole in my hand. My body went numb. Electricity pulsated within me. The rain didn't help heal the pain. The Overload was growing fiercer.

I was writhing on the ground when Conner said, "You okay?"

I remained silent and dealt with the pain. It felt like my head was going to explode if I didn't do something. I responded, fists clenched, eyes squeezed shut.

I said, "I'm fine. Let's keep going."

We shimmied on the ground a few more feet until we were able to get up and take cover behind some trees near Juliette. Bullets flew by as we pushed ourselves up. I was on Juliette's right, and Conner was behind a tree to her left.

"What's your plan, Juliette?" I asked.

The rain poured a little harder now. Her dark hair was soaked. Droplets of water streamed down her face, but that didn't cool her ferocity. There was a natural beauty that I have never noticed before in that instant. For a moment, I was a little jealous of Marcus.

She said, "I've been destroying these guys left and right, but they keep coming. I don't have much energy left. My head is beginning to ache, and the Recruits with guns can't really penetrate their armor and they're not very accurate."

"What do you want us to do, then?" Conner asked.

"I want you two," she pointed at us both, "to provide me with some cover fire while I charge up the rest of my energy. I can create enough javelins to kill most of them, then the others will most likely retreat."

Conner and I both nodded. Juliette nodded in return. I ducked back down and crawled to place myself in front of Juliette. Conner followed close behind me groaning along the way. The bushes concealed us well as the further away we got from Juliette, the more visible the Agents became. There were about ten or fifteen troops corralled behind the trunk of a large fallen tree. A few others were scattered behind other trees or just out in the open.

The closer we moved, the more risky it got for us to be seen. It came to a point where I felt that they could look directly down at us. The mental image was horrific. Their black facemasks took away their individuality and made them soldiers from some dark abyss that only wanted to take you back to their abyss.

That's when I heard rustling to our left but still ahead of us. There was a lone Agent troop making his way from tree trunk to tree trunk, his gun held against his chest waiting for an opening to take down Juliette.

I looked back at Conner and nodded towards the Agent that was locked on for Juliette. He shook his head back, and we quickly took our positions behind trees. While this was happening, bullets continued to fly down the alleyway that connected the Agency to the Recruits. I wouldn't have to cross that in order to stop the Agent, but I would have to be quick; otherwise, the other Agents may spot me.

Conner coughed slightly which attracted my attention. My heart pounded hard. I feared he just gave away our position! I turned around slowly to see Conner pointing at me and then at the Agents behind the tree trunk and the others. I gave him a confused look wondering what he wanted exactly. He then rolled his eyes and pointed at his gun, flustered, and then at the Agent which had just moved closer to us.

I finally figured out what Conner was trying to force into my head. He would take out the rogue Agent if I distracted the other Agents for Juliette. I quickly nodded noticing the Agent only a few yards away behind a tree. It was amazing that he didn't spot us yet. If he did, we would be forced to move, and the river of sailing bullets would turn us both into Swiss cheese.

Conner pushed his back up against a tree and held his gun close to his eye getting ready for the Agent to step out from behind his cover. I didn't have the time to worry about him. I had to trust that he had everything under control and could do what was so impossibly hard until your first time, kill a man.

I dropped to my heels, crouched on the forest floor. The guns from the Agents continued to fire sending bullets in a metal storm across the forest, blowing bark and other debris off of the forest surroundings. It was then that a girl screamed and a thud was heard. I turned back to face Juliette and saw blood pooling from behind the boulder, and Juliette looked terribly afraid. The girl continued to scream hoping the pain would go away. At least, she was still alive, I thought.

This was my time to act. I nodded to Juliette who quickly nodded back. The bullets ceased for a few moments giving me a window of time to distract the Agents. I charged up in my wet hands. Electricity arced and jumped across my skin causing my body to explode in pain, but I couldn't stop no matter how much the Overload crippled my body.

I didn't have much time to spare, as the Overload was tearing me to shreds, so I sprinted across the opening with my hands bursting with electricity. I reached my palms forward at the black suited Agents behind the tree trunk. Only a few of them were visible, and it was my job to scare them out. I unleashed my wave of electrical fury on the Agents before they had a chance to unload on me. The bolts fluttered in a deadly wave that collided with the trees, rocks, ground, and all other things that happened to be in the way of my blast.

The bolts blasted the large tree trunk carving deep grooves into its wooden shell. The Agents jumped out of the way into open view for Juliette. Other bolts exploded into the ground sending a shower of dirt and debris into the air making the atmosphere foggy. Two bolts each blasted straight through smaller trees that hid two Agents. They both jumped in the dusty opening for safety.

I crashed to the ground on the other side of the opening. I could hear the Agents panicking over what had just happened.

A few spoke through communication devices making them sound like machines. "Was that Laufor?"

"It must be. No other subject can harness electricity!"

I laughed a little to myself as I rested in a pile of thick grasses and dirt. They made me seem so important and special, but in reality, I was just like the other Recruits with far less experience in controlling my ability. It was just different than the other Recruits which made me an anomaly to the Agency. How can I be that big of an issue, though, were they really that afraid of me, I wondered.

That's when Juliette unloaded wave after wave of air javelins. I could feel the cool wind blow me back gently as each invisible dart flew through the air. Followed by each was an explosion that dropped an Agent to the ground. I shielded my eyes from the splinters of trees that shot at my face. Little cuts formed from the shrapnel coming from the explosions, but they resealed almost immediately.

The cries of the Agents who had fallen were horrifying. The deafening booms of the air javelins blocked them out, but only for a moment. After each javelin Juliette conjured and fired, one less scream was heard. The Agents were falling one by one to Juliette's power. A little blood sailed across my face just barely passing my nose. The thoughts of their mutilated bodies made me gag.

With one last blast, there was silence. All of the Agents had fallen. Slowly, I got to my feet, the Overload crippling me greatly but not overcoming me. I tried to brush off some of the wet dirt off of my cloak, but it only ended up smearing, leaving dark brown stains on it. I groaned in a silly manner, as if that was the worst thing that had happened to me that day, and stepped out into the shooting range.

Juliette was to my left helping the injured Recruits on the ground. She applied bandages quickly and put pressure where it needed to be. If I didn't know any better, I would say that Juliette was a mother at one point, just by the way she took care of the Recruits so fast.

She stood, the arm of the fallen boy Recruit around her neck helping him up, and said, "Zeke, I'll be right back. These Recruits are in no shape to fight. I'm going to take them out of the forest. If you're looking for Marcus and the others, they are that way." She pointed directly behind me.

I turned in the direction she pointed and saw the bodies of the Agents. It was absolutely disgusting. There was nothing left of them. Armor clung to different severed pieces of limb or chest. I covered my mouth and turned back around.

I said, "Thanks, I'll go that way then."

She nodded and was about to turn around when something caught her eye. Her eyes opened wide and quickly spun back to face me. "Zeke!" She screamed. "Behind you!"

I quickly spun around and saw an Agent standing tall with a gun pointed at my chest. My guts sank deeper inside me. It felt like the end was here for sure.

Suddenly, Conner stepped out of the forest, his gun held up to the Agents head, and pulled the trigger. I shut my eyes, but still heard the blast of the gun followed by the drop of a lifeless human Agent.

I slowly opened my eyes and saw Conner in front of the Agent massacre created by Juliette and him. He said, "Sorry about that."

"What was that?" I asked still shocked that I was alive.

He stared down at the only intact Agent body, minus the hole through his head, and said, "I didn't react fast enough. I had my sights on the Agent the entire time as he stalked us through the forest, but when he heard the explosions, he ran over here. He was too late, of course, but when you stepped out from behind the trees, he began to move in. I risked your life, Zeke, and it shouldn't have come down to that. I choked when it came to killing him."

I couldn't really be mad at Conner. He suffered from the same fears as I did back in New York when the Agents attacked us. It's really hard to kill a person even if they are coming after you. There's a thought that crosses your mind for just a split second, and even though it is just a split second, it feels like an eternity. Questions begin to formulate like 'can I kill a person?' or 'what will happen to me if I take their life?' It's almost maddening and in the end, everyone loses. You become less of a human by killing another person, and the other person is dead regardless of their views.

I spoke softly, "It's okay, Conner. We are all safe and you made the tough choice in the end. I can't really blame you because I had the same problem back in New York when the Agency attacked me. I've been there, and it is really hard to kill someone."

He didn't smile or show any kind of sympathy. He just kept staring at the lifeless body of the Agent he killed and said, "Thanks, I guess."

I looked back to Juliette who was no longer there. The other Recruits were gone as well. I began walking towards Conner, stepped over the dead Agent trying not to look at him, and said, "We have to go this way. Follow me."

Chapter 41

The rain kept pouring down causing my Overload to react terribly. If it wasn't for my ability healing me while destroying me at the same time, I would've been incapacitated long ago. No way any Regular could still be mobile with an Overload. The pain was so bad, my body was so destroyed, but my ability kept fixing myself up. Essentially, I was fine, just in a massive amount of pain.

Conner and I kept walking together, him following behind me, through the forest. Gunfire was all around us now. We were constantly on edge waiting for an Agent to wander by and attack. We had to be ready to fight back at any time.

There was a loud crack in the sky followed by a low rumble. The rain began to fall harder ripping leaves off of trees and filtering water through the canopy. The Overload hurt even more. Not ready for it, I stumbled and fell to one knee.

Conner walked up behind me and said, "You okay?"

"Ahh, yeah… I'm fine. Let's keep going." I stood straight up and continued to walk through the pain.

"That wasn't the first time you stumbled and winced in pain," Conner said. "I notice these things. Something is wrong. Does it have to do with what happened during the Gauntlet? Was that why you were trapped in that room?"

I groaned and said, "Yes, it was because of that, but it's nothing serious. Don't worry about it. It will pass soon enough."

I looked back and saw Conner staring at me intently. It was sort of creepy, but much scarier than creepy because Conner was catching onto something he shouldn't be.

He said, "There was a reason why you were in that room, Laufor. Whatever happened in the Gauntlet, that outburst of electricity, that wasn't a onetime thing. I know it wasn't. Otherwise, Callon wouldn't have gone to such great lengths to locking you up in that room."

"It's nothing," I repeated.

We walked for a few more minutes in silence which was probably for the best. The Agents were all over the mountain probably taking down Recruits left and right. I hoped I could find Marcus before it was too late.

Suddenly, there was a loud patch of gunfire coming from straight ahead of us. Conner and I nodded at each other and moved silently through the brush and trees hoping nobody would spot us when we got close to the fight. It was hard, though. The mud would squish beneath our feet and clunk when it fell off. Puddles were everywhere, and the small splashes we made sounded loud enough that everyone in Colorado could hear them.

An opening was coming fast. Conner and I crouched low and kept moving. We stopped just before the line of bushes that surrounded the rim of the opening and watched.

There was a small, rain filled pond in the middle. On the far side were Agents, a lot of them. On the near side of Conner and I were a bunch of different Recruits including Sarah, Trish, Riley, and McKayla! They were all still okay, but not for long. They remained relatively well hidden behind the shrub line and different trees like Conner and I were.

"Over there!" I whispered.

Conner nodded, and we began to move over in that direction. We looked back over our shoulder and kept track of where the Agents were moving. They were slow but strategic. They wouldn't make a move against the Recruits unless they knew they could capture or kill them all. They had the upper hand and were stronger, but they weren't going to take unnecessary risks. That made them even scarier.

McKayla saw Conner and I move silently through the trees and quickly told the others. The ten Recruits all looked in our direction and smiled, especially my friends. They were ecstatic except for Trish. She turned back towards the Agency and gave us the cold shoulder. She was upset, but not at Conner, at me. I knew this would happen, but I couldn't worry about that now.

Conner and I stood and approached the group of frightened Recruits. "We're here," I said through the roar of the rain. "Is everyone okay?"

Sarah nodded quickly. "We're all fine. There were gunshots being heard all over the mountain. I don't know if I can say the same for everyone else. Did you see anyone else on your way here?"

"Juliette," I said. "She was with a few other Recruits. Two of them were shot, but she took care of them."

"Good," Sarah said slowly turning to let Riley and McKayla in the group.

Riley said, "Zeke. Man am I glad to see you. We are in some deep trouble, and we don't have much time to figure out a solution."

"Yeah," McKayla interjected. "The Agents are moving in from across the small pond. We are being circled and trapped like rats. If we don't move soon, we will be killed."

"Any ideas about fighting back?" I asked.

Sarah shook her head. "No, that wouldn't work. There are too many Agents, and by the sound of things, there are more ready to retaliate even if we somehow beat the Agents approaching."

The troops could be heard even through the heavy drips of the falling rain. Their boots echoed like the falling drops sending chills up my back. A decision needed to be made now before it was too late.

"We are going to run," I said. "Run to wherever Marcus and Callon are. They will help us get out of here."

"Do you really think that's smart?" McKayla asked. "Callon just wants to fight. He wants to show the Agents how strong we are. We are his creations."

Sarah jumped in. "He will. He and Marcus are a lot alike. Once Marcus talks some sense into Callon, he will lead us out of here."

Suddenly, Trish chimed in with a dark comment. "We hope."

We all turned to face her, but she kept staring out at the Agents approaching. What happened to her, I wondered. Was this my doing? She seemed so dark and depressed.

Trish remained distant and kept focus on the Agents. Somberly, I said, "Yeah…"

I began to walk over towards her while the others talked when a low rumble in the ground beneath our feet began. We stood, startled, and stared at the ground. What was causing that, we all feared. The rumble grew louder and the Earth began to shake a little. It wasn't an earthquake. Colorado doesn't have earthquakes and if it did, they were rare.

It all became clear to me. This wasn't an earthquake. As we all stood near each other, the rumbling and shaking grew stronger with each passing second, I knew what was causing this.

"MOVE!" I screamed.

Suddenly, a large spike shot out of the ground and caught a Recruit through the chest. He was completely skewered. The sight was terrifying and disgusting.

"What the *hell* is going on!?" McKayla screamed.

"Nathaniel!" I yelled as the rumbling began again. "We need to move, now!"

Sarah ran back away from the opening of the pool of water and waved her arms in the air. That's when the gunfire began to ring out again. Trees exploded with splinters, and Recruits dropped to the ground for protection.

Sarah didn't move. She stood in place and dipped her hands low and flung them high into the air. A loud whooshing sound overtook the rumbling. I turned back and saw a large wave of water launch out of the pool and hang in the air unnaturally. Then, it dropped and took out half of the Agents firing at us.

"That should hold them off," Sarah said smiling while a little bit of blood dripped out of her nose.

"Sarah..." Riley said slowly. "Your...nose."

She wiped it off and said, "Don't worry about it. It took a lot to lift that much water. Now, hurry before the Agents get back up!"

The rumbling stopped as another earthly spike jutted out of the ground, but this time, it only knocked a Recruit off of her feet. Thankfully too, because it was aimed for Trish.

I ran up to her and helped her up onto her feet. "We need to go," I said quietly making it personal to her.

She pushed away from me and stared at me with anger filled eyes. "I'm coming. Let's go," she said again with almost no emotion.

My heart dropped, but at least she was okay. Another rumbling began as Sarah led us all through the forest, quickly away from the Agents and more importantly, Nathaniel.

The group of ten or so Recruits followed Sarah by running as quickly as possible through the trees. Hopefully, Marcus and Callon weren't that far away. Along with them, hopefully we would find Liam and Teddy on the way. The poor kid must've been scared out of his mind.

I felt almost ashamed as we hurdled over logs and ducked under tree branches and wiped dripping water off of our faces. The large male Recruit that was pierced with Nathaniel's spike was left alone. We didn't even try helping. We just tried to get out of there as quickly as possible. Was there anything we could've done anyways, I wondered.

Trish ran close to me but didn't acknowledge me at all. I knew she was furious with me for not telling her that she was my Bloodling. If she was anything like McKayla, then she would be mad at me for a long time. I didn't want that. My heart wrenched inside my chest. No matter how much running or fighting for my life that ensued helped ease the pain. I would talk to her, sooner or later.

We kept sprinting trying to remain in a close group but we stayed apart to make it easier to move. None of us came up with this plan. It just happened.

Sarah stopped immediately when she entered an area where the trees were thinner and tree trunks were on the ground laid in a zigzag pattern as if they were placed there on purpose.

"What's up, Sarah?" I asked catching my breath.

Riley said, "Good thing she stopped. This is where the Test takes place. It's the final leg."

It all came rushing back to me. I had to walk across the zigzag logs otherwise I would fall down the dark pit that seemed to stretch on forever. Callon must've reset the Test for Teddy to take at some point once the Gauntlet was over. On the bright side of all of this mayhem, at least Teddy won't have to take the Test.

"Should we go around it?" McKayla asked.

Riley said standing close to her. "No," he began to grin. "We can use this to our advantage."

We all began to think along the same lines of Riley. The Agents didn't know anything about Callon's insane examination of abilities.

"We better hurry then," Sarah said. "Let's run around and use ourselves as bait. When they approach, we turn and run and pray that we don't get shot."

The other nine of us agreed and quickly sprinted around the perimeter. We all ducked down behind the bushes along the edge of the small clearing and waited. We could hear the Agency moving closer and closer to us. At first, I wasn't worried, but as time passed and I could hear the Agents close in on us, I began to tense up.

We all waited in anticipation trying to remain as quiet as possible. Then, a few moments later, through the white haze of the pouring rain, the Agents moved in. They ran in straight, horizontal lines sweeping the forest with their guns held across their chests.

Water splashed up from underneath their black boots. Their helmets had small visors on their foreheads to keep water out of their tinted window covered eyes. They reminded me a lot like storm troopers from Star Wars, but that was just a movie. Those couldn't kill you.

We all looked to Sarah who seemed to be in charge of our group ever since we escaped the pond. She held up one finger and waited. We all did and watched as the Agents moved closer to the large trap.

They halted just before the clearing, and the zigzag logs began. The rows of Agents began to form a mass behind the first row. They looked around wary of what might be waiting for them. How could they know there was a trap waiting for them?

We looked around at each other and wondered what was going on and what to do. We didn't expect the Agents to stop their movement. The only option was to risk our own skin to get out of here and trap them.

Then, the rumbling came back. Small rocks on the surface of the ground began to bounce and shake. Terror filled all of our eyes when we realized who was responsible.

Without even thinking, Sarah stood and shouted, "Agents! Run!"

She took off in the opposite direction of the Agents. Unable to comprehend what was really happening, the rest of us remained crouched beneath shrubbery when bullets began to fly after Sarah. That's when I took off after Sarah staying low. The rest of the Recruits followed behind me. The bullets continued to spray over our heads.

It was crazy, brash, and stupid, but Sarah's plan worked. The Agents sprinted after us stepping onto the fake ground. They fell into the dark pit. They fell out of sight as if the hole never ended, but a splash could be heard. Callon must have put a pool of water at the bottom. At least he wasn't trying to kill us, that was comforting, but I wished that he was.

The rumbling stopped once half of the Agent mass fell into the pit. I could only hope that Nathaniel was in that mass with them. I didn't know. I just kept running trying to keep up with Sarah and the rest of the Recruits.

The gunfire stopped shortly after as well once the Agents were out of sight. The pit was large, and it would take a while for them to regroup and get around it.

We followed Sarah through the rain slickened forest for about ten more minutes before we reached the end of our trek. Unfortunately, we didn't all make it. A Recruit was pierced through the chest by Nathaniel. I didn't even know him, I thought to myself.

My thoughts snapped away from the boy and to the break in the forest. Another small, circular opening with small bushes and vegetation clung together. Tall grasses went to about knee high. Water droplets sparkled at the tips of grass and leaf blades.

In the middle, huddled in a small group, were people wearing long cloaks with grass stains and dirt marks on the knees. I knew who they were before I even talked to them.

One turned. It was the bald friend of mine, Marcus, and he was accompanied by Liam, Callon, Teddy, and a few other Recruits like Bruno.

I could've done without him.

Teddy waved to us, a few of his teeth missing in a cute, childlike, smile. Callon didn't seem to care that we were there. In fact, he went right on to talk to Liam who seemed genuinely intrigued that I was there. He was intrigued, not happy. It was odd. What was he thinking?

Our group approached Marcus and the others. Bruno glared at us; red burn marks ran up the side of his neck from the Gauntlet. It looked hideous, but I wasn't going to point that out.

Liam said as we stepped towards them, "Well, look who it is, if it isn't sonny and his friends."

Callon said immediately after, "What are you doing here? You were stationed at the small pond near the southern slope of the mountain."

"I know," Sarah said still being leader. "But, there was a problem."

"What kind of problem?" Callon asked.

We all looked at each other wondering how we should say this, but in the end, I just told him straight out. "Nathaniel attacked us. He killed one Recruit while his Agents marched after us. We needed to get out of there, or we all would've died." I directed that more towards Marcus. Maybe he would help us out and get us all out of here.

There was a brief, unplanned moment of silence for the Recruit lost, and then Callon said, "Did you try to fight back?"

Sarah shook her head. "No, there were too many. We would've been overrun in a second. We held them off, though. They fell into the pit on the final leg of the Test."

Liam chuckled to himself. "About time that thing paid off."

Teddy laughed next to him and looked up at me. I looked down and smiled at him. He was taking this well for such a young kid. He was taking it too well, actually. I wondered why.

Then, it occurred to me. "Did you see any Agents yet?" I asked.

Marcus shook his head. "No, we were stationed here the entire time, but no Agents made it this far which is probably a good thing considering how close we are to the cavern."

"Like it matters," Liam said. "It's practically destroyed now anyways. Nathaniel bombed us purty good."

I focused on Marcus. "We need to get off this mountain before they regroup. They'll be here any second!"

Marcus turned quickly to Callon, but Callon quickly said, "No, we will stay and we will fight. My Recruits have been through enough training to stand up to Nathaniel's Agents."

"Are you sure?" Marcus said. "Think about your decision Callon," he stepped towards him, "you are condemning these Recruits to their death! We need to leave. Forget your foolish pride and make the smart decision!"

A fight began to ensue. "And, you know so much, Marcus? You've been through one fight. No, half a fight. You gave up and ran in the opposite direction with your tail between your legs. You and your Recruits are weak. My Recruits are strong and will take down that traitor once and for all."

Marcus and Callon were nose to nose. They were the same height and each had the same vein popping out of their forehead. I was prepared to break up the elemental fight at any moment, but I didn't have to. A voice broke through the tension.

"You should've listened to Marcus, you fool."

We all turned, traumatized. Standing inside the circular clearing, Agents sprawled about behind him, was Nathaniel. His arms folded across his chest.

He was here, and we were dead.

Chapter 42

The Agents formed a semicircle around the edge of the clearing. Their guns were directed at us from all directions. Nathaniel was placed in the middle with an Agent at his side. He must've been his second in command. Nathaniel took a few steps forward and let his arms fall down to his side.

What made my guts churn was Nathaniel's face. Pieces of skin were gone showing pink muscle. Under his left eye was a vertical strip of removed skin that stretched to his chin. The top of his forehead was tinted a dark black. The fire must've caught him before he could escape. We did take the escape helicopter out.

Gabe didn't make it out... I look at Nathaniel, and see him.

Forming an evil grin, he said, "No running or screaming? I'm impressed with your bravery, but it is foolish nonetheless."

We were in a tight group preparing for the worst, which would be a shooting range for the Agents. That never came. Nathaniel, instead, took a few more steps forward and separated himself from the group.

Marcus stepped forward. "We are not afraid of you, Nathaniel. I just don't see why you are doing this."

"Why?" Nathaniel said scoffing. "It's because it is the smart thing to do."

"Killing your friends is 'the smart thing to do?'" Marcus asked.

"No, in fact, when I look down at your mangled corpses, I feel a touch of sadness, but this must be done. The Clade has had this coming for some time now. You couldn't have possibly thought that you would be surviving another decade, not with the power the Agency has. I was just making the smart decision. Friends or life? I would choose life any day."

"You're a monster if you think that this thing you are living in is a 'life,'" Marcus said turning back towards our group. "With no one by your side, how can it even be enjoyable to you?"

"I don't need anyone at my side, just allies," Nathaniel said. "When I look upon what you call 'friends,' I see a bunch of weaklings huddled together in a group with no hope of escaping this. Your day of reckoning is finally upon you and it has been coming since Greg Laufor broke us out of our prison!"

Greg Laufor!? He broke everyone out of a prison? There was more I needed to know.

"What prison!?" I said stepping forward exposing Teddy who was in the middle. "You talk about my father like he was Moses. Why do you think of him like that? How come you *all* think of him like that?"

There was silence except for the sounds of falling rain. Thunder rumbled in the distance, and a surge of Overload caused me to stumble, but I made my point clear. If I was going to die, I at least wanted answers.

"Laufor," Nathaniel said. The Agents all raised their guns in accordance with my name.

"Zeke," Marcus said. "Stand down. Let me handle this."

"No," I said confidently. "I want answers." I turned towards Nathaniel and said, "What about my father and a prison?"

"Well," Nathaniel began, "None of these people could tell you because they weren't there, but I was. I was there when your father broke us out of the prison the Agency held us in thirty years ago. It's because of that one act that made him the god he is to all of the Recruits, and all of the new Recruits are trained to be madly, sickly, in love with him."

"Sounds to me like your jealous, Nathaniel," Marcus said. "You always did hate him."

He growled. "I could've broken us all out of the prison! Anyone at that time could! He was just the first one to take the chance, and because of that, he makes every decision in the Clade. Well, no more. The Clade will fall!"

I responded, my anger growing for my father, "Sounds to me like you are insanely jealous. If you could've saved your friends from whatever prison you were in, why didn't you? It sounds like my father was the strongest one of all of you. That's why everyone looks up to him. He did something that everyone else was afraid to do!"

Nathaniel didn't like that. He spat and yelled in rage. "How dare you speak to me like that you little brat!? You are just like your father! Special only because everyone else made you that way."

He stepped back until he was almost touching the line of Agents. He faced Marcus and me, his face red with anger. In one quick flick of his arm, he moved the ground beneath Marcus' feet and flung him into the forest crashing into a tree, out of sight.

"Marcus!" I shouted.

I began to sprint after him, but the line of Agents shifted in front of me, their guns pointed directly at me.

"No," Nathaniel said. "You stay here. This is between you and me. I'm going to show you just how weak and pathetic you really are… just like your father."

Just then, I wanted to tear the rest of Nathaniel's skin off his ugly face. If he expects to insult me and my father after killing my best friend, he is sorely mistaken.

I began to charge up my electricity. I pictured it flowing through my veins. It circulated faster and faster through every bit of my body. The pain of the Overload was crippling. I wanted to drop, but my rage was so great it kept me going.

I sprinted at Nathaniel screaming at the top of my lungs, electricity radiating in the palm of my hand. I lunged forward with my right, electrified hand. Nathaniel just smiled and dodged it easily jumping to his right.

I didn't stop there. I turned to face him, and right when he landed, I unleashed a furious bolt at him. He ducked under it and the bolt fried the Agent behind him.

The Agents did nothing to stop our fight. Nathaniel was in total control, and he wanted revenge for what happened to him in New York.

"Not bad," Nathaniel said slowly standing up. "You have talent, Laufor, but you would need a lot more to stop me."

Nathaniel held out his hand and closed it into a fist. Suddenly, a rumbling like before came back. I could feel the ground coming together. I took off towards the group of Recruits in the middle of the clearing when a small mountain burst through the surface behind me. It launched me through the air, and I hit the ground hard. Water and mud flew through the air.

"You're weak, Laufor," Nathaniel said as he sprinted and landed on top of me, his knees dug into my back. "Get used to this position, on the ground, because you are going to be there for the rest of your life. Unfortunately," the rumbling began again, "it's going to be short."

I needed to get out of there quickly before Nathaniel's mountain skewered me like the boy back at the pond. I tried to wiggle myself free, but Nathaniel was too big.

The rumbling was growing louder. Soon, I would be done for. I shut my eyes and let myself think. I could hear Nathaniel laughing as if it was all over for me, but he seemed a million miles away in my head. I focused on my memories with Sarah and Gabe and then Trish.

Gabe...

No, I couldn't give up. I wouldn't!

I could feel adrenaline rush through my body along with a massive flow of electricity and a burning pain. With one forceful push and cry of pain, a wave of electricity burst out from around me.

Nathaniel was sent off my back, flipped, and landed a few yards away from me. He held his face and groaned loudly. The rumbling stopped along with that.

The Agents were ready to gun me down, but Nathaniel, slow to get up, held his hands high in the air. "Easy, I'm fine. That was just a cheap shot by Laufor."

My rage built, "Gabe." That's all I said.

"What?" Nathaniel asked confused. "What does Manson have to do with any of this between us?"

"Everything!" I shouted. I felt my electricity surging through me again the angrier I got. "He was one of my best friends," I paused, "and you killed him."

Nathaniel scoffed. "Ha, there is so much you don't understand."

What did he mean, I wondered. My rage built even more when suddenly, during the loud rumble of thunder overhead, my body lit up with electricity. Bolts shot over the heads of the Recruits, and a few got the Agents, dropping them to their knees. Marcus, getting out of the forest, dove to the side to avoid the electrical storm emitted by me.

I cried out. I couldn't hold it in any longer. The Overload was taking over. I needed to beat Nathaniel before it takes me, but it hurt so much. I dropped to all fours and held my chest where it hurt the most.

The lightning finally died down, but the pain didn't. I was still weak from the episode and remained on the ground. For a moment, everything was still besides the falling of rain.

Nathaniel stalked over grinning. "Well, look what we have here. I do say that this is probably the most interesting thing I've ever seen." He stared down at me and then said to everyone, "Laufor, here, has an Overload."

Everyone stared at me awkwardly not knowing what an Overload was except for Liam, Marcus, and Callon. They remained still with the others.

"Laufor," Nathaniel said cockily, "would you like to explain to your friends what an Overload is?"

I shook my head left to right still trying to regain my strength from the blow.

"Okay," Nathaniel said. "I will do it then. You see, Recruits, Laufor has an Overload. It's a condition that causes one's ability to 'flood' in some ways. An event occurs that causes an increase in his body's natural level of electricity. Now, that electricity tears him apart and he has episodes like this. Eventually," there was another pause, "it will kill him. Tear him to pieces, and I think that time is rapidly approaching."

I looked back to my friends as I slowly stood up. They all were opened mouthed, terrified. The only ones that showed no emotion was Callon (which was understandable) and Trish. It looked as though Trish didn't even care.

Conner said, "And that was why you were locked in that room when I found you. What you said earlier was true."

I nodded. "What happened in the Gauntlet when Bruno was blasted when he hit me was due to the Overload. It was outside my control, and it probably hurt me more than it hurt him."

Bruno laughed a little from the back of the group. "So, you are telling me you cheated, and I truly won that."

Marcus smacked him in the back of the head. "That's not important here."

Sarah looked at the ground. I could tell she was in deep thought. "The lightning," she said coming to a realization. "That's what caused the Overload."

"Yeah," I said. "That did it, but I didn't find out until just last week."

"And you never told us!?" Sarah said.

I took a deep breath. "I didn't want you to worry. I'm fine."

"No! You're not fine, Zeke! Didn't you hear? You could possibly die!" Sarah exclaimed.

I was quiet. I had nothing left to say. They knew everything now. Now, I wished I had told them everything the instant I found out about Bloodling's and Overload's myself. Maybe, things would have been different.

"Enough of that," Nathaniel said. "It's apparent that with the Overload increasing your natural ability to use electricity, I can't beat you. I submit to you, Laufor."

"What are you saying?" I asked shocked. "You're giving up?"

Nathaniel stepped back out of the fighting grounds and back in line with his Agents. "No, I'm not giving up.

How would that sound if I, an Original, was beaten by a three month old Recruit?"

He began to slowly follow his line of Agents and circle us in the center of the clearing. "I'm confused. Then, what are you doing?"

"What I'm saying is," Nathaniel said, "that I cannot take you on with sheer power of ability alone. That is a fight that I would not win. However," his face formed an evil grin, "a truly genius general doesn't just give up. He rethinks his strategy, and I know your weakness, Laufor. I'll just exploit that."

I didn't know what he was talking about, but I feared the worst. "What are you going to do, then? Pump my body with more electricity until I explode?"

He laughed lightly. "No. The Overload will kill you soon enough. Even now, I can tell that you are trying to hide the excruciating pain."

He was right. I tried my best, but my face still twitched and scrunched.

Nathaniel stopped at a ninety degree angle from the group. I didn't even realize he was circling towards them. If I knew, I would be in front of them protecting them.

A sudden realization hit me. I knew what he was planning.

The rumbling began. I took off and sprinted towards Nathaniel. The others moved as a group backwards away from Nathaniel knowing what was about to happen, but they were slow. They weren't going to make it.

"Yes!" Nathaniel yelled excitedly. "Your friends are your burden, Laufor! And soon, they will be just a memory!"

I wasn't going to make it. Nathaniel spread himself too far away from me, and the other Recruits weren't moving fast enough to escape.

I tried to release a bolt of electricity to stop Nathaniel, but the Overload wouldn't let me. My body jerked and jolted when I tried to build up energy. I ran faster to try and tackle him.

The entire scene flashed before me like it was a scene from an action movie. I was too late. I was only a few yards away from him when I heard the rumbling reach its climax. I turned around and watched as the ground began to lift and swell. Then…

…nothing but a lot of dust rose from the ground.

It was either a mishap by Nathaniel or a miracle. There was no mountain destroying all of my friends. There was only a dust storm that almost completely engulfed the group.

I looked back at Nathaniel who seemed as surprised as I was. "H-how!? They should be dead."

Suddenly, a voice from the group rose over us. "I'm afraid your little trick won't be of use here, Nathaniel."

"L-L-liam!?" Nathaniel stuttered falling backwards onto his back. His face was misshapen in a grotesque, horror-filled way.

Out of the group stepped Liam. He moved through them like a salmon upstream and stood next to me. "I'm afraid I can't let you hurt these youngins. I've grown rather fond of them, especially sonny here and the little one in the back." He pointed at Teddy who was terrified beyond belief.

Nathaniel, still terribly shaken, stood and said, "No matter. I'm with a stronger alliance now. You can't take me on anymore, Liam. Laufor has a better chance than you do." He looked Liam up and down. "You let yourself go."

Liam ruffled his dirty, gray beard and said, "I may have taken a short leave of absence, but everything happens for a reason, right?"

"What do you mean?" Nathaniel asked.

"Simple. If it wasn't for me living in the forest in Pennsylvania, I wouldn't have been able to save these fine Recruits from falling to their deaths. Also, I got to spend some quality time with my son. That's something I never got the chance to do, and he turned out to be a fine young man."

Marcus, who was standing a few feet from the group, smiled and turned a little red.

I interrupted him. "What do you mean you saved us? Didn't we just fall and get lucky?"

Liam laughed. "Sorry, sonny. You're strong, but you're not immortal. You see, my ability allows me to change the consistency of the earth." He bent over and picked up a chunk of wet mud created from the rain. "Watch," he said.

I kept my eyes on his hand. There was nothing to be seen other than the dripping pool of mud solidifying! He tossed it to me and it was solid. I tried to break it with all my force, but it was way too tough. It was like trying to shatter a diamond with brute force alone.

"Tough, eh?" Liam said still giggling to himself. "I didn't get to show that off in a long time."

"I still don't get it," I said still locked on the rock not even caring about Nathaniel or any of the Agents.

He took the rock from my hand. "My ability works both ways." Then, in another moment, the rock blew away in the wind in the form of dust particles.

Sarah commented, "That's how. You saw us falling and turned the earth from solid to soft."

"The girlie got it!" Liam said truly excited… for some reason. "I kept thinking 'water bed,' and sure enough, you landed on the ground that was as soft as a water bed. That didn't stop you from getting beat up purty good, but I can only do so much."

Liam suddenly was the coolest guy on the planet to me. Not only did he treat all of us with respect, but he was also silly.

Oh yeah, he also saved our lives twice now.

"Now," Liam said. "Would you mind joining your friends, sonny? I can handle Nathaniel."

"Umm… okay," I said. It was all that I could say. I didn't expect that out of him and it was usually me to fight Nathaniel.

He smiled at me while I stepped through the mud back to join Sarah and the others.

Liam and Nathaniel stared each other down for a few moments taking in their opponent who used to be their ally.

Then, Nathaniel made the first move. This time, there was no rumbling. A small mountain was about to burst out of the earth, but it was immediately turned into dust the second it reached the surface!

Liam shook his finger. "Ah-ah. I'm afraid abilities will be of no use here, Nathaniel. It'll be just like old times."

Nathaniel groaned loudly. Liam laughed a little to himself.

Maybe this is the chance we needed to beat Nathaniel once and for all. I didn't want to get my hopes up because something else will probably occur, but it was hard not to. This is the first thing that has gone our way in a while, and it came from a person I never would've expected.

All the Recruits stood back and watched Liam take on Nathaniel in a classic brawl.

Chapter 43

Nathaniel threw the first punch. He sprinted at Liam, mud flying off the heels of his boots, and swung with his right arm. Liam ducked under it and grabbed his arm and twisted it behind his back. Liam got behind Nathaniel and pulled him close.

"Your basic fighting abilities are lackluster," he said. "Has your new alliance not taught you anything?"

Nathaniel pushed off and broke free. "Your weak old man." He came back with his left, and Liam caught it. Then, Nathaniel quickly came back with his right, but Liam caught that as well.

Liam stepped back and released Nathaniel's arms. "Old man? We're the same age."

The fight continued, but this time Liam quit playing and began to go on offense as well. It was incredible. Liam, for being middle aged, was able to unleash a flurry of punches that seemed to be so fluid, it was like air. He struck Nathaniel on both sides of his face, and then swept his legs out from underneath him. Nathaniel fell to the ground with a splash and held his face.

I didn't realize it right away, but we were all cheering for Liam especially Marcus. He was really getting into his dad beating up on the enemy who was once his partner. It could be because it was a good fight, but no one forgot about what Nathaniel did to us. He deserved so much more.

Liam walked around the fallen Nathaniel. "You do realize you deserve this, don't you? This is for all of the pain you have caused us. You were our friend. Your betrayal might even be more agonizing than all of the lives you have taken."

Nathaniel let Liam continue to speak down to him. His eyes were full of fear as he realized that this was one fight that he probably wouldn't win. Liam already mastered his ability, and instead of working on his martial arts like Nathaniel should've, he continued to rely too heavily on his abilities.

I looked back to Callon during this moment. He just nodded and focused back on the fight. That was what Callon was trying to get through to us the entire time. Our abilities are useful, but the one's that win the Gauntlet are the ones that can survive even when they are outmatched through ability. We had to get strong and fight back in the classic style.

As I watched Liam circle Nathaniel like a shark, I couldn't imagine how hard it must've been for Callon to sit out of this fight. Nathaniel wanted me to fight him, and now it was Liam's turn, and he hated Liam more than anyone in the world. It's for the best, though. The Agents held their guns at the ready just in case one of us decided to charge in; although, it didn't appear as though we would have to. Liam was kicking butt.

Liam bent over and picked up Nathaniel by the collar and held him close to his face. "You deserve so much worse than this." Then, he let him go, but not before Liam got him in the chin with his knee.

Nathaniel flung backwards and dropped a few feet from Liam crying out in pain and grasping his chin. Blood poured from his mouth. His teeth stained with crimson blood. The rain did its best, but it couldn't wash away the massive amount of blood.

The weird thing is Nathaniel began to laugh. When Nathaniel opened his mouth, drips of blood came out. It was like watching a horror movie.

"What's so funny? You nuts or somethin'?" Liam asked stepping closer to him.

"You just don't get it, do you?" Nathaniel asked sarcastically. "I'm a tactician. I have planned for everything. There is no way you or your little rodent friends will ever escape with your lives."

"Now," Liam said, another plume of dust erupted from the ground turning into sticky mud from the rain, "do you really believe that? I don't know. You seem to think you are a lot of things, but the only thing I see is a traitor."

"Really?" Nathaniel said. "I guess I'm more convincing than I originally assumed."

"What do you mean, you snake?" Liam stepped closer.

Suddenly, Nathaniel swung his legs and swept Liam's legs out from underneath him. Liam fell onto his back while Nathaniel jumped up and landed on top of him. His knees pushed down on Liam's chest. Blood dripped out of Nathaniel's mouth and onto Liam's face.

"Get offa me!" Liam shouted.

"If you are wondering my old friend," Nathaniel said, "I have been practicing on my martial arts skills just in case I ran into you someday. It appears as though fate wanted this little showdown to occur, Liam."

Nathaniel began to throw punches down on Liam. With each blow, I swear I could hear thunder crackling in the distance, or that was my body crackling from the Overload. Liam was taking a brutal beating and he needed our help, but if we ran in, we would be gunned down.

I scanned the Agents in line. All of their eyes (or at least facemasks) were glued to us. None of us could do anything to help Liam, and if we didn't hurry, he would be killed for sure.

Liam's face was a mess of welts and black and blue marks. He couldn't fight back. His arms were pinned at his side under the weight of Nathaniel's body.

All of a sudden, there was a rustle in the bushes to our right next to the edge of the Agency line. We all looked that way to see who it was, but the person was too far back.

Then three loud explosions went off in front of us. Three Agents nearest the sound blew up leaving nothing but dead bodies and a huge, disgusting hole in their chests. It must've been Juliette!

Another flurry of shimmering air javelins flew through the clearing connecting with two more Agents and three trees behind them. The trees spun and toppled on two more Agents and almost hit Nathaniel and Liam.

Only ten Agents remained. Nathaniel pulled himself up from beating the hell out of Liam and said in a worrisome gasp, "Juliette!"

"Sir," said an Agent whose gun was raised and aimed in the direction of Juliette, "are we authorized to take her down?"

"Yes, you fool, before she gets-" Nathaniel was cut off by the sound of the Agent exploding and being sent twenty feet backwards.

"Ah, he was a loyal ally...," Nathaniel said sounding truly hurt.

Liam started laughing through his twisted, bloodied mouth, "How do you know anything about loyal allies?"

Nathaniel, angered by Liam's comment, threw another punch down. "Go after her!"

The troops began to move into the forest towards Juliette's position. Eventually, they were all out of sight. Everyone remained silent, and everything paused for a few moments. We were all glued to the swaying trees and trickling rain. Even Nathaniel stopped beating up Liam to watch and listen.

A few moments later, guns began to go off. We could only expect the worst. Juliette was grossly outnumbered. She was tough and talented, but she couldn't take on eight Agents with guns.

Slowly, the gunfire began to go away. What sounded like being on a firing range slowly dissipated into a tranquil forest. The rain drops were the only things heard through the cascade of leaves.

Nathaniel said, "And that is the end of Juliette."

"You're an evil bas-" Liam said before he was punched again.

Sarah grabbed me by the arm. "Do you think she is alright?"

I looked at the muddy ground and shook my head. "I have no idea. She's tough, but Juliette can't take on that many Agents all by herself. Could she?"

I turned back to see Trish still unmoving. Even the death of our friend couldn't stir Trish even a little bit. It pissed me off even more.

Then another rustle of bushes and breaking of sticks could be heard from the far left of Nathaniel and Liam. It couldn't be Juliette. She wasn't that fast, and with the Agents on her, I'm sure she wouldn't be able to move that silently giving out only a rustle.

All eyes were now peeled on the new rustling position. Nathaniel looked wilder than ever. His eyes darted from the new sound to where Juliette was, or at least, was supposed to be.

Suddenly an older woman with short, curly, blonde hair launched out of the woods screaming at the top of her lungs. She moved at an unbelievable rate. It wasn't like she was running at all. Instead, she was flying through the air with two jets of water spraying at the ground keeping her levitated. She was like a jet boat!

Barbara used the water on the ground and propelled herself rapidly at Nathaniel. Before he could open his eyes fully, Barbara rammed her shoulder and wrapped her arms around Nathaniel launching them both twenty feet away from Liam.

Liam rolled over and pushed himself up. He stared at the sky and let the rain fall and wash away some of the blood from the cuts under his eye.

He said, "Nice for you to join us, Barbara. Your timing couldn't have been more impeccable."

Barbara stood up leaving Nathaniel almost unconscious on the mud. "Sorry. I would've been here sooner, but there were a few Recruits that needed my help to fight off a few Agents on the opposite face of the mountain."

"How did you find us?" Callon asked.

"Wasn't hard," Barbara said joining our group. "Nathaniel's ego can be spotted from space."

We all laughed. Barbara focused on Sarah with meaningful eyes. "Are you alright?"

Sarah nodded. "I'm fine, mom." Sarah saying mom felt awkward, but Barbara seemed genuinely happy just like Sarah.

"Aw well, isn't that cute. Everyone is all happy," Bruno said behind us.

Callon spun around. "Quiet Jagger," and he shut up.

For one small moment, everything was right. We were all right where we were supposed to be, including Nathaniel, who was laying face first in the mud still dizzy from Barbara's hit.

One person was still missing though. Juliette was lost in the forest and never revealed herself after the Agents attacked and disappeared. Was she okay I wondered. I was about to go check when a dark figure moved about just beyond the tree line and stepped into the clearing. Juliette stood in front of us with a large, bloodied scratch across her cheek.

"Juliette!" Marcus shouted and ran towards her from across the clearing.

She brushed off her cloak and the two hugged in front of all of us. It was a little gross. I think Teddy covered his eyes even. Maybe it was my little pang of jealousy that made it gross, though. I wanted nothing more than to be with the girl that was over my shoulder, who was now awkwardly whispering to Conner, but she wanted nothing to do with me. Was it really my fault? It felt like it in my heart, but my head knew that was not the case.

Nathaniel began to cackle. Bubbles popped on the low surface of the standing water. "The whole happy group is back together. Perfect... for now."

"Trying to scare us now, Nathaniel?" Liam said. "You will not be tormenting us again. Your Agents are dead. You have killed hundreds of Recruits and possible Recruits who were only children. No, 'for now.'"

Barbara joined Liam. "You're time is over. You're lucky we don't kill you where you lay, Nathaniel. A monster like you doesn't deserve to live."

Nathaniel laughed again, but much more loudly than before. "This isn't over. This won't be over until the Clade falls."

There was an ominous pause. A lot of us didn't want to believe that there was a way for Nathaniel to escape, but he seemed to be skilled at escaping inescapable situations, like the forest fire in New York.

Then, confusing to all but Liam and Barbara, Nathaniel said, "*He* is on the way."

Liam and Barbara immediately looked at each other and gulped. What was Nathaniel talking about? If Liam and Barbara were scared, should everyone else be? Not even Callon, Juliette, or Marcus knew what they were talking about.

"We need to get everyone out of here now," Barbara said anxiously.

"Right. We have no time to waste," Liam said. He turned back towards us still in our small group and said, "Okay, we need to leave now. Split up and find any little Recruits that happen to be lost in the woods or hurt. We don't have time to waste."

"What's this about, father?" Marcus asked. "Who is Nathaniel talking about?"

"His boss," Barbara said. "The person responsible for giving the Originals like Nathaniel, Liam, and myself abilities, which led to your abilities and the origins of the Clade."

"He's that important!? He's responsible for all of this?" I asked.

"What's his name, Liam?" Callon asked.

"No time," Liam said with force that caused Callon to jump a little. "If he is here and with backup, we will all be eliminated. Callon, is there a way off of this mountain?"

"Yes," he answered immediately. "There is the path that leads to the diner, but that is most likely being blocked off by Agents."

"Anything else?" Barbara asked.

Callon thought it over and said, "Yes, there is one other way down the mountain, but it's a little more hazardous."

"In what ways?" Barbara asked.

"There is a path that goes around the cave. It becomes extremely narrow as it reaches the leeward side of the mountain. Then, there is a steep slope filled with rocks and a few sparse trees. We will have to zig-zag from different trees and rocks, and still, there is a large chance that some may fall down the slope and drop off the edge of the cliff to their deaths."

"Is it the only other way down?" Liam asked.

He nodded. "I'm afraid so. It was only used once as a test before. Never has it had to be used. It would take us to the same highway that the diner is on. An old bus is parked in a wooded area just across the highway. We can use that to get away."

"Okay," Liam said. "Barbara, find any Recruits within the area that aren't dead. Juliette, go find your team. Everyone else, stay here and help dispose of Nathaniel. We will meet at the cavern in five-"

Liam stopped when a mountain erupted between him and Barbara. They were both tossed to the sides of the clearing while everyone else in the small circle were thrown backwards. We landed with a splash and a large jolt from the Overload held me down much longer than the others.

I did get up, though in time to find Nathaniel getting help onto his feet by an Agent. Surrounding Nathaniel was a line of ten Agents that just appeared without anyone noticing. Then again, we didn't even feel the rumble before the mountain appeared. We were too engrossed in escaping.

Accompanied with the ten or so Agents dressed in full black armor was a man in a black business suit and a black tie. It was unusual to say the least. The suit looked expensive, and the rain would most likely destroy whatever material it was made out of.

The man wearing the suit was older than the Originals, probably in his sixties. He had gray hair that was pulled back and gelled to remain still like a soccer player's hair. His face had only a few white stubbles for hair. His eyebrows were bright white that were high above his bright blue eyes that resembled ice. I got a chill from staring at them for too long.

"Martinez," the man in the suit said, "is he okay?"

The Agent helping Nathaniel up said, "He appears to-"

Nathaniel cut him off. "I'm fine! I had everything under control. The subjects were just about to split up. That's when I would've taken them all out."

"Really?" The man in the suit said. "Because, to me, it looked as though they were about to kill you."

Nathaniel shook his head and brushed off some of the big chunks of mud from his cloak. "No, the subjects are too weak to do something like that to someone they once cared about and trusted." Nathaniel changed the subject. "We are both gentlemen here. When are you going to give me some of your black armor like the rest of your soldiers?"

"You will get armor when you can be fully trusted. As for now, you are still a subject to me just like the others."

Nathaniel looked away and cursed at what the man said. It appeared as though the man in the suit was in charge of Nathaniel and the Agents. Was this the man Nathaniel was referencing?

I think my guess was right when Liam said, "Crap."

Chapter 44

The man in the suit stared us down as if we were abominations. If what Barbara said was true, then this old man was responsible for creating abilities in all of us. How, I wondered. I don't have the slightest clue, and it appears as though he is leading the Agency as well. This man, standing in front of me, is responsible for everything that has happened to Recruits and the Clade the last forty or so years. It's odd for me to admit that I have a passion for the history of the Clade now.

Liam and Barbara began to walk back towards us when the man in the suit held up a silver pistol he swiftly pulled from inside his coat.

"Stay where you are Subject 6 and Subject 15," the man in the suit said. "One more step, and I'll have my troops unload on the other subjects."

The man had a fetish for calling all of us subjects. I'm guessing that was supposed to be a demeaning term because Nathaniel seemed pretty irritated when the man in the suit called him that.

Liam and Barbara stopped immediately and raised their hands in the air.

"Good," the man in the suit said. "If only you behaved this well thirty-five years ago. Then, we wouldn't be in this situation."

The man in the suit was definitely the leader and was responsible for this mess we were all in. Liam and Barbara, however, were the only ones that appeared truly frightened. Juliette, Marcus, and Callon just looked confused, but they knew the dire situation we were all entering. Things weren't looking good on our escape.

"Before we precede any further into the matters at hand," the man in the suit said, "I have some matters of my own to attend to among my own ranks."

With that, he turned and faced Nathaniel who appeared anxious waiting for the fallout to begin. His smile stretched from one area of missing skin to the next.

"Subject 13," the man in the suit said.

Nathaniel faced him and said, "Don't call me that anymore. My name is Nathaniel Rafford!"

"You will be called the name that was provided to you when you were born under my care, 13!" The man in the suit shouted. "I do not care about what name you have given yourself since the Fallout, but when you are under my ranks, you will be called what I want you to be called."

Nathaniel scowled and said, "Yes, sir."

The man in the suit didn't say "you're welcome" or give Nathaniel any satisfaction back. He just kept staring at him in rage.

"What's the problem, sir?" Nathaniel asked cautiously.

He shook his head. "We've been over this many times, Nathaniel. When I say 'eliminate the subjects,' I mean 'ELIMINATE THE SUBJECTS!' How many times have I had to clean up your messes, hmm?"

Nathaniel stuttered. "S-S-Sir, I have a-a-always followed my orders swiftly and without hesitation. I even betrayed my comrades at the time to follow under your command."

"That's only because you were scared of death," the man in the suit said, "and it appears to me that you still are."

"What, sir?"

"You heard me, 13." The man said, his voice increasing in volume. "When we caught you on your mission to '*Recruit*' Ulma Thurman, you begged for your life like a scared runt. That's the worst kind of soldier, one that will run when faced with death, because we are always faced with death."

"Sir, I-I-I was only trying to show you that I was loyal to your whim. I didn't want you to kill me before I could tell you about my loyalty to you and your Agency."

"Please," the man in the suit said, "stop calling it an *Agency*. I worked hard to build this business to where it is today, and I expect it to be respected as such."

"Y-Y-Yes sir."

Nathaniel was beginning to shake. It was so bad water was beginning to bounce off of his cloak and fall to the ground. The man in the suit, whoever he was, terrified Nathaniel. I just didn't see why, though. He may be the leader, but he could easily kill him using his ability. Why didn't he, I wondered.

"So," the man in the suit said, "are you telling me you really aren't afraid of death?"

"Yes," Nathaniel nodded rapidly while fiddling his thumbs.

Suddenly, the man in the suit lunged at him quickly and held the pistol against the back of his head. Nathaniel jumped and immediately held his hands in the air. His eyes were squeezed shut.

"Get on your knees, 13."

"B-B-But sir, why are you d-d-doing this?" Nathaniel asked slowly dropping to the ground.

"Why?" The man in the suit said. "It's simple, 13. I'm proving a point. Look at you squirm beneath the barrel of my gun. Literally an inch between my finger and the trigger, an inch between your life or death, and you are about to cry, break down, run away at the first chance."

"Sir, I-I don't know-"

Nathaniel was cut off. The man in the suit said, "Don't know? Look at you! You are a waste of my time. A soldier of mine would never squirm under such a fate. They would have their head up high as they accept their death, and, in their final words, they would tell the other subjects to go piss off."

Nathaniel didn't say anything. He just nodded and kept his eyes shut. It was as if he was beginning to accept his fate like the man in the suit said.

None of us tried to help Nathaniel. We all just watched with our hands up. Secretly, as bad as this scene was, we all wanted Nathaniel to suffer after everything he's done.

The man in the suit lowered the pistol and placed it in his jacket. "You'll live for now, 13, but you are on thin ice. I'm sick of your cocky attitude. It drives me absolutely crazy. You talk about how powerful you are when I'm always in the background putting out forest fires, dragging your ass barely alive, and now, finishing off the rest of the subjects in this location."

"Yes, sir," Nathaniel said slowly standing still not inhaling.

"Tell me, before we continue, what value do you really hold? How can you benefit me?"

"What?" Nathaniel asked confused, like he had so many times in this conversation.

"It's simple, 13. I'm a business man, and, currently number one on my agenda is the capture or extinction of all escaped subjects. How can you benefit me?"

It was a weird question, but it made sense. I guess I never thought of business like that. If you don't benefit the whole, then you don't belong.

Nathaniel answered, this time confidently, "Sir, I provide you the locations of the different concentrations of subjects while helping clear them out using the gift you gave me so long ago."

The man in the suit laughed. "Don't flatter me. Your talent for sliding the earth and creating mountains is a curse. It's the reason why you're in this position. I guess you do provide me valuable information about the subject locations, but you do not help extinguish them."

"Sir," Nathaniel began to plead. "I am always on the front lines making sure they are all destroyed. I hid undercover for ten years waiting for the perfect time to strike. Then, when Laufor's, I mean subject 7's son appeared, I knew that the time had come."

"Yes, you did a good job of working undercover. I am still amazed by how you were able to access the computer system in the old hospital without anyone noticing."

My mind flashed back to the computer system that contained the plans for Operation: Zeke Laufor on them. I guess that was how Nathaniel was keeping in contact with the Agency. There was one here, too. There must've been another use for those high tech, even for today's standards, machines.

"It's one of my many talents, sir," Nathaniel said smiling nervously. "Secrecy and sneaking about is one of my-"

Nathaniel was stopped by the man in the suit. "Here you go again, 13. Bragging about yourself seems to be your greatest talent; although, I wouldn't say it was your greatest."

Nathaniel shut up and remained silent for a long time. The man in the suit finally continued on to what he was here to do, eliminating all of us. He turned his attention back to us and began his rant.

"Subjects," he said to us in the circle, "you are under arrest for acts of treason against the United States of America. He then turned towards Liam and Barbara and said, "You are also under arrest for fifty counts of code 750.193, escaping from a federal institution of imprisonment."

"What did he say?" I whispered quietly to the group.

Riley answered, "He said that Barbara and Liam escaped from a place where they were legally contained, kind of like a prison."

"They were in prison?" I asked surprised.

Riley shrugged. "Must've, or he is making up excuses for reasons to shoot us all. Last I checked, I wasn't acting traitorous in any way. They are at the very least." He pointed cautiously to the Agents at his side.

"What do you have to say for yourselves?" The man in the suit asked.

Liam stepped forward and said, "I would say we're innocent and the only criminals on this rock are you and your soldiers, but that would only get me shot."

The man in the suit smiled. "This is very true. How about you both surrender and accept the laws you broke? Tell your followers," he pointed at us in the middle, "to do the same. At least you will have longer to live if the courts take up your case."

"Do you really think the United States court system will take up a case about people given superpowers out of selfish, evil reasons?" Barbara asked.

"No, but we'll just leave out the superpower thing," the man in the suit said.

"Do you think the courts will believe you?" Liam asked.

The man in the suit genuinely laughed loudly at what Liam said as if it was some kind of joke. "You really aren't aware of the kind of power my business possesses. I have my fingers in every branch of the government."

"That's not hard to do," Marcus said. "We have had allies in the government as well, undercover for us, taking care of our needs since the beginning of the Clade."

The man in the suit cocked his head and said, "I was not speaking to you, young subject." There was silence, and then he spoke again. "However, I do find the offspring of my subjects intriguing. At the time the abilities were given to the subjects like your father, I had no idea that abilities could be transferred from parent to child. Even the child of subject 7," he looked at me, "who was the offspring of a subject and a regular American citizen, that gained abilities different from all the others."

I stepped forward, but Callon held me back. He was speaking about my father and me. There was no care at all in his cold voice.

"I would like to examine how these abilities are transferred between generations," the man in the suit said beginning to walk between his troops. "If you weren't all so bent on revenge for what we did, then you could all live, but unfortunately that isn't the case."

"Don't you think we deserve a little revenge after what you did to us?" Liam asked. "We're not even stinkin' humans anymore!"

"Such insolence!" The man in the suit shouted. "I hate that most about you subjects. You don't understand that humans have freedoms and rights. You have no freedoms and no rights! You were and still are my property since the day your parents conceived you!"

"And you find no problems of morality here?" Barbara asked.

With force and a cutting tongue, he said, "No, none whatsoever."

There was a long moment of silence as we digested what the man in the suit said. He feels no wrong in killing what he believes is his. We weren't animals. We were people, and, apparently, he was responsible for the origins of all abilities and Bloodlings.

My rage began to build. Along with it, so did my Overload. My veins created bumps in my arms I was so enraged. If that man thought he could reveal himself to everyone (besides Barbara and Liam) for the first time and take control of us, he was dead wrong. I wouldn't let him.

Nathaniel spoke up, "Yes, there is no hope for any of you. Just surrender now, and we may be merciful."

"WHAT DID I SAY!?" The man in the suit bellowed, his face turning a dark shade of red. "I told you to shut your mouth, but you just can't, can you? And, you revealed your arrogance once again! This isn't a 'we.' This is all due to me and me alone!"

Nathaniel cowered and backed down. "I'm sorry, sir. I didn't mean-"

The man in the suit cut him off. "I know you don't mean to speak up and gloat the power you don't possess. It's in your nature, but I command loyal troops that keep their mouths shut! If I hear one more word from you, you're dead, got that?"

Nathaniel stuttered, "Y-Y-Yes, sir."

Suddenly, in a flash, the man in the suit pulled out his pistol from his suit and shot Nathaniel in the forehead. Nathaniel dropped to the mud in a crumpled heap with his eyes still partially open. A bullet hole dripped blood that polluted the water.

All of us stood frozen, completely shocked at what had just happened. Nathaniel, the enemy who was responsible for so many deaths, was dead, killed at the hands of his own leader.

The scariest part of all of this was that the man in the suit kept his evil eyes locked on us the entire time.

Chapter 45

A few moments passed, and the reality still hadn't hit me yet or anyone else. I was seeing, but I wasn't believing. Nathaniel was dead. A now clean bullet hole was the only evidence of what killed him. I didn't realize my mouth was hanging open.

"Now, where were we," the man in the suit said turning the gun back towards Liam and then to Barbara.

Liam said, "You're a monster."

"No," the man in the suit said, "As I was saying earlier. You are my property, not real people as *real* implies. If I wanted to terminate your life, I have every right to do so."

"Since when?" Barbara retorted.

"Since I made you who you are!" The man in the suit shouted. "You know what?" He said shaking his head back and forth. "I don't see why I bother trying to explain this to you over and over again. None of you are free. You all belong to me. I created you all, even the kids in the back."

Liam and Barbara didn't say anything. They didn't even move. The man in the suit continued to stare us down as he began to pace back and forth like he was deep in thought. He passed over Nathaniel's body multiple times, and I began to feel bad for him, but that ended shortly after I thought of Gabe... he never leaves my mind.

Finally, after what seemed like a lifetime, the man in the suit said, "The time has come subjects. Two of you have already fallen, only three left."

"Three left?" Liam said. "You're not going to kill all of us?"

"I don't have to," the man in the suit said. And, this was the moment that the evil man revealed his master plan to take down the Clade. "I realized that the only way to kill the snake was to cut off its head, and, thanks to my dead colleague," he waved his hand towards Nathaniel, "I found out that your pretend organization has only five members left that had abilities before the Fallout. If those five were to be extinguished, then the Clade would fall with it."

"How do you imagine that?" Barbara asked.

"It's my theory," the man in the suit began, "that if the 'Originals,' as you call yourselves are removed, there would be no one to carry on your organization. I realize that you elect others to replace them and lead like a few of you here, but you don't know the history of all of this. You have no idea where you came from or why you have abilities, other than I am somewhat responsible. The

Clade will fall, I will prevail, and the experiment shall continue again. Only this time, I'll be much harsher and cruel for your parent's actions."

"You're really going to continue the experiments? You already know that they were a success. What's the point?" Barbara asked.

"Simple, 15," The man in the suit said. "I continue the experiment, I get more money. It's the American way."

"You're sick," Juliette stepped forward. "You did all of this for money?"

"I'm afraid so. It's also your precious democratic, free government that is paying me," the man in the suit said. "Hmm... I would also love to experiment with how a subject is able to transfer abilities to another normal person."

I turned my head slightly to see Teddy cowering behind me. Tears were beginning to form in the pits of his eyes, but he wasn't mad. I wish I could say the same thing for Trish. Her dark eyes were burning. It looked as though she wanted to kill me.

"I think that's enough discussion for today. If you want more, surrender now," The man in the suit said.

None of us said anything. We just kept our hands up no matter how much they were beginning to ache and waited. We weren't going to surrender to him. I'll be honest, though, a part of me wanted to. I didn't want to die that day, not with so many questions still rattling around in my head.

The man in the suit looked genuinely upset when he pulled out his pistol and examined it. "Fine, then." He held it up and pointed it out at Barbara and then back to Liam and back again.

"Who will be first?" The man in the suit said.

Nobody moved. Liam stood tall, strong, and determined. He wasn't going to let that man get the best of him.

She was beginning to shake and shutter visibly. The man in the suit could see this too. He smiled and turned the gun in her direction.

He stopped halfway through though, and caught a glimpse of something in our group. He said, "Well, I didn't notice it before, but the daughter of subject 15 and subject 65 is here." He pointed at Sarah standing next to me.

Sarah stepped back a little when the man in the suit said, "Since no one volunteered to die first, or surrender, I will have to choose. I choose your daughter, 15."

Barbara's eyes opened wide while the man in the suit slid his finger down the side of the barrel until he reached the trigger.

"No!" Barbara moved. She launched herself using her ability to put herself between the man in the suit and Sarah.

She was flying through the air when a loud bang rang out. My heart dropped when I heard the sound. Barbara dropped to the ground and didn't move.

Everything that happened after seemed to move in slow motion. Sarah began to take off for her fallen mother, but I used all my strength to hold her back and keep her close. Teddy grabbed onto Trish as she tried to console him. Marcus and Juliette stayed where they were, but clenched their fists getting ready for a fight. Riley, McKayla, and Conner all stepped back, their mouths wide open, not believing what they were seeing. Bruno and Callon didn't move. They watched and waited as if they were planning something.

"Mom! NO!" Sarah cried out, tears immediately beginning to flow from the pits of her eyes.

"Sarah! Stop! Remember why she did that. She did it to protect you! Don't run out and get yourself shot!" I yelled at her.

She simmered down, but she continued to cry. "First Gabe... now my mom. We just started to get to know one another..."

"I know," I said softly. "I'm so sorry, Sarah, but we need to get out of this so she didn't get shot for nothing."

Suddenly, Liam shouted, "Run, NOW!" And with that, the entire line of Agents and the man in the suit fell into a large pit. Dust circled them as they disappeared into the ground. Liam used his ability to turn the dirt to powder.

We began to turn and run for the cave when a gurgle came from Barbara's body. "Sa-Sarah."

Everyone else already began to run. I wanted Sarah to come to, but she couldn't leave her mom.

Liam stayed next to Barbara, comforting her in her final moments. He waved to us. "Come, but be quick. That pit isn't deep."

We ran up. Sarah sprinted as quickly as she could and fell next to her mother. I looked down upon her and saw a bullet hole right in the center of her chest. Dark red blood covered the outside of her cloak. It hurt because there was nothing I could do to help her. Sarah would lose another loved one.

"Mom," Sarah said bawling, "I'm... sorry. I should've-"

Barbara forced out, "Sshh, don't. Not... your fault."

Sarah kept shaking her head like it was her fault. She should've been shot. Barbara was more important to the Clade anyways, and she only helped push the man in the suit's plan further.

Barbara said, "I would never... let... my daughter... die. I love you."

Sarah fell over her mother's dying body. "I love you too."

Barbara placed a hand on her head and said, "Run, baby. Run...fast."

Sarah nodded and hugged her one more time before she stood and began to run away.

I was getting up myself to follow her when Barbara whispered, "Laufor... come here."

Confused, I bent over her and said, "What, Barbara?"

She put her shaking hand on my face and said, "You... keep her safe. Defeat them. Save the Clade. Be the one we hoped... you would be."

And then, her chest deflated as her last breath escaped. Her hand fell through the air only to land in Liam's. He gently put it down over her chest covering the bullet wound and closed her eyes. She looked like she was sleeping. It was so beautiful my chest tightened.

Liam looked at me. "We need to go, sonny."

I jumped up and followed him in a dead sprint just as the heads of the Agents were beginning to pop up from out of their hole.

It hurt to leave Barbara's body behind. She deserved a proper burial witnessed by all of her companions and followers including Sarah. They were just beginning to get along and bond like real mother and daughters should. All of the years they missed would've been redone and all of the pain caused by the Clade would've been healed. Why did this have to happen, I wondered.

Sarah had lost two loved one's now, her special someone, Gabe, and her real mother, Barbara. I couldn't imagine how much pain she was feeling all at once. She still hadn't gotten over Gabe's death yet. I would have to make sure that I'm there for her if we escaped this mess.

I followed Liam through the forest for about a hundred yards where the rest of the group was waiting for us. They stood huddled in a tight group with Callon in the center giving out orders to everyone around him.

He spotted us and said, "About time. Where were you two?"

Liam said, "We had to pay our final respects…"

I noticed Sarah in the back wiping her eyes to no avail. More tears continued to flow. There was no hiding her sorrow. It cut her deep. She wanted nothing more than to stay with her mom even if that meant death for her as well.

My mind kept replaying the final scenes between Barbara and me. All the things she told me like keeping

Sarah safe and watching out for her seemed like such a difficult task now that she was like this. Saving the entire Clade seemed well out of reach to with whom we are dealing with, now that we know the true enemy.

Callon said, "Fine, I'll just tell you what was planned already. Stewart and Laura found us. I told them to gather as many Recruits, alive or injured, as possible and meet us at the cavern entrance. We are to meet them there in five minutes. It will probably take us ten to run all the way back, so we need to move quickly. Only Barbara and I know where the path down the slope is, and now that Barbara is gone," Callon lowered his head, "I'm the only one who does."

"Then, let's get our butts in gear, and go!" Liam said.

Callon nodded, "Right, let's-"

The bushes rustled to our right. We all turned just in time to see two Agent troops separated from their squadron.

One shouted through a mechanical speaking device, "Stay where you are!"

The other raised his gun, but he wasn't fast enough. Just as his partner was about to open fire, a strong gust of wind blew by. Suddenly, Marcus was standing behind the Agent with a knife stuck in the side of his neck. He removed it quickly and let the Agent drop.

He dove for the other Agent who didn't realize he was there and aimed at us as well. Marcus caught him in the side of his abdomen spinning the Agent clockwise, bullets being sprayed from his gun in the process. We all ducked and covered our ears to block the Agents cybertronic screams. A few moments later, he was dead.

We all thought Marcus had saved us, and we got a lucky, narrow escape, but McKayla's screams soon proved our assumptions wrong. Lying on the ground in front of Trish was Conner. A bullet hole was in his gut just below the right side of his ribs. His hands were dark red and shook when he grabbed his side.

Trish dove on him. "Why did you do that!?"

"I…" Conner tried to speak. "I couldn't let you get hurt."

"Why!? What's so special about me that you would do that?"

That's when everyone else rushed to Conner's aide including myself. I wasn't really paying much attention to Conner at the time, though. It sounds horrible since he was lying on the ground just after being shot, but Trish was speaking and moving. I haven't seen any emotion or sign of life since she found out I gave her powers.

We all crowded around Conner. Questions began to fly in so quickly that they sounded like a bad screeching sound. I didn't get most of them, but what I did notice when Trish asked why he dove in front of the bullet, he looked at me. He looked at me with distraught eyes that looked as though there was something he was hiding.

And, then it hit me. My mind flashed back to when Conner and I were on our way to find Sarah, Trish, and the others at the pond. He told me he keeps himself detached from all emotions and people because then there is no pain when they die, but that was changing. He was getting feelings for someone.

It was Trish.

My mind was trying to wrap itself around that, but it just wasn't happening. I always thought that Trish and I was sort of a "couple." Everyone knew I liked her because I made it obvious enough, and I thought she liked me too. Could Conner really like her even *love* her, I wondered.

"Pick him up!" Callon shouted. "Marcus, carry him until we reach the cavern. We need to move, now!"

Marcus wrapped his arms around Conner gently and lifted him up. We all began to take off for the cavern once again as quickly as we could move.

I could've been wrong. This was all just assumptions after all, but I couldn't help but shake the feeling I was right. Conner risked his life to protect Trish. I was grateful he did, but also jealous in that now Trish would notice him more that she would notice me.

My mind wouldn't let go of Trish and Conner being together. Like any jealous boy, those thoughts soon spread and blew themselves out of proportion. "It was obvious that now Trish and Conner would become something, and she would never talk to me again. Those kinds of thoughts flooded me.

I wouldn't have much longer to speculate on their futures together because the more jealous I got, the more anger that came with it; and, the more anger I felt, the more the Overload crippled me to the core. It was already tearing me apart before Conner was shot, and now, it was only getting worse. A few times I dropped completely on the ground. I just kept telling everyone I was a klutz and kept moving. They all bought it except for Liam, Marcus, Juliette, and Callon.

The rain would cripple me as well. The heavy part of the storm was just over the horizon and would soon destroy me. How much longer did I have before the Overload killed me? It wasn't long. I felt like dying right then and there.

Then, Conner was shot, and my anger rose from jealousy. My body channeled its electricity and began to grow in strength leading to a terrible amount of pain. As we ran, my legs began to visibly glow blue. They stung so badly I was prepared for Trish to slice off my leg with her flaming arm.

It only got worse from there. We were only a half-mile away from the cavern when the Overload finally won. I was towards the back of the line of Recruits when a huge bolt of electricity erupted from my chest blasting over trees and dropping me to the ground.

Marcus stopped in front of me and crouched over me while the others continued to run. "Zeke, what's wrong? Is it the Overload?"

Lightning bolts cascaded over my body jolting me and causing my body to spasm uncontrollably. "Stay... BACK!" I shouted as a surge of energy erupted off of me and blasted another tree. "It's the Overload! It... got me."

Sarah was the last in line and stopped as well. She stood back, same as Marcus, while electricity rippled across my skin.

"Zeke!" Sarah cried out. "Zeke! What's wrong? We have to keep going!"

I shook my head left to right while on my back. My neck jarred and stuttered while the Overload took over. "Can't... Overload... too STRONG!" Another tree was blasted down.

"You need to get up, Zeke," Marcus said. "The Agents are on their way. If we stay any longer, we're done for. C'mon. You are stronger than this. You've fought off the Overload so far. We are so close to the end, Zeke. I know you can do it."

Sarah added, "Yeah, Zeke. You have to come with us. I'm not going to lose another person close to me! Got that?"

Electricity kept bouncing on top of and around me. Dirt was upturned and blasted into dust around Marcus and Sarah's feet. Small trenches formed from the electrical outbursts.

"I… can't. Overload too GREAT! AAHH!" I cried out. "Please..." I couldn't believe I said this, "Kill me."

"What?" Sarah said completely stunned. "Why? We can help Zeke!" Tears formed in her eyes again.

She began to take small steps towards me. "I said get back!" I screamed. "The Overload… too strong! It's going to kill me, just go!"

It was hard on Sarah and Marcus to hear that. Sarah didn't know much about the Overload, and Marcus knew very little since Callon was in control of Shiloh the entire time.

Shiloh…wait, that's it! There is a cure to the Overload!

Marcus said, "Zeke, the Agents are coming. I'll carry you and get shocked if I must, but please come."

The electricity crippled my movements, but I managed to bend my arms and legs. I grunted and winced as I pushed myself up onto my feet. My upper body dangled and hung towards the ground while I stood. I swayed gently as bolts arced around me and blasted the environment. Marcus and Sarah both had to dive out of the way for a few of them.

It took even more work, but I was capable of standing completely upright after a few minutes of searing pain. I grabbed my chest and stomach trying to fight off the pain, but it was too much. I wobbled and began to fall but pushed myself back up.

"Zeke! Perfect," Sarah said, "now, let's go!"

"I c-can't," I pushed out. "Overload is going to kill me sooner or later, Sarah. I have a plan to cure it, though."

"How!? We need to go!" Sarah cried out.

"You... won't like it" I said.

There was a silence for a moment. Then, Marcus knew what I was planning. "Zeke, no, you don't mean you plan to-"

I nodded. Marcus knew right away that there was only one way to cure an Overload, and that's through death. But, there was more to my plan than just keeling over and letting the Overload take me.

Sarah said, "What then? What is it?"

I spoke slowly not for Sarah and Marcus to understand, but for me to grasp it as well.

"I... I have to let the Agents kill me."

Chapter 46

"WHAT!? Zeke, no, you can't be serious!" Sarah screamed. The tears began to fall once again.

"Zeke, you don't have to do that. You can come with us, and we will find a cure," Marcus pleaded.

I shook my head. "I'm sorry... both of you. This, guunnh, is hard for me to say, but it's the only answer. The Agents will come and find us eventually, but I can finish them all off... and the leader."

"How?" Marcus asked.

"When Shiloh was shot and killed, his body erupted in flame and exploded from the Overload. It killed the two Agents that shot him. I think my Overload... will do the same," I said.

"And, what if it doesn't?" Sarah asked. "What if you die for no reason!?"

"I'm going to die anyways, Sarah. AAHH!! At least, I can try to take out a few Agents along the way, right?"

Then, Marcus said something that truly surprised me. "He's right."

Sarah and I both looked at him in shock. My Instructor was agreeing with me to get myself killed for the possible good of the Clade. He knew there was no cure outside of this. It was all just false hope to keep Shiloh and me going. Our fates were decided when we were struck by lightning or thrown in the furnace.

"What!? How can you be agreeing with this, Marcus?" Sarah exclaimed. "You're telling Zeke it's okay to get himself killed!"

"Yes, because otherwise he will die a painful death, Sarah! I don't want him to go," Marcus said, tears also forming in his eyes, "but it's for the best. If he's going to die, let him go out with a bang and possibly save all of us in the Clade."

"But…" Sarah said, her watery eyes locking on mine. "I can't let you go, Zeke. You're the only true friend I have left. Sure, I've been in the Clade two years longer, but I was always alone until you and Gabe. I lost Gabe, but I won't lose you!"

A moment passed where the only thing heard was the sound of my wincing and grunting. Lightning bolts still arced off of me. In fact, nothing has changed in the last ten minutes other than I've decided it's best to let the man in the suit shoot me.

"I'm sorry, Sarah. Trust me. It's the right move for the Clade… and me," I said.

Sarah began to sob heavily now. She dropped to her knees and began to punch the ground. Water splashed up in her face mixing tears with the dirty water.

"Sarah..." Marcus began.

"Quiet!" Sarah shouted. "If all of my friends are going to die and leave me alone, why don't I just go with them? It's going to happen to all of us eventually!"

"Don't be like that, Sarah. We didn't plan for this," Marcus said.

"We didn't plan to have abilities or be Recruited either. No, this is just the way it is. We are doomed to be killed just because we are a little different."

"Stop it!" I screamed in pain.

Sarah stopped and looked up at me from off of the ground. I wanted to walk up to her and put my hand on her shoulder and comfort her, but I couldn't. The Overload wouldn't let me. I would kill her if I did.

I said, "So many people care for you Sarah and need you. I won't let you die. You don't know this, but your mother told me to keep you safe, protect you, and save the Clade, and dammit I'm going to for her!"

Sarah remained silent with her mouth agape. Her eyes leaked with fresh tears. Marcus held Conner tightly and stayed upright. He walked around my circle of electricity where the bolts were cascading and knelt next to Sarah.

"I care for you, Sarah. I don't want to lose you too. Please, come with me. We don't have much time left. We are going to be left behind."

Sarah cried out loud in agony. She looked up to me and said, "I'm sorry, Zeke."

I shook my head, "It's not you… fault."

She stood straight and walked with Marcus down the path the other Recruits took. They slowed down as I began to fade from their sight.

Sarah stopped and said, "Goodbye, Zeke. Is there anything you want before… you go?"

I didn't at first, but then I said, "Tell Trish, I'm sorry for everything. I didn't mean to do this to her. Also, come back for my body, okay? Make sure the area is clear, though. I don't want any of your lives to be risked."

She nodded. Then, Marcus said, "Goodbye, Zeke. You were a great pupil."

I cackled and said, "I was an annoying pupil, don't lie."

He laughed to. Tears began to fall out of his eyes as well. This is the first time I've seen Marcus truly cry. It was sad and relieving at the same time.

He said, "Okay, that is a little more accurate."

We all forced a smile. Then, Marcus and Sarah left. I wondered if it would be the last time I would see them, as if some greater being would keep me alive long enough to get a glimpse of them. Shiloh did it; why couldn't I, I wondered.

I forced myself back up straight. The time had come. I needed to do what I said I would do. No matter how terrifying it was, I would face the Agents and let them take me.

With one deep breath, I began to walk slowly, one step at a time. Each step came with an eruption of agony stretching from my foot to the top of my head. I kept telling myself that relief would be here soon.

Chapter 47

It was hard work for me to trek through the mud and pain. It was like sludge that grabbed my feet every time I would make a step and hold me there. It took extra effort to force another step, but I kept going.

I didn't realize it until I began my final walk, but my cloak was burnt to shreds. My torso was completely exposed and everything below my knees was showing. Everything between had large burns and seared patches that revealed a little of my skin. Hopefully, my friends would change my clothes when they buried me.

When people describe their lives flashing before their eyes, I never really got what they meant, but now, I think I do. It was not a flash. Maybe to everyone else and how quickly it actually happened it's a flash, but to me it wasn't. And, what flashed before my eyes weren't significant moments, it was people.

The first was my mom. At least, the person who was paid to be my mom. It didn't matter to me who she was. She took care of me and loved me the same as any parent would love any child of theirs. There were different memories of my mom that I would remember the most. My favorite was when I got to go to the zoo and name the giraffe Geronimo. I even got to pet him and feed him. I don't know why that stands out the most of all my memories with my mother, but it was nice. It made me happy.

The next person to flash in my mind was Thomas. We were best friends since elementary school ever since I stole his lucky pencil for a test because everyone thought it was magical. Turns out, he was just that smart. We got to know each other, and we ended up hanging out almost every weekend and almost always at Thomas' house because my apartment was rather small. I got along with his entire family and his parents thought of me as their "son they never had." We played a lot of video games and traded pokémon cards. As time went on, we began to switch our focus to girls. Emma Watson was always a wishful choice for us, but we knew that was always out of reach. So, we focused on girls that were only slightly out of our league like Trish.

Speaking of Trish, she was next. My mind went to when we were kids and I was at her birthday party. That's when I first began to develop feelings for her. Ever since then, I was hooked on her. No other girl was good enough except for her. I kept trying to go out with her, but she never got the hint. Then, middle school came, and we were separated for most of the years. I thought my chances had run out until high school came, but she started dating that jerk quarterback right away, and they were together, on and off, ever since until now.

Gabe and Sarah were together in my next vision. The most flashes occurred during the time that we snuck around at night and found the secret room 241F. We were silly and didn't realize how reckless we were being, but, if it wasn't for us planning our great escape, we would all be dead. We were the ones that discovered Nathaniel's heinous plans. I guess good could come from even the most serious of situations.

My final flash was a series of moments that combined Marcus and Juliette. They were always great leaders looking out for Gabe and me while we learned how to control our abilities. Our sessions with them ended early, but the moments didn't. Gabe vanished when we met Liam, Callon, and Barbara. Good for him because otherwise he would have had to go through the Gauntlet with me, Riley, Conner, and McKayla.

Riley, Conner, and McKayla reminded me of myself, Gabe, and Sarah back in New York. They each had something that made them a little bit different than each other but that kept them good friends. Soon, they became our friends. I didn't think that I would find friends here after everything that happened before.

Then, the moments vanished as if the fog was lifted from my eyes. To my amazement, I was almost back to where the Agents fell in the pit and Barbara died. I guess I was imagining those things for a while.

Light began to break between the green and brown of the trees and other vegetation. The clearing was just up ahead. I moved as quietly as possible trying to keep the groans to a minimum which was hard. Sometimes, they would just slip out.

I could hear the voice of the man in the suit just beyond the tree line. He was swearing at his Agents for letting us get away and formulating a new strategy.

The man in the suit said, "Subject 6 shouldn't be underestimated again! His control of his ability has surpassed what we originally anticipated. By now, the subjects are probably finding a way down the mountain."

I moved closer trying to be as silent as I could be. Half the time, though, the electricity radiating off my body would crackle and spurt giving off a low hiss of sound like a generator. It was annoying. At any moment, the Agents could hear me and take me out. I needed to make sure I had all of them in range of my final attack. The problem was I didn't know how large my blast radius would be.

I kept listening to the Agents speak as I approached.

"What shall I do, sir?" A mechanical Agent voice said.

The man in the suit said, "I want you and three of the best soldiers in your squadron to take the helicopter we landed in and circle the mountain looking for where the subjects are exiting. When you find them, take them out. I have no use for subjects that won't follow orders. I have enough back at headquarters."

The Agents nodded and said, "Yes sir," and began to call off the names of the Agents he would take on the mission.

I stayed low for a few more minutes taking in deep breaths and wondering how badly it would hurt to get shot. Hopefully, it wasn't as bad as the excruciating pain of the Overload. That was the driving force in this.

I began to get cold feet. Could I do this? Could I walk into the heart of the enemy and take a bullet for my friends knowing that chances are high that they would live a good life afterwards with no fear of being chased or killed? I wanted to believe I was. I always thought that I could do the right thing and fall on that grenade, but now, I don't know. The moment was here to prove myself, and I was shaking.

The four Agents began to group together and head out of the clearing. I needed to do this before they leave the clearing. They had to be taken out; otherwise, they would kill all of my friends. The time was here.

I stepped out of the forest and into the clearing. The Agents and the man in the suit were standing in front of the large pit near the center of the clearing.

They heard me walk near them and immediately held up their guns. I shut my eyes and choked. I couldn't be killed yet. I wasn't close enough to make sure they were all blasted.

The man in the suit raised his hand and held them off, though. He said, "Hold your fire."

He stepped forward to separate himself from the group of Agents. "This is awkward. I did not expect a subject to be so foolish to approach us. I figured that you would be trying to get out of here as quickly as possible. I guess I was wrong, but why?"

I didn't answer him. I wanted to try to remain as strong looking to him as possible even though I was ready to keel over. It helped that electricity jutted out from around me.

The man in the suit said, "Although your motives appearing for your own demise are unclear, I do believe you are the son of subject 7. Yes, you are. I can tell by your unique ability signature. You appear to control electricity which is unique compared to all of the other descendants of subjects or the infected."

"How do you know I'm the son of him?" I asked. "I could be the child of any subject that just happens to have electrical powers."

The man in the suit shook his head. "I'm afraid you are the offspring of subject 7. Our reports indicate that subject 7's offspring was unique in that he had relations with an American citizen. The only one of all the subjects which is very interesting to say the least. Our data then suggests that something else would be attained by having children crossed between a human and a subject. You were that something else."

My father seemed important to this guy as well. I wondered why? Nobody seems to give me a solid answer on that other than he led the escape from the controls of this old man. Is his ability crazy powerful; is he hailed for having a child with a Regular?

The man in the suit stared at me for a long time. The Agents didn't lower their guns yet either. Why wouldn't he just shoot me already and get this over with instead of bragging about how bad my father is?

I said, "Hey, I have a question for you to."

He lifted his eyebrow. "What might that be?"

"Who are you?"

The man in the suit laughed as if it was odd that I didn't know his name. It was also a pretty random question for the situation we were in; me waiting for death and all.

The man in the suit said, "My name is Victor Desmon. I am president and CEO of Generotech. A company that works in compliance with the United States government to advance the understandings and research techniques of human and animal biology."

So, the man responsible for all of the terrible things that happened to everyone with abilities, all Originals, Recruits, and Bloodlings, were because of a businessman infatuated with science. It was a little ridiculous to believe, but it must've been true. Why would he lie about it, I thought.

I didn't know what to say after that, so I just remained silent and let the Overload further cripple me, hoping that would cause a bigger boom.

Victor said, "So, if you are not going to talk, then I shall. I have been a part of this war since the beginning thirty, or so years ago. Eventually, your society will cease to exist. A kind like yours won't be able to survive even without my army coming after you. There is no way you could survive in this society. There would be panic in the streets, and people asking to lock you away. That is why it is best for us to just kill you."

I braced myself for the bullet, but it never came. "So, what are you waiting for?" I asked cockily. "Aren't you going to kill me?"

Victor said, "No, I'm not going to kill you. You are a fascinating specimen. I can see all of the possible futures that you could bring to us. Just look at the energy you are radiating. You could power all of New York City for generations with no harm to the environment. Think if we had more like you. There would never be any worry of global warming or coal."

As odd as it was, that's not what I wanted to hear. "You aren't going to shoot me?"

Victor laughed. "No, that would be ridiculous. We only kill the useless ones. You are unique. I plan on taking you in and studying you."

I groaned and not just because of the Overload overwhelming me. Everything that I had planned was about to go up in smoke if I didn't get shot. Not only would that end this war with the Clade on top, but it would also rid me of this Overload. It would cost me my life... but I knew it had to be done.

Victor waved his hand and the four Agents that were originally supposed to go to the helicopter began to move towards me. One of them took handcuffs out of his side pocket.

I had to do something before they took me in. They weren't going to kill me. I needed to figure out a way that would make them want to kill me.

I knew what I had to do.

My heart began to pump heavily and sweat formed on my forehead. It would have to be perfect, but it would still be risky. The Agents approached me with nothing to worry on their minds. I would soon change that.

This was it... the moment I had planned for. I told my friends that I would do this, and now, I have to. I promised Barbara, and I told myself that nothing would happen to Trish.

It was now or never.

The Agent unclipped the handcuffs and began to circle me when I unleashed two powerful bolts of lightning out of the palms of my hands. Two were blasted into the forest. I then bent my arms slightly and unleashed another bolt again and blasted the other two into oblivion.

Victor's eyes opened wide. "It's like you are asking for death, menace. I am allowing you to live. Let me take you in NOW!"

Two more Agents separated from the group and began to move towards me.

The Overload was about to take me down. I didn't have any time left.

"I'm... sorry... Victor. I'm afraid... I'm not going... with you."

Then, in one final move, I unleashed all of the energy that had been building up inside me since I was first hit by the lightning in Pennsylvania. I swung my palms in front of me and screamed as the searing pain returned.

Large bolts of lightning exploded from my hands. I could feel them tearing themselves apart from the inside. There was so much energy released in such a small space.

The Agents dove out of the way in a hurry, but they couldn't escape. Those hit by the large bolt themselves almost vaporized while the ones who were able to avoid the large bolts were still hit hard by the fingers that extended from the main bolts.

I held the bolts in place as long as I could. My head began to feel light, and I dropped to one knee. The Overload was taking me... my time was up. My vision became blurry, and colors seemed to fade from existence. Yet, I could still see the massacre that my Overload lightning bolts were capable of.

Victor lied on the ground covering his head while the bolts took out his troops. The bolts weren't meant for him though. I needed him alive. Just him.

My energy began to fade. The bolts began to slowly diminish. I tried to stand, but couldn't. There was no hope for me anymore. The Overload was going to tear me apart until my painful death.

Then, there was a loud bang. Suddenly, a rush of warmth filled my chest. My lightning bolts were cut off, and I grabbed the warm spot. I didn't feel anything, but when I lifted my hand, there was blood covering the whole thing.

I looked up slowly to see Victor rising off the ground putting his pistol back in his jacket. He shot me. My plan worked.

There was a crackling sound coming from deep within me. It grew in volume until I could tell that it was coming from inside the bullet hole. Suddenly, great pain followed the noise. I dropped immediately onto my back and cried out in pain. It wasn't the bullet. It was the Overload. It was going to happen. There was no stopping it now.

It rose and rose until it eventually tore at every bit of being that made me. I convulsed and my back arched. Light and energy poured out of the wound. More energy than I ever could produce on my own.

A great stream of lightning burst out of the opening and expanded into a huge ball of electricity. I cried out.

Then, the explosion occurred. Everything exploded into blue light. Everything burned deep.

And, my last thought was that I would never know my real father.

To be continued...

Coming Soon:
The Human Element Trilogy Book 3: Extinction

Sarah

The ride was long and exhausting. I couldn't believe that a little boy like Teddy could remain quiet for so long. I've always heard that little boys were rambunctious and wanted to wreak havoc wherever they went. He could've been well past that age. I didn't have any brothers or sisters, so I wouldn't know.

Marcus parked the truck and let it idle for a few moments. We waited in the rusted, red machine until he said, "We need to hurry. Chances are this will probably blow up in our face. But if you can find him, and bring him back here quickly, maybe then we can persuade him."

Trish said from the back seat, "We'll go quickly. That's not a problem. You stay here and watch the truck, and Teddy and Sarah will come with me."

We agreed on the plan and got out of the truck. I slammed my door shut and stepped out onto the sidewalk and immediately bumped into a pedestrian. They gave me a funny look and walked away just as my face was turning red.

The city was incredible. I slowly spun in place and took in the wondrous sights- the skyscrapers, people and traffic. How anyone could live in a congested area like this must be patient. The noise of the hustle and bustle echoed through the paved streets. I was never to a large city like this before, and it surprised me even more that there were larger ones than this!

Trish and Teddy stood next to me while Marcus shifted the truck to park.

He said, "You have ten minutes. The Agency has been on our tail ever since the Colorado division collapsed. Go now."

We didn't say another word to him. We turned and headed down the street wearing regular street clothes to help ourselves blend in. Trish took the lead since she knew her way around this city. Teddy and I just walked behind her. Teddy could barely keep up with his little legs. It was pretty amusing.

Teddy asked, "How far do we have to walk, Trish?"

Trish responded, "A few blocks. You heard Marcus. We couldn't park closer because the Agency is probably watching Zeke's apartment. We have to go on foot. They won't recognize us as much as they would recognize Marcus. Just try to blend in."

And, that's what we did. We remained quiet for the rest of the walk. I didn't feel like talking anyways. I was too taken in by the fantastic sights I was seeing. I was like a kid in a candy store as so many older people put it. My mouth hung open slightly in amazement at the view.

Trish then turned left onto another busy avenue with cars parked all the way down the street. I even saw a parking cop writing a ticket because of an expired timer on the meter. I never saw that happened before.

It was then that Trish immediately stopped and stared up at the skyscraper in front of us. Teddy accidentally bumped into her back and whispered, "Sorry." Trish didn't respond.

I looked up as well wondering what she was looking at. The building was about twenty to thirty stories high with big glass windows looking into small living rooms all the way to the top. It appeared to be an apartment building. What was so special about this, I thought.

Trish sighed and said, "If you're wondering, that window right there," she pointed to one of the middle windows on the seventh floor. "That is where Zeke used to live before he disappeared. Well, he didn't disappear. According to the letter, he moved away and didn't have time to tell anyone."

The significance began to sink in. This was the remnants of Trish's old life. Before she even met me or ever heard of the Clade, Trish was walking around these streets with all of her friends worrying about whom to take to a dance or something cliché like that.

Trish looked around too make sure nobody was watching us and said, "Alright, let's keep moving. We have about four blocks until we reach our destination."

We followed her lead and kept walking. Still, I found myself constantly looking back to that apartment building thinking about Zeke and his life before Marcus recruited him. What happened to his mother? Would his friends still care? Who was living there now having the life Zeke had taken away?

It was then that I thought about my own life and realized that the same questions could apply to me. Except, I know for fact, my pretend parents were dead.

We never did find Zeke's body. The handful of Recruits that survived at the base of the mountain watched in horror as it began to crumble from the bombings when, suddenly, there was a burst of bright blue light. It shot out from the trees into the air like a pillar and erupted into an electrical storm. It was then that we all knew that Zeke had given the ultimate sacrifice.

Most of the Recruits were in the dark about Zeke's decision to stay back. He only told Marcus and I before he hastily stumbled back to face the man in the suit.

The man in the suit... his horrifying image kept reappearing in my mind; His short white hair, aging wrinkling face; his icy blue eyes that made me unravel. He was the reason for Gabe's death and now, possibly, Zeke's.

After the explosion, all of the Instructors and Head Instructors made their way back up the mountain. All of the helicopters had disappeared over the surrounding mountains giving us clearance to search. The explosion was huge. They moved quickly while the rest of the Recruits waited at the bottom of the mountain.

We waited anxiously hoping that they would find some evidence that Zeke was alive... or at least dead. That way, we would know, but I didn't want that. I couldn't lose another good friend. Zeke had always looked out for us. He was a truly good person with good intentions.

I looked back to Trish who was talking with Conner. She seemed really into her conversation with Conner even after hearing about Zeke from Marcus and I. It was like she started to not care anymore just because she was Zeke's Bloodling. She needed to get over that. Zeke didn't ruin her life. We all knew that Zeke wanted nothing more than to give her everything, but she appeared to be oblivious to him.

I wanted to walk up to her and punch her in the face.

However, I controlled myself, and as time passed our hopes that Zeke survived grew slimmer and slimmer. It wasn't until Callon returned that we knew something was wrong. He told us that Zeke's body wasn't found and with all the scorched earth, toppled trees, and electrical feeling in the air, he could've vaporized himself.

The news was hard to take. I almost dropped to my knees, but Riley was there to hold me up. McKayla embraced Conner and began to cry. Bruno didn't care one bit, and it looked as though Trish didn't either. She just kept staring ahead into the eyes of Callon.

Did I mention I wanted to punch her?

But, what Callon said next really brought me down. "Sarah," he said softly. "We did find someone up there."

He stepped to my side and let me watch as Stewart and Laura carried down the body of Barbara Irving.

My mother.

The memories of her began to swarm my mind. I remembered when I first met her, and how she never spoke to me, only watched me. Then, she was watching me during the Gauntlet, and how she opened up to me later during our escape. I saw her drop to the ground when I was about to be shot.

I rushed over to her body. Stewart and Laura gently placed her on the ground next to an alive, lush tree that created an immense area of shade. I wrapped myself around her shoulders and cried for a long time. Nobody cared. They knew why. We had finally started to accept the other's mistakes. Why now, I kept thinking? Why now?

I stood back up and forced Callon to keep searching for Zeke.

"He *has* to be up there! Keep looking!" The tears kept falling.

Callon shook his head. "I'm afraid there is nothing more that we can do. We checked everywhere. Even ground zero. But, there was no body or signs of life found."

It was then that Callon said something I thought I would never hear him say. "It's a shame... I was really starting to believe in that kid like Marcus did."

After that, Juliette found the truck we parked behind the **Wintry Slope Diner** three months ago and began giving small rides back to the nearest town. It took a couple of trips, but we all made it safely with no Agency involvement at all. From there, we took a bus and went back to Liam's home in Pennsylvania which was almost completely demolished now.

It was there, two months later of trying to survive off of the land and trying to find a safe way to reach the third division of the Clade (our money for busses and other forms of safe travel had been diminished), that a plan was made.

Fall was right around the corner. The sun was beginning to set behind the tall trees. The house was beginning to reek of mildew, smelly Recruits, and decay when Marcus said, "If we had money, we could make it to the third division in Florida and warn them before it's too late."

"It's already too late," Callon said. "I want to believe that there is hope, but with our numbers diminished to only one hundred and some, I doubt that the Agency will have trouble finishing us off."

Juliette said, "It's not too late, Callon. We just need to come up with a way of making money."

He scoffed. "You mean getting a job? Hate to burst your bubble, Juliette, but we aren't technically citizens anymore now that the Agency knows that we all have abilities."

"Not like that," Juliette said. "I'm thinking we need help from a Regular."

Marcus, leaning back in his chair, said, "Really? A Regular? I don't think that is such a good idea. It may work, but who would ever want to donate money to an underground society filled with individuals with abilities currently at war with the government?"

"It sounds crazy," Juliette said. "But, maybe there is someone out there who would help? Who knows? All we need are some funds to get a few of us a ride down to Florida."

Marcus shook his head. "I… I just don't know, Juliette. I'm sorry. I want to believe, but after Zeke died… I just don't know what to believe in anymore. He was our chance at a real life, and now he's dead."

"I agree with Marcus," Callon said. "Dragging a Regular into our mess is ridiculous. No way would they help us. The Agency would be knocking on our doorstep the minute we asked."

"You don't know that Ezekiel is dead!" Juliette jumped out of her seat; the table shook. "If what Marcus and Sarah told me was true, then Zeke said that Shiloh was still alive after he erupted. The Overload crippled him, but he lived for a short time."

Marcus slowly stood up as well beginning to see where Juliette was going. "Are you suggesting that Zeke lived, but so did an Agent?"

Juliette nodded. Callon laughed. "Again, we need to start thinking logically. The chances that Laufor lived are slim if that. If he did live and an Agent took him, then he killed him and took his body. That I believe."

"We need to believe in something, Callon," Marcus said.

Callon stared at the ground. His arms were crossed over his chest. He exhaled deeply and said, "I just… don't know."

"What do you say then?" Juliette asked. "We ask a Regular for help. Someone we can trust. They provide us with funds to get some of us to Florida and warn Sissy and Layona them of the attack. You heard Victor. It looks like his goal is to kill all of the Originals. That would eventually lead to our separation and end."

Callon thought to himself for a long time. I watched his eyes dart across the floor. I kept wondering what he would say. He was at war with himself, but all that Juliette and Marcus had said was giving me hope as well. Could Zeke really be alive? I hoped they were right. I couldn't accept the fact that he was gone too.

"Fine," Callon said definitively. "I'm in. Now, we just need to find a Regular that will listen to our god awful story and beg for money."

Marcus said, a smile starting to form on his face, "Don't worry. I know the perfect person."

And, here we are now. Marcus drove the truck to New Haven to find the Regular we needed to help us get to Florida and potentially save the Clade...

... and Zeke.

Trish led us to a street lined with actual houses. Most of them were older, two-story homes of different colors. Behind me was a school that Trish said that Zeke and she went to. For a minute, I was almost envious since I had the world's best tutors. I missed out on a lot in my life, but maybe I could get that all back.

I forced myself to think about the mission at hand as Juliette turned onto a walkway that led up to a white door. We had reached our destination. The house was bright blue with a small garage detached from the house around the back. The sight gave me a warm feeling. It was a lot smaller than my old home, of course, but that's what I liked. My mansion wasn't what I wanted. There was no sense of family. For a moment, I thought that I would much rather choose to be a Recruit than live my old life again.

That all changed when Trish knocked on the door and a young man stepped to answer it. He was slightly taller than me with thin, round, glasses. He had short, light-brown, hair and wore a collared shirt. His acne stood out beyond his freckles.

His eyes opened wide. He stepped back and caught his breath. "T-T-Trish… where have you been? Everyone thought you disappeared… You've been gone for almost six months and didn't tell anybody you moved until a few days later."

He looked around at all of us and then said, "Who are your friends?"

"Look, we need your help," Trish said. "There is a lot we have to explain to you. A whole lot. But, you're the only one that can help."

He looked confused and shook his head. "What are you talking about?"

"I have no time to explain. You just have to trust me!"

Thomas looked around. "Why? What are you hiding? Where did you go for the last six months?"

"You keep questioning me like it's my fault! It's not! I just had to go, and Zeke needs your help too!"

"Pff," Thomas said slowly shutting the door. "You're going to need a better argument than that. Look,

I don't know why you're here, but it better be for a reason other than Zeke. He left without even telling me. Did you know he was the only friend I had? Thanks, but no thanks. I'll tell everyone at school you said hi."

The door was almost completely shut when Trish pushed her arm through the crack and held her hand right in front of his face with a bright orange flame crackling in her palm.

He gulped and slowly reopened the door. "How... How can you do that?"

"Like I said," Trish said, "I can't tell you yet. You just need to trust me. We need your help and so does Zeke... will you come with us?"

He stared at us for a few moments and then turned back and yelled, "Mom! I'm going out with a few friends from school! I'll be home soon!"

He stepped outside and said, "How can I help, Zeke? What's wrong?"

"A lot," Trish said. "Like, the lives of hundreds of people, including mine, hang in the balance."

"...wow," he said in disbelief.

"So, you're with us Thomas?"

Thomas looked at all of us and then said, "What do you need me to do?"

About the Author

Kevin Van Camp is currently a 20 year old boy living in Madison, Wisconsin where he is attending the University of Wisconsin-Madison. He is double majoring in Biology and English. Kevin's hometown is Freedom, Wisconsin. No one really knows where that place is unless you live there or in the area of Freedom.

This novel is the sequel to The Clade published by Kevin Van Camp. He is very excited about it, and he hopes to continue his hobby of writing stories for other people's enjoyment. He hopes that his writing aspirations will grow and become a full-time job someday; however, he does have backup plans just in case.

Currently, he also has a blog where he posts short stories every two weeks just for the enjoyment of the readers.   This   site   is   http://vancampstoryweb.blogspot.com and is free to everyone. Make sure to read the stories and post your comments.

Kevin's hobbies, when he is not writing, include playing video games and hanging out with his friends, playing soccer or any other sports in the summer, swimming, and enjoying a good laugh every once in a while.

Enjoy Overload?

Then, tell a friend about the Human Element Trilogy before it's too late!

Book 1- The Clade

Book 2- Overload

Join the Human Element Trilogy group on Facebook for more from the Clade.